COLD
GIRL

COLD GIRL

A B.C. BLUES CRIME NOVEL

R.M. GREENAWAY

DUNDURN
TORONTO

Editor: Allister Thompson
Design: Laura Boyle
Cover design: Laura Boyle
Cover image: ©Ollyy/shutterstock.com
Printer: Webcom

Library and Archives Canada Cataloguing in Publication

Greenaway, R. M., author
        Cold girl / R.M. Greenaway.

(A B.C. blues crime novel)
Issued in print and electronic formats.
ISBN 978-1-4597-3437-1 (paperback).--ISBN 978-1-4597-3438-8 (pdf).--
ISBN 978-1-4597-3439-5 (epub)

I. Title.
PS8613.R4285C65 2016   C813'.6   C2015-905331-5
                                               C2015-905332-3

1   2   3   4   5   20   19   18   17   16

  Canada

We acknowledge the support of the Canada Council for the Arts and the Ontario Arts Council for our publishing program. We also acknowledge the financial support of the Government of Canada through the Canada Book Fund and Livres Canada Books, and the Government of Ontario through the Ontario Book Publishing Tax Credit and the Ontario Media Development Corporation.

Care has been taken to trace the ownership of copyright material used in this book. The author and the publisher welcome any information enabling them to rectify any references or credits in subsequent editions.

— J. Kirk Howard, President

The publisher is not responsible for websites or their content unless they are owned by the publisher.

Printed and bound in Canada.

VISIT US AT
Dundurn.com | @dundurnpress | Facebook.com/dundurnpress | Pinterest.com/dundurnpress

Dundurn
3 Church Street, Suite 500
Toronto, Ontario, Canada
M5E 1M2

To Daniel

Prologue

FALL FAIR

SHE WAS THE ONLY PATCH of stillness on the planet, to Dion, the dark-haired girl sitting on the far wing of the bleachers, second to lowest tier, watching the band play.

She wasn't alone, surrounded by people on all sides, but she was a break in the pattern that had caught his eye, her solidity and forward gaze, while all around her the crowd pitched and bobbed in response to the music, volume up so high it vibrated the blood in his veins. Clouds drove across the dimming skies and the lights from the fairground beyond flickered and twirled. People danced on the grassy patch in front of the stage, and above them the Rockabilly Princess leaned into the mic to sing the bouncy refrain. Something about small change and love letters. Much of the crowd sang along.

Seated next to Dion, high up on the bleachers, Penny sang along too, loudly and not so well, arms lifted high to clap. Dion didn't sing or cheer but tried to clap his hands to the beat now and then, following procedure.

Proof that he was as present as anyone. He'd come out tonight determined not to brood or drift. He worked on listening to the music, and it was lively and noisy, but it really wasn't great, and he couldn't stay with it. First his ears went out of sync, then his eyes. He checked Penny's profile, saw that she looked happy, then surveyed the crowd and saw more than heard the chaos and motion, all but the dark-haired girl down there who sat perfectly still, her attention fixed on the band, the singer, the guitar player. Unlike Dion, she was completely in sync. Just another fan, he decided. But one of the silent ones.

He looked down and sideways at the pink denim of Penny's skinny, pumping knees, but the thoughts kept ticking, not in words but little kicks of anxiety. It was all part of the healing process, this constant kicking, ticking, and going in circles, and now he was at it again, watching the girl down there. She was native, he was sure of it, while most of the fairgoers were white. And there was something else that set her apart: baggage. Next to her he could just see the hump of some kind of bag, a large backpack or duffel, which said that maybe she was just passing through, a drifter. From his position seven tiers up he could see little of her face, only the full curve of her cheek. Her long hair was loose and whipping in the breeze. Nothing special about her, a woman in her twenties, probably, on the heavy side, in faded jeans, and in spite of the chill just an ice-blue T-shirt.

He told himself he wasn't obsessing, just whiling away the time as he sat through a long stretch of rockabilly noise he couldn't tune in on. Maybe it was a good thing, a throwback to better days, when it had been his job to analyze situations, pull out the anomalies and turn them over till he had it figured out. He frowned down at the dark-haired girl. When she turned and glanced up his way, he felt caught out and flicked his gaze away, back to Fling.

The pop and boom of the monster speakers frayed his nerves, along with Penny's pumping knees and the sea-like motion of the crowd. The song came to an abrupt end, there was another round of applause, and in the lull he could breathe easier, like coming up for air. As the band fussed with their instruments, gearing up for the next assault, Penny touched his arm, got his attention, and pointed at the heavy bank of clouds moving in over the mountains. "Snow's coming, I can smell it in the air."

She said it like it was a good thing. He glanced at the heavens and saw them hung with some kind of floating debris catching the last of the sunlight. The only smells he could pick out from the general fairground pong were cow dung and candyfloss, and the occasional whiff of suntan lotion and sweat.

What did snow smell like? What did it feel like? How would he survive it?

A new hailstorm of notes from an electric guitar made him wince and stare back at the stage, at the guitar man working the strings again, hard.

"My lord, he's a hottie," Penny said, "that Frank Law."

Dion leaned elbows on knees, no longer clapping along, no longer trying to fool anybody. He pulled the brim of his baseball cap lower, checked his watch, and did the math. Six songs so far, just a couple more to go. The dark-haired girl was still down there, a stillness in a choppy sea, but he'd lost interest in whoever she was and wherever she was headed.

Touch didn't come easy to him, these days, but he made the effort, grabbed Penny's hand, found it warm, and interlocked her fingers in his. She responded by leaning her shoulder against his. The music ramped up, and he could feel through his body the thumping of appreciation from the crowd, some three hundred fans shaking the frail structure like they were working together to bring it down. He thought about steel rods criss-crossed and linked to suspend too much weight too high, and about metal fatigue, the chain reactions of a snapped bolt, the carnage that would come with collapse, and his own death, twice in one year.

The next song was slower, its lyrics turning from hanky-panky to slow romance, and the thumping stopped too. Dion took a breath. Penny looked away to the midway rides, the languid revolving silhouette of the Ferris wheel. "It's Kiera's take on 'The Banks of Red Roses,'" she said, sounding distant. "It's song nine on her CD. It's about murder. It's *so* depressing. I always skip it."

Penny hated violence. She liked romance novels and happy news of rescued animals. She seemed to believe that men were faithful and good, which bothered him. He'd tried to educate her, being a man himself, knowing well how unfaithful and ungood men really were. The average man follows his dick and grabs what he wants, and if he appears to behave, that's all it is, appearances. Rein it in to hang onto the job, or marriage, or whatever he values. He had explained it all to Penny just the other day, and then put it to her: if a man has nothing to lose, then what?

Kiera finished her song of murder and yelled into the mic, "Thank you, Smithers, you're the best, see you next year, hey?"

Penny said, "No way she's going to leave it on that crummy note," as singer and band walked off, and she was right. Enough of the audience came to its feet and demanded an encore that the band filed back on stage. Kiera took up the mic again and crooned, "I love you too. Here's one more for the road. I wrote this one especially for you cow-babies."

She closed her eyes and swayed. Penny recognized the intro and said, "Oh, geez, I love this one. The blown kiss. Watch Frank."

Dion did as he was told. The song was much like all the others, wild and discordant. The Rockabilly Princess was flipping her skirts, showing her legs. The boys in the crowd whistled and cheered. Frank the guitar man leaned into a second mic, and the song became a lovers' duet. Frank stopped playing long enough to kiss his palm and blow that kiss at Kiera. Kiera reached up and caught the kiss and made to blow it back, but Frank missed the obvious cue. Distracted or ill-rehearsed, he failed to catch the kiss but kept strumming at his guitar strings, looking not at his lover but down into the crowd. Kiera twirled and sang on.

"Ouch," Penny said. "She's not too pleased."

Frank was bowing back into his guitar strings, playing hard for the song's climax. Maybe he knew he'd screwed up, or maybe not, but Dion found the missed kiss funny. He looked at Penny to see if she did too, but her eyes were fixed on Frank with what looked like pity.

Frank was the love of Penny's life, on some level Dion couldn't understand. She had a glossy Fling concert poster pinned to her bedroom wall showing the Princess dancing aggressively into the camera lens in denim dress and cowgirl boots, and next to her Frank in clingy tank-top, electric guitar slung across his chest. Penny had pointed to the poster on one of Dion's rare visits to that bedroom and said, "Only in my dreams."

Maybe he should have taken offence, but he didn't then as he didn't now. He looked down again and saw the native girl was gone, and so was her bag. In the middle of a song. Cutting out early struck him as strange for one who'd been watching so keenly, even if it was the last song. But probably he was wrong and she wasn't a fan, was just *here*, like him, drawn into these bleachers by circumstance and killing time. He gave one last look at the spot she'd vacated, and then at the benches just above. One row or maybe two up from where she'd been sitting was now an empty patch, where before there had been a fairly even spread of audience.

He looked westward, scanning the milling fairground crowd, and spotted her as she passed through the blare of concession stand lights, not so far off yet that he couldn't recognize that long hair flipping like a black banner, that ice-blue T-shirt. She moved from one patch of light to another, weaving through the crowd, crossing the midway, carrying her bag, not a duffel but a packsack. He searched for a pattern of motion at her back and saw it, a solitary figure scything through not far behind her, passing beneath those same patches of light and closing the gap. Tall, male, Caucasian, wearing a baseball cap much like Dion's. Black, he thought, till a spotlight hit it square for a fleeting second, and he realized it was red.

He stood to see better, and Penny tugged his hand, saying, "Hey you, it's not over." He sat and looked down at the stage, but his heart was hammering. The girl was going to meet friends in the beer garden, that was all. Or heading for her car parked on the well-lit lower level plateau. Around him people went on stamping to the beat, and somehow he was sure she wasn't meeting friends, or climbing into the safety of her car, that she was alone and she was on foot and her destination was the highway, either by one of several paths that cut through field or forest, or the long gravel road that led away from the fairground to the west, dark and empty, the perfect place for the man to catch up, reach out, take hold.

"I'll be back," he said into Penny's ear and stood and edged along the bench past a dozen sets of knees until he was on the steps, thudding down, now jogging across the midway, seeking a red cap following a girl in blue.

But she was nowhere, and he stood amongst the fairgoers and listened to the happy din, conversation on all fronts, the music from the rides, screams from the Haunted House. Behind him Kiera cried breathlessly over the loudspeakers, "Thank you, I love you," and she went on to remind her fans of her upcoming CD, on sale by Christmas. "It'll knock your socks off, people, I promise." The applause followed her off stage as Dion made his way back up, climbed the bleachers, edged past a dozen sets of knees, and sat next to Penny.

"You see somebody you know?" she asked.

"Maybe," he said.

A man was on stage now, introducing The Old Time Fiddlers. Some people rose, shuffling toward the stairs, but most stayed seated, bringing out the lap blankets and Thermoses. Penny said, "Well, what d'you think?"

"I think we should go."

"No, about Fling. Now that you've seen 'em play."

A cold missile hit Dion on the nape of the neck, and he stood, mind set on departure. Penny gave a happy shriek as she was hit too. It was an icy rain, not quite the snow she longed for. Holding hands, they made their way along the planks to the steps, and by the time they'd left the stage behind and were heading down the midway where the rides spun and clanged, the water came down hard as hail. They took shelter under a canopy by the mini rollercoaster and watched the kids hurling along its rails.

"Have you been to the PNE?" Penny asked. "Bet you rode the big one. I always wanted to but never had the nerve. Did you?"

The noise of the fairgrounds and the rain had drummed out her words, or the meaning of them. He said, "Sorry, what?"

"You grew up down there...." She always did this, pressed patiently on through all his lapses, and he couldn't understand why. He and she were a bad match. She was fun and lively, and he was barely here. Last month he'd arrived in this town, 1,149 kilometres from where he wanted to be, and was down at the post office signing up for a mailbox because they didn't do door-to-door here. She'd been working behind the counter, and gave him the paperwork and key. He'd been bewildered and emotionally raw and she'd been chatty and welcoming. She'd talked him into a night at the movies, then dinner at her parents' house, and already he was caught, a misconception more than a boyfriend, with no easy way out.

She repeated a question he must have missed. "And you're a big, brave guy, so you must've, right? Rode the giant roller coaster, I'm saying."

He looked down at her in distracted wonder. Penny didn't know, because he hadn't told her, who he was and why he was here. Hardly a big, brave guy, and no new recruit with a rosy future. As far as the force was concerned, he was a rehab experiment with low odds.

A flicker of colour brought him back to the moment, a red ball cap approaching. He studied its wearer but saw this guy was too young and too heavy to be the stalker, which wasn't a stalker at all but a flight of fancy. His temples throbbed, and his back was sticky with sweat. He recalled with regret that other thing he'd done tonight, or failed to do, further proof he was no longer a detective: he had looked away just as she had looked up, the lone girl in the bleachers. His one good chance to see her face, and he'd blown it.

There was a clatter and shriek, and a carload of kids flew by. Penny was still next to him, but she'd given up on conversation. He pulled her into a brief hug then pointed a thumb at the glum roadie at the gate. "I'll get you a ticket, if you want."

He was joking. This was a travelling fair, with break-down rides, and its roller coaster was only fit for six-year-olds. "Thanks but no thanks," she laughed.

Heavy streaks of clouds muddied the night skies, and he sought Penny's hand again, planning to tug her toward the parking lot, but she had escaped. He saw her over at the bumper cars, talking to friends. She beckoned at him and called out, "Hey." He shook his head and flicked a hand at her, meaning *go ahead without me, I'll wait*.

The last thing he needed was another crash. He leaned against the metal rail and turned away from the noise and action. He touched the left side of his head, just over the ear, feeling with his fingers the unevenness of the surgical mend, always worried it would come undone, and whatever he had left in there would come seeping out.

Behind him the cars slammed into each other, set to Def Leppard. He puffed out a breath and couldn't help being there again, driving too fast down the long, straight roads of Surrey — or maybe it was Cloverdale — middle of the night, chasing someone, and it had come out of nowhere, a flash of red torpedoing in off the right out of what had to be a concealed side road. He recalled spiking the brakes, when in hindsight he should have stepped on the gas. He recalled shouting to Looch, but shouting what?

Last words.

Later he found out he'd been comatose for six days. Nobody would answer his questions or show him photos or share whatever the traffic analyst had pinpointed on speed and degrees of fault. They'd asked a question or two, but it was hardly the interrogation he was ready for, and that worried him too. All they said was, why were you in Richmond breaking the limit? Where were you guys going to, coming from? He'd said he remembered nothing of the day of the accident. He didn't expect to be believed, but they seemed to do just that, believe him.

The flip side of claiming amnesia was that he left himself in the dark. He couldn't ask those pointed questions he wanted to, and now he knew nothing of the investigation except the names of the deceased. He'd missed Looch's funeral. He'd left town without a word to Looch's widow, Brooke, or Looch's mom or dad or sister or brothers. They wouldn't have forgiven him anyway, but at least he should have tried.

So now he was back in uniform, pretty well healed, good to go. There was no brain damage, they said, and they seemed to believe it. He was trying to believe it himself, but he couldn't. He was changed, rearranged, not himself. It would be a while before he could start climbing his way back to the top, be once again that smartass cop in suit and tie, integral, admired, the keenest eye on the team …

He brought his hand around and found it wet with cold rain, not warm blood, which took his worries in another direction: the winter weather and how he was going to steer his wheels through the coming snowfalls. Aside from training at Regina ten years ago, he wasn't prepared for northern driving. He imagined snow coming down thick, coating the roads, concealing the ice. It would send him into a tailspin, another crash, another coma. How many comas could one brain take?

The knot tightened. He told Penny as she rejoined him that he needed to get home, get some sleep; he had work tomorrow.

On the gravel road to the upper parking lot they joined other fairgoers walking slowly out into the dark.

Holding his hand, Penny said, "It was the best, though, wasn't it?" The colourful fairground lights reflected in her eyes as she looked back, still spinning away in the distance. "Seeing them play?"

"Seeing what?" he asked.

"Them play."

As always, the dots didn't quite connect. "Who?"

"Fling." She'd lost patience, probably for the first time since they'd met, maybe the beginning of the end. "Fling, the whole point of this day, remember?"

They walked in silence toward the vast muddy field that had been turned into a jam-packed parking lot for this fall fair weekend, no longer holding hands, and he kept an eye out for the native girl and the man who followed her, both long gone, leaving nothing to chase but a really bad feeling.

One

FEBRUARY CALLOUT

DAVID LEITH BROUGHT the phone to his ear, standing in his living room by the big picture window, looking out at the winter scenery. Not his personal phone but his work phone, the police-issue BlackBerry, and that meant this Sunday, his day off, was probably shot.

"Leith," he answered. And sighed, and listened, and continued to watch the falling snow.

He liked snow — maybe even loved it. As a boy he had skated through it, slid on it, built with it. He'd grown up and joined the RCMP and been bumped west from Saskatchewan to Alberta's Slave Lake, then farther west to B.C.'s Fort St. John, and finally all the way to the coast, to this rugged little city of Prince Rupert. He'd got married, settled down, and until this year had continued to be one with the snow. Till now it represented *fun* to him, and *beauty*, one spoke in the great wheel of life. There was nothing like standing out there first thing in the morning, dazzled by a world cleansed in white, and feeling one with nature.

"Be there in ten," he said, and disconnected.

Snow in Prince Rupert didn't hit hard, as it did inland, this being the oceanic climate, and usually melted as it hit the ground, but now and then there was a great dump of the stuff, and it stuck. This last dump was sticking, and it was no longer fun or beautiful to Leith. These days each new snowfall just pissed him off, the way it found its way into his boots and behind his collar and brought him crashing to the ground from time to time as he forged to work and forged out on investigations and forged out to the supermarket and forged home again. Snow tracked into the home with all the other stresses of the day and dirtied the carpet and made Alison bitchy.

No, that wasn't fair. She was never bitchy, no matter how dirty the carpet got or how low their spirits fell. She would go mute, though, which only made him louder. They had never argued in the Februaries of their younger years, and it worried him that something had gone so badly off the rails — and how bad exactly would it get? Maybe having a child too late in life had upset the balance. Leith was forty-four, Alison thirty-eight, and Izzy was just turning two, and had morphed not into cuteness but into a tiny, blond-ringletted monster with powerful lungs. Ear-splitting lungs. Alison blamed it on the Terrible Twos. Leith blamed it on the species and dreaded the next twenty years.

So this call from the office at midday on this, his first day off in a while, didn't bother him as much as he made out it did. He cursed aloud and told Alison he had to go out. She didn't seem disappointed. He pulled on soft-shell, then outer jacket, then sat on the foyer bench to lace up the waterproof boots. "Bye-bye-bye," he said and stooped toward Isabelle where she stood staring up at him on the dirty grey stretch of hallway carpet. She raised a threatening fist and spoke in tongues. Alison gathered the child up and didn't bother to see him off on the doorstep where she used to stand smiling, back when they were in love.

At noon, Prince Rupert seemed steeped in dusk. He drove to the station, parked underground, walked up into the stuffy over-lit main, and on down to Phil Prentice's office, where he found his boss on his feet, speaking to a stranger. The stranger wore glasses, a black suit, white shirt, no tie. He was bigger than the average cop, and bulky, kind of bear-shaped, head ducked down as if he was self-conscious about his height. He looked to be about Leith's age, maybe a year or two younger.

He was vaguely familiar, too, like Leith had seen him somewhere recently. Maybe on TV? A journalist? Prentice made introductions. "Mike, this is my main man, Constable Dave Leith. A real get-it-done guy."

The stranger looked pleased, shook Leith's hand, and said, "Sergeant Mike Bosko, up from North Van for the border security conference. How ya doin'?"

"Good, thanks," Leith said. A big man himself, he stood nearly eye-to-eye with the stranger, who he now in fact recognized. Couple nights ago Mike Bosko had been up at the podium at the Highliner Inn, talking fluidly about something important. Exactly what, Leith couldn't say, even after taking notes. "Heard your talk, sir. Amazing stuff."

"Amazing what we got accomplished in three days," Bosko said with a smile. Too smart, too self-possessed, and thankfully soon to be gone, Leith thought. He turned to Prentice to ask why the call-in on his day off.

"Yes, sorry about that," Prentice said. "Another girl's gone missing, inland."

"Hell, no. Where and when? Same place?"

"The Hazeltons. Reported missing last night."

The Hazeltons lay in the colder, snowier interior of the province, northeast of Rupert by a good four hours' drive. As Leith understood it, the Hazeltons were composed of Old Hazelton, New Hazelton, and South Hazelton, and the smaller offshoots of Kispiox and Two Mile. Of course that four-hour drive could stretch into eight in a blizzard. He took the bulletin Prentice had thrust at him and looked it over, a photo of a young woman with all the stats typed up below, which he now scanned. "It's out of his range," he said, and already felt the ice receding from his veins. The killer he'd been hunting for two years had centred his hits around the Terrace area, so far, which sat midway on the highway between Rupert and the Hazeltons.

"Sure, but what's a few miles for a man with a truck?" Prentice said. "Thing is, her vehicle was located up on a logging road, Dave."

A logging road in the winter was bad at best. Linked to the MO of a serial killer, it was dismal. Leith looked at the bulletin again, photograph of a young woman with a dazzling smile, warm eyes, a tumble of glossy brown hair. The image was professionally lit, more a publicity head shot than something out of a family album. The stats said she was twenty-two. The name, Kiera Rilkoff, rang a distant bell. "She's a bit of a celebrity? A singer?"

Prentice nodded and said for Bosko's benefit, "She's quite the talent, too. Our local pride and joy. My daughters are huge fans. Country and western stuff, I think."

Leith had learned not to take many of Prentice's adjectives at face value. Like *huge*. If asked, those daughters would probably agree that, yeah, Kiera's pretty good, why?

"Oh, sure, the Rockabilly Princess," Bosko said, snapping his fingers. "There was a piece on grassroots music on CBC Radio just before Christmas. She gave a short, man-on-the-street type interview, and they played a track from her first CD. Self-produced, I think. She seemed excited about the future of the band, and they had a second CD coming out. Did it ever happen?"

"No, I think it got nixed for some reason."

Bosko didn't look surprised, Leith noticed, and then it clicked that he'd actually seen the singer play, which was one better than hearing her on the radio. "I caught her act at last summer's Seafest," he said. The event filled his mind, the sunshine and crowds, the barbecue aromas, little Izzy on his shoulders gripping his hair and trying to knock off his sunglasses. He'd been more interested in the food than the music, frankly, but he'd stopped to watch the pretty girl on centre stage. The music itself was fairly run-of-the-mill country yowling, as he recalled, and he hadn't stopped for long.

He shook his head, handing the bulletin back to Prentice. "She's not victim four. He wouldn't go for a celebrity. What's with her vehicle?"

"Parked near a trailhead on Kispiox Mountain," Prentice said. "They got a spare key up there and checked. Engine wouldn't turn over."

"What's the matter with it?"

"No news yet on that yet."

"Must be deep snow up there. Any tracks?"

"Mess of tracks, Giroux tells me. Terrace sent two Ident guys over for a look. Should be there by now. Problem is family and friends went tramping about before we were brought in. Doubtful there's anything left."

A trashed crime scene was a terrible beginning, and already Leith knew this was going to end up bad. Unless she was incredibly inconsiderate, the girl hadn't caught a ride with somebody, hadn't met up with friends, wasn't simply out having too much fun to call home.

"Why d'you say he wouldn't go for a celebrity, Dave?" Bosko asked.

The "he" they all spoke of was the so-called Pickup Killer, as dubbed by the press because it was about all the police had on him so far, that he drove a pickup. And even that was little more than circumstantial say-so. Leith eyed the stranger, not keen on this first-name-basis thing — it's *Leith* to you, buddy — let alone case-note sharing. But Prentice wasn't objecting, so Leith pulled in his shoulders and gave the stranger the abridged version, just short of rude. "His last two victims were pretty well loners, down-and-outers, which buys him time. Grabbing Kiera is not only way out of his abduction territory — it's not his style. This is something else altogether, and that means it's not my file, Phil, and I'm going home. Bye."

His last few words were directed at Prentice while stepping across the threshold, but Prentice sharply called him back into the room. "It happened in the Hazeltons, where for all we know he's based," Prentice said. "What about the logging road? It's a link we can't ignore, and right or wrong, we need you out there, if only to sign off on a no-go." To Bosko he explained more pleasantly, "Dave heads up the Pickup task force. He's immersed like nobody else. If there's one incriminating fibre to be found, he'll find it."

Leith stood embarrassed, for however immersed he might be and whatever responsibilities he shouldered, he wasn't much of a cop, as his rank pointed out. At his age he hadn't even made corporal. Couldn't pass the exams, couldn't make an impression on those who mattered. He lacked some quality, elusive as charisma. Maybe it was just inherent laziness or a basically crappy IQ, but he wasn't well read (though he tried). Or well travelled (though he dreamed). He wasn't suave, wasn't patient, wasn't lovable. Worst of all, he wasn't intuitive.

If one word could sum him up, it was dogged.

His personal phone buzzed, and he glanced at it, a coolish text from Alison telling him to pick up another bag of sidewalk salt, and he reflected that a few days away from home might not be so bad. "Right," he told Prentice. "I'll go pack. Call Giroux and tell her I'll be on the road in an hour. ETA, no idea."

He was nodding goodbye to the stranger Bosko, but Bosko wasn't done irritating him and said, "Hold on a sec, Dave. I've run this by Phil already, and so long as it's fine with you, it's fine with him. I'm wondering if you'd mind if I rode along with you."

"Rode along? To where? The airport? The airport's that way."

"New Hazelton. From there I could catch the next available sheriff run to Prince George and hop a plane.

Wouldn't mind seeing the interior up close. Never really get the chance. Always flying over." He smiled.

The room's windows looking out to sea were solid grey but for the white bombardments of sleet, and Leith could hear the muted howl of February pressing against the double-glazed window. The roads would be murder, the view obscured by haze, and it wasn't much of a view anyway, a monotony of ice-rimed trees with the occasional glimpse of ice-jammed river.

He tried to send the stranger a *fuck-off* message with his eyes. "It's a hell of a long drive, this time of year. Hours. And in this weather you won't see much but taillights. It'll be slow going. Gruelling."

"For once in my life, Dave, I've got time."

Leith shrugged and glowered. "Okay, then. Meet back here in forty minutes?"

"Absolutely."

The only thing worse than a winter drive to the Hazeltons, Leith reflected as he made his way to the parkade, was a long winter drive to the Hazeltons with a man who answered grim propositions with *absolutely*. Damn.

* * *

"Thing is, I don't have to be back at the office till the end of the month," Bosko explained, settled next to Leith in the passenger seat, his specs reflecting the oncoming headlights. Prince Rupert was behind them now at two thirty, and they hadn't yet sped up to highway limits. "The conference wrapped up quicker than we expected, as you know, which opened up this great window of time for me, a whole week, and my first impulse was to call up admin right away and top it up. But then I got to thinking. I walked down to the harbour, watched the waves crashing in, and it occurred to me how little I know of these parts, and how I wouldn't mind some eyes-on exploration. I've called B.C. home for the last decade, yet I haven't driven north of Cache Creek, would you believe?"

"Huh," Leith said.

"And I'm not the only one. I don't know how many superior officers I've talked to down on the coast who've seen Disneyland but never drove the highways of B.C. It becomes a problem when those who run the show forget about the practicalities of working under conditions such as you guys face on a daily basis. I'm stating the obvious, you'd think, but there's a genuine disconnect, Dave. There's real time and distance involved. It's not like moving the cursor across Google Earth. It's distance you can feel in the small of your back." He grinned, watched the cruddy snow-plastered trees pass for a while, and said, "So what do you know of Kiera Rilkoff?"

Leith could sum up what he knew of the missing girl on three fingers. She was attractive, popular among the local youngsters, and had aspirations. He said as much, padding it out with extra words, trying to sound smart, feeling Bosko's eyes on him.

After a beat Bosko said, "The track they played on the radio back in November was pretty rough on the ears. By the sound of it, I'd say it was done up in a home studio, and not too well. Kiera promised their upcoming CD would be a professional burn, that they had sunk money into it, and maybe had acquired an agent, I think she said. Or was it a manager? Does that mean anything to you?"

"I haven't been following her career," Leith admitted. "Sorry."

"No, and unfortunately I wasn't really listening at the time," Bosko said. "But if anyone's interested, it can probably be pulled from the archives."

Who needs archives when you have the amazing Bosko's hi-fidelity recall, Leith thought enviously. His own memory was good on things that mattered, but recount some random bullshit he'd heard on the radio three months ago?

Bosko asked more smart questions about the logistics of operations in the area, search and rescue, continuity issues with thin staffing, response times in various conditions. Leith did his best to answer, not so well, and soon enough the big man from the city went from asking questions to a kind of running soliloquy on whatever was on his mind at the moment. Northern demographics, poverty issues, the border security conference and how it had gone down, who had spoken, upcoming shifts in policy and legislation. As Leith was learning now the hard way, Mike Bosko abhorred a vacuum.

Half listening, grunting occasionally, Leith pressed on, away from the ocean, into the bleak wilds of B.C. There was no colour in the sky, no colour anywhere now that they'd left the port city behind and the temperatures had plummeted. The roads were slick but manageable. He drove faster than the traffic pattern, passing when possible, until a line of loaded B-train freight trucks slowed him to sixty on the straights and a mind-numbing thirty through the curves. And Bosko's low, plodding voice droned on. As well as knowing pretty much everything about the universe at large, he seemed to have the scoop on the local crime scene. He spoke of the Pickup killings, knew the bodies had been found on forest service roads, knew the names, Karen Blake, Lindsay Carlyle, Joanne Crow, and the stories their bodies told of forceful takedown, bondage, and strangulation. Leith wondered if Mike Bosko had gotten hold of the files at some point, and if so, why? He wondered if Bosko was privy to the holdback information that had been kept back from the press, known only to the inner circle of investigators so far, the killer's quirk. He said, "You've done your research."

Bosko either didn't hear or didn't care to answer.

The Pickup Killer case had gone cool, if not cold, and these days Leith only worked it if something new turned up. Nothing had for over a year now, except faint whispers that kept him awake some nights. The whispers said the beast was still in their midst, still crawling the streets of Terrace.

As they passed through that very city, the killer's known hunting grounds, darkness fell and the snow came down in earnest. Terrace fell behind, and they were again in lonely wilderness, with another two hours to go before they reached the Hazeltons. Bosko switched to historian mode, telling Leith all kinds of interesting things about the area, Hazelton being rooted in the Omineca Gold Rush, the sternwheeler that ran the Skeena once open a time, the turn-of-the-century search for Simon Gunanoot, much of it news to Leith.

He shifted in his seat and sighed with relief as the lights of their final destination approached, the broad, slow highway that cut through the main settlement of New Hazelton. Passage through town would take about two minutes if a person drove the speed limit, which nobody did, except Leith now, slowing to sixty, then fifty, losing the tandem trucks ahead, which ploughed through and disappeared up the big dark hill that merged again with black forest, probably heading for the mills of Smithers.

"We're here," he said, sounding smarter than ever.

There was scant traffic out and about as he cruised the SUV under the orange glow of tall lamp standards, past a gas station and shut-down supermarket, a few darkened restaurants. He pulled at last down a side street and parked in front of the New Hazelton detachment. He shut off the engine and looked at Bosko, hoping the shabbiness of the place was a crushing disappointment to the man. Bosko looked fresh, pleased, and enthusiastic.

Inside the small RCMP detachment they were met by a sleepy-looking auxiliary constable who told them that Renee Giroux, the local sergeant in charge, was up on the Matax with a small search team. Leith said, "Matax, what's that?"

"Hiking trail heading off the Bell 3," the auxiliary told him. "Where Kiera's truck was found."

"Bell 3 …"

"The logging road."

Leith told the auxiliary to contact Giroux and let her know he was on his way. The auxiliary said, "I'll try. Can't guarantee a connection. The airwaves are thin up there." She supplied him with a map, marking it with Xs, one for the Bell 3 turnoff and one for the Matax trailhead. Leith thanked her.

"It's going to be tedious," he told Bosko as they headed back out to the truck. "You'd be better off checking into your room and kicking back. They've got us booked in at the Super 8 over there. I'll just drop you off?"

"I'll tag along, if that's okay."

They left the town lights behind, and Bosko got a tour of the Hazeltons as they passed through the settlements of Two Mile, Old Town, over a canyon into the heavily forested Kispiox area and beyond, where Leith was soon lost, in spite of map and GPS. With Bosko's help he did manage to locate the Bell 3 signpost, the words nearly obliterated by driven snow, and took the turn, geared the truck down, and the high-suspension, fat-tired V8 police truck began to climb the snowy road beaten flat by previous tires. The incline steepened steadily and the road narrowed until even Bosko sat mute as the headlights lit the banks falling steeply away inches from his right shoulder.

The second X on the map wasn't far in theory, a mere 9.7 kilometres of straights and switchbacks, but it was a crawl to get there, and nearly an hour passed before a pylon glowed in the headlights. A moment later a row of vehicles came gleaming into view, a couple of police SUVs and a black four-door sedan that didn't look fit for the terrain. Leith pulled in behind the sedan and stepped out onto the road, wincing. Crystals fell light but fast, tiny daggers lashing his face. Upslope and deep in the woods a hard light pierced the darkness, a signal to follow.

"Not a good place to break down," Bosko remarked. He stood now at the nose of the truck, taking in the scene. Leith shone his flashlight toward the man and saw how out of place he looked in urban overcoat, collars turned up, glasses flecked with snow and his short hair flipping about, but no fear on his solid, pale face. Bosko checked his cellphone for signal and confirmed what Leith already knew. "Not a single bar."

The pylons pointed the way to a parking area for trail users, ribboned off with crime-scene tape, the ground here churned by tires, but no vehicles occupying its space. Leith swung his light about low and caught another line of pylons, and these led him up on a short trek into the woods. Here as everywhere the forest floor was disturbed by foot traffic in every direction, silent evidence of the searchers who would have been and gone, criss-crossing the wilderness, calling out Kiera's name and blasting whistles.

He and Bosko reached a clearing, a kind of muster zone, and arrived at the lights and action they had seen from afar. Officers were spread out in the trees, marked distantly by the bobbing of their flashlights. The muster zone was lit by heavy-duty portables on stands, and under their raking glare stood a roundish bundle named Renee Giroux.

"My big-city detective at last," she called out as the men arrived before her. She stared past Leith at Bosko. "And you are?"

Leith made introductions, and the little First Nations CO forgave Bosko for being a stranger enough to shake his hand. "I was just leaving," she said. "Good thing you got up here to see what we're dealing with. But this," she said, and scanned about the site, which was a confusion of crime scene tape strung between bushes, "is going nowhere fast." She pointed to where several officers were concentrated, performing a finer grid search. "Possible burial site there, snow heaped about, but no body. Her friends and family from here to kingdom come were up yesterday and spent the night looking for her. Natural enough, but what a disaster. SAR made a couple passes overhead, and they're on the ground now, team of eight, doing the crags and crevasses. Reason I'm up here is Dash drove in from Terrace about half past four and yanked his handler into the bushes, where we got us a game-changer." She pointed to where two constables were searching the forest floor. "Found it over at that marker. Which is, what, a hundred feet from her car. So all of a sudden it's looking not like a girl lost in a woods but a girl taken by persons unknown."

Leith told Bosko that Dash was a tracker dog from Terrace and that actually it was probably the dog's handler who drove, and asked Giroux what exactly the game-changer was.

"A cellphone," she said. "Looks new, and I'd be stunned if it wasn't Kiera's. Haven't looked at it yet, was waiting for Big City to show up and do things proper."

Big City was her nickname for Leith. She grinned fleetingly, not pleasantly, and looked around and again pointed. "Dash said there's nothing of interest beyond that point, so that leaves us with two scenarios. A) She lost or discarded her phone, then got a ride with some-one we don't know and is some *place* we don't know, safe and sound but phoneless and for some reason unwilling or unable to get in touch. B) She was abducted and lost her phone in the struggle."

She paused, and Leith knew she would be thinking of the faint but frightening possibility that the Pickup Killer had moved in. Here, to her zone of responsibility. Bosko said, "We didn't see her vehicle on the parking flat. It's been towed down, has it?"

Giroux nodded. "Fairchild's call, not mine."

Leith told Bosko that Corporal Fairchild was head of the Terrace Ident section. He was on scene now, over-seeing the search.

Giroux said, "Duncan's sent their big rig and came and got it. Had my doubts, but got lots of pictures before it was touched, inside and out, and figured we'd be better off giving it the once-over in the garage."

Bosko scratched his ear as if he had his doubts and looked at Leith. Leith nodded shortly at him. "Life in the outback, sir. They use Duncan's Auto Repair around here for tows."

"Anyway," Giroux said, "Fairchild wants us to get that phone down to a signal and see if there's any messages. Where's my exhibit man?" She turned and bellowed at her crew, "I'm taking the phone and going down. Spacey, shoot it over."

A figure approached from the shadows, and the ex-hibit man, it turned out, was Jayne Spacey, a regular constable Leith had once worked alongside. Spacey, in heavy fur-lined parka, pulled off a mitt and handed an exhibit baggie to Giroux. She noticed Leith and smiled a crooked hello at him, which impacted him now as it did every time they met, taking his breath away. That was young Jayne Spacey, her face asymmetric like she'd suffered a stroke, but all the more beautiful for it.

Before he could fumble out a greeting, she turned to go, saying something about another missing person she had to go search for and rescue.

Leith called after her, "What?"

She walked backward a step or two, grinning. "Just kidding. Our temp, Constable Dion, from Smithers. Went off into the woods and didn't come back. Kinda cute but not too bright." She laughed, faced around, and trudged away into the dark.

He watched her go. He heard a murmuring of voices from the possible burial area and looked sidelong to see Corporal Fairchild beckoning him. He left Giroux and Bosko talking and joined the man and a small crew of Giroux's constables, who stood by a square of land about ten by ten, marked into a search grid with pegs and string.

Fairchild was near retirement, shorter than average, with a heavy grey moustache and gloomy eyes. He looked at Leith and said, "We got glitter, Dave."

Which to anyone else might sound silly, but filled Leith with dismay. "Damn," he said. "What colour?"

"Take a look." Fairchild pointed with his penlight beam, and Leith crouched and aimed his own penlight at the same clumps of snow within the grid. He angled his beam this way and that until the light bounced back at him in a pink flash.

It was the holdback info, the quirk, the fact that traces of body glitter had been found on two of the Pickup Killer's victims. Lab work had tracked it down to the same brand in both cases, and even to the chain store that sold it, if not the store itself. The store was found in just about every mall in the province.

He stood, swearing. Fairchild said, "Doesn't necessarily mean anything. Lotta girls wear it these days. And pink's a popular colour. Could be from lip gloss, or they put it in their hair, on their fingernails. They even glue it all over clothes. We'll scoop what we can, send it in, see if it's Hello Kitty."

Even if it matched the brand, Leith realized, it wouldn't be definitive proof. Up here shoppers didn't have a huge choice in anything when it came to the more esoteric products. If you were after body glitter, as he knew from those earlier investigations, Hello Kitty was pretty well what you were stuck with. Fairchild was right; maybe it meant nothing. But it sure didn't make him happy, those tiny sparkles of pink in the snow.

* * *

Dion was in trouble. He'd lost track and was wandering in circles, every step a struggle in the deepening snow. She had sent him this way, but how far was he supposed to go, and how far had he gone? He ploughed along farther from the lights, farther off the trail and into darkness, until there was nothing but his flashlight beam for company, and the woods were dense, the sky blacker than he had imagined possible. He swore at his own feet that couldn't seem to keep him upright, at the ear-popping elevation, the chill, the gloves he'd left behind. At himself for telling his CO back in Smithers that he was up for the challenge, and at the CO for believing him and sending him this far north. It had been a murderously long drive on slick roads, where logging trucks barrelled at him like monsters from the darkness, wood bits flying in their wake. He'd nearly lost his life on that road, lost traction twice, fishtailed once, then slowed to a crawl till his cruiser gathered a parade of headlights at its rear. But he'd finally arrived, two hours and fifteen minutes later, not the "one hour max" they'd told him.

The town they'd sent him to was called New Hazelton, about a quarter the size of his Smithers posting. From the New Hazelton RCMP office — the smallest detachment he'd ever stepped foot into — he'd been sent still farther out, twenty kilometres of back roads and then up the scariest mountain he'd ever faced, and now here he was, swallowed in wilderness, searching for a famous person. Famous locally, at least, far as he knew.

He skimmed his light through the trees. He reminded himself how grateful he was for this first real chance to prove himself. "This is fantastic," he said aloud, and his voice came out thin and quaky in the heavy silence. His boots slithered again, this time almost taking him down. He steadied himself and swore again. His teeth started to chatter, and to stop the chattering, he gritted them, but the shivers only moved into his shoulders. The light beam he was scoping through the spaces between the trees flickered, came on again strong, then blinked madly. "No, don't!" he shouted. He banged the torch on his thigh and thought about batteries. How could he forget such a fundamental as putting in fresh ones and packing spares? His heart began to thud.

"No big deal," he said and was reassured by his own adult voice, low and angry. "Walk back, follow your tracks."

He turned to head back to where he thought the distant main lights should be, thinking about wolves, and now his heart banged harder because he couldn't see his own tracks in this dim, wavering light beam. He turned the thing off, in part to conserve what juice was left and in part to make him less of a sitting duck to the nocturnal eyes that watched from the wilderness on all sides. He'd heard the predatory noises, the secretive shifting, the low breathing, the salivating, the circling. The sounds came from here first, then there. He turned, turned again, looked back, looked sideways.

Listening hard, he could now hear nothing but himself existing, the blood coursing through his system, the nylon of his jacket squealing with every shallow breath. Then something else, a distant crunch-crunch climbing toward him. Not a wolf, but maybe worse. He turned with measured speed and breathed out heavily as he saw that it was only her, the local constable, Jayne Spacey, who'd met him on the logging road some hours earlier and given him his instructions. She was following her light beam in his direction, calling out his name. He waved overhead. "Here."

The light landed on him. She crunch-crunched to a stop before him and cast her beam down so it bounced off the snow and lit her up like an actor before the stage lights, the angel saviour with one eyebrow tilted. She said, "What're you doing standing in the dark? Been gone so long I thought you froze to death out here."

"My light's dying," he said.

To prove it he raised the torch and clicked the button. Light flared like a small sun, catching her full in the face, making her squint. He shut if off again as fast as his cold fingers would let him, and Spacey said, "Well, lookit that, hey? It's fixed itself."

"Sorry about that."

He tested the light on the snow, the trees, the sky, and she said, "So I guess we're at a dead end, right?" She was nodding, agreeing with herself. "Yeah, we're on that thing I like to call the unlikely perimeter."

"There's tracks," Dion said, something he'd almost forgotten. With the light strong now, he found his way back to his only discovery, the mysterious, fairly fresh footprints cutting through a small clearing in a strident way. Spacey leaned to see where they went and then waded through bracken and crouched to inspect the boot prints closer. She smiled back at him and said, "I was hoping they're yours. That would be really funny. But they don't match."

She made her way back, looking at him with new interest, maybe concern. She said, "But we're just looking for small stuff, not tracks, remember? This area's been swept. The tracks, they're just SAR doing their rounds. You okay?"

"Fine. I was just heading back."

She stood watching him, scanning for some kind of information he couldn't supply. Her hood fur-fringed, and the fur was lashing about, along with a stray lock of gold hair. Her cheeks were rosy, her eyes gleaming as she maybe saw through him, saw that he wasn't fine, that he was cold and confused, just a step away from petrified. "First days are always rough," she said kindly. "But it'll get better, promise."

The words stung, *first days,* but worse was the sympathy. He nodded and tried to sound grateful. "Good to know."

She laughed and reached out to knock him playfully on the shoulder, the punch slowed by too many layers of clothing. She said, "It's getting onto eight thirty. Big meeting at the Catalina Cafe. Did you book accommodations yet? You're just an hour away, Smithers, right? Most staff just day-trip it, but the boss says there'll be no commuting on this one right now. Waste of time, she says. And makes no sense moneywise. She gets a deal at the Super 8, cheaper than manpower miles, even with the per diem. If you like, I'll take you out later, show you the town, all two minutes' worth of it. You won't fall in love, but at least you'll have a map in your mind."

He'd lost most of what she said, except the time. He angled his flashlight to see the hands of his wristwatch, and she was right, it was only half past eight, nowhere near midnight as he'd thought. "Meeting?" he said.

"Basic briefing, not mandatory for you, but you'd better come along, familiarize yourself with our reign of terror called Renee Giroux. I have to tell you, she's nothing like that nice white-haired NCO you got running the show at Smithers. He treating you right?"

Spacey's voice was young but husky, like she'd been a heavy smoker for years. Her speech patterns were snaky and hard to track, almost as bad as Penny McKenzie's, but she seemed nice, and if he was lucky he'd be shadowing her for however long he was stuck here, three days, four, before they found the missing girl, the singer whose name he'd already forgotten. He almost forgot the name of his NCO too, but it came to him now, as they hiked downslope toward the portable lights. "Willoughby, yeah," he said. "He's great."

Back in the brightly lit clearing, Spacey spoke with some members from the Terrace Ident section who stood by awaiting instructions. There was nothing left to do here tonight, Dion heard. They'd pack up and go, with a reduced crew to return in the morning light. Packing up everything but the crime-scene tape to mark the spot, the team carted out gear bags and went about powering down the lights. The generator grumbled to silence, and the last halogen faded to black. Flashlights came on, and all members prepared to leave the site, leaving only Dion kneeling in the snow, struggling with his designated task, packing a set of mattocks and spades into something like an oversized hockey bag. The task took him longer than it should, because his hands were numb, and the tools had to be laid just so or the zip wouldn't close.

Finally, he bullied the thing into shape and got it half-closed, then stood with it hoisted over his shoulder and gave the darkened scene a final scan, and it struck him with a wash of horror: they'd all leave, and she'd be left alone, if by some freak chance she remained trapped in some hidden nook or cranny. He imagined her reviving, crawling out into these terrifying woods, crying out, being met by silence.

Strange how he'd seen her in person, just a few months ago, at the Smithers Fall Fair. He pictured her now, the pretty girl dancing about the stage, singing her heart out. Kiera, that was her name. As it turned out, it was Kiera who needed help, not the black-haired girl in the bleachers he'd fixed on so pointlessly. If he'd been looking at the stage, not the crowd, maybe he'd have seen something that would lead to some conclusion now that would save the day.

He snorted at the idea and dug at the trampled snow with the heel of his boot, testing it for give. The ground below was hard as iron, so she couldn't be buried deep anywhere hereabouts. And the mountainside had been combed by dozens of searchers, so she wasn't buried shallow either. She'd been taken away then. He knew it. Maybe on foot, but likely in a vehicle. From what he knew, which wasn't much, he believed she was dead.

Somebody shouted, and he listened, but was distracted by the forest noises, almost voice-like, wordless mutters and whispers, and a low, demented whistling. The flashlight beam guttered again, and distantly, up on the logging road, he heard car doors slam shut and an engine turn over. He could imagine them forgetting to do a head count and departing without him. He saw himself alone in the woods, following Kiera's footsteps into the wildest mystery of all. A moment longer he hesitated, and then shifted the gear bag to his other shoulder and headed up the trodden path, almost at a run, to join the departing team.

* * *

Leith and Bosko arrived at the Catalina Cafe, its big yellow sign a blazing landmark on the highway cutting through town. Leith was tired, hungry, and aggravated.

He had spent the last hour in conference calls from his new desk at the New Hazelton detachment, and his vocal cords were strained raw. He wanted to return to Terrace and dive straight into the Pickup lead, now that they had a solid link to the Pickup Killer. Phil Prentice thought otherwise, reminding Leith that holding back information could be a valuable tool, but it could also cause havoc. Leaks happened, and supposedly confidential clues could be used and abused, and nothing should be taken for granted at this point. For now, pink glitter be damned, Leith was to remain in the Hazeltons and explore all the other myriad avenues, keeping in regular contact, of course, with the Terrace task force that would be chasing down the Pickup Killer full-tilt, headed up by Corporal Mel Stoner. Furthermore, the glitter angle was to remain, at Stoner's discretion, held back from the press and disseminated only to the core team.

The back room at the Catalina was too warm, and Leith shed his several layers of coats, jackets, and sweaters, hung them up, and took a seat. He had missed lunch and was glad the briefing would be bracketed around food. Hardly gourmet grub in a place like this, but he didn't care so long as it was greasily rich in salt and starch. Giroux said the food was great as she sat across from him, but she had to say that, knowing the owners; she knew everybody here. That was the advantage and disadvantage of running a village in the middle of nowhere: familiarity.

They were a party of ten, a few faces Leith didn't know. Giroux said she'd used this room often for meetings such as this. It was also used for weddings and whatnot. Sound-wise, it was well insulated, private, and the staff knew all about discretion. The one long table they sat at was draped in white. The walls were panelled in fake wood and hung about with genuine mounted animal heads, which in turn were hung about with cobwebs. Swing doors separated this room from the kitchen, but the kitchen sounds were distant enough when the doors clicked shut. Music from a local pop station played, but barely audible.

Coffee was served and orders were taken, and Giroux made introductions, naming herself in charge of New Hazelton. She would be dealing with issues in her community but would be at hand to lend assistance to the team when possible. She introduced Leith as lead investigator, the one who'd assign tasks, make all procedural decisions, and liaise with Sergeant Phil Prentice in Prince Rupert.

She introduced Sergeant Mike Bosko, the brass from the Lower Mainland who was joining the team in a sort of unofficial advisory capacity until further notice. A few brows went up, and Corporal Fairchild from Terrace asked jokingly, "What, just happened to be passing by?" the joke being that nobody *just passed by* the lonely Hazeltons in mid-February.

Leith watched Bosko for reaction to the jibe and saw the irony had gone right past him. "Pretty well," Bosko said. "Dave was heading this way, so I hitched a ride."

Giroux charged through the remaining introductions and then gave the floor to Jayne Spacey, who had opened the file and knew it best. Spacey stood to talk, skimming fast over Kiera Rilkoff's particulars, since they were all there on her stat sheet: age, height, weight, the colour of her hair and eyes, address, identifying marks. She went on from there. "At twenty-two she still lives with her parents and her sister Grace on 12th Avenue. Sergeant Giroux and I were there early today, and on a preliminary look-around there's nothing out of ordinary in her room."

"The family's completely flummoxed," Giroux put in. "And devastated. We don't have to focus on them whatsoever."

Spacey said, "Kiera's a high school grad. She has plans of attending music school in Vancouver somewhere down the road. Good reputation in the community, no criminal history. She'd been employed at the Chevron gas station until last summer, when she quit to devote herself to her music. We all know Fling's a successful band and seems to be going places. Her parents support her financially and morally, it seems. I haven't taken full statements from them yet, but like the boss just said, we have no reason to focus on them at this point. Kiera's dad is with the Ministry of Forests, and her mom's a physiotherapist at the hospital, so they're financially secure."

Leith admired how Spacey had progressed since they'd last met. He wondered if her straight-shouldered stance and lucid delivery had anything to do with the presence of the brass from the city. He wondered if his own blustering did as well, and hoped not.

Spacey said, "Now for the here's-what-we-know part. Kiera's boyfriend is Frank Law, who's the guitarist in the band. She spends much of her time at his place in Kispiox." She passed around several copies of a map marked in red with points of interest. "It's the 'L,' and I've been there as well today. It's a good-sized house on an acreage he shares with his two brothers, Leonard and Robert, better known as Lenny and Rob. It's here Fling has been rehearsing since the house was built, about four years ago. They were rehearsing there yesterday when Kiera left the house, alone, drove off, and didn't come back. She left at the lunch break, around noon, but nobody can give a precise time. She was seen driving northwest on Kispiox Road about an hour later by a friend of the Law brothers, Scott Rourke."

She went on detailing the eyewitness account of Scott Rourke, who had been riding down Kispiox Road on his motorbike when Kiera had passed him in her Isuzu, upward bound. Leith had heard most of this up on the mountainside, but he made notes now. Most everybody at the table did the same, except for the dark-haired uniformed constable at Leith's left, who couldn't seem to find a pen. Leith gave him his spare and said to Spacey, "A motorbike? In these conditions?"

"More like a dirt bike," Spacey said. "And Rourke's a maniac." She went on. "Also on the map you'll see an 'RL' up on Kispiox Mountain. That's where the Law brothers, more specifically Frank's older brother Rob, run a logging show. We have reason to believe she was heading up to see him when her truck broke down at the 'M' you'll see there, the Matax hiking trail. Kiera and Frank texted briefly around one thirty, and that was their last communication. We got it off Frank's phone."

Another photocopy was passed around, a printout of a direct screenshot from an iPhone. Bosko looked it over and then passed it to Leith. The text came from Kiera at 1:26 p.m.

Kiera: "Screw U. Find yrsf another lead"
Frank: "WTF? Where RU?"

Spacey said, "Kiera didn't reply, and Frank more or less put it out of his mind till later in the evening, when Rob Law came upon her black Isuzu Rodeo at the Matax trailhead as he was coming down from the cut block around seven. He got home at seven thirty. That's when Frank collected Chad and went up."

She paused as the waitress brought food. Not a moment too soon, Leith thought, his stomach grumbling. The constable to his left, the one who'd forgotten his pen, was in his mid-twenties, maybe, pale-skinned but dark-haired and dark-eyed, beat-up looking. He was staring with doubt at the Denver sandwich placed before him, and in a low-grade epiphany Leith realized this was the guy Jayne Spacey had called "kinda cute but not too bright." Dion, the temp in from Smithers.

The long-awaited "Special" burger with extra fries landed in front of Leith, and he dug in. Spacey ignored her wrap, still on her feet, and went on briefing the team. She told them who had been at the house yesterday at noon when Kiera walked out: Chad Oman, the drummer, Stella Marshall, who played fiddle, and Frank Law's younger brother Lenny Law, who was seventeen and home-schooled. Lenny wasn't involved with the band, as far as Spacey knew, and there was some question about whether he was present at the time Kiera left.

Giroux told Spacey to sit down and eat, which Spacey did, and for a while there was only the sound of forks and knives hitting china, munching, sipping, and the distant twitter of pop music.

Leith chomped at his burger faster than he should. Down the table, Mike Bosko ate a much healthier salad of some kind and made conversation with Corporal Fairchild, Ident Team Leader, at his side. Constable Dion picked up the first quarter of his Denver and devoured it in two big bites, then closed his eyes and looked ill.

Bosko left his conversation with Fairchild to ask Spacey, if she didn't mind, about more general background on the band itself. "I've heard they're putting out a CD?"

"Was supposed to come out at Christmas," Spacey said. "There were some delays, and I'm not sure where that's at right now. Mercy Blackwood would be the one to talk to, the band's manager. I'll set her up for an interview."

Leith added the name Blackwood to his list of interviewees and listened as Constable Spacey described a barrette she'd found in the snow near where Kiera's cellphone was found. Both barrette and phone would have to be fingerprinted, and Kiera's family would be asked to identify the items.

Leith scrubbed the mayo off his mouth and told the team of the critical clue, the body glitter, possibly linking up this disappearance with two of the three Terrace murders. Some discussion followed on the importance of eliminating or confirming the link, then he turned to the cellphone, now Police Exhibit 1, which wouldn't give up any secrets till he got it unlocked. "Nobody knows her password?" he asked Spacey. "BFF, family, boyfriend?"

"Not so far," Spacey said.

Bosko said, "And who is her BFF, by the way?"

Corporal Fairchild said, "What the hell is a BFF?"

"Best friends forever in teen-speak," Spacey told him. "And WTF is what the fuck."

"Everybody knows what the fuck," Fairchild said testily.

Spacey ignored him and said to Bosko, "Her BFF would be Frank. She's got tons of Facebook friends, I know because I checked, but not a lot of real up-close and touch-em people in her life. The band is kind of insular in that way. They stick together."

Leith was thinking about the cellphone. He told Fairchild, "If you could find out who her provider is—"

"Rogers," Spacey said. "I checked."

Leith nodded at her. "Contact Rogers," he told Fairchild. "Crack the code, get a printout of her call and text history."

"I'll get on it," Fairchild said. "I'll see what I can do about a data dump, but it may take a while. For starters I can grab some screenshots. How far you want me to go back, Dave?"

Leith suggested a month.

Fairchild put the question out about the Isuzu — which was being scoured for evidence by his team even as they spoke — why it had stalled, whether an engine could be sabotaged without leaving a trace. Leith didn't know the answer. Nobody did, not even the fountain of knowledge named Bosko. Giroux said she'd ask Jim of Duncan's Auto Repair; he'd know.

Spacey passed around a snapshot of Kiera Rilkoff and Frank Law. Leith had only glanced at the photo earlier, and he took the time to study it now, Kiera smiling gorgeously at the camera, her boyfriend seated beside her, also smiling. Frank's smile could be judged gorgeous too, he supposed, if the judge was a young girl.

Frank Law, like Kiera, was white, in his early twenties. He had longish hair, dirty blond, and in the photo he wore a clingy black short-sleeved shirt, a thorny tattoo banding his upper bicep. Leith angled the photograph to Giroux. "Any kind of a record on this guy?"

She nodded. "Pretty minor. Assault, few years back. Got one year probation and a stern eye from the judge is about it."

"Domestic?"

"No, he pushed a guy. Or punched him, depending on which one of them you believe. The guy fell down. It was just stupid, really, but this guy who fell down was a building inspector. We couldn't just let it slide. Building inspectors have it rough enough, without letting it be known you can push 'em and get away with it, eh."

Leith passed the photo sideways to Dion and said to nobody in particular, "Girl like this could have her share of stalkers, right? Even without the celebrity status."

Across from him Corporal Fairchild added to the thought. "She could have her share of *anybody*. Maybe she did, and maybe Frank didn't like it. Why is nobody asking why she was heading up to see his brother?"

The team canvassed the issue, but it entered the realm of conjecture, and Leith, suffering the first pangs of indigestion, didn't take part. The waitress came by, checking if anyone wanted refills. Nobody wanted more coffee except Giroux, a woman who bragged she only needed four hours' sleep a night. Constable Dion asked for another Coke and ice, and when he received it and

COLD GIRL

stuck the straw in his mouth, Leith felt obliged to turn to him with a warning, thinly disguised as chummy advice. "You heard the latest on sugar, right? They've discovered it makes lab rats stupid."

He didn't feel chummy about it at all. He was genuinely concerned about stupidity in the ranks, and this man, he could see at a glance, needed to hold onto as many brain cells as he had left.

Constable Dion set down his glass and gave him a blank stare. "'Scuse me?"

Too late, Leith thought. "Forget it," he said, and watched Dion do just that, returning to the sandwich like it was some kind of do-or-die challenge. Leith glared at him a moment longer and then told the team, "Tomorrow first thing I'll talk to Frank out in Kispiox, and if he's agreeable, I'll get Forensics in there, the sooner the better." To Giroux he said, "I wouldn't mind if you came with me to do the introductions. After Frank, we'll just have to plough through the rest of the band as fast as we can. I also want to talk to Frank's brothers, Rob and Lenny. Especially Rob."

Spacey said, "Getting hold of Rob isn't easy. He's a workaholic, spends a lot of nights in the Atco up on the cut block. He's there now, and I can't reach him to call him in for an interview. No cell service up there, and his satellite phone's either down or disconnected."

"Well, somebody's gotta go haul him down here, then," Leith said, hoping it wouldn't be himself doing the hauling. He wasn't afraid of Rob Law, but he was afraid of that fucking road, the painful crawl along a precipice, tires thumping over the rough-furrowed snow. Nobody around here seemed much fazed by that particular road, but he was a prairie boy, and verticals just weren't in his genes.

Fairchild shook his head. "Get him on his trucker chat-channel. Or one of his crew's. Get the message out that he's to come and see you or face a warrant. We don't have time or resources to go chasing our witnesses up mountainsides. Not here, not now."

"Amen," Leith said. "I'll leave it to you, then."

"No problem," Fairchild said.

"Well, maybe we can work it into a viewing of the trailhead tomorrow," Bosko offered, countering Fairchild's great suggestion in that long-winded, easy-going manner that was starting to grate on Leith. "We could go up and take a look around the crime scene in the light of day, then head up to the cut block, if that's what Rob Law prefers, which might be preferable for us too. Sometimes it's better talking to people on their own turf. What d'you think, Dave?"

Leith eyed him coldly. "That works too."

He went about dividing up the rest of the inter-views, with Spacey making notes. The songs playing distantly on the radio were melancholy, making Leith crave beer, but drinking wasn't in the cards tonight. The meeting began to wind down, and there followed some less formal chit-chat and housekeeping matters. Giroux talked about disbursements and accommodations for the out-of-towners, Leith from Prince Rupert, Bosko from the Lower Mainland, Fairchild from Terrace, and the dumbass temp from Smithers, Dion, who was too busy cramming the last of his sandwich to notice he was being addressed, which made Giroux raise her voice in irritation and flap her hand at his face. "Constable. Yes, that's you. Did you get yourself a room yet?"

With mouth full, Dion stared across at her.

A familiar anger began to crawl in Leith's veins, and for good reason. Sometimes, somehow, a real bonehead crossed the recruitment hurdle and made it onto the force. Dion was one of those, just out of training, shell-shocked by the grim reality of his job. Probably expected respect, glamour, fun. Probably on day one he'd been posted roadside for eight hours with a radar gun in his hand and was already balking. *Well, fuck you, we've all done it*, Leith thought.

Maladjustment was just the base of the problem; the reputation of the force was at stake, and by extension the reputation of Leith. As though scandals and leadership issues weren't bad enough, last year a bonehead rookie such as this one, under his command, had blown an investigation, costing the Crown a rock-solid conviction. It was a big case, and the acquittal still left a genuine twinge of pain in Leith's chest when he thought of it.

So no, he didn't find stupidity in the ranks funny. And neither did Renee Giroux, who barked at the temp now, "I take that as a no. So, not for the first time, please get yourself booked in over at the Super 8 and bring in the paperwork. Got that? It's right across the highway there."

Everyone watched Constable Dion absorbing the instructions, and Corporal Fairchild asked him, "Up from the city, are you? Touch of culture shock? How'd I guess? Easy. You got that *what's with all these fucking trees* look about you. Where's the malls? Where's the Starbucks?"

Jayne Spacey laughed and blew ice water through her straw at Dion's face, making him blink. Mike Bosko looked at the temp with brief interest — and maybe only Leith caught his slight double-take — then turned back to Giroux, who was asking him something.

"So where exactly do you call home, Mike?"

"I'm kind of between homes right now," Bosko told her. "I was in Vancouver for four years, with Commercial Crimes, and I'm making the move over to North Van to help rewire their Serious Crimes Unit. Just needs some tweaking here and there, but it's not as easy as it sounds."

"From white collar to SCU to clambering about in the mountains," Giroux said. "Impressive."

Spacey leaned forward in a sparkly way, getting Bosko's attention. "Does your rewiring include seeking out new talent by any chance, sir?"

He smiled back at her. "It certainly does."

The exchange got Leith's attention, and he checked Bosko's face, trying to see if he meant it about the talent search. If so, it might mean an opening for him too. He wasn't so sure he wanted it, these days, a radical move to the glittering metropolis. Fifteen years ago, leaving his home in North Battleford, Saskatchewan, to join the RCMP, he'd set his sails for the bright lights of Vancouver, but now that he was comfortably lodged in Prince Rupert, a place he liked, the idea of leaving seemed about as doable as relocating to Mars. Or maybe he was just scared.

He shifted back in his seat, vaguely depressed, imagining being stuck in dingy backrooms like this for the rest of his working life. On the other hand, stalwarts like him were needed here as everywhere. Missing kids like Kiera Rilkoff needed him.

His depression deepened, no longer for himself, but for her. Whatever anybody thought, he knew this would be no happy ending. The girl had crossed paths with somebody bad, and was either dead or in that person's control. He heard Bosko and Spacey discussing North Vancouver, what a great city it was, that buzzing beehive to the south, and from the corner of his eye he noticed Constable Dion had become interested for the first time in something other than his own plate, and the something was Mike Bosko's face. Was there recognition in his stare, along with a touch of anger? Leith looked at Bosko, thinking he must surely feel the heat of attention, but apparently Bosko didn't.

Anyway, Leith realized, it wasn't a stare so much as a sustained glance, and already Dion was tuned out again. But Bosko's earlier double-take, together with Dion's sustained glance, told him something about these two: They either knew each other or knew something of each other, and yet neither wanted to admit it. It was a puzzle, but probably just his imagination at work. And even if it wasn't his imagination, it was certainly none of his business.

The remaining dishes were cleared from the table. An old Harry Nilsson song was on the radio, muted and sad. The SAR people were out there, working hard through the night, FLIR-equipped choppers raking the mountains. APBs were broadcast and reinforcements were on their way for a search that was going to spread ever outward till she was found or resources ran dry. There was nothing more Leith could do right now but rest up for tomorrow. He declared the meeting over and ordered everyone to get a few hours of sleep. All team heads would be up and at it bright and early, for if the Rockabilly Princess was being held by a predator with a pickup truck, there was no question about it: her time was fast running out.

Two

QUESTIONS

TALK AT THE CATALINA Cafe had gone on past midnight, and Leith hadn't made it to his motel bed until one thirty. He woke in the morning when it was still dark out, missing Alison, and missing her more as he stood, toothbrush in hand, and observed the lumps and bumps of his homely face in the bathroom mirror. He'd forgotten all the domestic unhappiness and slamming of doors and the howling child and his aching head. All he knew was he missed them both. Ali and Izzy, his girls.

His home away from home was a room on the second floor of a long, boxy, two-storey Super 8 motel set right on the highway, mid-range, furnished in the usual murky browns and golds like every other inn Leith had ever been stuck in, not a destination but a contingency for the working traveller. Depending on how things went, he could be struck in this Gyproc haven for days, maybe weeks, along with a growing legion of out-of-towners. For now the team was relatively small.

The corridor outside his room was hushed and empty, a hive of sleeping souls. Downstairs in the diner he found Fairchild and Bosko already with coffee in front of them. The only other resident out-of-towner on the case so far, Constable Dion, was nowhere to be seen. The three men had a quick breakfast, asking each other how they'd slept, exchanged motel horror stories, then sat in their vehicles and crossed the silent highway to the small Hazelton detachment.

Small was an understatement. It was a low, squarish building probably built sometime in the seventies, posted with the backlit RCMP signage out front, but otherwise innocuous as a laundromat. The kind of place that would make wandering criminals feel right at home as they cased the town, Leith had told Giroux last night, still seated in the Catalina's back room with her and Bosko following the dinner briefing. "It's better than anarchy," Giroux had answered. Anyway, it would soon be replaced with something bigger and better, and she'd passed over photos not of her nieces and nephews but the architectural rendering of the project to be. In a few years, she said, no more little straw house. She'd be living in brick. "That makes you the smart little pig," Leith had pointed out.

Unfortunately, for now they were stuck with the straw, hazy under the pre-dawn glow of lamp standards. Inside, he left Bosko and Fairchild in the main room, busy on their respective BlackBerrys at their temporary desks, and found Giroux in her little office, moving colour-coded magnets around her organizational white board. Like the detachment itself, the woman put up an unlikely face of the law, a little middle-aged Métis lady with slightly crazy eyes that always seemed widened on the verge of outrage. Leith, like probably a lot of people, had assumed Renee Giroux had gained her office via reverse discrimination, a local native, female, getting the boost to show the RCMP's non-sexist forward momentum and open-mindedness. But Phil Prentice had once enlightened Leith to the truth over beers: Renee Giroux had got where she was by the sheer digging in of her stubborn little heels. And she wasn't local, either, but had blown over like a travelling weed from eastern Canada, made this her home, and refused to budge. She'd started out as a constable at the age of twenty-two and served under a score of commanding officers, mostly big white guys like Leith himself, and against the odds her wit and hard work and loyalty and sheer *rootedness* had finally paid off, and she'd made corporal, and then sergeant, and now she was officially the queen of this little mud-hole called the Hazeltons.

"Why are you so set on it?" Leith had asked her last night. They'd left the Catalina and were standing at their vehicles, hunching against the bitter wind funnelling down the broad highway, no sign of life in this poverty-stricken little shanty town of hers. "Awesome place," she'd said, and pointed up to what Leith saw only as midnight skies layered with clouds of thunder grey. "Stood under that mountain there and fell in love, said this is where I'm going to die."

That was what she said last night. Now she said, "Morning, Big City. You're late."

On some level, Leith liked the nickname she'd stuck on him some years ago. It flattered him, which in turn made him feel foolish, because Prince Rupert, City of Rainbows, was hardly a big city; it was a largish funky fishing village on the stormy north coast. He wasn't awake enough to bandy about cheerful greetings. "You said six thirty."

The crazy eyes widened at him. "Yes, which means six fifteen. Okay? So Spacey's organized herself and Thackray to canvass the Bell 3 for any workers that slipped our radar last night, and I got whatshisname, Dion, out looking for Lenny Law. Sound good?"

Lenny Law was Frank Law's younger brother, one of many witnesses who needed to be rounded up. An important witness, one of the last few to see Kiera on the day of her vanishing. Leith said, "Oh. I figured he slept in."

"Who?"

"Dion."

"No, actually, he was in bright and early. Unlike you."

This was Giroux's territory, but it was Leith's case, and he knew there would be some jostling before they got comfortable in their roles. So far the jostling was fairly amiable, and if they didn't bite each other's heads off first, it should stay that way. "Fine," he said.

"Great. Then I'm ready to go tackle our prime suspect, as you called him last night about five times without any grounds whatsoever."

She pulled on her RCMP-decalled jacket as she spoke, heavy-duty blue nylon, and Leith said, "Yes, and I stick to my guns on that. And by the way, we're going out there without backup. Should I be worried?"

The jacket swamped her, made her comical. She said, "Worried? About Frank? No. He's a musician."

"Last I heard, musicians can be mean too. He's got a police record involving fists, and I saw the picture. He's covered in the kind of tattoos that say 'make-my-day.' I don't get along well with people covered in tattoos. You ask me, we should err on the side of caution and take along a uniform. What we in the big city call 'backup.'"

She laughed. "Get real. I know Frank. He's a sweetheart. You got a gun, don't you?"

"I'd rather not use it."

She snorted, and with that won the argument.

They sat in her vehicle, the dinged black Crown Vic he'd seen parked up on the mountain last night. Like her jacket, the steering wheel looked a couple sizes too big for her. "They live over the bridge and deep in the woods," she said, conjuring up another children's classic to brand the boys neatly. "I call 'em the three bears."

Rob, Frank, and Lenny Law.

"Bears," Leith said, regretting he hadn't insisted on that backup. An extra 9mm at the sidelines would be nice, at least till he got a feel for the players in this thing. Being in unfamiliar territory didn't help. He had worked in the Hazeltons before, but never in depth. The land here was huge and wild, dense with pine and poplar, riddled with rivers and gorges, and within all that chaos of nature sat this starburst of small communities linked by long, meandering roads, much of it barely charted. So, yes, he was a little uneasy.

"And I say it again," Giroux said. She had fired up the Crown Vic's eight lusty cylinders and lunged the car out through the chain-linked lot onto the avenue. "And this is why. He's got an alibi for the time she went missing, unless it's a three-way conspiracy, which I guess we can't discount. And he was the first to put on his boots and go out searching. And he searched till he bled," she added, the Queen of Hyperbole. "They had to drag him in half-dead from the cold. If that's not sweet, what is?"

Leith sighed.

"It's your case," she added. "But my people. So just keep that in mind."

By *my people* she meant all the registered locals, he realized. Not just the dark-skinned Aboriginals that populated much of the north. Whites were the minority in the Hazeltons, but not by far, and they too belonged to Renee Giroux.

Clouds had gathered, thick. A few flakes fluttered down, not nearly the whiteout of last night. Giroux steered them through Two Mile, through Old Town, over the bridge that spanned a rather gut-wrenching canyon, and on for another quarter hour down a narrow, snowy back-road, finally turning into a driveway made of tire ruts.

The driveway seemed to go on forever, dead straight through a young poplar forest, ending in a clearing, and through the windshield Leith saw a big ugly rancher set down amongst the trees with all the grace of a beer can on a beach. Powder blue, vinyl-sided, green metal roof sloping at a shallow pitch. Machinery and cars and clut-ter in the yard. The kind of place a pit bull would run around looking for man-sized snacks. He kept an eye out but saw no animals lurking in the gloom.

"Been out here before?" he asked.

"Once," she said, puffing vapour ghosts. "About four years back. That incident I told you about. House was just bare bones then. The Law boys built it pretty much on their own. Dispute with the building inspector became a verbal firestorm and ended in Marty — that's the inspector — on his ass. Frank did his penance, and far as I know it never happened again. Far as I know, Frank and Marty still drink together."

Up on the porch, Giroux rapped her knuckles on the door. Leith, listening for dogs still, saw deck chairs, ashtrays, beer cans, and what was probably a mega-gas barbecue under a tarp. The three bears enjoyed their house in the woods, it seemed. Heavy wool blankets thrown over the deck chairs suggested they enjoyed it even on a cold winter day.

The door opened, and he got his first look at his only real suspect so far, Frank Law. The guy was twenty-three, still at the concave-gut stage of life, a lanky powerhouse. Tallish, lightly bearded, eye sockets dented by what was maybe exhaustion, maybe guilt, maybe a good brew of both. "Anything?" he asked.

"Sorry, nothing yet," Giroux said. "Frank, this is Constable Leith, up from Prince Rupert. He's come to make sure we look in all the right places, okay?"

Frank looked far from reassured but allowed them in with a good show of manners. In the living room, among more macho mess and the not-so-faint smell of pot smoke, they took seats.

Leith fiddled with his pocket recorder, prefaced the recording with date and time and who all was present, and asked Frank to take them to the beginning, starting from the day before Kiera had gone missing, that being Friday. "Just take your time," he said, "and give me a visual replay of everything you can remember, okay?"

"Friday," Frank said. His voice was husky and sore. "Helped Rob up on the landing all morning, bucking some old windfall out of the way for the crew. I left for home about four. It was getting dark. Rob stayed on alone, breaking his own rules. You don't work alone in this business unless you got a death wish, but there's only so far you can push him, and he just shuts you out. That's Rob. Anyway, he's got these new lights set up there, wants to get his money's worth. Told me not to worry. So I didn't." His frown deepened, and he seemed already lost. Giroux prompted him with an encouraging murmur, and he gave a start and carried on. "Friday night. Came back, had dinner with Lenny and Kiera. She came over for dinner."

He didn't recall the conversation around the dinner table or what they'd done that evening except watch some dumb show on TV. Leith asked if Kiera had mentioned anything out of the ordinary happening in her life, if she'd met anyone, even just a casual encounter. Did she have any special plans for the upcoming days?

Frank didn't recall anything unusual in their conversation. Kiera went home pretty early, around ten o'clock. Frank went to bed soon after.

Leith asked him about the day that really mattered now, Saturday. "Just go through it, minute by minute. What happened?"

"I got up about seven thirty, had toast and coffee."

"And Rob had stayed up on the mountain, right? What about Lenny? Was he around?"

Frank scowled. "Sleeps like a pile of rocks these days. He's seventeen. Such a shitty age. Used to be our soundman, and a good one, but lost interest. Lost interest in everything, pretty well."

Leith studied Frank's downturned lashes, the troubled lines of his face, his shoulders, that almost visible inner quaking of emotional trauma. Not a cruel man, but possibly a killer. Anybody could be, really.

Frank went ploughing on, talking in machine-gun bursts now, like all he wanted was to get this over with. "So Lenny was in his room, and Kiera came over a bit later than she said, nearly nine. We'd agreed on eight thirty."

"Was that unusual?"

He shrugged. "Kind of. No big deal. I was already setting up the equipment. We went over some of the music, played a bit, waited for the others to show up."

"You have an in-house studio?"

"Top of the line," Frank said, sitting straighter and flicking hair out of his eyes. "Just finished last November. To die for." He looked pugnacious as he said it, as though daring Leith to contradict him. Now he was glum again. Leith prompted him back on track.

"Chad and Stella showed up minutes after Kiera, around nine, quarter after," Frank said. "Chad's wrecked his truck, so he caught a ride in with Stella."

Chad was Chad Oman, the band's drummer. He was native, local born, once a bit of a troublemaker, according to Giroux, but nothing worse than the usual teenage *joie de vivre*. Now that he was in his twenties, working at the Home Hardware, and with a great career as a drummer on the horizon, he was behaving "pretty good." And Stella was Stella Marshall, also a band member, also local born, also in her early twenties, who apparently played the electric fiddle.

Frank described how the band had rehearsed for a couple of hours, till lunch break. More to get a sense of the group dynamics than anything, Leith asked if it had been a good rehearsal. The answer was short, snappy, and surprising. "No," Frank said. "It was crappy. Got nothing accomplished. It's the pressure. We need to get this demo put together by the end of the month because the last one bombed, so we were all just on edge. Especially Kiera. So we took an early break, and I put out some food, but nobody seemed hungry. Kiera said she was going out for a while, and she just took off. Drove off in her truck. It was just after noon, I guess."

"Did you see which way she went?" Leith asked, though he knew the answer before Frank shook his head. There was only one way she could have gone by vehicle, and that was off down that long, tree-shrouded driveway. Unless somebody followed her, they couldn't know which way she went once she hit the narrow two-lane Kispiox Road, whether it was south toward town or north toward the Kispiox Range, where her truck had been found.

"What did she say, exactly, as she left?"

"Not much. 'Back in a while.' That's about it."

"She was upset?"

"Not upset. Fed up."

"With who, or what?"

"Like I said, the music wasn't coming together. They're upbeat tunes. You can't force upbeat, can you?" It was a black, rhetorical question. He said, "Stella said there wasn't much point sticking around, so she and Chad left. Lenny crawled out of his room, grabbed a sandwich, went off with Tex to Prince George. That was my idea. I wanted him out of there. Last thing I needed was a sullen teenager hanging around."

This part Leith didn't know so well, but he'd seen in the statements taken by Spacey, drafted up for review, that Tex was Lenny's buddy who'd picked up Lenny and taken him off to Prince George for the day. So far neither boy had been reached, and it wasn't for lack of trying. He also knew that both Lenny and Tex were homeschoolers, so they chose their own reading assignments and wrote their own schedules, which also made them harder to pin down. "What time was it they took off?"

"About half an hour after Kiera left, I guess."

"What does Tex drive?"

"Old Toyota station wagon. Silver."

Leith asked why the boys were going to Prince George.

"There's stuff to do in George. Tex has family down there. His dad's there, has a big place, so they go there whenever they can."

Leith told him to carry on, and Frank was slumped again, eyes closed to help track his memories. "I had a bite to eat then called Parker in to see if we could salvage anything from what we had so far. Parker had a listen and said pretty flat-out, no, we couldn't fix this. It was garbage."

"Parker?" Leith said, taken aback. "Who's that?"

"Techie, works at the college, does our post-op mix for us."

Leith got the gist. He asked for Parker's full name and address, but all Frank had was a cell number, which he read out from his phone. Leith wrote it down and asked for a timeline for Parker's attendance. Frank looked at his phone again and said he'd called Parker at 12:50, and the guy had come by within about fifteen or twenty minutes.

Leith said, "So Parker comes over, listens to your recording. Now what?"

"Like I told Constable Spacey, Kiera texted me. 'Screw you. Get yourself another lead.' Didn't take it too seriously. She was just sulking. I texted back, asked her what that was all about. No answer."

"Right," Leith said. "I've seen the texts. You didn't press her for more. Why? Weren't you worried?"

"I was wondering where the hell she was off to, but I wasn't going to play any head games. I figured she'd be back eventually, and we'd kiss and make up like always."

"Were you surprised when her truck was found up on the Matax?"

"Totally. I guess she was going to see Rob. She wouldn't be hiking the Matax, not at this time of year. Not dressed like she was. Unless she went home and changed. Which she might have, for all I know, because she was gone quite a while before she texted, and she couldn't have texted from up on the mountain. No signal."

Leith said, "She hadn't mentioned visiting Rob before she left?"

"No, never, and I have no idea why she'd want to see him."

"How do she and Rob generally get along? Are they close?"

Frank shrugged, cracking his knuckles. "They get along okay, as much as Rob gets along with anyone. Don't have much in common, except me. I've got no clue why she'd all of a sudden go up to see him. Maybe she had something to tell him that she couldn't tell me. I just can't say. I asked Rob. He says she didn't call, didn't talk to him beforehand, and she never showed up there. I think she's only been to the cut block once, me just showing her the operation last summer. You can ask Rob yourself, but he'll say the same thing. He hasn't got a clue."

Along with the knuckle cracking, there was a vicious undertone to his words that Leith made mental note of. It made him wonder, was there something between the lines he should be reading? He now went about angering Frank by backtracking for further detail, such as what was served for lunch, food and beverage, stuff that could be pertinent only in the grim event of an actual autopsy. Frank didn't know what Kiera had or hadn't eaten or drunk. Leith next asked about the pot smell. "Who's the smoker in the house?"

"None of us smoke."

"I'm not talking cigarettes."

Frank crossed his arms, an irritated man, paddling his feet on the floorboards.

Leith said, "C'mon, Frank. I'm getting stoned just sitting here."

Frank sighed. "We all smoke. Everybody in the world smokes a bit of herb."

Except me, Leith thought. He wondered about the drugs, their source, whether they figured into the abduction at all, but it was a diversion he didn't want to take quite yet. Except for one more question, relevant to nothing but his own concern for the welfare of a young person. "Does that include Lenny?"

"Definitely not Lenny," Frank said. "I won't let him touch the stuff."

He said it adamantly, and Leith believed him and was slightly cheered. "Glad to hear it. So Kiera's texted you. Go on from there."

"Parker left. I think I just worked on a song till Rob got home, saying he'd found her truck up at the Matax trailhead. Then I got scared."

At this point Giroux said she could smell coffee. Would it be okay if she helped herself to a cup? Frank nodded at her, and she rose and went to the kitchen, just visible from the living room through an opening in the wall, and banged around in the cupboards. "Carry on," she said. "I can hear you from here."

Leith asked Frank to describe what Kiera was wearing when she left. Frank described distressed jeans, grey T-shirt, the heavy shapeless cardigan that looked straight off a homeless man's back but was actually a pricey piece of steampunk she'd bought in Vancouver. And the boots to match, the army-of-the-future look. If she had a coat, she'd left it in her truck.

There was no coat in the truck, Leith knew, so it was probably still on her back. What about her hair, he asked. Did Frank remember how was it done up that day?

Frank shrugged. "She usually ties it back, for practice. Keeps it out of her face."

Giroux was back with a coffee mug between her palms. Leith said, "Photos. Were any taken on Saturday? Of Kiera, I'm interested in mostly."

Frank checked his phone and found one shot he'd chanced to take during the rehearsal. Leith had a look, and

from what he could see Kiera's hair was in a ponytail and
clipped to one side with a barrette. The colour of the hair
clip was indiscernible, and he suspected that no amount of
pixel-tweaking would tell them if it matched the metallic
blue clip found on the mountain. Still, it was something.

He asked if he could skim through the shots, and
Frank didn't care, so he did, flicked through a few weeks'
worth and found typical pictures that young people take
of each other and themselves, mostly out of focus and
chaotic. A talented photographer Frank was not. It did
tell him that however gloomy they'd been on the day of
Kiera's disappearance, they'd been happy enough in the
days before. Of course the metadata would tell him a lot
more, but he couldn't get the metadata without a warrant, and he wasn't even close to that yet.

He asked if he could keep the phone for a day or two,
upload that photo of Kiera? Frank looked at him aghast.
"No way. I can email anything you want, but no way
you're taking my phone."

"Cool," Leith said — not the word he had in mind.
He handed over his business card. "Send me that shot,
but soon as possible. Okay?"

"Sure, I can do it now," Frank said, and he sat there
tapping at his phone, transferring the shot to Leith's
email address off the business card.

Leith said, "Once you heard from Rob of the Isuzu at
the Matax, then what happened?"

"I picked up Chad, and we dressed up warm and got
flashlights and went up to have a look. Got there about
eight thirty. Pitch black already. Her truck's cold as ice.
Doors were unlocked. She's careful about stuff like that,

locking her car. There was no notes, no keys, no handbag. Saw a bunch of footprints in the snow going down the slope toward the trail. There's that little dip there before it climbs. So that's where we went."

"Did you touch anything in the truck?"

"No."

"See her coat there?"

"No. Wasn't looking for her coat."

"In the snow, how many sets of prints?"

Frank rubbed his face. He'd said it before and didn't want to say it again. "It was too messed up. Tracks overlaid and snowed upon. Then where the trail started there was lots of tree cover, so not enough snow on the ground to leave tracks. Farther in where the snow got thick again, we didn't see any tracks, and we were looking for 'em hard. We walked around the woods yelling her name. Then went back to town and called you guys. Talked to Constable Spacey there. No search team till morning, she says. Couldn't believe my ears. Still can't." He gave Leith a nasty stare, his eyes raw and sore. "So we gathered friends and family, many as we could, nearly a dozen, went back up and did it ourselves."

He was wilting again. He directed his next words toward the window. "I should be out there now, fuck me, looking for her."

"I think the Search and Rescue guys have it covered."

"Then I might as well get back to the block, help Rob get the trees in. The guy wants to shoot me. This is the last thing he needs right now."

"Why?"

"Wood," Frank said, dully. "Gotta get in as much wood as we can before spring melt."

Leith asked if he could take a look around, see the studio where they rehearsed, and whether Frank would be okay with a complete forensic search of the house and property, say this afternoon?

Frank didn't seem to care. "I can show you the studio now."

Down a hallway toward the end of the house, Leith and Giroux followed him into a large room, lofty, tidy, and professionally set up as a recording studio. Leith looked at the mixing boards, the drum kit, keyboards, and computers, what were probably acoustic-boarded walls, pricy-looking speakers and microphones, the heavy coils of cable, and a stack of black cases for taking the show on the road. He said, "How much does something like this cost?"

Frank crossed his arms and pulled a face. "A lot."

A more definitive answer would be nice, but Leith left it for now.

As they left the studio and headed for the front door, he said, "One more thing, Frank. Where's Lenny? We tried the numbers you gave us. The first one's not in service, and the others don't seem to lead anywhere either."

A complicated new emotion flashed in Frank's eyes, a visible ramping up of confusion and grief. Frank Law knew nothing of his brother's whereabouts, and Lenny too, it seemed, was gone without a trace.

* * *

As Dion had it written down, Leonard Law was the younger brother of the missing girl's boyfriend, which was a bit of a mind-bender, but not his problem. The great thing about being a nobody is the assignments are simple, the answers black and white, and nothing much matters anyway. You're given a destination and a set of questions to be answered, you scribble it down, go back and type it up, then drink coffee till the next simple task. Perfect.

There was a more immediate problem, though, in that he was lost in a strange town, the smallest town he'd ever worked within, population below a thousand, a number he'd had to double-check. He turned the tourist map of the Hazeltons upside down, finding it lined up better with where he had situated his cruiser on the shoulder of the highway. The car was GPS-equipped, but either the thing couldn't pinpoint the address or he'd punched it in wrong. The five-minute drive had taken him half an hour, so far, and counting.

His eyes found the road on paper, a little dead-end spur way over there on the other side of town, on the road to Old Hazelton. He pulled out a pen and circled it, then clamped the map under the sun visor and turned again onto the empty highway that shone like dull steel in the morning light, and after a few more wrong turns found himself on the right track. And there at last was the road itself, unpaved, and according to the number on the mailbox that was the house in question, a little pink bungalow under a white cap of snow. Dion peered through the windshield and saw on the front lawn a gathering of small lumpy people, four of them standing all in a row, dead still, wrapped and bound in heavy cloth. Leaving the car and taking a closer look, he found them to be skinny shrubs, covered in burlap and tied with twine.

He climbed the three steps and knocked on the door. A woman, small and bottom-heavy, opened the door. Behind her a tall, lean figure stood, dark and mysterious and still, like a continuation of the shrubs in the yard.

Dion presented his ID and asked the woman if she was Clara Law.

"Yes, I'm Clara Law," she said. "This is my husband, Roland. How can we help you?"

"Constable Dion, RCMP," he said. "I'm looking for your son, Leonard Law."

"Leonard?" Her eyes pierced him, puzzled. "Leonard Law?"

He brought out his notebook and studied what he'd written down. He looked at the brass numbers hammered to the siding, and down again at the small woman. "You have a son named Leonard, ma'am?"

"Yes, I have a son named Leonard," she said. "But he's not here, for heaven's sake. Why would he be? Why are you asking?"

"Leonard was at a house party that's under investigation. We haven't been able to contact him."

"Why didn't you phone and ask, save yourself a trip?"

"I think there were several calls placed, with no answer."

"They might have called, Clara," the big man behind the short woman said.

She looked around at her husband. She glared at Dion and said, "You're letting the cold in. Please come inside so I can shut the door."

The interior was too warm. He removed his police cap and scraped his boots clean on the welcome mat. He followed the couple along a plastic runner to the opening into the living room. The room was darkened by fuzzy-looking wallpaper and heavy curtains. Clara Law told him to remove his footwear and sit, gesturing at an armchair. He chose to keep his boots on and stand on plastic.

The place smelled sour. A huge grandfather clock ticked in a corner. Roland Law stationed himself behind the sofa his wife sat on, and the two of them watched Dion standing on plastic at the threshold of their living room. He said, "When's the last time either of you saw or spoke to Leonard?"

Roland Law startled him with a voice like a foghorn. "We haven't seen Leonard for months. Haven't seen any of the boys for nigh on twenty years."

Leonard Law, Dion had thought, was only seventeen. He began to ask for clarification, but Clara Law interrupted with, "Sweet Jesus, Rolly, let me do the talking."

"No," Roland said, a huge finger in the air. "Wait. I did see him. In the gazebo. Looked out the kitchen window and seen him just starin' out at me, then he just up and disappeared."

Clara smiled at Dion, whose attention was divided between her and her husband, now mostly on the husband. She said, "We haven't seen the boys in probably a year and a half, and through no fault of ours, either, because let me tell you —"

"My birthday," Roland boomed, patting at his chest, his thighs, looking for something lost. "And where is it?" he said, still patting. "I'm looking for the damn thing, Clara, to show the man."

"Dresser," Clara said. "Top drawer with your vests."

Roland stepped out, and Clara said, "All our boys moved out of home at sixteen. Except Robert. He moved out when he was just fourteen and went to live in those welfare rooms near the highway where the Indians live, where frankly I wouldn't let a *dog* live. He stayed there probably getting buggered by Mr. Heston who he worked for who runs the machine shop who got arrested for peedeefeelya. When Robert got big enough, he came over with a hunting rifle and threatened Rolly and took over Rolly's logging outfit, and far as I know bought some land over near the reservation and built a house. Which doesn't belong to Robert, of course. It belongs to the Royal Bank and always will. He was always very independent, very moody. The schools hereabouts are godless mills of crime and corruption, so we home-schooled all three. But Robert, who was born in a hospital, came into the world with a violent streak you couldn't whip out of him and a tongue you couldn't clean with soap or Tabasco, and when he turned his back on Jesus and family I banished him from my heart and changed the locks on the door. Frank was different, born by a Christian midwife. A good boy. My favourite. The prettiest baby, and smart as a whip. No Tabasco, no spanking, a listener, an angel spreading light into the world. Very talented, very musical, always with a guitar in his hand. He left the day he turned sixteen, and I cried for days. It's Robert lured him away with alcohol and prostitutes. And then Lenny, my youngest. Lenny is slow in many ways, and such an ugly duckling. Not handsome like Frank. But he did write some nice poems. He wanted to leave with Frank, but I hung on for dear life, went to the government, and the government made him stay. The day he turned sixteen there was nothing I could do to save him, and Frank came by in his pickup and without a word took my youngest from salvation to Hell, and now they are all lost to me. All of them, stolen by sin, and not a word on Christmas or birthdays, and I can tell you that come Easter Roland and I will be kneeling here alone."

Dion didn't doubt it. Something moved in the shadows, and he saw that Roland had stolen back into the room with an object in hand, a pipe, its bone-white bowl carved into a human head. The man held out the pipe to Dion like a gift. Dion looked at the pipe but didn't take it.

"I only smoked it once," Roland said. "Didn't like it. Don't smoke, generally. Never did."

"Why are you showing me a pipe, sir?"

Clara said, "It was a gift from Lenny on Roland's seventieth. On Frank's sixteenth birthday I made his favourite cake, and I cried rivers. He ate his cake with his bags all packed, and he gave me a hug and walked out the door. My favourite baby boy. A slap in the face. We were a very close-knit family when the boys were growing up. One year we went to Nevada. They loved Nevada, especially Frank. We have pictures of them on packhorses. I'll show you."

She started to rise, but Dion stopped her. "Really, I just need to know, can either of you think of any friends or relatives Leonard might have gone to in the area?"

Roland answered. "My sister Mabel. Mabel Renfrew. Always very close to the boys."

Dion raised his brows at him. "Whereabouts does she live, sir?"

"Vernon, B.C."

Dion wrote it all down, asked for an address, and watched Roland Law's long, dark face break into a chuckle. "Last known address," the man said, "Pleasant Valley Cemetery, Vernon."

Dion drew a line through Mabel, and Roland went on to contradict everything his wife had just explained about sin and corruption and hostile takeovers. "Don't know why you're looking for Lenny. Good boys, all three. Always were."

Cap back on, notebook tucked away, Dion thanked them for their time and turned to leave, but Roland had one more nugget to offer. "Maybe they gone up the Dease," he said. "Lenny and his wife, the injun. That's where she's from, far as I know. Dease."

Dion looked back at the man. He didn't want to pursue this. He wanted to run. The room was making him seasick, the grandfather clock banging at his brain. "Pardon, sir? What?"

"Oh, for god's sake, that's Robert," Clara snapped. "It's Robert married the Indian lady, not Lenny. Honestly, Rolly, your mind is going in leaps and bounds."

Roland swooped both hands downward in go-to-hell anger and left the room. A door down the hall slammed shut. Clara hurried after her husband, and Dion stood alone in the sour, trapped air, listening to the ticking of the clock that he could swear was not keeping time with the rest of the world. And then a distant, muffled argument.

He saw himself out. The gloomy morning now seemed over-lit, hard on the eyes. He got into his car and began to write out a summary of the disjointed interview in his notebook, but stalled after the bare basics because the rest, it seemed to him, was garbage.

He'd woken this morning with renewed ambition. Showered and shaved and buffed his boots and went in early, but everything dragged him down, the new computer with the power button he couldn't locate, the complicated short-term transfer paperwork, and meeting the local constables who met his short greeting with their own. Whatever was left of his waking spirit had been trampled flat by Clara and Roland Law.

He studied the paragraph he'd written, knowing there was something he was missing. Something he'd heard that he'd meant to follow up on. But his handwriting had gone to ratshit along with all his other skills, and whatever it was had been washed away in the stream of Clara's words.

Did it matter, though? The Laws didn't know where Lenny was, hadn't seen any of their sons in a while, and even if they had, they wouldn't know it. He checked his watch and wrote down time of departure, precise to the minute. The time seemed wrong, so he checked it against the dashboard clock and found it was off by several minutes. Just like himself, just like the grandfather clock in the Laws' living room, his watch was having trouble keeping up.

* * *

Two o'clock and the snow was coming down again, big flakes hitting the earth like slow-motion bombs, adding to the mess on the mountainside. Leith was behind the wheel of the SUV, with Sergeant Mike Bosko beside him. They were headed once more up the Bell 3 logging road, first to see the Matax trailhead in the light of day, and second to pay a visit to Rob Law, who wasn't making it easy for them, keeping to his cut block and returning no calls.

The drive was as slow and gruelling as it had been the first time up. The light of day made it easier than last night, but the occasional logging truck coming down made it much, much worse, forcing Leith to pull over on the narrow track, as close to the drop-off as he dared, and hold his breath as the truck lurched past. Worse, he had no choice on one occasion but to reverse downhill till he could find a pullout.

At last they reached the flat spot that was the parking area for the Matax trail, where Kiera's truck had been found. They left the vehicle and stood looking about. Leith was ready for the cold, as always, in long johns under his jeans, hiking boots, fleece, and storm jacket, hood pulled up against the snow. Bosko was still dressed for a stroll down city streets, in overcoat, baggy black trousers, and Oxfords.

There was nothing to see here, in Leith's eyes. The forest had been searched last night, searched again today, and if there were anything to be found, it would have been. Before him stood just another hectare of woods in a hundred thousand hectares that stretched out in every direction, and a gravel road with banks of dirty snow spewed by truck tires. Beyond this clearing for parking there was a dip down, and then a rise toward the Matax trail. Not an inviting hike, by the looks of it, but Renee Giroux had said it got really nice after about an hour's trek. She'd told him he should try it sometime. In late summer, when the wildflowers were at their best. "No thanks," he'd answered. He didn't like hiking — it amounted to nothing but sore feet, sweat, bears, and mosquitos — and even if he did, this place would be forever haunted to him. Even if this case ended well.

Standing now on the road with no sound but the wind singing in his ears, he was reminded of the absurdity of one of their scenarios. He said, "What are the odds she gets stuck here just as a serial killer is cruising by? This is not the kind of place you'd trawl for victims."

"Or, as we discussed last night, it could be he works in a logging outfit up here somewhere, or drives truck," Bosko said. "A case of the wrong time, wrong place."

Or, Leith supposed, the Pickup Killer could have broken his pattern of targeting the unknown and unwanted and become fixated on the exact opposite, this beautiful young singer, loved by everyone. Started following her around. Followed her up the mountain, and then … then what? Gambled that her car would break down and leave her vulnerable?

Last night the ident section had found the reason for the Isuzu's engine stall: a dislodged electronic fuel-supply sensor. What they couldn't say was if it was entropy or sabotage that did it. Taking the sabotage theory to its conclusion, did the killer mess with her Rodeo while it was parked at the Law residence, when the band was inside rehearsing, again gambling that it would die in some remote spot instead of in the local IGA parking lot? Or did he force her to a stop, get her immobilized, and then sabotage her truck to divert suspicion?

He mentally balled up the theory and trashed it, and it was back to scenario one, an age-old story: the boyfriend did it. Or in this case, maybe the boyfriend's brother.

They returned to the vehicle and continued up the road. After twenty minutes, it forked without signage, and Leith had to consult his forestry map to learn he'd want to go left. They didn't reach the logging site run by Rob Law, called RL Logging Ltd., for another ten minutes of bone-jarring ascent, and here suddenly was life and noise, the churning of an active logging show amidst a clearing.

Again they stepped from the truck, and they found it was colder here, windier. Just the altitude, Leith supposed, or the lack of shelter, brought the temperature down. A crew of five or six pushed large machines through the snow, and a worker in yellow rain gear swung off a Caterpillar to ask their business. Leith asked to speak with Rob Law, and the worker indicated the loader toiling away a hundred yards uphill, swinging logs from the great pile of timber on the landing onto the long spine of a waiting rig. "That's him there. Why? Got some news? Kiera …"

"'Fraid not," Leith said. "Could you call him over for us? Just a few questions."

The worker got on his radio and forged off through the dirty snow. Bosko said, "I understand Rob and Frank inherited the company from their father Roland eight years ago or so, and that Roland's no longer involved. Is that right?"

Leith hadn't a clue. "That's what I understand," he agreed. He watched a man he assumed to be Rob Law approaching. He wore a plaid mack jacket and jeans, hard helmet on, pulled low. *He's going to be difficult*, he thought. He said, "D'you want to take the lead on this one? I'd rather do the observing."

"Sure."

The logger took his time making his way over, pausing to talk to his crew, kicking at a piece of machinery, but finally stood before them, face tipped back with what looked like challenge. He wasn't so tall, about five-ten, but solid. Renee Giroux called him antisocial and/or misogynistic. Any time she encountered him in town he'd be ducking his face, she said, and she believed it was more to do with her sex than her rank.

Leith introduced himself and Bosko. "You're a difficult man to get a hold of," he added. "You didn't get our message to come down and talk, sir?"

"Busy," Rob Law said. He swung the Thermos he was carrying toward a portable workstation set up on a nearby slope, what Jayne Spacey had called the *Atco*. "We can talk in there. You're supposed to wear lids, eh." He rapped his own hard hat.

"We won't tell," Bosko said.

Rob led the way around pulverized wood debris and coffee-coloured ice puddles, climbed the set of fold-out stairs leading up to the Atco trailer's door, stomped the soil off his boots at the threshold, shoved open the three-quarter size aluminum door, and stood aside to let them pass. The trailer they found themselves in was a long, near-empty room that apparently served as his on-site headquarters. Heat and light were provided by a grumbling generator. A kitchen table with mismatched lawn chairs was set at one end, a ratty sofa at the other, everything else in between. Deck of cards on the table, coffee maker on the counter, small fridge, mini-sink. *Supernatural BC* wall calendar. Without asking, Rob cleared the table of paperwork and set three cups of coffee on the Arborite tabletop, one cup in front of each folding chair. Bosko took the cue first and sat. Leith took his own chair and watched Rob step away, shove open the door, and leave the trailer without so much as an "excuse me."

Leith left his chair to watch through a window, making sure their subject wasn't fleeing, and saw Rob walk back toward the trees and step into a bright blue Johnny-on-the-spot. If this was an arms or drugs charge Leith would be worried, but it wasn't. Under his breath he said, "Real king of the castle here, aren't you."

The king of the castle returned, washed his hands more meticulously than Leith would have expected, took his chair at the head of the table, dried his palms on his jeans, folded his arms, and waited.

As Leith had suggested, Bosko did the questioning. Leith wondered now why he had suggested it, really. True, he wanted the opportunity to sit quietly and ob-serve Rob answering questions, but more so he wanted to see how Bosko operated. There was anxiety too, in that he feared he'd make an ass of himself in front of Bosko. He could be abrasive, he knew, and his interviewees could be too, and now and then his questioning sessions became shit-slinging contests. He didn't want that to happen here.

He wondered further why he cared what Bosko thought of him, and it took another moment of self-analysis to get it. Simple, really: Bosko was look-ing for talent for his new Serious Crimes Unit down on the Lower Mainland, and Leith wished to impress him. Ergo, Leith wished to leave the north, which in turn came as a big surprise to himself, something he'd have to consider later.

He sat and observed the men, Mike Bosko and Rob Law, as they talked. Rob was not bad looking, in a rough-hewn kind of way. His hair was longish and un-kempt, face moody and unwelcoming, a bit of a worker troll. Bosko explained to the troll in a level, respectful way that there were no leads on what had happened to Kiera. He described where the investigation was at. Finally he asked for some background information: How long had Rob known the girl?

The logger's face slewed into an exaggerated sniff. "I don't know. A while."

"What's a while?"

"Years. Who knows? Why? It matters?"

"Well, I can tell you," Bosko said, "it might seem pointless to you, and maybe it is. But we have a lot of blanks to fill in right now. I can also tell you that I've only got about ten short questions, but if you answer each one like this, we're going to be here for a lot longer than you probably want."

He said it nicely enough, but Leith expected a back-lash. None came. The veiled anger in Rob's eyes neither darkened nor lightened, but he seemed to get the message. "I've known her as long as she and Frank got togeth-er, which is when they were teens, so whatever that is."

"Good," Bosko said. *Good* was a reward word, a tool Leith rarely used. He watched another degree of tension leave Rob's face. "Tell us about Saturday," Bosko said. "The day she went missing. Give a timeline of what you did that day, starting from when you woke up in the morning."

"Timeline." Rob said it with distaste, maybe just not keen on fancy words applied to his unfancy life. "Got up with the light, got to work. Worked all day. The crew knocked off at six and took off home. I did my paperwork and went down the hill about seven. On the way I found her wheels parked off to the side. Checked it out a bit and then went down and told Frank about it. That's about all I know. Frank went off looking for her. I'd have gone and helped, but I was dead on my feet. Went straight to bed."

"You didn't take part in the search?"

"Other than looking at her truck there when I found it and hollering out her name, I never joined the party, no. If a dozen guys with dogs and whistles can't find her, I sure couldn't either."

Bosko paused, maybe thinking what Leith was thinking, that Rob by his own admission was alone at the Matax at 7:00 p.m., and it was only his word that he hadn't found Kiera there at that time and done something with her. It was unlikely but worth a follow-up.

"Did you notice anything else in the area that night, besides her vehicle?" Bosko asked. "Tire tracks, footprints, items on the ground, anything out of the ordinary?"

"No. Wasn't looking, didn't notice. Never crossed my mind anything worse had happened than she'd broke down and gotten a ride back to town with somebody. Probably one of my crew, heading home."

"The big question on everyone's mind," Bosko said, "is why she was heading up the Bell 3. The only possible destination is this worksite, don't you think? Did she communicate with you in any way, that day or before, that she was coming to see you? Were you expecting her?"

Rob sat stone-still and drilled his eyes at Bosko for a long moment before giving the shortest possible answer. "No."

"You can't think of any reason, then, for her visit?"

"No."

"Was she friendly with any of your crew?"

"Not that I know of."

"Did any of your crew leave the site between noon, say, and shut-down?"

"Not that I know."

"If they had, would you know it?"

"Definitely."

"Any logging trucks leave or arrive without the usual paperwork?"

"'Course not."

Bosko had one more question, the one that had been put to Frank earlier this morning. "Your brother Lenny, do you know where he is? We can't seem to find him."

"Hey?"

For the first time, something other than obstinance crossed Rob's face, a flush of anxiety maybe. Leith took over then. "Frank tells us Lenny's gone to Prince George with a friend, Tex. But we haven't been able to track down either of them. Does Lenny generally let you know of his whereabouts?"

"We don't always know where he is, no. He's kind of useless that way."

"You seemed startled."

"Yeah, I'm startled," Rob said with anger. "We're talking about Kiera being seriously missing, maybe dead, and you mention Lenny in the same breath. 'Course I was startled. But no, if Frank says he's in George then I believe it. Goes there with Tex whenever he can. Tex has half his family down there, so there's places to stay."

"Doesn't he leave some kind of contact number when he takes off like that, normally?"

Rob grinned suddenly, and his teeth weren't great, jumbled and stained. "That's right, now you mention it. It's Lenny's way of giving me the finger. He had a smartphone, loved it more than life itself, but I took it away from him last month. Cost too much. Told him he can have it back when he gets a job. So he decides he'll take off and not stay in touch. Payback time. Let us worry ourselves to death, see if he cares."

Leith watched the alarm fade and knew that Lenny's payback wasn't paying back well at all. "So now you're not worried, then."

"He's seventeen. An adult."

"If he needs a job, couldn't you give him work up here, help bring in the timber? Frank says you need all the help you can get right now."

"Over my dead body," Rob said. "Too dangerous."

The two bigger bears watch over baby bear, Leith decided. The brothers were close, cautious, and defensive. Could it be that whatever had happened to Kiera somehow tied in? He said, "In any case, it's important we talk to Lenny, soon as possible. He was at the house around the time Kiera went missing. You can't help us out?"

Rob shook his head. "Can't. And when you find the prick, tell him to call me, on the double."

The men thanked him and left the trailer. "I'm keeping that one on my list for now," Leith said as they made their way back to the SUV, shortcutting across the clearing. Progress was awkward, the ground chopped by truck tires, frozen into lumps, hollows filled with snow, puddles turned into mini ice rinks.

"Definitely have to keep our eyes on him," Bosko agreed, walking in front, talking over his shoulder. "Watch your step, Dave. It's pretty slick here."

Slick for a city slicker, Leith thought, and for a brief moment he enjoyed an image of the big man in front of him losing traction and doing the famous midair northern reel.

Ha, he thought, and his foot went out from under him.

Three

THE THREE BEARS

COMING BACK FROM THE LITTLE pink house of Clara and Roland Law, Dion crossed paths with Constable Jayne Spacey. She was just heading out to grab a bite, she told him, and invited him along. Of all the people he'd met here in the Hazeltons, Spacey was the friendliest. She would catch his eye, as she did now, and smile, and for the moment he would feel okay. He climbed into the passenger seat of her cruiser and snapped on his seat belt. "Thanks."

"Not a lot of choices here, you may have discovered," she said. "But I'm going to take you somewhere *really* classy." She drove hardly a minute down the highway, passing the Catalina — the food was way too greasy for a girl watching her figure — and stopped at the IGA supermarket. "They actually have some pretty good deli here," she said as they left the truck. "And a place to sit down. And music."

Inside they bought sandwiches and took a table. Spacey asked him about himself, a question he always dreaded but had planned for. He'd been with the RCMP for a year and half, he would tell people in casual conversation, not the ten years he'd actually served. That way he could avoid the crash altogether. Then he'd bulk out his early years of adulthood with vague odd jobs that nobody would care to pursue.

He gave Spacey the spiel now, and then went on in the brisk and cheerful way he'd been perfecting lately in the privacy of his own room. "Got posted in Smithers last October, and it's great," he said. "Nice place, nice people. Love it here."

Spacey sized him up for a moment and said, "You're what, twenty-six, twenty-seven? Kind of late start with the Mounties, isn't it? But that's cool. I joined right out of high school. Never done anything else."

He was twenty-nine but didn't say so. He told her it was beautiful here in the north. Strange words for the setting, a brightly lit supermarket deli with Muzak playing and shoppers pushing their carts past. But it was something he'd heard said a lot, how beautiful the north was, and a part of him meant it. Sometimes he found himself staring at the land in disbelief, and maybe it was just that, this wraparound beauty that made him — and by association his problems — small, insignificant, nothing at all. Spacey put down her fork and said, "Bullshit it's beautiful. It's a pit. It's part of the circuit. It's penance. I can't wait to get out of here."

She told him of her big family back in Canmore, Alberta, and her husband Shane, or ex, to be precise, a cheating creep she was happily divorcing. "He's still crazy about me, but too bad, schmuck. You're history."

"No second chance?"

She laughed and shrugged. "I gave him a second chance, but he's not getting a third. And this time he really blew it, 'cause it was Megan he fooled around with. My best friend. Or was. Can you imagine that? Can you imagine screwing around with your best friend's husband? I mean, how can you live with yourself?"

Her words were serious but her expression was careless, and Dion wasn't sure she wasn't making it all up. He said, "Shane's an idiot."

She nodded. "As most men are. Are you an idiot, Constable Dion? Don't answer that, it's a trick question. And how's *your* love life? Got a sweetheart somewhere?"

The woman who came to his mind's eye wasn't Penny, but Kate Ballantyne, whom he had broken off with after the crash. She still wrote to him sometimes, but he didn't have the nerve to read those letters. And of course the longer he waited, the harder it was to approach them, so they remained in a box on the shelf, three so far. Meanwhile there was the relationship with Penny McKenzie from the post office, which he saw as nothing but a long date going stale. He summed up with, "No, not really."

"Tell me another lie," Spacey said. She reached out to touch a crumb off the side of his mouth, and now they were sitting knee-to-knee, eye-to-eye. She said, "Hey, you're not religious, are you? Or a teetotaller?"

Neither religion nor drink had any power over him. He shook his head no to both questions, and Spacey was delighted. "Perfect, 'cause I'm going to take you out tonight, show you the town. Game?"

He hesitated a moment and said, "If I'm caught drinking and driving, it'll be the end of my great career."

"'Course not. I'm driving, and you're sitting back and watching the scenery. Later, if we get along okay, we'll park the car and take a cab out to the Black Bear for a beer. The Black Bear's out on the Kispiox River. It's where all the big-game hunters hang out. Heli-ski base and all that."

"Sounds good."

"Fucking fantastic." She wiggled her upper body in a victory dance. She stopped abruptly, bit into her sandwich, and chewed a moment, watching him. "You're part native, aren't you?"

"Native? Me? No."

She chewed a moment longer and then shrugged. "Doesn't matter. Give me your phone."

Wondering what didn't matter, he handed over his personal cellphone, a fold-up Motorola. Spacey entered her number into its databanks, aimed it at herself, snapped a picture, and gave it back. She told him to call her about 8:00 p.m., and they'd arrange to meet. She checked her watch and said, "Oh my god, we better get back. I forgot to tell you, Constable Leith slipped on ice and banged up his hand, so he needs a scribe. Which is why I'm making myself scarce. But you don't have my kind of leverage around here, so you'd better run along."

She dropped him off back at the little detachment, and her cruiser scudded away. Dion climbed the steps and went inside. The reception area was noisy with young people, slouched, standing, talking, drinking pop. Passing through to the main office, he was flagged by one of the local uniforms and directed to go see Sergeant Giroux.

Giroux's office was a small room, ten by ten at best, mostly taken up by an L-shaped desk and filing cabinets. She was at her desk, and in a chair across from her sat the terse blond detective from Prince Rupert named Leith, the one who had called Dion a lab rat. Leith was slumped, jacket and tie removed, shirtsleeves rolled to the elbow, his right hand swathed in tensor bandages. Both officers fell silent and looked at Dion where he had stopped in the doorway. Giroux remained seated and said, "Looks like you and me need to have a talk about lunch breaks and punctuality. How's your handwriting? And your stamina?"

Neither were great, but he didn't say so, and as directed followed Constable Leith down the hall to the first of two small interview rooms. There were no windows here, no sharp objects, ropes, or combustibles in sight. Just a desk and some chairs and a lot of stern posters on the walls. Leith took a chair, slapped down his notebook, and studied what was written there. "We'll start with Chad Oman," he said at last.

Since the crash, words had become Dion's greatest enemy. Sometimes they came together easily, but often he needed some catch-up time. Already Leith was looking at him, losing patience, spelling it out more clearly. "Chad *Oman*, our witness. If you'd get him, please?"

Dion went to the reception area and called out the name, and a bulky native kid stepped out from the gathering of youths. Oman followed him to the interview room and sat across from Leith in practiced fashion, like he'd been interrogated before and knew the drill. Leith asked Dion if he had a tape recorder. Dion didn't have one of the newer digital devices, which he found hard to figure out, but had an old-fashioned mini-cassette type with simpler controls.

"Good," Leith said. "Take care of it."

Dion checked that the blank tape was rewound to the beginning, thinking about the North Vancouver detachment, its many interview rooms hardwired for audio-visual, and adjacent monitoring rooms, and usually extra staff to man the controls. Smithers' one-room set-up was far simpler but modern enough. New Hazelton was a shocker, barely an empty closet, no Mirropane, no camera. He started the recorder and set it down, angled toward the witness, got pen and paper ready, and jotted down the preliminaries.

Leith told Oman that the conversation was being recorded, and for the benefit of the record gave time, date, place, and name of witness.

"Yeah, that's me," Oman said. "Whatchoo do to your hand there, bud?"

"My feet went south," Leith said. "On ice."

"Hooya, that's a bitch," Oman said gravely.

Leith grimaced. "I'll get you out of here soon as possible. Just a few questions. Let's start with Kiera Rilkoff and Frank Law. When and how'd you get to know them?"

"Knew Frank since grade eight," Oman said. "We were always into the music, eh. Him on guitar, and me, I liked hitting things, so I got to be the drummer. We wrote some wicked tunes that looking back now, man they were bad, evil crap. But we got us a bit of a following. We were called Frankly Insane then. Stella came in with her fiddle, and then Kiera one day got up and took the mic from Frank, and we found out she could sing not so bad. And she's got the looks too. I mean, talent is one thing, but ballsiness is everything else. She made it a show. That day at the school dance she opened her mouth and yodelled out 'Soulful Shade of Blue,' we knew we were magic. We changed the name to Fling, her call, and everything was great. And last summer it got even better when we got talent-spotted. For real, man. That lady talked to us after that fundraiser gig at the rec centre and told us what we already knew, that we're really good, and we oughta get serious, market ourselves and whatnot."

"Ms. Blackwood, is it?" Leith said.

"Mercy Blackwood. She's huge. She launched Joe Forte and the Six-Packs. You know them, right?"

"Oh yeah," Leith said. He didn't really, but they sounded like a flash in the pan. "Whatever happened to them?"

"Forte got killed in a freak boating accident."

Now Leith recalled the story. Forte wasn't a flash in the pan. He was up-and-coming, but he'd died young. He said, "That was a long time ago. So she's been in the business a while. She's living here now?"

Oman nodded sympathetically. "I know, you're thinking what's a person like that doing in a place like this, right? She come up here to look after old Mrs. Trish Baldwin last year, who's her relative or something, who's gone now. Mercy says she'll probably move on soon as the old house sells, but in the meantime she's helping us out in a big way. Got us a bunch of sound equipment, made up our website, put our name out there. So, yeah, all of a sudden we're not just high school rockers; now we got a future. Which is kind of funny." His smile faded, and he finished on a quieter note. "So that's about it. It's so unreal, I can't stop cryin'. I forget she's missing, and every time I remember I just start cryin' all over again."

There were no tears in his eyes, but Dion got the gist, and Leith seemed to as well. "What's kind of funny?" he asked.

"Nothing. What d'you think happened to her?"

"We're working hard to find her," Leith said. "What's kind of funny?"

"Nothing, hey. I'm just so freaked out here, just can't think straight."

Oman was a fast talker, and Dion flexed his wrist. He wondered how many interviews he'd be on today. How long before his scribbles turned to garbage? *Just get the key points*, he told himself. Oman was describing for Leith the Saturday when Kiera walked out of rehearsal without explanation, and Dion's key points fractured into point form, then finally random hieroglyphics. It didn't matter, though, because the tape was getting it all down. Notes were just for backup and quick reference, memoranda for the continuation reports that he would be typing later. He rubbed his temple and flipped a page.

Oman talked about the new demo they were working on after the big disappointment in December when that Vancouver record label backed out of a deal. "Mercy says don't worry about it, just carry on, write some new material, work harder, which is what we're doing now, working on the new, improved demo that's going to make us a big name."

"And how's that going?"

Oman shrugged, which said it all.

Leith said, "I was in the sound studio at Frank's house. It's an impressive setup. You're saying Blackwood funded all that?"

"I'm not sure how that's all worked out. They have a contract, I think. Frank could tell you. Are we done soon, because I want to go home and shoot my brains out."

"Why?"

"Because I have a feeling Kiera's not coming back, which means so much for making it big, which is super depressing, if you have to know."

Leith told him gravely not to go shooting his brains out. He asked for more details, specifically if Oman recalled anything Kiera had eaten or drank or smoked, and what she was wearing as she left, and how her hair was done up, and her mood at the time. Oman didn't know if Kiera drank any beer or smoked any dope. He didn't recall what she was wearing, in particular. Jeans and a baggy sweater, probably, and those battered Blundstones of hers. He didn't recall her leaving with her coat on. She left alone. He agreed that Frank was in a bad mood, but not angry or anything. They were all glum. Soon after Kiera left, Oman left with Stella, and later that night Frank buzzed in a big panic, and Oman had put on his winter gear and gone up the mountain with him to look for Kiera. They hadn't found her, and that was that.

The interview wound down and Dion was breathing hard, as if he'd just jogged up a steep hill. The witness was having a few last words with Leith and seeing himself out. Dion reviewed his notes and felt the familiar sliding chill of defeat. The witness was gone, and Leith was by the door, studying him. "There a problem?"

"Couldn't keep up so well at the end there," Dion told him.

"It's just for reference," Leith said irritably, coming around, taking his seat, prepping for the next interview. "You got it recorded, right?"

Dion rewound the recorder to check with a brief playback. Nothing issued forth but a faint hiss. His pulse went into overdrive. He must have pressed *play* but not *record*. He looked at Leith and saw the kind of restrained anger that was worse than a blowup. Leith took Dion's notebook, looked it over, and tossed it back at him. "I'll dictate what I recall of the conversation. You write."

They spent half an hour getting down what had been said, and Dion discovered that Leith had an excellent memory. When it was done, his nerves were still jangling, but the stifling fear had lifted. He said, "I'm sorry. It won't happen again."

"Not a big deal," Leith said curtly. "Just be happy it wasn't our prime suspect."

Dion nodded, and Leith devoted himself to his file documents.

"He was lying, there. I think," Dion said.

Leith stared up from his papers. "What?"

The stare was direct and unsettling, and whatever lightbulb had been burning in Dion's brain blew a fuse and went black. He said, "It just seemed … no, probably not. I thought … but … sorry."

The detective's unfriendly blue eyes stayed on him. "Thought but what?"

"Nothing. Sorry."

"You just said you think he's lying. Lying about *what*? What makes you say that?"

Dion was starting to sweat. He searched his mind for something, anything, but all he found was more dead air. He said, "Actually I forget."

"You forget *what*?"

They were staring at each other now, the inevitable answer to the question lying heavy and silent between them.

With a slap on the tabletop, Leith said, "Just get Stella Marshall in here, please."

Stella was a tall, solidly built woman in her early twenties with white-blond hair. Her eyes were pale and bulgy. Her pink skin was blotched, and a fine white down picked out by the fluorescent lights ran down her cheeks like vague sideburns. She spoke much slower than the drummer, to Dion's relief, glancing his way from time to time as if to be sure his pen was keeping up. Sometimes she smiled at him. "I've known Frank forever," she told Leith. "I joined his band in grade ten. I played bass guitar then, but I've gravitated toward fiddle, and I think that worked better in the long run. It branded us country and western, but that's okay. We're very popular around here. Produced our own CD. Didn't exactly go viral, but we get some good paying gigs. And as you've heard by now, we've hit the big time with Mercy Blackwood coming along to back us. She's got connections. She's going to put us out there. Have you heard us play?" she asked Dion.

Leith brought her attention back his way, saying, "Let's go over Saturday again. Give me a play-by-play of what happened that day, start to finish."

Her narrative paralleled that of Chad Oman. Kiera had left rehearsal prematurely. She was in a bad mood, but her nastiness didn't seem directed at anybody in particular. She hadn't eaten anything or drunk any beer or smoked any pot. She might have been wearing a coat when she left, but Stella couldn't be sure. Her hair was definitely tied back, and maybe pinned back too, on one side. Stella and Chad had left soon after lunch because there was no point hanging around. Frank had called her later that night, about eight, asking if she'd seen Kiera, and saying something about the Rodeo up on the Bell 3. Stella had taken part in the search deep into the night.

She tilted her head, and her long blond bangs swung. "They're saying it's the Pickup Killer. But I don't believe it. Way up there, in the middle of nowhere? Do you want to hear my theory?"

"Sure," Leith said.

"I think she had engine trouble, and she was walking down the road, and maybe decided to cut through the woods to avoid the switchbacks, and fell and twisted her ankle or something. She's probably alive, just can't move. She's very outdoorsy and savvy about survival. But I imagine your SAR guys have checked the area far and wide with a helicopter and dogs and the works, right?"

Leith said yes, they had, and Stella said in that case she didn't have a clue. She said that she was glad she'd kept the day job, and now she was done too and was allowed to leave, wishing Dion a good afternoon and ignoring Leith.

A man named Parker Chu came next. Chinese-Canadian, thin and unsmiling, a self-admitted nerd. Parker told Leith he wasn't friends with Frank or the others, that it was just a job for him doing their sound work. He was employed at the community college some days, teaching computer, but it wasn't great pay. He was planning to move to Alberta soon as he could pin down a better job.

The band paid him by the hour, he said, though the hours were running thin. He recounted how Frank had called him up Saturday just before one, and he'd gone right over, because work was work, and listened to the tracks, which weren't tracks at all, but random noises. No, he exaggerated, he said, with a smile. But it was bad. He'd talked it over with Frank, trying to be diplomatic about it, and left within the hour.

Yes, he recalled Frank's phone pinging, and Frank sending a text moments later. Just one, two at most. He looked kind of peeved as he did it.

Parker left, and before Dion could go out to fetch the next interviewee in line, one was brought to them by Sergeant Giroux. She darkened the doorway with a boy in his late teens at her side, tall and solidly built, his brows bunched into a thundercloud of anger.

"Look who showed up," she told Leith. "This is Leonard Law, better known as Lenny."

She left, and the seventeen-year-old took the interviewee's seat. His brown hair was long at the front and short at the back. He wore skinny black jeans and a bulky black hoody covered in bold white graphics. The hoody looked new, to Dion, and expensive.

"I just got back," Lenny said, nearly spitting the words at Leith. "And Frank says Kiera's missing and you guys are looking for *me*. You think *I* did something to her, is that it? 'Cause I didn't do nothing, and I got an alibi to say so, and I want a lawyer, and I want it now."

Leith opened his mouth, but the boy wasn't done. "I don't have to say nothing till I got a lawyer. And I want a real one, not your Legal Aid joke-in-a-suit who can't get your name right, let alone what you're supposed to have done."

Leith said, "Sit down, Leonard — should I call you Leonard or Lenny?"

"You can call me nothing, 'cause I got nothing to say. I get one phone call, right? I think your talking to me before I get my phone call is a breach of my rights, and none of this can be used against me in court, and you know what? This is all you're getting from me from here on in." He stood looking combative, mouth turned down and arms crossed tight.

Leith said, "Take it easy. Would you sit down, please?"

The kid uncrossed his arms and dropped hard into the chair.

Leith said, "It's just we're talking to everyone who was at the house on Saturday. You're not being charged with anything. You're just a witness. Honest."

Lenny sat, thinking hard. Dion rotated his writing wrist. Leith continued to watch the boy, waiting through the silence as though he knew it wouldn't last. He was right.

"But I'm *not* a witness," Lenny burst out. "You say she's missing? I didn't even know it. I was in Prince George. With Tex. I don't even have a phone, 'cause Rob cut me off, so I was five hours away and didn't even know you were looking for me."

"Yeah," Leith said. "I know."

The colour was returning to Lenny's face. He cleared his throat and said, "Sorry."

"That's okay," Leith said.

"So what's happened to Kiera?"

"We don't know what happened to Kiera," Leith told him.

Lenny sat for a moment, staring into nothing, then without warning his face crumpled and he was crying like a frightened child. Dion was glad, because his writing hand was sore as hell, and tears didn't need transcribing.

* * *

Leith was fried. He shut down the interviews for a time out to talk to his colleagues. He sent Lenny Law on his way and met with Bosko and Giroux in Giroux's office. The others sat, but he paced. He'd had enough of sitting for a while.

"The kid was mighty defensive," he said. "You told me he hasn't been in trouble with the law before."

Giroux at her desk shook her head. "Hasn't even lifted a candy bar. But it's what he grew up in, eh? The three bears were estranged from their parents early on. If you met them you'd know why. So they moved into their big house in the woods and far as I know stay out of trouble. Rob was never caught committing a crime, but probably everyone he was close to as a youngster had done time. And as we know, Frank's got that assault thing. So if Lenny's edgy about the police, you can see where he gets it."

Leith described the boy's crying jag, which was understandable, maybe, but didn't quite jibe. "All these people, for some reason I'm having a hard time reading them. Why do I get the feeling they're holding back?"

Bosko asked, "What did Lenny have to say, once he pulled himself together?"

"Nothing new. He was in his room all morning and left after Kiera was gone. He didn't witness anything."

"Did he tell you about Prince George?"

"Not really. Like his brothers said, he goes there a lot. Nothing strange there."

"Sure," Bosko said. "Did he give any reason why, here in the communication age, nobody could reach him for two whole days?"

"I did ask him about that. Lenny's lost his cellphone rights. Tex doesn't answer his dad's home phone, as a rule, and it happens he wasn't picking up his cell either because he was trying to avoid some girl, and he doesn't have caller ID, so he wasn't screening either."

"All of which you're going to verify with Tex," Bosko said, a question without a question mark attached.

Leith hadn't planned on verifying anything except the trip itself, but gave a nod. "Spacey's tracking him down right now."

Bosko said to Giroux, "That reminds me, how are you doing for manpower? You have a village to run, and we've stolen your troops. Are you getting everything else covered, or should we call for more help?"

"More help would be good," Giroux said. "We're down one rookie 'cause this ass slipped in the mud and broke his hand, so he needs a scribe."

Leith said, "Slipped on the *ice* and *sprained* my *wrist.*"

"However you want to say it, we're down one guy who's taking notes for Dave here instead of out doing his own interviews, which is too bad, 'cause there are plenty of minor witnesses on my list that even he could handle."

"Dion?" Leith said with contempt. "I wouldn't let that halfwit make coffee. What are they letting out of Regina these days? He can't work a tape recorder. Scares the hell out of me that he's in charge of a loaded gun."

Bosko lifted his brows. "What's he done, exactly?"

"It's not so much what he's done," Leith said. "We all make mistakes. It's what he is. He's slow, and he's absent. You haven't noticed?"

"I've noticed him," Bosko said, not quite answering the question. "Do you feel you should write him up?"

"No," Leith said after a moment's consideration. "Not at this point. But I'll definitely be keeping an eye on him."

"And maybe have a talk," Bosko suggested.

A counsellor Leith was not. He grimaced and moved on. "First impressions on everyone I've talked to so far. Frank Law's still my first choice, but he's got at least one good alibi, Chad Oman. I don't think Oman's lying to cover him. Stella Marshall I'm not so sure about. Parker Chu is solid. I'm more interested in Rob Law right now. Think of it, he's up at his worksite, not far from Kiera's truck. He couldn't have gone down to meet her without being seeing by his crew, and nobody saw him leave, but he was there after everyone left. Maybe he met her then, down at the Matax, or she'd made her way up to the site, waited till everyone left before going in to see him."

Giroux and Bosko looked doubtful, and Leith knew why. A logging road in mid-February was no place to hang about for hours, even in the shelter of a vehicle. He sighed, checked the memo that had been handed to him in the hallway, and recalled he had one more interview to cover off. Not a band member or family, but Scott Rourke, a friend of the Law brothers who lived just up the road from the Laws, now waiting out in the reception area. Rourke was the last one to see Kiera alive, if he could be believed, but he'd already been cleared as a suspect, and so far Leith had seen no need to question him himself.

The facts were simple enough: Rourke had been riding his dirt bike from his mobile home toward town when Kiera had passed him in her truck. The time, as far as he could narrow it down, was just before one in the afternoon. She hadn't acknowledged him, probably hadn't recognized him as she approached, just sped past. It was about all he could say then, but now apparently he had something to add, and this time he wanted to talk to the lead investigator.

Rourke was a name Leith was all too familiar with from his many long days of weeding through the listings in his search for the Pickup Killer. This one he'd pulled and run through the system more than once because of its history, but nothing had panned out, and he'd moved on. He said to Giroux, "Our biker. We all know this turkey, but I haven't talked to him in person yet. What can you tell me about him?"

He saw a shadow cross her brow, and she made a noise, something between a spit and a hiss. "Where do I start?" she said.

* * *

Leith ushered Rourke into the interview room, gave Dion the name, and took his seat. Scott Rourke was an ugly sucker, face rippled by a nasty scar. He was somewhere in his late fifties, with yellow hair going silver. He wore skinny jeans, battered cowboy boots, a white muscle shirt, and a black leather vest with a large, grubby bird's feather — illegal eagle, Leith suspected — laced to its lapel. First Nations people could possess feathers and whites couldn't, and Rourke was white as white could be. He draped himself loosely over his chair, gnashing on a wad of chewing gum, stared across at Leith, and said, "Well, let's get started."

Leith told Rourke to state his full name, age, and occupation.

"What's what I do for a living got to do with anything?" Rourke said.

Dion the scribe wrote it down.

Leith hardened his voice. "We won't know until we know, will we?" He studied the scar bisecting the witness's face, starting from the forehead, skirting the inside of the left eye, running down the left side of the nose, crossing the mouth, not quite centre, ending off to the right of the chin. Somebody had done a job on him, but a while ago. The scar looked old.

"I'm self-employed is what I am." Rourke's brown arms were crossed, every tendon popped and delineated. "I fix things. Okay? Anything I can fit on my workbench, I fix. Small engines, clocks, microwave ovens, you name it. Well, okay, maybe not microwave ovens. Okay? But everything else under the sun, it's broke, I fix."

"All right," Leith said. "Self-employed fix-all. Was that so bad? See, I ask you questions, you give me answers, he writes them down, and we move on. That's how it usually goes."

"Thank you for educating me on the fine art of interrogation. So move on."

"You said you have some information for me about Kiera Rilkoff. I've got your statement about seeing her drive past on Kispiox Road. What else d'you know, sir?"

"It's not so much what I know as what I want to know. Time is of the essence, right? The first forty-eight and all that. I don't see a lot of action happening here, you all sitting around, questioning people like you're writing some fucking book. What a waste of time. It's not people that got her, it's that bastard, and she could be still alive, and you people better get your ass in gear and start turning over rocks."

"What bastard got her?"

"You know the bastard I'm talking about. Mr. Pickup, who strangles young girls and leaves them in shallow graves. He's been having his sick kicks for two years now, and with all your equipment and your brains and manpower, you keep letting him get away, and now he's got Kiera, thanks very much."

"Is that your *information*, Mr. Rourke? Are you done? 'Cause I have a few questions myself. You live about a stone's throw from the Law brothers, is that right?"

"If you call kilometre and a half a stone's throw."

"You're a close friend of Kiera Rilkoff?"

"That's why I'm here, you fucking genius!"

"Keep your hair on," Leith snapped. "This is a police station, not your local watering hole, get that straight. When did you last see her?"

"You guys already asked me all that."

"I'm asking you again."

"Last night, then, to be exact. It was a hot day, blue sky, and her and Frank were standing in the river, okay? Down at the S-Bend, up to their navels and side by side. I was on the beach in a purple tux, reading them their vows from a podium made of Popsicle sticks. That's the last time I saw her."

Dion the scribe was clearly not keeping up. Leith picked up the tape recorder, checked its little bars were hopping, and set it down again. He leaned toward his witness and said, quietly, "That's fascinating, sir. But see, this fellow has to take down everything we say, and he thinks you're giving him a load of writer's cramp for nothing. And he doesn't think it's cute. And neither do I. So let's stick to facts. Okay? Not dreams, not your artsy-fartsy sarcasm. Fact."

"I thought I'd share an interesting dream."

"I don't want to hear your interesting dreams."

Rourke shrugged. "Who the fuck knows the last time I saw her, besides her driving past me on Saturday. On the street maybe, few weeks ago, stopped to chat, whatever. Or I was over there for dinner, or they dropped by. We just bump into each other all over the place, helter-skelter, willy-nilly."

Dion's pen fell to the floor with a clatter. Leith waited till he was back in business and said, "Your relationship with Kiera. In your mind it's a little more than just friends, isn't it? You've got ideas about you and her. Fantasies."

Rourke straightened in indignation. "Fantasies? Me? I'm old enough to be her grandfather."

"Ever heard the term 'dirty old man'?"

"Ever heard the term *libel action?* Because, sir, I'm just itchin' —"

"All I asked you," Leith pointed out, "is if you've ever heard the term. What were you doing Saturday?"

"Nothing. I worked on my projects. Fixing things."

"Anybody with you?"

"A friend."

"Name."

"Evangeline Doyle."

"Contact information?"

"She lives with me, so get it from your file."

Leith gave Dion a nod to flag the name. "Anything else?"

"When I heard about Kiera, I went up the mountain and searched it high and low, doing your guys's job for you, which is just plain hair-brained, 'cause that mountain should have been turned inside out on that first night, not by a bunch of amateurs, but by a bunch of cops who could have maybe found a clue or two before it got destroyed, because guess what, there's a murderer at large. But no, I guess you got your protocols to follow...."

He had plenty more, and Leith argued with him for a while, but mostly he let the man rant. He didn't like Rourke, a man with a bad criminal record, but for now all he had against him was his own, sorely biased contempt. He watched Rourke's mobile and badly scarred face, the rolled-up sleeves, the scrappy hands, oil-blackened and rough, and the muscled arms flexing with every angry word. There was a rhythm to his words, a drumbeat that was saying more than it was saying. The missing girl wasn't his only grievance, or the shortcomings of the police service. It was something bigger and meaner, and it was wounded, and just as Leith was getting a sense of what it might be, Rourke seemed to short out, tossed his hands one last time, and said he was bloody done here.

Leith said, "Glad to hear it. Thank you, sir, for your time. And do yourself a favour, lose the feather. Next cop you meet might not be so nice."

"I got Mohawk in my blood."

"Good for you."

He watched Rourke leave and then smiled briefly at Dion, who was already clearing up to leave. "Got all that?"

Leith wasn't a great smiler, never had been, but he thought he'd give the rookie a chance. If he could make contact, find something of value, some tiny glimmer of intelligence, he could maybe start on the road to positive mentoring.

In the next instant, he wished he hadn't bothered, as Dion nearly stumbled in his haste to rise and said sharply, "No, I didn't *get* all that." He didn't look well, his pale face flushed, his hair sweaty and spiked, dark rings under his flashing, angry eyes, and for the first time he had plenty to say. "Nobody could *get* all that. You let your witness off the leash, throw sticks and watch him run, just for the fun of it, and you expect me to *get* all that?" He removed a tatty duty notebook from his pocket and flipped it across the desk at Leith, who was still staring at him in dumb surprise. "Read it, if you want, circle all the mistakes, and send me to hell, if you want. Frankly, I don't give a shit."

He strode out, leaving behind the little spiral notebook in its leather case.

* * *

"Hell," Dion said again, hands linked behind his neck as if to save himself from toppling backward. From his second-floor motel room window he could see a volcano -like mountain rising up, a dark mass in the night sky, its peaks glowing a paler blue, a two thousand and seventy metre-high rock called Hagwilget Peak, according to the tourist brochure he'd read front to back this morning over coffee.

The motel was right next to the highway, and even through the thick glass he could hear the grunts of trucks decelerating and the occasional noisy exhaust of an older car barrelling by. There were muffled screams and gun blasts from the TV in the room next to his, too. But mostly there was silence, immense and smothering.

He was thinking about his last exchange with Constable Leith, just an hour ago. He had doubled back moments later, partly to face the music, but most-ly because it wasn't his duty notebook he'd left behind, but his private one, the one where he kept track of per-tinent names and dates, random statistics, and what-ever else he needed to keep the facts and fictions of his life in order.

Leith was still in his chair, just finishing a phone call, lodging a complaint of insubordination probably. He'd looked up, and Dion had spoken loudly to keep the tremor out of his voice. "Is that it, then? Should I pack my bags? You want my badge?"

Leith had observed him blankly for a long moment, and finally said, simply but coldly, "No. Why?"

"Anyway, I just wanted to apologize." Dion had moved closer to the table and saw the notebook lay as he'd left it. He'd reached out, picked it up, tucked it behind him.

Leith didn't seem to care about the notebook or the apology. He left his chair abruptly and walked out, and that seemed to be the end of the matter.

Another freight truck roared by, breaking the limit. Jayne Spacey, Dion thought. Eight o'clock. He checked his watch, comparing it to the radio clock on the bedside table, and saw that the watch hands were off by over ten minutes, confirming his fears. It was a special watch, older than himself, all gears and leather. He adjusted it and gave the stem a bit of a wind, whistling a careless tune.

He changed into jeans and sweater, boots and jacket, and went downstairs, hoping not to run into any of the other officers lodged at the Super 8 — Fairchild, or Bosko, or especially Leith. But there was nobody around, not in the halls, the stairwells, the lobby, or next to the lobby in the motel's small diner — Western food, gingham motif — run by a thin, aloof Korean named Ken.

Dion took the only booth in the place, the one by the window. There was nothing to see outside now but the occasional passing truck, vehicles going from point A to point B, passing through Hazelton by necessity. Everyone broke the limit, leaving arcs of slush or swirls of crystal in their wake. He ordered dinner, roast beef for the protein, salad for fibre, all the trimmings for the calories. Filling himself out to be the man he'd been before was one of his major goals. Gaining weight wasn't as easy as it seemed.

After dinner he walked along the cold, blustery highway that formed the backbone of the town. The lamp standards blazed their dead orange-grey light along the four-lane strip, and the banners banged and clanged in the wind. The businesses along the highway were closed, all but the Catalina Cafe, lights on bright, the stout silhouettes of diners against the drapes. And the Chevron, the twenty-four-hour gas station/convenience store where Kiera Rilkoff had once worked part time. Youths loitered on the sidewalk, smelling of cigarettes and weed, and Dion worried about being swarmed. They didn't even look his way.

From inside the Chevron he phoned Spacey, and her little blue Toyota RAV4 pulled up soon after. He climbed in the passenger seat, and they were off, exploring the great spread of land that made up the Hazeltons. Her uneven smile lit by the dashboard, Spacey said, "In the city you get entertained. Here you have to entertain yourself. Wheels help, big-time."

The drive turned out to be a nice break from routine, though she barrelled along the backroads too fast for comfort. In Old Hazelton they stood in the snow in a darkened park ringed by enormous dark trees that rustled their dead leaves and whispered. Spacey told him about the totem poles and longhouses, the preserved Gitxsan village of Ksan. Later she took him to a viewpoint over a chasm and told him of a dramatic rescue that took place here. She drove down to a winter-dead meadow with train tracks and a river, and they walked southbound along the ties and talked, mostly about her life and troubles. But she was funny, and she didn't seem worried that he wasn't laughing or had little to say, as though she knew he appreciated her even in his silence. He looked across at the trees growing on the far riverbanks, leafless, tall, and ragged. The trees looked like a tribe of giants deep in conversation. Black cottonwood, Spacey told him, following his eyes.

A train came and went, also southbound, and it was while it flooded past, shaking the ground they stood on, that Spacey put an arm around his waist and stood close, tilting her face for a kiss. He wrapped her in both arms to complete the embrace, and completed the kiss too, feeling the warmth of arousal as their mouths met, and something even better: a dramatic change of mood, a teasing sense of bliss.

Spacey pushed him away with a smile and said it was high time for a drink. They returned to the RAV4, and she drove along a road that followed the river a ways, pulling into the parking lot of a large post-and-beam structure that glowed like a cruise ship in the dark. The Black Bear Lodge. A couple dozen vehicles sat in the snow, all of them four-by-fours, and Spacey said, "More traffic than you'd think, even in winter. You got your heli-skiers and skidooers and hunters. And a few locals, anybody with extra money in their pocket. This place isn't cheap."

Inside they found the bar was doing good business, even at this hour, nearly midnight. The lights were warm and the music just loud enough to add milieu without hammering the eardrums. Spacey said she'd only have one beer, and she'd make it last, no problem; it wouldn't even touch her bloodstream. Afterward, they'd go to her place and play Scrabble. She said it with a wink.

His first clue that something was wrong came as he followed Spacey through the bar and she reached back to grab his hand, guiding him to a table with a good view on the brass and glass of the long bar itself, at the attractive, brown-haired woman mixing drinks there, who was looking across at them with what looked like stony-faced wonder.

"Why's she staring at us?" Dion asked as he took a chair, returning the stare.

"Because she's a nosy, jealous bitch," Spacey told him. "That's Megan."

Megan, if Dion recalled right, was Jayne Spacey's ex-friend, which made this spot the worst possible choice in the whole bar. Before he could object, Spacey leaned across the table and kissed him on the mouth. Then she sat back and grinned at him. "It's okay. Kind of awkward, but she won't bother you. I will have to ask you to go up and order, though, since she and I aren't speaking."

He pushed his chair back. "We can move. We'll sit over there. I don't need her glaring at me like this."

"She's not glaring at you, she's glaring at me. You she likes. She's always had a thing for native guys, like my ex, Shane."

"I'm not —"

"Whatever. Just smile at her nicely and make her twitch, horny little cow." She tilted her head, reading the doubt on his face, and her voice went smoky. "C'mon, do me a big favour and play along. I'll pay you back in a big way."

Understanding was jolting through him now, followed by amazement, followed by mute anger. This wasn't friendship, and it wasn't even sex. He was a prop, and she'd brought him here to fling daggers at the one who'd hurt her. He opened his mouth to argue, but shut it again, knowing anything he had to say would only take the situation on a fast downhill slide. He would play along for as long as it took to drink one beer, then he'd insist they leave.

He stood and dug out his wallet, walking up to the bar. He ordered two draft pints from Megan. He didn't smile at her, and she didn't smile back. He left a generous tip, brought the mugs back to the table and settled in, his back to Megan. He drank his beer and let Spacey do her thing, chatting and posing, showing her ex-friend what a great time she was having with her new boyfriend.

About halfway through his beer, just when he was getting used to the idea of being a prop and deciding he actually didn't care, a hulk of a black-haired man in black leather walked up to their table, glowered at Dion, and said to Spacey, "Get over here and talk."

So this would be the cheating husband Shane, still crazy about her, the Shane who she'd never forgive. Spacey stayed in her seat, and Dion remained next to her, mouth shut, marvelling at how she'd fixed this scene. He listened to Spacey telling her ex, "You're looking kinda desperate, Shane. Why don't you go poke Megan in the ol' beaver pelt? Looks like she could use the exercise." She put her arm through Dion's as she spoke, and it was here he messed up badly by losing patience, removing her arm, and standing up, telling her he was done.

Outside, a cab stood idling and wreathed in vapour, its roof light on to net the drunks who spilled out like clockwork around closing time. He climbed in and said "Super 8."

Back in his room, he turned off the phone, not checking the messages. He didn't call Penny, breaking another promise. He turned on the TV and found an old movie that he couldn't follow, black and white, a man and a woman talking wildly at each other. He sat on the bed and watched and listened, without seeing or hearing. He thought about the train hurling by, and the black trees having their conversation, and a strange notion of wanting to join them, learn the language, stand in their midst, and let the elements take him.

He pushed the thought away. All that really bothered him right now was the twenty-five-minute difference between his wristwatch and the time on the cabbie's dashboard clock. "Doesn't matter," he said, studying the watch up close. His face felt feverish and his airway was tight. He lifted the watch to his ear, and it ticked softly, *chk-chk-chk*, pretending to do its job. Such a simple job, to stay with him, keep track of the minutes and display them. Not much of a conversation, but a conversation all the same, and it couldn't even manage that.

It was a black-faced Smiths military watch. It had been old when he'd got it from Looch seven years ago, a birthday present, and like everything with moving parts, it had a life span. It'll outlive you, Looch had promised, but apparently Looch was wrong.

He took the watch off to adjust the time, giving its stem a clockwise winding, carefully, slowly, stopping when he met resistance and giving it a little back-off twist, as he'd been taught. Held it to his ear again, and it sounded fine now, so everything would be okay for a while. He sat on the bed with the watch in his hand and the TV light strobing over him, battening down the fear.

Four

WILLY AND THE WATCH

HE WOKE BEFORE THE ALARM went off. Most every morning he woke with resolve that today he'd find his bearings and start walking into the light of normality. But today was different, and he felt defeated before he opened his eyes. When he did look, the sky was pitch black and the clock radio said six thirty. He rolled, fumbled for the light switch, and under its fuzzy blare checked the Smiths. It told him it was 4:02. The TV was still on, now playing a morning talk show just loud enough to not raise complaints from the other guests.

With two hours before shift, he showered and shaved and dressed with care, and went downstairs to the Super 8 diner, picking up a newspaper from the stand by the door. News in the north was never hot off the press, since delivery took a while, but it kept him current enough with the city. The restaurant was empty except that his favourite place, the sole window booth, was occupied by an old native man smoking what looked like a giant doobie.

Dion stopped by the table and could smell cheap, harsh tobacco. He gestured with his newspaper at the red pictogram placard on the wall, a crossed-out cigarette in a circle, and said, "Sir. It means no smoking."

The old man looked up. He wore a rough-looking scarf around his throat and a canvas coat that sagged open. His hair was white and chaotic, and his eyes looked damaged. He gazed at Dion directly and said something, a full and complex sentence with not a single English syllable thrown in. It sounded like chit-chat, so the man was either partially blind or incompetent, not seeing what stood before him, a white man wearing a hefty gun belt and full patrol uniform. Not someone to chat with, especially if you were native.

"No smoking," Dion repeated. "Okay?" He crossed the room, took a table of second choice, and waited for Ken the Korean-Canadian waiter/proprietor to come and take his order. He asked for eggs over easy and dry toast, nothing on the side, and coffee, then added with a gesture toward the smoker as he told Ken, "It's your restaurant, and you know the rules. Enforce them, would you?"

Ken dropped an ashtray in front of the old man and said, "Put it out, Willy." He went off to the kitchen to start cooking, and the old man named Willy crushed out the cigarette, sending up a stink like a dumpster on fire, directing more gibberish at Dion across the space between them. Again there was no hostility there, just babble, like English spoken backward, this time ending in a question mark. Only one word stood out as recognizable to Dion's ears, the name *Johnny*.

"I don't speak your language," he said, loud and slow. He flattened his paper and tried to read the stale news.

The next time he looked over, Willy was turned away, looking out at falling snow. Dion looked down at his wristwatch and compared it to the Dairyland wall clock facing him. He unstrapped it and held it to his ear, shook it and listened again, and what he heard chilled him, a fatal arrhythmia.

Ken set down a breakfast plate with a clatter. "Watch problems?"

"The beauty of old stuff like this," Dion told him, almost viciously, "is it's fixable."

"Good jeweller over at the Copperside."

Dion thanked him, but he wasn't really listening. He already had someone in mind, a guy who could fix anything. Except microwaves.

* * *

The fix-all's address took Dion farther into the wilderness than he had expected, across that spine-tingling chasm that Jayne Spacey had shown him on her tour, and along a road of hard-packed snow with rock wall on one side and forbidding woods on the other, but by the time he'd figured out how impractical the errand was, it was too late, and he had arrived at his destination, a mobile home on a cleared bit of land all fringed by woods.

A hand-painted sign was posted out front, roadside, attached to the wooden fence. It said, "Northwood Repairs Incorporated," with an "NRI" logo shaped into a wrench and spewing yellow flames. The yard was full of old shop signs, car parts, the bones of appliances, some grouped in categories and others heaped untidily amidst weeds and snow. Dion parked his car in the open space in front of the trailer, stepped up three aluminum stairs onto an aluminum landing, and rapped on an aluminum door, then stepped back to make room for the door to swing outward. While he waited he looked about, trying to imagine who would buy a piece of land like this, set in shadow, damp year-round. A great breeding ground for mosquitoes come summer. If summer ever reached this bitter land.

He had given up waiting and was crossing the soggy grounds back to his car when the aluminum door shrieked behind him, and the man with the scar was up on the mini-landing, scowling down. Rourke was wrapped in a striped terrycloth robe in burgundy and blue, and looked like he had a backache the way he stood gripping the door frame, yellow-grey hair sloped messily to one side.

"Sorry," Dion called across the yard. "I didn't mean to wake you."

"Well, you woke me, so now tell me what you want."

"We met yesterday, but actually —"

Rourke interrupted with a snap of his fingers and pointed at Dion like a warlock casting a curse. "That's right, the cop with the writer's cramp. What's this then? More goddamn pointless questions? What size goddamn shoes I wear, which way I goddamn vote?"

Dion brought the Smiths from his pocket and held it out. "It's running slow. I thought you could take a look at it for me. If you have time."

"Very smooth," Rourke blared. "Give it up, Mountie. We all know what's going on here. I'm way up there on your suspect list, and if you haven't figured out that I've figured it out, you're stupider than I gave you credit for. That's the only reason I went down to see you yesterday, to save you the satisfaction of dragging me in yourselves. Cops," he spat. "You're all cut from the same cloth, two-faced, underhanded, self-pandering bunch of dipshits. I'll be writing some letters, you better believe it."

Dion listened through it all and then thrust the watch back into his jacket pocket, as it had dawned on him that he'd made a mistake, and a clumsy one: Scott Rourke was in no frame of mind to be fixing things. The missing girl was a close friend, and he'd have no room for anything else at the moment but worry, and all Dion could do now was apologize and back off. "Of course," he called up. "I'm sorry. You're not open for business at a time like this. It honestly never crossed my mind. Sorry."

He moved again toward his car, but Rourke brought him to a stop with a shout of, "Hang on now." He'd flung the door wide so it caught and held. "How about some answers? Where are we at? You got any leads? We all have a right to know."

Dion stood on the grass, car keys in hand, his mind already elsewhere. What time did the Copperside jeweller open, for one. The repair was hardly an urgent matter, but he needed to know, as soon as possible, if the thing could be saved. He tuned in and realized Rourke was still bellyaching at him, asking questions he couldn't answer. He cut in sharply, saying, "I'm just a temp, and you're going to have to direct your inquiries to the office. You need that number again?"

"No, I got the number," Rourke snapped.

Dion squinted into the sky, which had stopped pelting snow but was a solid chalky white, maybe just holding back. He looked again at the pissed-off man in the bathrobe and said, "I've heard there's a jeweller at Copperside. Is he any good, d'you think? With watches?"

"He's a charlatan," Rourke said. "And a thief. You want a watch fixed around here, you gotta come to Scottie."

"Right, and I did, but you're not taking on work right now, which I perfectly —"

"Did I say I wasn't taking on work? Death and taxes. What d'you have there, a fucking Rolex?"

"It's a Smiths," Dion said. "I'll pay extra. This watch means a lot to me."

Rourke walked back into his aluminum palace but left the screen door locked open. Dion stepped in, shutting both doors behind him. He had been in a lot of trailers over the course of his career, all shapes and sizes. They were like condensed houses, with plenty of plastic and tin stripping, but kind of appealing, some of them. "Everything you need and not a bolt more," he said as he followed his host down a narrow, dingy corridor, giving a wall panel a thump with his fist.

"You got that right." Rourke led the way to the end of the trailer, the living room fuzzy with morning light, where his in-house workbench was set up. "I'm happy here. It's home, anyway. Home is where the heart is, they say. Have a seat while I look at this watch of yours."

Dion gave him the watch and sat on a kitchen chair near the workbench. Looking around at the clutter, he saw that Rourke was a packrat but kept the place in fairly good order. A glut of old snapshots was tacked to one wall, and he looked away in case there were images he really didn't care to see. Next to him on the bench stood a trio of bright toys. A little tin black man pushing a wheelbarrow, a duck driving a red car, and a yellow school bus.

Rourke followed his gaze. "Job for the second-hand guy. Clean and tune. Puts bread on the table, okay?"

"Are these worth something?"

"Not a heck of a lot. Except the duck. It's well preserved, and it's got historical significance of some kind. Don't ask me what."

The collar of Rourke's bathrobe sagged as he leaned forward, showing a bony chest. He studied the Smiths draped over his hand and gave a low whistle of admiration. "This is a fantastic watch. The last of the great British military line. Nice. But it's in shitty shape. Where'd you steal it?"

"A friend gave it to me. Long time ago."

"You shoulda boxed it up and kept it in your attic. Might be worth something now."

"It's worth more on my wrist."

Rourke looked at the back of the watch, hunting for access. "Don't expect miracles. You put it through a few wars, have you? Rain, snow, gunfights, and the odd dunk in the bathtub. It's old, older than I'm used to dealing with. I'm not saying old is bad, necessarily. But in this case you might be better to just —"

"I'd rather have it fixed."

"I mean, for the cost of repair you could get yourself a real nice —"

"Oh Jesus, open it up and do what you have to do."

Rourke grinned at him, the grin bent out of shape by his horrific scar. "This friend of yours, was she good-looking?"

This friend of his was Looch, in fact, a big loud-mouth cop going prematurely bald. Lucky Luc, Luciano Ferraro, hilarious guy, sorely missed. Dion crossed his arms and said, "His name's Luciano. We go way back, and I can't read time unless it's off this watch. Are you going to fix it or not?"

"I tell you what. Leave it with me, and I'll see what I can do. Though to tell the truth I'm kind of up to my arse in projects right now as it is."

"What, wind-up toys?"

"And three lawnmowers due for overhauls. Yes, lawnmowers. In a couple months they'll be all the rage."

Dion was having second thoughts. What he should have done was pick up a cheap substitute, get the Smiths fixed when he was back in the city, however many years down the road that might be. There in the land of plenty he could take it to a professional, get it done right. He said, "I'm just here for the short term. I could be gone tomorrow. We'd better just forget it."

"No, you leave it with me tonight. I'll see what I can do. You picked the worst day of the year, you know, what with Kiera."

"I realize that. Thank you. I appreciate it." Dion checked his wrist, already forgetting it was bare, and his heart skipped a beat. He stood to go. "Better get to work."

They walked back down the shipshape corridor to the exit, and in passing what must be a bedroom door Dion heard a woman's sigh as she tossed on squealing bedsprings. He glanced back at Rourke, who said, "You can mind your own damn business."

Outside, the sky had grown lighter, no longer snowing. Dion stood on the deck, found his keys, and started down the steps. Rourke remained out in the fresh air by his screen door, saying, "So now I've done you this big favour, you gonna do me one back and keep me in the loop with Kiera?"

Dion turned to give him a businesslike smile, in no position to start throwing out promises. "I'll do my best."

"Bah," Rourke said.

At the side of his car, Dion remembered the one question he had to ask in order to tie off the loose end on an overdue report he should have submitted yesterday. Or at least try to confirm if it had any basis in the real world. He turned back to Rourke in the doorway. "Your friend Rob Law, is he married?"

"No. Why?"

"I heard he's married to a native woman."

"You're talking about Charlie?" Rourke glared northward. "They weren't married, but it was in the plans. She took off in the fall, back home to Dease. Rob's like me. Can't keep his women."

Took off in the fall. The words jolted Dion six months back, to that blowsy afternoon with Penny at the Smithers fairgrounds. He had waited in the following days for reports of young women gone missing from that particular time and place. None had, and his fears had faded. Rourke's words now brought back an illogical drift of anxiety.

"Charlie…?"

"West."

Inside the trailer a phone rang, and Dion, one leg in the car, looked up in time to see the screen door swing shut and through its mesh the shadowy figure of a woman with long, wild hair approaching Rourke, her hand outstretched. He hesitated, considering this could be the missing singer, but screen and main door were both closed now.

Scott Rourke had mentioned someone he lived with, a Ms. Doyle. That's who it was, no mystery. He sat behind the wheel and wrote in his duty notebook, *Charlie West*. Then he realized by the clock on the dash that in about two minutes he would be late for work, and the drive back was at least twenty. He fired up the engine. One step sideways and two steps back.

* * *

Leith had two main roads to pursue, as well as a few minor alleys. One main road was the Pickup Killer, and another was Fling. This morning he would be focusing on Fling because of a tip that had arrived at the crack of dawn. The tip came in the form of a middle-aged waitress who worked at the Catalina Cafe and had overheard an argument between Kiera Rilkoff, Frank Law, and Mercy Blackwood sometime last week, a few days before Kiera's disappearance. Most of the loud words were between Mercy and Kiera, with Frank just sitting on the sidelines. The waitress recalled a few lines verbatim, from the argument: Mercy called Kiera a waste of time, and Kiera called Mercy a frog. "A frog?" Leith had asked, cupping an ear.

The waitress insisted that was what she heard, frog.

An interview of Ms. Blackwood was on Leith's to-do list anyway, if only to firm up some background info, so now he would ask about the argument as well, kill two birds with one stone. But first he would get Frank's take on it.

Frank Law showed up when the grey of dawn was just flooding over the mountains and promising another day of half-light in the Hazeltons. Leith had a cramped and cluttered workstation in the main room. He sat Frank down here, gave him a cup of coffee, flattened his notebook, and wrote down the opening particulars. Leith had been accident-prone his whole life, so his body was conditioned to fast healing — that was his theory, anyway — and already his wrist was good enough that he could take his own notes, which spared him further contact with Constable Dion, whom he had come dangerously close to shooting yesterday. He told Frank about the overheard argument at the Catalina and asked for an explanation.

"Argument?" Frank said. "What argument?"

Leith refreshed his memory for him. "You were in a booth on the south wall of the restaurant. You were seated next to Kiera, and Mercy Blackwood sat across from the two of you. Mercy and Kiera were arguing. Quite loudly. There was some swearing."

Frank looked tired and uninterested. "Okay."

"You had coffee. Kiera had tea and a cherry Danish. Mercy didn't order anything but brought her own drink in a Thermos." All this the waitress had recounted for Leith this morning before her early-bird shift. She didn't like the drink-in-the-Thermos part, and no, she admitted, she didn't like Mercy Blackwood. "Mercy accused Kiera of wasting her time, and Kiera called Mercy a frog. Mercy's not French, is she?"

Frank's mouth hung open. His short, rakish beard was becoming just plain scruffy. "French? I don't know, maybe."

"Seems kind of a racist thing for Kiera to say, doesn't it? Does she have a thing against the French?"

"Who doesn't?"

"And why would Mercy say Kiera's a waste of time? That's pretty harsh."

Frank said, "I don't remember much. Probably they were arguing about the demo, which wasn't going well."

"I don't get that, why it wasn't going well," Leith said. "You guys have been playing together for years. You're popular, have a lot of fans. What wasn't clicking?"

Frank shrugged. "We're trying for a recording. Kiera's a show girl. Without an audience egging her on, she's kind of … flat. Me and the others, we tried all kinds of tricks to get her spun up, and she tried, but it just doesn't seem to work." He hesitated. "That's what they were arguing about, I guess. Mercy thought maybe I should do lead vocals, Kiera would sing backup. And we'd ditch my songs and try something else. None of which Kiera accepted for a moment."

His eyes shifted about, a man thinking of things he didn't want to discuss, and Leith considering harassing him further on the issue. But really, it was all sidetracking. Scott Rourke, for all his rattiness, had a point when he said to stop wasting time talking to *people.* It was a monster they should be looking for.

* * *

Next in line was Fling's manager. Maybe it was the aggressive ring of her name, but Leith had envisioned a battleaxe, and Mercy Blackwood was anything but. She was a reedy, intelligent-looking woman in her late thirties, possibly, with a fine-featured and pleasant face, intense grey eyes, and grave manner. She wore black slacks, brand-new looking snow-boots, a fine-weave grey sweater, and a puffy white parka with fake fur trim. For the pretty librarian look, she wore gold-rimmed spectacles.

"I'm glad to finally meet you," she said and held out a hand in a jerky sort of way, as if she had doubts about physical contact. "I've seen you from afar." She didn't smile. He shook her limp hand and invited her to remove her coat and sit. She kept the coat on, saying it was chilly, but placed herself primly on the hard wooden chair next to Leith's desk. He could see how out of place she was. He recalled she was from Vancouver, up here to care for a dying relative, who had then died. He also recalled she was primed to sell her dead relative's house and return to the city ASAP, where she quite clearly belonged.

She watched him and waited, still and expressionless. To break the ice, he said, "I hear you worked with Joe Forte and the Six-Packs, way back when. They had a great thing going while it lasted. Too bad about Forte."

She nodded, still not a sign of smile on her attractive face. She said, "They were the first group I worked with, went from bar gigs to the Commodore. Amazing talent. I learned a lot from that experience."

And made a lot of money, too, Leith thought. "Who did you work with after that?"

"Lemon Heart," she said. "Goldie Weatherstone, who you may know better as Goldie Hawkins. The Midlanders, you know, Jerry Robinson and his fellows? That's about all. Once I got on with the Midlanders, I worked with them exclusively, as I had worked with the Six-Packs."

It all sailed over Leith's head, names that meant nothing to him except possibly the Midlanders, a fairly big name on the music scene. He said, "And now you're here in the Hazeltons representing a little country rock band called Fling. Why?"

"Terrible name," she said. "I want them to change it before it's too late. But they're quite stuck on it. I'm here because I had to give up the Midlanders. Medical issues. Plus I had to care for my grandmother."

He was reading her face as she spoke, and thought he saw traces of fear and dismay. Not surprising, considering what brought them to this room. Or maybe it was just physical discomfort. Or, like Fairchild had suggested to Constable Dion, culture shock. Whatever it was, she looked miserable. He offered coffee to warm her up. She declined.

He asked her to tell him about Fling, where they were going, what the plans were, that sort of thing.

She studied him for a moment in a cool, analytical way, before answering. "I'm not sure you care to know, but I'm only up here for the short-term. Or that was the intention. It's a full year ago I first chanced to see Fling perform, at the high school auditorium, the Valentine's dance. I had to get out of the house, away from Granny. Do something. Move. You know? Anyway, back to Fling, I guess you'd say I was smitten, or more like swept up in the moment. They shook the auditorium, and the audience loved them. Sometimes the music is secondary. That can be worked on. Personality and verve, you either have it or you don't. They did. Do. You will find her, won't you?"

"We're doing our best," he said.

She looked doubtful, and he could understand why. The whirring gears of the investigation, based in Terrace, were all but invisible to residents of the Hazeltons. A chopper flew by now and then, shiny trucks arrived, strangers reined someone in, asked questions, and were gone again. Meanwhile, Leith and his team looked like plods, and frankly, Leith was worried they were. He said, "How do you find working with them, Frank and Kiera?"

"Lovely," she said. "Both of them. Very down-to-earth, but gung-ho."

"They were thrilled when you took them under your wing?"

"Thrilled is the word," she said, and there she should smile, he thought, and still she didn't. She said, "There are difficulties, of course. They're lovers, for one thing, which complicates things. They're both stubborn. And I hate to say it, but they're not reliable. I foresaw problems, but I guess I underestimated their unreliability."

"Things are not going well, I take it," Leith said.

"Things need fixing," Blackwood said gloomily.

"Can you elaborate for me?"

She gave him another studious gaze, with no reply at the end of it. She said, "People are saying it's the Pickup Killer."

"That hasn't been crossed off," Leith admitted.

"I've also heard it said the killer lives right here in the Hazeltons."

"That's possible too."

"And he's responsible for all those missing girls from Prince George to Prince Rupert."

"Highly unlikely," Leith said, and that was true. The profilers had crunched the data, what little there was of it, and concluded the Pickup Killer was not responsible for the atrocities that had plagued Highway 16 for so many years, as yet unsolved. This killer was localized, new to the area, employed in Terrace, maybe, but could live elsewhere. The profilers believed he lived within a two-hour drive of Terrace, which encompassed both the Hazeltons and Prince Rupert. Leith banked more on Prince Rupert, his own home base, but the Hazeltons remained under close observation. The population of the area was scant, and he had probably looked at the name of every male in the area at least once over the last two and a half years. Nobody had jumped out at him or held his attention for long.

Mercy Blackwood sat silently now, pondering him. He had received nothing of value from her so far and didn't expect much from his next question either. He said, "I have to ask you, Ms. Blackwood. I've been told you were heard arguing with Kiera, on February the fifth, which is eight days before she went missing. I need to know what it was about."

She frowned in a worried way, casting her mind back. "Yes, I guess we did raise our voices somewhat."

"What was the problem?"

"Disappointment, clash of ambitions, reality checks. Unhappily, nothing was working. The Vancouver label pulled out because the CD just wasn't good enough, which I should have known, and I feel bad about that. We're brainstorming, trying to get back on our feet. My suggestion was a radical change of direction. Kiera didn't do well in a studio setting, for some reason, and I thought the best route was to try new songs and new lead. A new persona, really. Frank could take lead vocals and Kiera could sing backup. That was my plan, and they both said hell no. So there you go. I wished them luck, said I would hang in through the making of this second demo, and then I would leave them to find their own way from there. And that's where we stand."

Everything she said lined up with Frank's version so far. Leith said, "Worst case scenario, Kiera doesn't come back, will you continue working with Frank and the others?"

"Too soon to say. Frank can go places on his own, if he puts his mind to it, and I'll work him through it, if that's what he wants to do. We'll see."

Leith's notebook told him he'd come to his last query, and it was a touchy one. "D'you have any French in you?" he asked.

"French," she echoed. "Me? No. I speak some French, but that's as far as it goes. Why?"

"During the argument Kiera called you a frog. I'm wondering why."

Her cool grey eyes didn't leave him for a moment. She was one of those maddening interviewees who kept their emotions tucked neatly away, surprise, anger, and amusement. "Frog," she echoed. "Wow. I don't recall that."

He said, "Also, you called her a waste of time. Sounds like quite a battle."

Now, finally, she showed herself; her brows went up and she almost smiled. "Ah," she said. "I recall now, yes. I was fed up with her stonewalling all my ideas. I flung up my hands and said she was a *perte de temps*. She said, what? I translated, waste of time. I guess 'frog' was the meanest comeback she could think up on the spot, followed by bitch and cow. Well, I've been called worse over the course of my career, working with artists, you know."

For the first time she grinned.

* * *

Jayne Spacey glanced up, and her face was smooth and sweet. She didn't look angry, but she was, and even the indoors felt frigid now to Dion. She hated him; he could feel it as he walked up to her at her computer with his apologies. She stopped typing to listen to what he had to say and continued to look smooth and sweet, but the chill kept spreading.

"I didn't want to get into the middle of it," he said. "Sorry."

"Well, I must say you have great comedic timing. Shane and Megan couldn't stop laughing. Sure, I'd like you to go to hell, and you know what? That's where you're going, judging by the things I overheard them saying about you."

"Who saying?"

"Those who matter," she said. "But chin up, baby. I hear security guards are in high demand, and it's better than minimum wage. No thinking required. Briefing in fifteen, by the way, and the boss has made a note that you're late. Better have caught up on your reports. She's a stickler for the twenty-four-hour rule."

Those who matter would be Giroux, he knew, and Leith. Or was it Sergeant Bosko from the Lower Mainland, a presence that had bothered him from the start, back at the dinner briefing at the Catalina, when Bosko spoke of his latest posting, North Vancouver, Serious Crimes. What was a man of his stature doing here in the sticks? Just hanging around, helping the locals with a missing persons investigation, just for the hell of it?

No chance. Sergeant Bosko had bigger things on his mind.

Dion was back at his own station, a temporary set-up jammed between filing cabinets and a fax machine, and he got to work on his last, overdue report. His time was coming to an end; he could see it approaching like banners of war fluttering on the horizon. At least he could get this report in. Late and full of typos, but better than nothing at all.

Five

THREE VOICES

LEITH THOUGHT ABOUT MURDER and its aftermath, all the damage done. There were the victims themselves; that went without saying. Then there were those left behind, their lives forever bent out of shape. The family of the killer, also in tatters. There were the cops, working night and day and getting ulcers. Like himself. Last October, back in Prince Rupert, stomach pains had sent him first to the doctor, and then, for the first time in his life, to a counsellor.

He hated being sent for counselling. He didn't believe that any external advice could fix any internal problem of any healthy man. He didn't like being told how to breathe, how to think, how to relax. As he'd said to Alison afterward, what a stinking bunch of hogwash. To avoid a return visit to the shrink, he'd determined not to get another ulcer, and so far hadn't.

This gloomy afternoon, sitting eating lunch in Giroux's office, he felt something gnawing at his gut again, and it wasn't just all the takeout he'd been down-ing lately; it was the proliferation of trucks in the north.

All eyes were open for reports of suspicious pickups, but every other person drove a pickup, and with a little imagination, every other person could look suspicious. A map lay before him, in his mind the constellation of burial sites and the voices of three women telling him what they'd been through as their time ran out. Joanne Crow, the last known victim, had the most to say. *This evil man raped me, held me captive for days, bound and gagged me, starved me and let me freeze. Look at my hands and toes and nose and cheeks, destroyed by frostbite. He didn't even have the heart to put me out of my misery. I did not go easily.*

That was the big thing to consider, the evidence of es-calation of this man's tormenting, again as whispered by the dead. The first killing had been vicious but relatively swift. Abduction, rape, and strangulation. The second had been kept alive for maybe two days, possibly in a house, possibly in a vehicle, but most likely a shed with rotting floors, according to trace evidence. The third, Joanne, had endured at least a week before exhaustion and the elements got her. There had been no rotted wood fibres found embedded in her wounds. She had died in her zap-strap handcuffs and been dumped in the mud, some-what farther to the north from Terrace than the first two.

If the killer had taken to keeping his victims captive, it followed there was a good chance that Kiera could still be alive — in that house, that cabin, that cave, that vehicle, wherever the hell he had her — and if Leith's days were long and difficult, hers were eternities of sheer, unthinkable hell.

"Still bothers me that Kiera's grabbed over here," he said, speaking more to himself than Bosko over on the other wing of Giroux's enormous desk. "While the others happened over there." In the Terrace area. "Is he expanding his hunting ground, or was he just passing through?"

The question belonged not to him but to the Terrace task force, Corporal Stoner, and it had been beaten to death here, there, and everywhere, really not worth putting to words for the hundredth time. Bosko was on his laptop, communicating with his home office, but present enough to look at Leith and say, "Might be worth it to go over the timeline again."

The timeline was fixed in Leith's mind like a fiery branding. "Karen Blake was taken March of 2008, two years ago. Lindsay Carlyle, nearly nine months later, November 2008. Joanne Crow just two months later, December 2009. And nothing since. Nothing for over a year. We found Joanne over fourteen months ago, on Christmas Day. It's not much of a pattern."

"But a pattern, however you look at it," Bosko said. "And it's more likely opportunity than urge that's dictating when he strikes. That should prove helpful."

Leith got his point, of course. If it was a pattern, there weren't enough hits to make even a rudimentary shape, but it was the ABCs of profiling. Use the pattern as a template against the comings and goings of anybody who might come under suspicion — truckers, hunters, forestry workers — and it could help sift out the perpetrator. These were all winter kills, sure. That, if nothing else, stood out loud and clear. When it came to the Pickup Killer, death was tied to the seasons.

Bosko asked how many light-coloured pickups were registered in the area between Terrace and Smithers, a question that took Leith back to the pain in his gut.

"Every other guy has a pickup," he said. "I have a pickup. And every other pickup is light in colour. Like mine. There are lots."

"I've noticed," Bosko said.

"Rob Law has a tan pickup, but it's pretty new. Both sightings say it was probably an older model. One tip, from November, says it's white; the December tip says silver. Different trucks or just a trick of the light, who knows. Neither witness knew much about vehicle makes and models."

Bosko spoke of how important it was not to get in a rut with this truck-sighting business. "Like you say, Dave, there are only two leads in that direction, both tenuous. Now, if we had a third sighting —" he added, and it was at this exact moment, at least as Leith later recalled it, that Constable Jayne Spacey stepped into the room with news, and the timing was surreal.

"We got a truck sighting," she told them, flapping her notebook. "Dean Caplin. I've got him in the interview room. He's a driver for Whittaker Contracting, working in the cut-block above the Law outfit. He was pulling a loaded rig down the mountain at fifteen twenty hours on Saturday afternoon —"

Which fell, Leith knew, some five hours before the search for Kiera got underway, and his interest was definitely piqued.

"— and he passed Kiera's Rodeo on the lookout, which stood out to him, because it's hardly tourist season. But it's what he saw a couple minutes later you gotta hear. He passed her Rodeo, and two or three minutes later, that's his best estimate, he came up behind a vehicle driving down the road ahead of him. We missed him earlier because he was out of town, just got back, heard we wanted to talk to him, called in right away. You're going to want to talk to this guy, like, now."

Leith was already on his feet, inviting Spacey to join him.

The witness, Dean Caplin, stood when they entered, a man who fell into the "good citizen" camp, in Leith's snap-judgement opinion. Introductions were made, hands were shaken. Caplin's hands were huge, calloused, cold, and oily. Not only a good citizen but a hard worker.

"Yeah," he told Leith when they were all seated around the table. "It was a white pickup, five, ten years old, some old Nissan or something, two-wheel drive, had no business on them roads. Couldn't see who all was inside because rear window was some kind of custom job, black glass."

Leith had laid out a forestry map, and he asked Caplin to pinpoint as best he could where he'd first seen this pickup with the black window.

Caplin pointed to a spot just down from the lookout where Kiera's Rodeo had been found. "It was going pretty slow till I came up behind it, then it shot off, eh. Kind of fishtailing a bit. I thought it was going to go over the bank, and I'd be picking up the pieces. I probably lost sight of it about here, around this bend." His finger traced a short line and stopped.

"I don't suppose you caught —"

"Christ, no, sir. Licence plate was covered in mud. And even if it wasn't, I wouldn't have made note of it. Had no idea it was a crime in progress. Sorry."

When Caplin was gone, Leith made some phone calls, talked with Giroux and Bosko, and decided it was time to take this last bit of info to Terrace and upturn the files again, see if it clicked anywhere, small white pickup with black rear window. He'd go himself, he'd go now, and preferably he'd go alone.

"I might as well join you," Bosko said. "Does that work?"

"Does it ever," Leith said, two thumbs up. "Wonderful."

* * *

By mid-afternoon a hard wind was blowing, and the undersized detachment seemed to creak and strain on its foundations. Dion had been aware of some excitement earlier, something that had taken Leith off in a hurry to Terrace, the small city farther to the north. The search for Kiera seemed to have settled already into a lower gear, and the crowds were gone, the place hushed but for a woman sobbing in one of the interview rooms down the hall, an unrelated case. His fingers were smashing at the keyboard, spell-checker racing along and underlining half the words he laid down. He had been tasked with assisting Constable Thackray with exhibit documentation, and he was in a trance of words and numbers when something came clomping over and hovered into his left-hand peripheral vision, too short to be Thackray, too graceless to be Spacey. He looked sideways and stopped typing.

"We're going out," Sergeant Giroux said. "Witness interview. Take a fresh pen."

Outside, small vapour ghosts raced over the tarmac, forming lines and breaking up again. The sergeant had marched to Dion's cruiser, to the passenger side, which meant they'd take his car and that he'd be the driver. He stood by the driver's door and searched himself for keys, a minor pastime of his lately. The keys weren't where he expected, and he had a lot of other pockets to check, and it wasn't long before Giroux shouted across the roof at him from the passenger side, "Just pretend this is an emergency callout and people's lives are at stake. What's the matter with you? You don't like driving?"

He looked aside, between buildings and signposts, toward what he could see of the highway, its surface glittering in the dull light of day like it was strewn with crushed glass. "No, ma'am. It's pretty icy."

He'd found the keys, not in any of his jacket pockets or duty-belt but in his trousers, and beeped the locks, but too late because Sergeant Giroux had struck off across the parking lot toward an older model sedan. "We're taking my Celeb," she called back at him. "*Sacre!* I'm not riding with a man who's afraid of a little ice."

When he was in the passenger seat, she said, "Never before met a constable afraid of the road."

"No, ma'am," he said, and fastened the seat belt.

Giroux cranked the key, and the engine woke with a ragged snarl, mellowing to a purr. She drove off the avenue and onto the highway. The trip to Hazelton's Old Town took about ten minutes, a distance they covered in silence. She parked in front of a pint-sized Royal

Bank. Inside the bank Dion waited next to a stand of brochures, not sure why he'd been brought along, while Giroux sat in a cubicle dealing with the bank manager for nearly twenty minutes, poring over a computer monitor and making notes.

After she was done with the computer, she stopped at one of the two teller stations and spoke to the young woman there, who Dion now recognized as one of the band members who had been interviewed by Leith — the violinist with the white-blond hair, looking different in the context of work. She had given him a friendly wave some minutes ago, and he'd nodded back, but still hadn't placed her.

"Afternoon, Stella," he heard Giroux saying. "Howarya? Just a couple questions."

Dion remained standing at his distance and didn't hear much of their conversation, something about an argument with Mercy at the Catalina. Mercy was a name on the file, but he couldn't put a face to her, or any significance.

He consulted his second notebook, the one he kept separate from his duty notebook. This was the one he'd nearly left with Leith by accident, where he listed names from any file he was assigned to, in chart form, to keep them in order. Nadia, his rehab professional, had told him not to be ashamed to keep notes of even the most minor details. Anything to get you through the day. And it worked. On top of field notes, he had reminders of all sorts of crap that hampered his day-to-day living, PIN codes, and basic computer procedures. He even had a necktie-knotting diagram, which was embarrassing. Still needed it once in a while, when he lost the moves and stood with a tie end in each fist, no idea where they were supposed to go next. That was when the panic set in.

Giroux was done, leaving the bank, so he followed. When they were in the car, breath gusting white, she snapped at him, "Why didn't you join me? It's your job to pay attention. You're a highly intelligent sponge, not a dumbass doorstop."

He wasn't so sure about that, so he couldn't agree. Even apologizing seemed futile. He busied himself with his seat belt instead.

Giroux's voice hardened. "This is off the record, Constable Dion. I worry about you, maybe because you're First Nations, and I'm Métis, and we're different creatures from the present governing race, and we have to look out for each other. I want to help you. So how can I put this nicely? There's something wrong with you. Are you on drugs?"

He stared at her, trying not to gape. "I'm not First Nations."

"Sure you are."

"No, ma'am."

"You've got Cree eyes. Take that as a compliment, if you want."

She seemed to mean what she said, and he began to wonder if he *was* First Nations. Spacey had suggested he was. The old guy in the Super 8 diner had jabbered at him like he was. And now this. And maybe they were all right, and he was wrong. He looked at his own hands and saw the skin was white as ever. His father was white. His mother was maybe on the dark side, from what he could remember, her arms going around him, tight, hair cascading over him, black, on one of her good days, few and far between. He knew nothing else about her, really, and had made no inquiries, and never for a moment had he considered she might be native.

Giroux said, "So you protest your bloodlines but not the drugs, so what are you on?" Her palm went up, a stop sign. "No, I don't want to know, because you're right, I couldn't let it slide if you fess up. But take this as a serious warning. If you're on something, get off it. Now."

"Ibuprofen," he said with anger, pointing hard at his own temple. "That's all. For headaches." He crimped his mouth. "I'm sorry. I wasn't sure what you wanted me to do, take notes or guard the door."

She blinked at him. "Hover, Constable. Look, listen, analyze. You should know that. I'm not going to be directing your every move. Be interested. Nobody can make you be interested. It's got to come from within. Are you interested? At *all*?"

"Yes, ma'am."

She looked unconvinced. Worse, she looked sympathetic. They both gazed forward, and for a moment it felt to Dion like a first date gone wrong, stuck in Lovers' Lane with nothing to say. Giroux said, "Actually, I owe you an apology, because I know nothing about you, and I should. I'm supposed to review files of all my people, even if they're short-term, but I didn't. I'll get to it sooner or later, probably after you're gone when it's too late anyway. Whatever, never mind, doesn't matter. I'm just trying to tell you something here. It's a tough job, and if you don't walk into it with a sure stride, you'll fall behind. Get me?"

"Yes, ma'am."

"And the fact is this job's not for everyone. There's no shame in admitting it's not your calling, pet. Better sooner than later, is all I'm saying."

He looked away, out the passenger window at parking lot, and beyond that to the drab little village smothered in snow.

Giroux started the car and drove away from the Royal Bank, turning onto yet another small byway that connected the communities. Dion watched homes and ranch land, river and roadside bushes blur by. Nadia had said, "Don't look too far forward or too far back, one step at a time, sweetie." That's what she'd always called him, *sweetie,* in her South Pacific accent. He'd taken the name at face value until it dawned on him that was what she called everyone she was trying to bend back into shape. *Sweetie.* It meant nothing, like *pet* meant nothing from Giroux.

She was sharing her thoughts again as she drove along, maybe because she wasn't giving up on him so easy, but more likely because she was in the habit of talking to herself aloud. "Poor Kiera, if that sick freak from Terrace got his hands on her. At least now we have something to work with, hey?"

Dion turned her way and tried to sound smart, not with the usual *yes ma'am* but a full sentence, complete with theory attached. "The pickup sighting, right. Black glass, that should narrow it down. In fact —" he said, and the words were knocked from his head as the world went into a skid. He grabbed for the dashboard, heart slamming, and found that instead of slithering into the second catastrophic collision in his life the car was idling safely at the side of the road.

"Damn," Giroux said. "I forgot all about them. The photos."

Without explanation, she carved a U-turn on the frosty asphalt and headed back the way they had come.

"It was inadvertent," she said, not so much to Dion as to the windshield, which wasn't clearing properly, fogged at the edges. "They were right there on the counter by the coffee maker, and I wanted to ask Frank if I could look at 'em, because maybe they were from the day in question. But I put 'em in my pocket and forgot."

They crossed the frightening chasm bridge to an area Dion was familiar with, the road to Scottie Rourke's trailer, but turned instead down somebody's driveway, where Giroux slowed to a crawl, for it was barely a lane tunnelling through branches. A minute later, no house in sight, she stopped the car and let it rumble on standby. Here she sat rock still, hands on the wheel, looking up. Dion followed her stare at the clouded sky, chopped by branches. The branches were fine, pale and leafless. Giroux said, "Well, since I have 'em, might as well take a quick look. Hand me my bag there, would you?"

He watched her draw a white drug-store envelope from the handbag, about six inches by eight, and from it she brought a thin stack of what he saw as glossy photographs. "Who does the snapshot thing these days, with all your digital slideshows and whatnot?" Giroux asked herself. "Nobody but my Aunt Jean and the three bears, I guess. They're probably Lenny's, actually. He's the sentimental one in the family. The reader of books, the poet.

The historian." She shuffled through the pictures, shaking her head, giving a brief running narrative. "Nope, nope, not even from winter, obviously. There's Kiera. What a pretty smile she's got, hey?"

She showed him the picture, but too fast for Dion to absorb, and kept shuffling.

Excluded, he sat waiting. Out the side window, high up in the endless grey, a hawk of some kind wheeled in a slow drift out of sight. The Chev had settled into waiting mode and purred quietly. "These are from the summer," Giroux said. "Rob with his new truck, looking like a proud dad. Frank jumping in the river. Kiera again." She paused on a photograph and said, "Who's this? Don't know this girl at all."

She angled the shot at Dion, and he caught a glimpse of a young woman in an ice-blue shirt, native, the young woman from the fall fair, and Giroux had maybe noticed his inner lurch, because she searched his face. "You okay? Going to be sick? For god's sake, get out of my car and do it in the bushes."

"No, just …" he said, and stalled. The girl in the photo wasn't the girl at the fair, of course not. That would be crazy. But she was a reminder of a sick feeling past and a sick feeling present, that he hadn't done up the report, a double failure.

Giroux was still fixed on him, sharp-eyed, peeling back his thoughts. She tapped the picture at him. "This picture startled you? Why? You know her?"

He didn't take the photo from her but looked at the image, a black-haired girl, somewhere in her late teens or early twenties, hard to judge. The ice-blue T-shirt he'd seen at first glance was actually a sky-blue summer dress. She had soft round shoulders and had turned her face down with the reticence of so many native girls he'd dealt with in life, all in the line of duty, down in the Lower Mainland, where most native guys he confronted were belligerent, and most native girls looked they would rather disappear than have to face the world and all its tough questions. The girl in the picture didn't look like she was in a bad place. She was at a kitchen counter here, cutting vegetables, and though she hid from the camera, he could sense she was smiling.

He squeezed his eyes shut for the beat of a moment and saw the girl at the fair like it was yesterday, walking away. How could someone forever walking away never go away? She would keep walking away and dragging him along till she pulled him under. He spoke heavily, looking pointedly at the photograph. "That could be Charlie West. Rob Law's fiancée, or was, from Dease Lake. She left him last fall. I meant to type it up."

Giroux drew in a loud breath. "And how the hell do you know all that?"

"Scott Rourke told me. I had meant to put it in my report —"

"You already said that. Why didn't you? You forgot?"

Worse than forgot, he'd procrastinated. "It didn't seem important," he said. "Sorry."

"And what the hell conversation is this, with Scott Rourke?"

"I have this watch, needs fixing, just asked him —"

"Yeah, okay." The woman in charge of his life sighed, and in that breath he felt himself dismissed, papers to follow. "You don't make calls like that, what's important and what isn't, till you've got some status," she said. "Which doesn't look promising. Though I'm not much of a role model, am I, grabbing evidence without a warrant? Better get this back to them before I get sued for trespass."

She rolled the car the rest of the way down the driveway, where a boxy blue house sat, and climbed out of the car. Dion followed. She walked up the steps, knocked on the door, then banged on it, and eventually a boy opened in tank top and pajama bottoms, the youngest brother, Lenny Law, looking wretched and under-slept. Nobody else was home, he told Giroux, letting her and Dion pass inside. Frank and Rob were up there, he said, gesturing vaguely to heaven. Working. The house was cold. Giroux asked him why he wasn't in school.

"I am," he said, crushing an eye with a palm.

"Oh right, I forgot," she said. "Homeschooler. I won't keep you. Just wanted to stop by and see how you're doing, okay? You and your brothers. Can we sit down a minute?"

He rolled his eyes and made a show of just how baggy-faced and irritable he was feeling, but nodded.

"It's an icebox in here," Giroux said. "Go put on a robe or you'll catch pneumonia."

"I'm okay."

"That's an order."

He went off to do as he was told, and Giroux slipped into the kitchen. She came back with a cup of coffee in hand. "Always coffee on the go here," she told Dion with a wink. "It's terrible. You want some?"

He didn't want coffee. Lenny returned, swaddled in not a robe but a heavy cardigan, and Giroux said, "Tell me about Charlie West."

His brows went up. "Charlie? What's to tell?"

"I don't know. Maybe nothing. But if she knew Kiera, I want to know about it. That's all."

The boy shrugged. "She was Rob's girlfriend for a while. They were supposed to get married, but it didn't work out. She left at the end of last summer. Went back home. To Dease."

Dion watched the boy, wanting to pin him down on her date of departure. Did she go straight home? Any chance she'd go south instead? While he was considering opening his mouth to ask just that, Giroux said, "Does she stay in touch?"

"No way. And if she tried, she'd get blown off. She's burned her bridges in this house, leaving Rob like that."

"You have any photos of her, so I can have something for the file?"

"I did," he said, with sudden anger. "They disappeared. Probably Rob got rid of them."

"Well, have another look around," Giroux said. "How did Charlie and Kiera get along?"

Another shrug. "Fine. Charlie was quiet. She was always just kind of there."

"D'you have her contact info? I'd like to talk to her all the same."

This was what Dion was waiting for. He held his breath.

"I don't know why you'd bother," Lenny said. "What, you're thinking Kiera and Charlie ran off together?" He brayed a snarky laugh. Dion stopped holding his breath and frowned, watching the kid laugh, and watched the smile fade back to glum, and willed Giroux to get tough, ask more questions.

Giroux said, "Get her number for me, would you?"

"She doesn't have a cellphone."

"How about a home number?"

"You'll have to get it off Rob," Lenny said. "He might have something. Unless he threw it away, which he probably did. He was pissed off when she left."

"Well, tell him to look for it and call it in to me, okay?"

Lenny nodded and saw them out. Out on the driveway, Giroux gave Dion the car keys and said, "Better get used to it."

Driving back, a few clicks slower than Giroux seemed to appreciate, he reflected on the look on Lenny's face when he'd opened the door, a kind of fear he'd seen before and should be able to categorize, but couldn't quite. And the strange laugh, full of contempt, but concealing some kind of pain. In the passenger seat Giroux said, "'Course Rob won't call in with that number, but like Lenny says, why bother. Just look up her stats for the file and fill it in as best you can. Think you can do that for me, fill in the blanks?" She didn't sound optimistic.

"Yes, ma'am," he said, and for a change he was one step ahead of her. "I will."

* * *

Once all the sleuthing was done, the rest, Leith realized, was basically a crapshoot. A chance sighting of a pickup truck heading down a mountain, for instance, can take a case out of the fridge and back onto the burner. Which always got his blood coursing. He was in Terrace, the middle-sized city that sat between Rupert and the Hazeltons, probable base of operations for the Pickup Killer, though probably not his home. Because of the pickup sighting by Dean Caplin the trucker, Leith was here turning the stones over once again, re-interviewing witnesses, having all local security footages reviewed from the last weekend, scrambling the map points and timelines and trying the gestalt thing. He wasn't great at gestalt, but it didn't stop him trying.

But he'd been at it too long without a break, back here in Terrace like a recycling bad dream, and he could see himself running into yet another brick wall. He tried not to punch something in frustration, but when deep breaths and happy thoughts didn't work, he hammered his own thigh with a fist hard enough to hurt. Mike Bosko, standing at the pin board nearby, said, "Problem?"

"All it's done is throw doubts all over my best leads," Leith complained. "I have to start a whole new category of what-ifs now. Frankly, it's bullshit. I don't think it's him."

"Well, that's a good thing, isn't it?"

Yes and no. Ironically, Kiera had a better chance of being alive if she was with this particular lunatic, who liked to savour his prey for days. But it was the ugliest silver lining Leith could imagine. He didn't answer.

"There's this fellow, Andrew Blair," Bosko said. He was facing the board where all the key info was pinned. "Why isn't he front and centre?"

"Because we looked him up, down, and sideways. All we got on him is he said something to somebody which led to a Crimestoppers tip, which led to nothing."

"What did he say?"

"Something about women and where they belong," Leith said. "Something any natural-born dickhead in a bar would say when talking to his buddies." He didn't add it was something his own misogynistic asshole buddies might say in bars, in fact.

"And what did he say when you asked him about it?"

"Not much. Apologized and admitted he's a dickhead. Maybe not those exact words." Leith flipped through files until he had the statement and handed it over.

Bosko sat and read through it, then set it aside. "I don't know. You're right, there's nothing to grab onto here. And I'm no profiler by any means, but he's the only one that clicks in place for me."

"I talked to him myself," Leith said, the uneasiness filtering back in, tightening his belly muscles. One of his most enduring fears was that he would be the sloppy one, the detective who couldn't read the evidence, the one to let another murder happen on his watch. "No alarms went off," he said, and knew it wasn't true. He reviewed the statement with a scowl, closed his eyes to see the big picture, and conjured up Andy Blair, that *person of interest*, and he felt it again: Blair was one of the faces that had continued to nudge even when cleared, if only in the back of his mind. Blair lived in Terrace, and the profilers said the killer didn't, but profilers could be wrong. "Yes," he said. "We should at least check where he was on Saturday."

Bosko said, "The guy's got the resources, anyway."

And that was a big reason it nagged. Blair had access to trucks. An assortment of them, new and used. Which might explain the variations in the witness reportings.

Leith reached for the phone to round Blair up, but Bosko stopped him. "Hang on. Let's save him the trip and see where he works."

They drove together to the Terrace Chev dealership owned by Blair's father, where Andy did anything that needed doing, apparently, from selling cars to detailing them. "There's a lot of used trucks here, as well as new," Leith said as they left their SUV and headed for the glass doors of the showroom. "They gave us access to the records, and we found nothing in them that jibed with the abductions. But Blair being second in command here, he could fiddle the numbers and we'd never know. Believe me, I looked into it. Nothing panned out."

They found Blair inside at the main desk, feet up, chatting with the receptionist. The woman, like most car dealership receptionists, should have been a runway model. Blair was nowhere close to runway material. He was thirty-seven, on the comfortable side of ugly, had no criminal record, wasn't a troublemaker, had a long-term girlfriend and a healthy set of friends. Lately, he drove a little Ford Focus.

Blair rose from his chair with a salesman's grin, which didn't cool even as he recognized Leith as the cop who'd harassed him no end some months ago. He reached, shook hands, nodded as Bosko introduced himself, and took them to a sleek little office with a set of chairs, desk, and computer. He offered coffee, cracked a used-car-salesman joke or two, and waited for the questions Leith would throw at him.

"There's been another disappearance," Leith said. "So we're basically re-canvassing old ground, right?"

"What, another girl?" Blair looked at Leith, looked at Bosko, snapped his fingers and said, "Kiera Rilkoff? It was in the paper. She's kind of a big name down in Hazelton there, so they made a big deal about it. You know, I've seen 'em play, her and her band. They did a gig at a benefit concert here, I forget for what. She was outstanding, if you're into that kind of thing. Terrible. So you're thinking it's the Pickup Killer strikes again? Hazelton's a bit out of his usual range, isn't it?"

"It's really not that far," Leith said. "If you have a truck. So what were you up to this past weekend?"

Working, Blair explained. The girlfriend was away, and he'd watched an amateur game at the local rink, had a buddy over for beer, Friday night. Was alone Saturday, nursing a bit of a hangover, and didn't see anybody and didn't go out.

Which left him without an alibi for the critical time. Leith said he'd like to look around the lot. "Be my guest," Blair said. "Especially take a look at the newest Camaro. Very hot."

Colourful flags with Chev logos flapped under a dull winter sun. The detectives walked the entire car lot like a pair of hard-to-please buyers. They looked into the shop, asked to see the recent sales records, and even checked the side avenues for overflow inventory. There was no white pickup with black glass in sight.

Leith was feeling one part energized and nine parts spent. He had found the devil — he believed it, if for no clear reason — but was nowhere near able to rattle its bones.

* * *

The evening took Dion back to Rourke's neat junkyard, parking his cruiser alongside the dingy trailer. He was off duty now, in civvies except for the work boots and rugged RCMP parka, which he needed against the cold.

Rourke told him to come on in. He followed the fix-all into the depths of the trailer and met the woman he'd seen only in silhouette before, the one with the wild hair, not Kiera Rilkoff at all. She rose from a heavy velour armchair and said, "You're the cop with the watch Scottie was talking about, right?"

"That's me."

"Evangeline Doyle, meet Dudley Do-Right," Rourke said and took his place at his workbench. "Just putting this thing back together for you, Dudley. Two minutes. Make yourself at home. Get 'im a beer, Evie. And me a fresh one."

She was young and pretty, in a pampered way. Far too pretty for an old greaseball like Scottie. And very pale. She belonged on a stage with a name like Peaches 'n Cream, twirling the chrome pole. She brought a beer for Dion and returned to her chair, gesturing at him to take the tatty loveseat across from her. The trailer was warm, and she wore only a gauzy green dress that showed off her long, solid legs. The fabric was shot through with metallic threads so that it gleamed in the lamplight. Her hair, even wilder than he'd seen in silhouette, was orangey-gold. She sat comfortably and watched him with interest. She said, "So, you guys getting anywhere finding Kiera?"

"Not yet," he said, about all he was willing to say about the case. "Sorry."

"She's dead, isn't she?"

"I can't say that."

He considered asking Rourke and Evangeline about Charlie West again, but there was really no point. His assigned task to locate the woman had been taken off his hands by Jayne Spacey within minutes of his first attempts, when he was leaving a message with the Dease Lake detachment. Spacey was working on crushing him. She confiscated his duties whenever she could, didn't want him claiming any accomplishments, even small ones. She would tell the boss that Dion couldn't cope with even this, tracking down contact information, that she had to do it herself.

In the end, it hardly mattered. He'd checked Spacey's file notes and saw that she did manage to reach Charlie West in Dease Lake, which meant Charlie wasn't the girl walking away from the fall fair, which didn't surprise him, brought no comfort, only crossed out one of a million possibilities.

A space heater hummed, roasting the air. The beer Evangeline had given him was cold. Rourke brought over the Smiths and handed it to its owner, almost tenderly. "You're lucky," he said. "It's not every repairman who keeps every bit of junk he ever comes across in his whole godforsaken life. I got a shoebox full of watch corpses. Happened to find one that matches close enough, and I replaced the gizmo, there, and put it all back together. I don't guarantee eternity, but she's got another ten years under the belt, easy."

Dion listened to the watch ticking, and it sounded robust. He strapped it to his wrist and felt whole again, ready to take on the world. Rourke was back at his workbench, beer in hand. "No sir, they don't make things like they used to. It's a setup. Everything you buy self-destructs on deadline, otherwise known as warranty expiration. Right, Evie?"

"Absolutely," said Evangeline from her armchair. She pulled a knee up and embraced it, smiling at Dion.

He returned the smile briefly. He was running on an empty stomach, and even a few sips of beer, combined with the relief at having his Smiths back in running order, made him feel light, happier than he'd felt in months. He said to Rourke, "Are you really incorporated?"

"In a manner of speaking."

"Watch it, Scottie," Evangeline said. "He's a cop."

"You could *say* I'm incorporated," Rourke said. He was tinkering with something at his bench, back turned on his guest. "In the broad sense."

"He doesn't even know what incorporated means," Evangeline told Dion. "Leave the guy alone. It just sounds good. Like you tack 'esquire' behind your name, when you're for sure no squire."

"Oh, I'd never do that," Dion said. He swallowed beer, taking in the environment, feeling present. Integral. Evangeline's arm moved and her bracelet caught the light, shooting turquoise sparks into his eyes. "So, are you Scottish?" he said to Rourke's back. Rourke wore overalls and a tank top, neither flattering his ribby frame.

"Sort of Norwegian-Mohawk strain," Rourke said. "Bit of this, bit of that."

"He's a mongrel," Evangeline said. "But no Scot in Scottie. You can ignore the name."

Rourke said, "And what kind of a name is *Dion,* anyway? *Dion.* Sounds girly."

"It's my surname."

"Well, obviously," Evangeline said. "You got a regular name?"

He downed more beer, watching her watching him, safe enough at the moment, with Rourke's focus down his magnifying glass. "No, I don't have one, actually."

"Like hell you don't have one," Rourke said. "Everyone's got a first name. It's the law."

"It's probably a really goofy name he's embarrassed to say," Evangeline said, eyes gleaming. "Like Jasper, or Stanley. To go with the haircut."

Dion checked his watch once more and compared it with the satellite-perfect time on his cellphone. Dead on. "You fixed it, Rourke," he said. "Guess that means I'd better pay you." He pulled out his wallet and riffled through it. Not that there was much to riffle. His pay rate had been chopped since November, since vehicular triple somersaults and crash landings and diminished capacity. The short-term disability payments had stopped the moment he'd been cleared to return to full-time employment, and none of it mattered a bit anyway, now that he was back in working order. "How much do I owe you?"

Rourke turned around. "Honestly, the time it took me fixing that thing, you'd owe me your next ten paycheques. But give me thirty and we'll call it even."

"Scottie's such a shark," Evangeline said and lazily noodled an index finger around her temple, for Dion's eyes only.

"Thirty-five," Rourke said.

Dion gave him a fifty and said to keep the change.

Rourke snapped the bill and held it up to the light. "No, come on, fifty?"

"Keep it. It's worth it to me."

"Boy, you really are attached to that ticker, aren't you? I guess you being a cop, I'd better give you a receipt, right?"

"Forget it." The mean northern wind had blown up over the last little while, gathering force, and was now rattling the trailer. The windows were pitch black. Dion looked at the pitch-black windows and thought about a pickup truck with a black rear window. He could hear something outside, sounded like those voices again, trying to tell him something, and his transient sense of well-being began to slip away. "I should get going."

"You should have another beer," Rourke corrected, scribbling a receipt. "Evie, get our guest another cold one."

"So long as he knows he's going to have to arrest himself for DUI," Evangeline said but did as told, rose from her armchair and wandered to the kitchenette.

Next to Dion the wall was covered in photographs, the ones he'd seen on his first visit, all stuck up with push-pins. Now he threw caution to the wind and had a better look, thinking of Sergeant Giroux's remark. *Who does the snapshot thing these days?* But Rourke was a bit of a throwback, didn't belong in the digital age. Many of the snapshots here were old and faded anyway, he saw, their colours washed out to blue. Quite a few newer shots of Kiera, but Kiera was a celebrity, and the camera loved her, and he didn't think obsession could be read into it. Kiera on stage, singing, backed up by her group. Kiera embracing friends, including this old greaseball, Scott Rourke.

Kiera crouched down chatting with a toddler, riding a horse, grinning at the camera. There were pictures of Frank Law, too, one person of interest Dion hadn't met, other than seeing him down there on the stage last fall.

There was a recent-looking shot of Evangeline, and several of the Law brothers over the years. This was Lenny, probably, as a boy, couldn't be more than four or five, which meant Rourke had known the brothers at least a dozen years. There was a more recent picture of Rourke standing between the two older Law brothers, Rob and Frank, an arm hooked around each of their necks and pulling them to him, like an affectionate dad with two grown sons horsing around in the backyard.

There were even more faded shots, probably from Rourke's childhood, and some of his years as a young and not-so-bad looking man, before the scar. None of Rourke's dead wife, though. Naturally enough.

Evangeline delivered the fresh bottle of Kokanee to Dion's hand and stood so close for a moment that he could smell the soap and perfume and the slight mildew of a dress grabbed from a pile on the floor. Rourke was talking about what he'd do to the bastard responsible for Kiera's disappearance when he got his hands on the sick piece of trash. Rourke was 99 percent certain the Pickup Killer was responsible. "And let me tell you," he was saying. "It's not just me. There's a whole posse of us ready to hang him high. You can bet your cotton socks on that, my friend. And there's nothing you bleeding-heart cops are going to be able to do about it. Somehow or other, that sonofabitch is going to get himself strung up from the tallest tree in the valley."

"I wouldn't talk like that if I were you," Dion said, not quite serious, but not quite joking either. "Not with me around. I'll have to remember this conversation when we're cutting that sonofabitch down."

"Yeah, Scottie, keep your big mouth shut," Evangeline said, back in her chair. And flapping a hand at Dion, dismissing the death threats, "Don't listen to him. He talks big, but he wouldn't hurt a fly."

Oh, he'd do a lot worse, Dion thought. Not quite twenty years ago, Scott Rourke had come home a day early from a hunting expedition and caught his wife with a lover. He'd grabbed a baseball bat and clobbered the shit out of the man. The man had lived, but like Dion, he was left with a badly altered trajectory. And the wife, well, she was collateral damage: jumped in a lake and surfaced dead. Dion had heard mention of it in the Wednesday night briefing, and had checked his computer for the details on his own time. If Evangeline was unaware of the violence in her boyfriend's bones, somebody ought to tell her, and soon.

"You live in this area?" he asked her. "I get the feeling you're not from around here."

She rested her chin in her palm and challenged him with a stare. "What gives you that feeling?"

She looked and moved and talked and smelled like city, that's what. "I don't know," he said. "Just —"

"Just quit chatting up my woman," Rourke interrupted with mock menace, arms crossed, staring across the gloom at Dion.

There was not much fun in the mock menace, though, and Dion made sure to keep his eyes and conversation, if not his thoughts, well off Scottie's girl.

Six

AAM NIIN
(YOU ARE GOOD)

MORNING HAD BROKEN, and down in the Super 8's diner over coffee and toast, Dion had folded aside his paper and was mostly listening.

"I had a pal once," the old Indian named Willy told him, turtle-slow. They were sitting at the window booth, sharing the view on highway and windblown litter. "He's Gitxsan. Looks lot like you. You got some Gitxsan in you, not so far off."

It was a statement, not a question, and probably as wrong as Giroux calling him Cree. "Lot like you," Willy repeated, nodding. "Name is Johnny."

"Oh, so that's why you keep calling me that."

"Hey?"

"Forget it. What happened to him?"

"Dead. It's years ago, before you came into this world. He's dancing now … at the big powwow in the sky."

Dion shut an eye in case his collar was being yanked. But Willy's expression, side-lit by the low morning light and gnarled by age, gave nothing away.

"So how'd he die?"

No answer came. Willy seemed to go adrift, unlit cigarette clamped between his puckered lips. Dion dropped
his attention back to the news of the day, stale breaking news from the Lower Mainland, all that murder and
mayhem he was forced to watch from the sidelines.

"Drowned," Willy said, minutes later. "Twenty-two."

"That's too bad. Was he a good friend?"

"No. He's a liar and a cheat and he drinks too much.
We worked together. Deckhands. Trawlers, just out of
Rupert."

"Oh. So it happened on the job, did it?"

"No. Fell in the river, down here." Willy's bluish left
eye and semi-clear right eye stared at Dion fiercely, as if
he'd had something to do with the tragedy.

"So how did it happen?"

Again no answer, and this time it seemed there
would be none any time soon. Willy was looking at his
own hands on the tabletop, cradling the cup of coffee
Dion had ordered for him.

"Well, tell me about it tomorrow," Dion said. He
pushed Willy's book of Eddy Lites across the table. "It's
bad for you, you know that? Bad for me too."

"I know. Tried to quit. Can't."

"Go ahead, few puffs, then put it out."

"Aam niin," Willy said, slowly. Slow even for him. It
was an annoying habit of his, teaching. "You are good,"
he translated, and waited.

"Aam niin," Dion said. "You are good."

Willy struck a match to light his hand-rolled. He took
a pull then sat back pluming smoke like a chip-burner.

"I will teach you not Gitxsan," he said. "I will teach you Nisga'a, my language. But close enough. Don't want to lose the language."

"Thanks, no. I have a hard enough time with English."

But the old Indian sat there being willfully deaf, nodding to himself, making plans. "It's a good thing," he said. He put out his cigarette and tapped at his own chest, somewhere over his heart. "Time to come home, eh?"

* * *

Andy Blair was being watched, everywhere he went, and the surveillers weren't shy about it, ranged around the Chev dealership in their shiny cars and trucks. "Maybe now he'll break a sweat," Leith said from the office, pushing papers around, waiting for something to give.

In the afternoon it gave, in the shape of Andy Blair's father Clive, local big shot, owner of the dealership, with Andy pushed and prodded in front of him through the police station doors. "Little asshole has something to tell you," Clive told the desk constable and marched out.

Andy Blair's hair and clothes hadn't settled back into shape after whatever shaking he'd just received. Leith sat down with him in the nastiest of the Terrace interview rooms and said, "What is it your dad wants you to tell me, Andy?"

"Nothing. He thinks I've been taking cars off the lot without permission and joyriding. Not true. I grew out of joyriding long time ago."

"Oh, so your dad's just assumed you're the Pickup Killer for no reason, is that right? You have nothing to say to that except he's wrong?"

"He didn't say I'm the Pickup Killer. He said I have something to tell you. Which I have not. That's where he's wrong."

Leith chose to lose his patience at this point, a faster escalation than usual, but he didn't have the luxury of time. "I'm here investigating the Pickup Killer," he blasted. "And your father knows it. He's not going to turn you in for some minor infraction, is he? What's it about, Andy? You need a lawyer? You want me to get you a lawyer so we can get to the truth without fucking around here?"

Blair's eyes widened. "Oh, c'mon. I didn't do anything."

"Is that what your father's going to tell me?"

Blair's thumbs twiddled fast, like whirligigs in a storm. "I maybe helped out a friend once or twice, let him take a truck out. Not the good ones. The trade-in junk from the back of the lot. And it wasn't for any killing sprees, that I can swear to." He lifted the left hand in oath and switched swiftly to the right, and grinned, not a criminal, just a charming brat.

Leith sat for a moment, looking at the brat, wondering. Blair could be a sociopath, but he didn't think so. "Who's the friend?"

He expected more waffling and instead got a straight-up answer, at least a partial. "John. Not a friend, really. Just an acquaintance."

"John's got a last name?"

"I don't know. Knew him on first-name basis only."

Leith stood with purpose, and Blair said, "No, wait, I remember. John Portman. No, Porter. No, Potter. Yeah, Potter. John Potter."

Leith was back in his chair, asking who exactly John Potter was and where he lived. The name was familiar in only the foggiest way, one name of thousands he'd maybe read on a list in the course of the investigation. But that was good; if the name were on a list, they'd find him. They'd drag him into the light and scrutinize him, if this was actually going anywhere.

Blair said he didn't know where Potter lived, but he had the feeling it wasn't close. Or what he did for a living. Some kind of a contractor, he believed.

Leith said, "So you helped him out. Go on."

"He wanted to buy this old trade-in truck, it was a 2004 Tacoma, I think, not in good shape, which I told him so. But I slapped on the plates and let him take it for the spin. Around the block, he said. It must have been a pretty big block, 'cause he brought it back about a week later. So we had a fight about it and came to terms. It was a misunderstanding, okay? A miscommunication. He acknowledged that and paid me under the table for the inconvenience. Which I declared on my income tax as 'other,' by the way. You can check."

Leith didn't care about the payoff at this point. He wanted more on Mr. Potter, and he wanted to tread softly now. Treading softly wasn't his forte, so he did as Blair did, twiddled his thumbs. Not fast, but slow, a kind of metronome. "You grabbed a copy of the guy's BCDL, I take it, before he took the truck out?"

Blair seemed to gaze into the past. "Hell, I must have at least looked at his driver's licence. Might not have copied it. Not for a spin around the block." He flung up both hands in surrender. "I know, I know, it's the law.

But I spent my week in hell. Learned my lesson. Never cut corners again. Dad never found out, 'cause I'm in charge of inventory. So in the end I thought, hey, no harm done. No big deal, right?"

"Can we narrow it down to a date, when Potter took this Tacoma?"

Blair smiled. "Nope, sorry."

But he was nervous, Leith could tell. No longer twiddling, but twitchy and damp. "So why'd you let him take a vehicle a second time, if he caused you so much trouble on the first one?"

"Huh? What second time? I never said there was a second time."

"You said once or twice."

"Manner of speaking. I meant once."

Leith stood again, this time with no show of threat. "Hang on a moment. Be right back. You want a coffee?"

In the case room, he sat down with Bosko and told him what he had. "He's lying. He thinks he's a smooth operator, but he's a fool. It lights up in flashing neon across his forehead, *I'm lying now.* He's always been like this, cocky but scared. The fact he's scared is interesting, because there's no paper trail, and we can't prove anything. So whatever it is he's covering up, it's serious. I think he's trapped into this lie. I think he wants out, but he can't make a move. The question is, should I charge him now so I can lean on him properly? Or keep cajoling."

"Keep cajoling," Bosko said. "In the long run, it'll be faster."

Leith was eying diagrams in the air. The diagrams were vague, maybe cryptic, and he was trying not to look lost. "I don't agree. If I suspect for one moment he's in on the killing, I'll have to charge him. And then we're stuck. I just don't want to waste time playing ball for nothing, if we're going to end up going the long way round anyway." With warrants and waiting, he meant. Lawyers and stone walls.

"I don't think he's in on the killing," Bosko said, and briefly Leith wondered how he could reach that conclusion with such limited info and seem so sure about it. He crossed his arms, said nothing, and Bosko went on in his firmly meandering way. "And the worst you'll get him for is conspiracy after the fact, and that's not your focus. Let him know that conspiracy after the fact is nothing compared to what he'll be facing if another girl dies because of him holding back. Sounds like you've hit pay dirt, but dig with care." Bosko had his phone out and was making a call. "I'm going to get the team on to Potter right now. Get the video set up for the rest of the interview, and I'll monitor, just to add a second set of eyes."

Leith arranged for video and then filled two cups of coffee and returned to the interview room. Blair focussed on sweetening his coffee, and Leith, sitting once more across from him, did as Bosko had suggested, cajoled and warned in the same breath. Then he asked, "So, how many times in all did you let Potter take trucks out?"

Blair was maybe too smart to insist on his "once" statement and dithered about for a while before recalling that yes, there was a second time, maybe the next summer.

"With all the paperwork done up this time?" Leith asked.

"Well, no," Blair admitted, losing his veneer. "I knew him now, so I agreed to kind of a handshake deal."

"Details."

Blair launched into another lie about Potter applying for job interviews, being down and out, needing a vehicle, and Leith reminded him of the peril he faced. Blair began to tire, to roll his eyes, stammer, and contradict himself. He didn't have the advantage of pen and paper, and Leith did. Leith cross-referenced the lies and threw them back at the suspect until the suspect became trapped in confusion, and his facial muscles softened. Andy Blair could see a jail cell in his future, either way he jumped. The sooner he jumped, the shorter the jail time, he would be thinking now.

Leith used the moment and asked it again. "You had an idea what he was using those trucks for, didn't you?"

"Not till lately," Blair said, barely a mumble now. "Lately, it occurred to me. But I thought, no, couldn't be. Not John. He's a nice, quiet guy. Friendly like hell."

"But the timelines bothered you."

Blair nodded. "He said it was for drug runs down to George and back. Didn't want to use his own vehicle. So he took trucks off the lot."

"What did you get in return?"

"Bit of weed. Recreational use only."

"Weed?" Leith said. "Really? Weed's cheap, and you can get it anywhere. What did you get in return, Andy? You want me to repeat those warnings for you?"

Blair nodded again. "Coke. A smidge, enough to share with a friend or two, no charge. Personal use only. But it was good stuff, and I believed him a hundred percent, that that's all he used the trucks for, and as far as I knew, he was only getting it for personal use too."

Leith believed that Blair knew the trucks were used for killing, at least toward the end. But he'd barricaded himself in with indecision, and if once the charges might have been dropped altogether, they now would stick hard. "He borrowed trucks three times, didn't he?"

Blair began to sniffle a bit and wipe his eyes. *Not for the dead girls*, Leith thought. *Not a tear for them.* "Spit it out, Andy."

Blair spat it out. "It was March, year before last, when he took out the shitty Tacoma. Then a couple times last winter, different vehicles, and I could give you more exact dates if I could look at my calendar."

"On your phone? Go ahead."

Blair reached for his pocket and paused, still a charmer, the little creep, even with his eyes wet with self-pity. "You won't shoot me?"

"I won't shoot you."

The car salesman studied the calendar on his phone for some time and was able to give Leith the dates, which he could extrapolate because that's when he got the free coke, which was when he'd thrown house parties. Three great house parties that aligned with three dead girls to a tee.

Leith felt something other than blood coursing through his veins, some kind of high-octane mix, and he sped up matters, pressing Blair for descriptions of the vehicles, and soon had it scrawled in his notebook, in chronological order: silver Toyota Tacoma, white Chev Silverado, dark blue Nissan, older model.

He took another break to step out and talk to Bosko, who had a report already on John Potter. Bosko handed it over and said the ERT was prepped and ready to hit the road. "He's a registered gun owner, Dave. Be careful."

"Everybody in the north is a registered gun owner," Leith said.

Pacing, he read the report and saw that John Potter was thirty-two years old, an ex-oil field worker from Alberta, moved to the area three years ago, bought a house, not in Terrace but Kitimat, seventy-three kilometres south on Highway 37. He worked off and on for Sherbrooke & Sons Roofing, a local Terrace company. No criminal record. He'd been canvassed, as all men in the area had been, but checked off as okay.

But it was futile to worry about errors and omissions now. What was really great was the piece of paper Leith now held in his hand, which gave him an address, a line of attack, and with pedal to the metal, he and the Emergency Response Team would be out there in no time flat. Half an hour, forty minutes max, they'd have their man in a bag.

* * *

Giroux had ordered Constables Thackray and Dion to accompany her to an event she worried might become a problem. Thackray told her he didn't see how a candle-light vigil for a pacifist like Kiera Rilkoff could get out of hand, but Giroux told him she'd seen stranger things happen when a bunch of emotional and probably stoned kids got together.

Now it was dusk, and the two constables in uniform stood getting pelted by sleet in the village's memorial park, down by the little covered stage. Friends and admirers of Kiera took the mic and said a few words about the woman they knew and loved. They sent prayers for her safe return into the drizzle. Music played too, starting with Kiera's up-beat CD, which hardly set the mood. Giroux had posted herself centrally, solemnly holding a candle, but Dion and Thackray stood at the sidelines with their collars up high against the elements, their hands free. "So we can battle this crazed uprising," Thackray murmured.

Dion observed the crowd, which numbered about a hundred and fifty, so many faces under-lit by flame. Hardly a bunch of kids, these were a fair mix of old and young, and none of them looked stoned or rowdy. He recognized several from their appearances at the detach-ment over the last few days. There were Kiera's parents, looking frozen in place. Lenny Law and Scott Rourke and Evangeline Doyle clustered together near front centre, with the drummer Chad nearby, head bowed. He didn't see Frank anywhere. Stella the violinist stood to one side of the crowd talking with an individual he didn't recog-nize, man or woman he couldn't tell at this distance. Their conversation looked animated, maybe angry. He asked Thackray who the unknown individual was.

Thackray squinted. "Looks like Jim from the garage," he said, and squinted harder. The individual was bulked by winter clothes, hood up, but turned more their way so the face was exposed, and Thackray grinned. "No, it's her. Well, they're twins, right?"

"Who?"

"Jim and Mercy," Thackray said. "That's Mercy. You can tell by the lack of moustache."

Mercy, Dion thought. That word again. He tried to put it together with recent thoughts, but it didn't mesh, and it was moments like this he despised what he had become. Fragmented. Unwhole. Next to useless.

Thackray seemed to notice he was struggling and dropped a clue. "She manages the band. Well, *did*. I'm not sure there's any band left to manage."

Dion watched the fiddler Stella and the band manager Mercy, the way they talked. They were trying to be discreet with their argument, he saw. The hand gestures, though angry, were short jabs, then hands jammed back into coat pockets. With their hopes of success trashed, he supposed, no wonder they were angry. Still, this was the time and place for prayers and grieving, not anger and recriminations. Bitching at any vigil was disrespectful. He checked the other faces in the crowd and found them devout, like churchgoers, listening not to a sermon right now but to a rockabilly love song blasting out over the speakers. Many were crying.

A young woman in Sorel boots and bundled in a heavy parka stopped in her passage and handed Dion a glass. There was a tea-light barely glowing within the glass, faintly blue. "For Kiera," the woman said, and moved on, distributing her candles to all those who stood lightless.

Seven

UP IN SMOKE

THEY DIDN'T KNOW ENOUGH about Potter to tackle him scientifically. He lived alone far from downtown, out in the country, up a long, straight road that shot away into the foothills. Leith was seated in car two of a fleet of six, passenger side. Bulked out in Kevlar, he stared ahead and worried that the man, if he was the killer, could be on his toes, braced for this pending Armageddon. The team had considered a surreptitious approach, but the long, straight road posed a problem, with nothing on either side for cover but scraggly fields now smothered in snow. Sneaking up would be an elaborate operation, would take time to arrange, and time was too precious right now to waste. So it was the shock-and-awe approach, carom in fast and roust the bastard; he'd be face down on the floorboards before he knew what hit him.

The house that came racing into view through the dusk was small and cute, white and turquoise, with a generous deck, lots of lattice and neat landscaping, and something about it jarred Leith as he stared forward. The little house was backed by dark woods and a steeply ascending rock wall, and all was still and silent and unlit. A truck sat in the driveway, fairly new looking. Leith ordered the vehicles to a stop here at a good distance, and he jumped out of the SUV and stood in the snow and stared at the little white house, not taking his eyes off it, because whatever it was that prickled at his nerves, intuition or superstition, or simply a wealth of bad experiences, he was certain the place was booby-trapped.

The standoff continued, unilateral and surreal. The ERT commander joined him, and together they watched the little house at the end of the driveway, the parked truck, the closed drapes. They were discussing Leith's gut feeling and the approach they'd take when lights came on in the house, in a slow-blooming way, from darkness to dull orange. "Aw, shit," Leith said, starting forward, stopping when he saw it was too late. The ERT was making a call. The dull orange glared bright, the curtains flared, and there came a thud of internal explosion, and another, and a third. Car doors opened and closed and the team was out, a band of helpless spectators as the house became engulfed in flames.

Was she in there? Was she going to burn? Was that all they had accomplished?

Leith conferred with the team, and they spread out to explore the perimeter of the burning building. He was called over to view the fresh snowshoe tracks at the back, leading up into the mountains. One set. He and four others took up pursuit but found the trail was narrow, the snow deep, and the risk too great that Potter would be waiting ahead with a scope and nothing to lose. So they turned back to make a plan, wait for the dogs and gear and reinforcements. Leith stood watching the frantic swivelling of red and white lights from fire trucks approaching along the beeline road. Potter would have had the same kind of view, would have had maybe five minutes to splash the gasoline, light the fuse, and grab his bag, pre-packed, and take off. He wouldn't be far, but every moment now he was adding distance.

He was probably one of those goddamn survivalists who could burrow into the scree for months, catching rabbits and sipping melted snow. Leith spent ten minutes on the phone, calling in choppers and dogs and as many hands as he could rope in on short notice to search the property for Kiera or the clues that would lead him to her.

And then he joined in the search himself.

* * *

But she wasn't anywhere on the property. The dogs arrived, and it was a dog that found Potter, or at least drew them close enough to his hiding spot that Potter opened fire, three blasts, rapid-fire, and by the sound of it the fugitive had not only the registered bolt-action Browning but an unregistered semi-automatic.

They had forged high enough on the mountainside that the air felt thin in Leith's nostrils. The blasts had come horribly close, had frozen him in his tracks alongside the others in the posse, nine in all, and in the time it took for the sound waves to disperse, he went through his half-second mantra, always there for him when things got dicey, to bring scant comfort: That he would have to lead the way, might die, Ali and Izzy would have to carry on without him, but luckily his insurance plan should cover them well, even put the kid through university if she was so inclined.

On that note of slight comfort he could go forward now, in ERT mode. Some days there just wasn't enough manpower and he had no choice but pitch in, join the front lines, and today was one of those special days. Possibly his last. The plan of the hour was simple: encircle the hideout, give Potter nowhere to run, and then try talking him out. Failing that, because time was of the essence, Leith would fire a warning shot. Failing that, he would coordinate moving in by cautious degrees. He didn't have to remind his team that it was imperative Potter be taken alive. Nor was there time for a nice leisurely siege.

He gave the signal and began to climb, upward and around, through dense woods. The climb was hellish. His vest was bulky, his gear catching on the underbrush, branches scratching his face. And god, he was no ninja, every move a snap, crackle, and pop, and he could only pray foolishly that if he should come into the sights of Potter's gun, he would see it first.

Twenty minutes later they had found their spots, and he was within shouting distance of the lair. Without a megaphone he had to bellow: "John Potter. I'm David Leith, RCMP. D'you hear me?"

The answer was a barrage of bullets. As the echoes faded, his men reported in, all safe. Potter was desperate, and this was going to end badly. Leith stayed low, a leg already starting to cramp, and shouted, "It's over, John. We're not here to hurt you. You need help, I understand that. I'm here to get you that help. You're surrounded now, man. Get out here with your hands up where I can see 'em and let's get to somewhere warm and dry where we can talk in peace."

Silence. Maybe Potter was reloading. Maybe he was eating a sandwich. Maybe he was setting a bomb that would blow them all to hell. "Potter," Leith called out. "I'm coming down so we can talk, okay? Just stay where you are."

There was another blast, and this one had a different sound, a different sort of finality. A sharp, clean handgun blam. Leith swore out loud, notified his men, and went scrambling cautiously through muck and bracken down the slope.

He found Potter hunkered deep in the hollow formed by two firs, head bowed forward between his knees as if ashamed of the big bloody mess he'd made of his life.

Leith made his radio call, bringing in the medics. Then he mirrored Potter in a way, head hung, nothing left to do or say.

* * *

Some hours later, from the case room in Terrace, he called Giroux to tell her about Potter. Not just the death, but what had been found in the remains of Potter's burned down house. "Convenience store receipts," he said. "For cigarettes. Dated Saturday. Checked the security footage, and we got Potter alibied, no doubt about it. We've almost certainly got him on the Pickup killings, but he wasn't involved in our girl's disappearance, and we're back to square one. Bosko's just dealing with some stuff here, then we'll head back to Hazelton. Be there in two hours, max."

Giroux spoke quietly, which was a departure for her. "I'll put on a fresh pot of coffee, Big City. See you soon."

* * *

With all hands on deck for a full-team briefing, the small detachment was filled to capacity. The air was overtaxed, dry and hot. Leith's nose was stuffed, a new discomfort to go with the headache, the guilt, and the dull pain in his wrist left over from the sprain. Any spiritual satisfaction he might have felt for stopping John Potter in his sadistic tracks would just have to wait. Right now his focus was on Kiera.

Outside the snow pelted down on New Hazelton, thick and fast, blanketing the village afresh. Four names were up on the board now: Frank, Stella, Chad, and Rob, four young people suddenly cast in a far harsher light. Bosko had suggested the approach to be taken, and Leith spread the word to the team. "We don't want the tenor of our relationship with these kids to change just now," he said. "But we'll have to get fresh statements, and this time we're going to trawl for inconsistencies."

Jayne Spacey asked how that tenor was supposed to go unchanged. "They're going to know about Potter. Right? We can't lie and say he's our man. They're going to know they're now in the spotlight."

Leith said, "There are still enough distractions. There's the white truck, our potential mystery abductor. And there's the question in the back of all our minds: What if Kiera ran away? We'll just give the impression, at least, of focussing on those two avenues for now." He directed his words to Spacey. "We'll need the phone records of Chad Oman, Stella Marshall, Frank Law, Rob Law, and Lenny Law, so if you'll bang out the production orders."

"Yes, sir."

"They'll know they're being looked at, and they'll be upset and need soothing," he told the team. "Let them know it's only procedural and hope they accept it. Any interview I'm not at personally I'll be monitoring, so make sure they're all well recorded. And I mean press 'record.'" At the back of the room, Dion didn't look up to meet his glare. "At one point we may turn on the fear," Leith finished. "But you'll get fair warning. It's got to be coordinated."

The team, which had doubled in size over the week, listened and nodded, and probably more or less got the message. The expanding investigation brought more members every day, and soon Leith feared he would have to commandeer the school gym or some other space with breathing room. The facts were building up like sediment, none of it helpful. All had been put before the team, in hopes that it might snag a real lead. The fingerprints on the cellphone belonged to Kiera only. Same with the barrette. Hairs had been caught in the barrette, and they belonged to Kiera. Fibres had been extracted from the snow, along with the pink body glitter. The fibres were synthetic, from a so-far unknown fabric, and the glitter was no match to that found on John Potter's victims, or to any known body-glitter brand.

Leith glanced at Sergeant Mike Bosko, always trying to gauge the man's mood. The gauging had something to do with his own ambitions, and something to do with a growing apprehension of the real reason for Bosko's presence. When Bosko wasn't giving advice from the sidelines, he was out there like a journalist, asking questions. Getting to know the beast, he'd said over drinks.

Now Bosko stood at the crowded perimeter, hands in pockets. He was looking not at Leith but toward the back of the room, either at the Mr. Coffee machine or beyond it to Constable Dion busy making notes. He had no good reason to look at either.

Leith was sore from talking. He rapped on the white-board behind him and closed the meeting with a final word of inspiration for the troops: "There's the strategy. Now for the action."

* * *

Fortunately for Dion, he didn't have to worry about strategy or action. Following the briefing, he was back at his computer, going through vehicle registrations for the area in an expanding radius, listing the owners of trucks and making phone calls. Others were following up on that list out in the field, actually eyeballing those trucks. The north was huge and sparsely populated, and there was a lot of driving involved. He was just grateful not to be out battling the wind and ice and slippery asphalt.

There was a Post-It note stuck to the glass of his monitor on which he had written the vehicle description, to keep him focussed. Without that Post-It, in no time he would end up looking for something like a late-model blue sedan among all these names and numbers, instead of ...

He glanced at the sticky again. *Wt pickup, 10+ YO 2-wheel drive, blk glassed rear window.*

In one of the briefings, somebody had said they thought the black glass was maybe just temporary, that peel-off crap. Somebody else had pointed out from personal experience that that peel-off crap was not so easy to peel off. A person would have to spend a day scraping, steaming, and vacuuming to get rid of all traces of the stuff, and even then on a forensic level they would fail. And according to the transcription on file, the trucker, Caplin, had been re-interviewed, and he said it wasn't that peel-off tinting crap, in his opinion. That stuff had a purplish tinge and wasn't, whatchoocallit, opaque. Even with a bit of ambient light from high-beams glaring off snow, you could see shapes through it and whatnot. No, this, he said, was *black* glass, as in black.

Dion didn't think the truck would ever surface, at least not with telltale black glass installed. Whoever was driving it that night down that mountain would have known they'd been spotted, and if they had just committed a serious crime like abduction, they would know they would be tracked down eventually. The glass would have to go.

There were other ways of making glass dark, aside from the tinting film. You could spray-paint the window. That would make it opaque, and the paint could potentially later be removed. Or an even faster and easier fix, duct-tape up some kind of dark material, paper or fabric, or even, say, black garbage bags. Fabric would be more light-absorbent, though. Black velvet. At night, in the headlights, glass covered in black velvet would look simply black. Like the night pressing in on Scottie's window. Black.

It wasn't likely permanent custom-installed black glass. If a truck with black glass for a rear window was driving about, somebody would have seen it previously and remembered it. Neighbours would for sure remember something like that, let alone friends or family. So unless it was from out of town and just passing through, which he didn't believe was the case, then it didn't exist. Which meant the glass was darkened temporarily, which meant the abduction, or *an* abduction, at least, was premeditated.

Were the other windows tinted? Probably not, for the same reason: People would remember an older truck with all-tinted windows. What would be the good of blacking out the rear window, then, when there were front and side windows to worry about as well?

He considered further, pen in hand, doodling cubes within cubes in ballpoint, until he'd answered his own question. *Because it was better than nothing.* It simply cut down the odds of being identified.

So the crime was premeditated but rushed. Haphazard. He was almost there, almost had the answer, but he was distracted, and it slipped away. He could sense a superior in the room, somewhere behind him, and he sat straighter and got back on task. Except he'd forgotten what that task was and had to check the sticky once again. *White pickup, ten years or older …*

* * *

Hazelton didn't have a "soft" interview room, exactly, a place set up to relax the subject rather than intimidate. But somebody at some point had read the new guidelines and made the effort, placing two chunky upholstered chairs against one wall with a coffee table in between, fake flowers and an array of magazines. The effect was odd, at best, like chandeliers in a fast food joint. The classic hard table and three hard chairs remained in the centre. Frank Law sat in one chair, Leith and Bosko occupying the others. This final re-interview, like all the others they'd ground through all day long, was being video-recorded.

Frank hadn't shaved, apparently hadn't showered, probably hadn't slept much since Saturday. There were not just rings of shadow around his eyes, but grooves, like a super-fast aging. Leith's opening approach was gentle. "You've been dating the girl forever and probably know her better than anybody. How does she deal with stress? Does she bottle it up, let it all out? Does she sulk, get drunk, go for a jog, or what?"

Interestingly, Frank wasn't swallowing the *ran away* scenario. "Number one," he said. "She doesn't get stressed. Anything bugs her, she talks about it. She's stronger than anyone I know. If she had a problem, she wouldn't run away from it. She'd run *at* it and wrestle it to the ground. That day she went away to think things over, but she wasn't running away. You can forget that idea."

"Right. So what's the alternative? If she'd gotten lost on the mountain, we'd have found her by now, dead or alive. But we haven't. An unidentified truck was seen driving down the road just down from the Matax in the hours of her disappearance. And you're sure you don't know a truck of that description? Forget the black glass, just the truck itself?"

Frank shook his head. "Can't think of anybody owns a truck like that, other than that list I gave you already."

"None of which were white."

"Well then, I can't help you."

Leith opened the folder he'd brought with him, thick with documents cluttered with columns of numbers in what looked like two-point type. The production orders for the phone records had given him what he wanted, a kind of numerical eagle's eye view of all the chatter that had gone on between the parties in the days leading up to Kiera's vanishing. It also documented the silences. He said, "You two used to text or call several times a day. Lately I'm seeing a lot of gaps. You were pissed off with each other, and it came to a boiling point on Saturday. There was a fight. She was injured. Is that what happened?"

Frank's face twisted in disbelief. "Are you kidding me?"

"Now's the time to tell me, Frank," Leith said.

"Now's the time to show you this," Frank said, and gave him the finger. He got up and walked out.

Leith didn't stop him. With Frank gone, he gave instructions to Spacey to apply for warrants, and then joined Giroux in her office to make it official. "Things aren't happening on their own. Guess it's time we made them."

Eight

TURN ON THE FEAR

LEITH PLANNED TO MAKE things happen by picking up Frank Law the following morning and placing him under arrest, searching his house again, making a racket. The arrest wouldn't hold past twenty-four hours, but maybe, as Bosko suggested, those twenty-four hours would stir the waters. Being a pessimist at heart, Leith expected they'd just muddy them.

A meeting was held, all staff including auxiliaries and temps crammed into the case room again at the crack of dawn so they knew what was happening and how to deal with questions about the arrest from the public. Or abuse, or death threats. The warrants had been approved, and after the meeting Leith and Giroux and two constables in battle gear, Spacey and Ecton, drove out in separate vehicles to the Law house in the woods and made the arrest. Behind them came the search team.

Frank and Lenny Law were both at home, but Rob was absent. Frank was silent and grim but submitted to the arrest and went along without a fuss. The fuss, Leith fully expected, was yet to come.

* * *

The search warrant had gone through, and Dion had his first real look around the Law home. It wasn't tidy, was well lived-in and messy, which kept him well occupied in his role of searching the living room. So far, nothing stood out within the mess, nothing the warrant gave him permission to seize. He studied the floorboards near the woodstove and crouched to pick up a tiny shred of paper that stood out from the other debris. The Law brothers fed paper trash into the woodstove, he guessed, and this had fallen out of the latest bin or bag.

The shred was about four inches long and not even a quarter-inch wide at one end. Good quality paper, not newsprint. Sharp-edged, not ragged. Kind of like a shredder scrap, except it narrowed to a point. It had plainly been slashed from a book, maybe using a straight-edge for cutting, but without mathematical precision.

He read the partial printed sentence. *It is vitally important not to believe them, or they will suddenly*

It sounded like some kind of instruction manual. *Don't believe who?* he wondered. *Suddenly what?*

He showed it to the exhibit custodian, one of the latest members to join the expanding team, a Sergeant McIntyre from Terrace. McIntyre shook his head, not interested.

Dion stood holding the bit of paper, feeling homesick. As an investigator, he should have some say whether this was interesting or not. It was interesting because it was from a book, and this was a house without books, except for the few lined up on a shelf in Lenny Law's bedroom. So what was the book, and who had cut it up? Had Lenny? Why? All valid questions, it seemed to him, that deserved at least some inquiry.

Anything not seized had to be left where it was, so he wrote the line into his notebook, dropped the scrap on the floor by the woodstove where he'd found it, and continued his search, looking for anything Corporal McIntyre considered worthy of a second glance.

* * *

The fuss Leith expected began soon after the arrest of Frank Law. Lenny had spread the word, and the word flew. Within half an hour, the detachment's phone started ringing. Journalists were rerouted by reception, and all other calls were patched through to Giroux's desk. Bosko happened to pick up the first of the calls, since Giroux had stepped out for a minute. She returned as the call ended, and Bosko picked up a Danish to go with his coffee before relaying the message, in what sounded like an accurate paraphrase: "Rob Law's coming down here to get his brother out, if it means killing us all."

Bosko didn't seem alarmed, and neither did Giroux, who muttered, "Rob's not exactly the brains in the family."

Was nobody but Leith thinking about bulletproof vests and pepper spray, or maybe just a good hiding spot? He said, "Kill us all? *All* of us? Did he mean it?"

Bosko shook his head and spoke around a mouth full of pastry. "No. But he's upset. He's got a bit of a drive ahead of him. He'll calm down by the time he reaches us."

Leith took the next two calls. Stella Marshall asked him what was going on. She got no satisfactory answer and ended up the call saying they had the wrong guy, that it was typical police scapegoating, and that she knew a lawyer from the city who'd make sure the Hazelton detachment was sued so hard, it would spend the rest of its life picking up pop cans for a living.

Mercy Blackwood phoned, not to rant but to reason. She asked what was happening and insisted Frank was innocent and didn't belong in jail. She knew Frank wouldn't hurt a soul. Leith promised her that Frank was speaking to a lawyer right now, and there would be no abuse of process.

Rob Law appeared within the hour, but he didn't kill anybody or even overturn a desk. He spoke with Bosko for fifteen minutes or so in the privacy of Giroux's office and then left quietly enough.

An anonymous tip came in, too, in the form of a note stuck to the windshield of one of the cruisers parked along the curb. The note said:

We seen Lenny Law Saturday night on Two Mile Rode

Leith found Two Mile Road on the map and followed it along with his eyes from start to end, thinking Lenny Law couldn't have been there on Saturday night, because he was loitering about the malls of Prince George with his pal Tex.

Tracking down the writer of the note would be tough. He or she would be one of the hundreds of residents of the Hazeltons who had been canvassed in the first days of the search and asked about Lenny, amongst other things. Now, with the heat coming down, the writer of the note was afraid of being implicated in a lie, and since that person hadn't been alone when they'd supposedly seen Lenny, as the note said "we," the writer of the note feared their companion would talk first.

The simple but complicated logic scrolled through Leith's mind as he looked at the wet and grubby little note, and it left him irritated. The writer was mistaken, or Lenny was lying about where he was on Saturday. Either way he would have to be brought in, along with Tex, and questioned once more. Leith called Jayne Spacey and told her to hunt him down.

There was more drama in the late afternoon when Scott Rourke made a personal appearance, the kind that sent papers flying, and had to be escorted out by Constables Thackray and Ecton. Thackray and Ecton returned, dusting their hands and laughing, and Spacey came along soon after, accompanied by a truculent Lenny Law.

Leith sat down with the kid in the interview room. The best approach was direct, he decided, and he laid the note on the table, read it aloud, looked Lenny in the eyes, and said, "So what about it?"

Lenny Law's approach was even more direct. Arms crossed, he looked Leith in the eyes, and said, "Yeah, so?"

"Yeah, so why'd you tell us you were in Prince George?"

"I was supposed to be is why. Frank thought I was there."

"You're going to have to explain yourself. I'm confused."

Lenny sighed. "I get up Saturday, and Frank's decided I should go to George with Tex. I said no, I don't want to go. He said yes, you damn well go, and in fact he'd already called Tex, and Tex was on his way over. He gave me a bunch of spending money and practically pushed me out the door. I know why he wanted me out of there, too, because the rehearsals were shit, and they didn't want me sitting around hearing them doing fuck-all for Ms. Blackworm."

Leith opened his mouth and shut it. The boy was glowing with emotion, angry as a bee, but he was on a roll, and it was best to just let him spew.

"You want to know why the rehearsals were shit?" the boy went on. "Because of her, Ms. Blackworm, coming around, telling them to be like this, be like that, Kiera should go on the treadmill, Frank should cap his teeth, add some theatre to their act, get professional, making them think they're something they're not. She wants them to use other people's songs, and far as I know, that's called intellectual theft, right?"

Leith thought it wise to agree and nodded his encouragement.

Lenny finished on a lamer note. "They're all on edge, ever since she came along with her big ideas. That's why I didn't go to George."

"I don't get the connection," Leith said. "Sorry."

Lenny steamed in silence for a moment and then said ominously, "Something was going to happen. I could feel it. I couldn't just leave them here by themselves, could I?"

"Something as in what?"

"I don't know."

"Something between Frank and Kiera? Were they angry with each other?"

"No," Lenny snapped. "Frank and Kiera are the most in-love people in the world. They'd never do anything to hurt each other, ever."

Leith knew all too well how the most in-love people in the world could hurt each other. He said, "Where was Kiera when you left the house with Tex?"

"She was gone. Everyone was gone except Frank."

"And you didn't go to Prince George?"

"No. I got Tex to dump me just outside of town and walked back. He promised he'd cover for me, but that's all. He didn't do anything wrong, so don't go harassing him."

"You walked back home to Kispiox?"

Lenny smirked. "No way, man. Frank would be pissed if I showed up there after he'd sent me packing. I went to my parents' place."

"You stayed with your parents?" Leith asked, surprised. He'd read an interview with Roland and Clara Law, typed up by Constable Dion, which said in black and white — albeit Dion's black and white — that they hadn't seen any of their sons in years.

"I stayed in their old gazebo thing," Lenny said. "Out back. I stash a bag there, a book or two, hang out sometimes, whenever I want to get away from Frank. He can be a real old lady."

Leith briefly marvelled that there existed a teenaged boy who read books, and without a cattle prod. "And your parents don't know you're there?"

Lenny Law gave a mean laugh and asked if he could go now. He said he was hungry and tired, and Leith had no right to detain him.

Leith let him go and sat thinking. Lenny's words hadn't shed new light on the situation, exactly, just a different pall. The tension within the band was ramping up, if Lenny could be believed. Kids could be wildly inaccurate in their statements, but usually Leith could find a grain of truth in there worthy of follow-up.

The day ended and nothing further came in, not from Frank Law's mouth or further anonymous tipsters or the community at large. *Nothing but a higher stone wall*, Leith thought, gloomily enjoying his metaphors, and the waters were indeed muddied. Still, Bosko seemed pleased. He had told Leith in an aside, "They sure do love Frank, don't they?"

Across the squad room, the big man was now talking to Giroux about something less serious. Beer, it sounded like. Leith scowled and eavesdropped. Microbreweries, calories, and warm versus cold. Giroux maybe saw him scowling and called across the room to him, "So we're going up to my place to confer about all this stuff further. Top brass only, but you're invited too. Coming?"

* * *

As he pulled his jacket on, Dion asked Jayne Spacey out for a beer, thinking that after a pint or two maybe she'd edge toward forgiveness. But she was great at holding a grudge, it seemed, and told him that no, she'd love to except she'd stepped in a big pile of dog crap and was looking forward to spending the evening cleaning her boots. There was wit and sarcasm in that, but there was also true hatred. He'd noticed the other constables seemed to like him less too, even easygoing Thackray, and Pam the desk clerk. No smiles, no attempts at small talk. And maybe it was just himself, or maybe it was something Spacey had said about him, a half-truth of some kind. Or outright lie.

He signed out, drove to the IGA for a deli wrap, then returned to his car and followed his fold-up tourist map northeast out of town, looking for somewhere wild where he couldn't possibly run into anybody he knew. Using the cruiser for recreation wasn't permitted, but this wasn't recreation any more than driving out to the Black Bear for dinner was, and they all did that. The map led through Kispiox, more or less where Scott Rourke lived, but splitting off onto a different gravel road. He landed on an outcrop of rock, where he left the car and walked down a steep trail criss-crossed with dirt bike tracks, down to where the map said a river would flow. And it did, broad and ice-cluttered, green and strong.

From studying maps and brochures, he knew this water had shed off the mountain ranges to the north, joining forces to become this, the Skeena. The river travelled through the land, past his boots, down around that S-bend, and on for another five hundred kilometres before releasing into the ocean at Prince Rupert.

He felt bloodless, not quite alive, and his eyes were watering in the wind. The cold day grew colder as the sun went down, leaving the world steel grey and thunder blue. He sat on a fallen log with a first-class view of the water coursing by on its endless journey. On the far shore those ragged black trees towered into the sky. There was a muted feel to the place, as if his ears were plugged, but he could hear the throaty roar of the river and the clack and thud of rocks in its depth, shifted by the current. The river had muscle, and resolve. Nothing would stop it getting to where it wanted to go.

He sighed and looked down, pushed back the cuff of his jacket, and looked at the face of his watch, knowing what he'd see. Not quite an hour ago he had adjusted its hands as he waited for his deli dinner to be wrapped and bagged. The watch told him forty-five minutes had passed. With sinking heart he checked it against his phone, and there was the living proof. The watch was off by seven minutes, and Scott Rourke had failed in keeping it alive, and so would the greatest surgeon in the world, and what good was a watch that couldn't keep time?

The light was fading fast, and Dion was alone. He un-strapped the Smiths. Down by the edge of the water he coiled back his arm and released with a hoarse shout of rage. The watch arced out and down, into an open patch of water and disappeared.

He stood a moment longer and then grabbed up the deli bag and walked back through light forest and across the wild-grass fields and up the steep four-by-four trail to his car.

Having no watch, and not wanting to be always check-ing his phone for the time, he drove to the drug store in Old Hazelton, stepped into the store, and spun the watch rack for a while, choosing a black plastic Timex with LCD display and backlighting. Water-resistant up to two hun-dred metres, it said, and it had a one-year warranty.

The watch cost him $49.99, plus GST, a blowout spe-cial. He drew out his wallet and chanced to look around and meet the stare of the woman in line behind him. She was tall and solid and pale, bundled in a long, puffy parka and fluffy pink scarf. Her hair was long, almost white-blond, her arms loaded with a supersized pack of Charmin TP, and it took him a moment to place her as Stella Marshall, the fiddler in the band.

"Well, hey," she said. "Just the man I wanted to talk to."

He nodded hello, found his debit card, gave it to the teller. When he was handed the receipt, the fiddler said, "Don't run off, now. I'll just pay for this stuff and be with you in a sec."

Darkness had fallen by now. He waited outside by his cruiser, removing the packaging of the Timex. He still hadn't figured out how to set it to the correct time when Marshall approached. She threw the TP into the back seat of a beat-up red Sunbird and came over to him, saying, "Here, let me."

She set the time in a few moves and gave it back to him. He thanked her and strapped it on. He tested the backlight button and pretended to be impressed. She said, "Now you owe me one. You can start by telling me what's going on. Why are you charging him? What proof do you have? Tell me that."

The instructions from the early morning briefing were simple. Frank was being arrested. If approached by the public with questions about the arrest, the question-er was to be directed to the officers in charge, Giroux or Bosko or Leith. That didn't mean Dion couldn't chat with people who had information to offer, and he probably should, and probably would have, if there had been any steel left in him. But there wasn't. "I'm just a temp," he said. "You'll have to go down to the detachment and talk to somebody in charge. Or I can give you the number."

Out in the open parking lot, the air was icy cold. Marshall's long hair and pink scarf took turns lifting then plastering across her face. She elbowed the tangles away and pointed across the road to a fish and chip joint that looked closed, not least because of the flip-around sign that was flipped around to *closed.* "Let's go sit down before we freeze to death. I have to tell you something, and it's a matter of life and death."

"Like I said —"

"And like I said, I have something to tell you, and you're going to listen. That's your job, right? To listen to the good citizens of the world?"

"I think they're closed," he said.

"They're not closed, just stupid."

They crossed the road and stepped into the little restaurant. The doorbell tinkled, but nobody emerged. A radio was playing on a pop station. Marshall turned the sign around to *open* then went behind the counter and poured two cups of coffee. She brought them around and ordered Dion to sit. Not there. There. He sat in the booth she'd chosen, and she sat across from him. She said, "They actually serve really good fish and chips, if you can catch 'em. Now, get out your notebook and write this down."

He brought out his duty notebook, found the first blank page, and wrote down the date and time. Marshall said, "He didn't do it. Write that down."

He wrote down nothing. He said, "What d'you have to tell me, Ms. Marshall?"

She sipped her coffee in silence for a minute, watching him watching her. She spoke softly. "Please call me Stella. Say it. Stella. It's not so hard."

"I told you, and I mean it, I'm not the right person to be talking to." He took the cellphone from his jacket's breast pocket and showed it to her. "Here, I can put you in touch with the office right now, and you can arrange to talk to someone who can be more helpful."

"I don't want to talk to someone more helpful," Stella Marshall said. "Giroux is a nasty little beastie, and those two goons she's got running around asking questions, I don't like them at all. I like you. You're like this spectacular angel-being come out of the blue."

"Well, thank you. But —"

"I'm not saying that to be nice. It's just the truth. You're very uneasy, I can tell. Like me. We're akin that way. Well, I have no excuse, I was born antsy. But you? You have every right to be uneasy, when you come flapping down expecting sunlight and butterflies, and instead you drop in the mud. New wings, huh?"

Uneasy was a wild understatement. He tried again to end this interview that was going from bad to worse, but stopped and was silent, seeing something wrong; it showed in her pale bulgy eyes and the pulsing of the artery at her throat. Her stream of nonsense was some kind of shield. She was afraid.

She had maybe caught the shift in his demeanour, from shutting her out to listening in, and she seemed to relax, and he wondered if it was all a game with her, and she'd just scored a point. She closed her eyes, and her lashes were white. Not to look at her colourless lashes and not to be duped any further, he looked outside. Past his own reflection, he saw things scuttling and spinning down the street, bits of garbage and clouds of snow crystals racing toward the river.

When she finally spoke, she was no longer coy and bossy, but calm and direct. "Frank and Kiera split up a few months ago," she said. "It wasn't official, and they didn't want anybody to know. But I knew. I also happen to know it was mutual, and it was amicable. There was no jealousy, no anger, no hostility whatsoever. I also happen to know that she was seeing somebody, secretly, because he was married. So they'd meet in different places."

Like the Matax trailhead, he supposed. He got his pen ready. "What's his name?"

"That I'm afraid I don't know."

"How do you know all the rest of it?"

"I'm inquisitive and have great hearing."

"And Frank knew about it and was okay with it."

"Yes. Like I say, they both wanted to move on."

He saw in her eyes that she loved Frank Law. She had to, to be sitting here making up diversionary bullshit like this, cheapest trick in the book. Unbelievable. He paraphrased her information into his notebook and snapped it shut. "Okay. I'll pass this on, and somebody will probably be contacting you for a full statement."

"Oh my god," she said, dully. He couldn't interpret the remark, nor would he pursue it. He watched her heave a theatrical sigh and slump back, maybe disgusted with him, or maybe just depressed. "Yeah, okay," she said. "Thanks for listening. Take care."

He put money on the table and left, driving back to the Hazelton detachment. Night shift was on duty, two constables he had only met once or twice and whose names he had forgotten. Under the annoying buzz of the fluorescents, he sat at his computer, wrote out the brief report, and filed it. Then he went back to his accommodations across the highway at the Super 8. Passing the room he knew belonged to Sergeant Mike Bosko of the Serious Crimes Unit, North Vancouver, where he had come from himself and where he belonged, he paused and stood before the door, considering its surface. He pulled in air, raised his knuckles, gave a light rap.

Nothing happened. And had that door opened, what would he have said? He wasn't even sure.

Back in his room, he turned the TV on for company and managed to get some sleep. Sleep was pocked with disturbing dreams, haunted as usual by Looch, who stood on the pavement below the Super 8. Dion looked down and saw the car parked curbside. The river ran beyond instead of the highway, black cottonwoods ranged along the far shore, dense as a wall. Looch wore a dark overcoat and was packing something in the car's trunk, an awkward parcel like a side of beef bundled in tarpaulin. Looch was leaving town, and Dion was crushed. The wall of trees was a wall of stone looming high into the sky. A figure appeared on the sidewalk, approaching Looch from behind, and Dion tried to open the window to either shout a warning or jump out, but the window wouldn't open. The figure was nearing and would soon be at Looch's back, and Dion banged on the glass with both palms until the strain of his foiled efforts woke him.

He had shifted across the bed in a tangle of blankets. He sat and stared at his own hands, pale blue and flickering in the light of the TV. Just a nightmare, but the message in the dream remained, a sour fear in the pit of his stomach. All the things he'd done wrong, the mistakes he'd made, they weren't buried deep enough. Like the figure on the sidewalk, they were slowly but surely catching up.

Nine

THE WALK

SUNRAYS SLASHED ACROSS the village in the morning, but Leith had a feeling it wouldn't last. Still, there were sparrows twittering in the bushes and at least a remote sense of spring on its way. He stepped into the diner downstairs off the Super 8 lobby, which was empty except for some old guy by the window — no colleagues, no Dion — and had a quick breakfast.

Across the highway at the office, a fresh-faced Renee Giroux handed over an occurrence report for himself and Bosko to look at. Leith went first, scanning over a single paragraph so riddled with typos and incomplete sentences that he had to read between the lines. "'STELLA MARSHAL,'" he read out, "'Avised Constable Dion that KEIRA RILKOFF spilt up a few months ago with FRANK LAW. It was by mutual content and.' Okay, sure."

"*Split*, I think," Giroux said.

"He spelled Rilkoff right," Leith said. "And mutual. Impressive. Ends the second sentence with 'and,' which is probably grammatically incorrect, but hey, what do I know?"

"Mm-hmm," Bosko remarked, taking his turn reading the report. As he did too often, he seemed to catch Leith's words but not the inflection, and Leith could never figure out how much of the misunderstanding was deliberate. "Interesting. Dave, you want to talk to the girl, get this story nailed down?"

Leith did not. There weren't many people he dealt with who made him feel foolish, but Stella Marshall was one. She only had to roll those pale blue eyes in his direction and he felt oversized and dim. "Sure," he said. "No problem."

He argued with her on the phone. She was at work and couldn't come in, so he agreed to meet her at her place of employment.

She was a teller at the Royal Bank in Old Town. The bank wasn't yet open when he arrived within the hour, but she unlocked for him, let him in, saying, "Good morning, Officer Leith." She locked the door behind him, mentioned that it was an exceptionally cold morning, and offered coffee.

"No, thanks," he said. "This'll be quick. I wanted to talk to you about the statement you gave to Constable Dion last night."

There was nobody else in the bank, and Stella led him to the manager's office, a posh little set-up. She lounged in the big leather chair, and Leith sat before her like a man seeking a loan. A man without equity, in his case.

"I haven't anything to add to what I told Constable Dion," she said.

"Well, I have things to ask."

"So do I."

He paused, already thrown.

She said, "I understand you want to see my phone records. Am I a suspect?"

"Ma'am, you're definitely not a suspect. We're looking at everybody's records right now, not for anything incriminating, but to help piece together Kiera's day around the time of her disappearance. It's a procedural thing. No worries."

"Okay. Thank you. Your turn."

He wanted her to pinpoint the date of this alleged lovers' break up, and she couldn't, since it was more a slow dissolution and nothing official, and probably nothing Frank was quite ready to admit, at least not to the world at large. "But think about it," she said. "It was inevitable. He and Kiera have known each other since they were ten. How can you stay in love with someone when there's nothing left to discover? They both wanted out, and they were very cool-headed about it, and they remained close friends."

"I heard they were engaged."

"It was just talk."

"You say she was seeing somebody else, a married man. It sounds like you know who that person is."

"No, actually, I don't. I'm not supposed to know any of it, and I have to say, maybe I'm way off base. It's just stuff I pick up. Big ears. As I told Constable Dion."

"You think Kiera met this guy on the Matax on Saturday? Is that what you're saying?"

She shook her head. "I really don't know."

But it was what she wanted them to think. She could be lying, Leith realized, about all of it. Frank Law was under the gun now, and one way she could deflect that suspicion would be invent a new suspect and throw him into the mix, like nuts into the cookie batter. The mystery man on the Matax. He said, "Did Frank have a love interest of his own?"

"Not that I know of."

"Was Frank upset with her when she left rehearsal on Saturday?"

"Yes, just like Chad and I were. It wasn't great timing on her part. But what could we do? The demo's a bust anyway. I think we all knew it."

Leith heaved a sigh. "How about giving us some names we can discreetly check out, at least. There can't be that many local men she could be seeing on the sly."

She only shook her head, swivelling in her bank manager chair, eying him in that way that made him feel so foolish. "I have no idea. He may be an out-of-towner, a travelling businessman, say. Or a cop. He may be yourself, for all I know."

Leith was done, and he stood. "Thanks," he said. He felt absurdly like a man who'd just been turned down for a loan, stiff and offended, as he turned and walked out of the bank.

* * *

The phone records hadn't yielded much of interest. The ream of paper was more a bog than a useful tool. There had been a flurry of calls between all subjects on Saturday evening, after word spread that Kiera was missing. Leith was more interested in the hours and days leading up to the disappearance.

As far as he could see, communications between Frank and Kiera had been fairly frequent and friendly. The texts printed out from Kiera's phone neither proved Stella Marshall's story of a rift nor disproved it. They weren't steamy texts at all, but neither were they cool.

Another call stood out to Leith. At 12:25 that Saturday, soon after Kiera had so inexplicably walked out, around the time Chad and Stella had left the house as well, and possibly Lenny as well, Frank had made one short call. The number turned out to belong to Scott Rourke's landline, and it lasted about half a minute.

"Gotta get Rourke's records too," Leith told the wall, and made a note to self.

Frank Law had spoken to his Legal Aid lawyer, Jack Baker, and now he was brought into the New Hazelton interview room, sat down, and given his warnings once again.

Leith put it to Frank that he and Kiera were no longer a couple, and watched the response with interest. It was odd. Frank yanked his mouth out of shape, blushed, and said, "What? That's bullshit."

Yet he wasn't completely surprised by the allegation. It wasn't news to him at all. So, was it true? Maybe, maybe not. Leith followed up on a new suspicion. "Your band is on hold for now, I know that, but do you guys still hang out, you and Stella and Chad?"

"Not much."

But some, and some was enough. "It's Stella's idea, isn't it? She told you to tell us that you and Kiera have broken up. Right? Why would she do that?"

Frank remained pink-cheeked with anger. "She never told me to say that."

"Maybe to throw us off what really happened, d'you think?"

Frank pulled in a breath and then inclined his upper body forward to give thrust to his question, loud, bitter, and sarcastic: "And what *really* happened, d'you think?"

The last thing Leith wanted to do was rile the man up. The interview was being videotaped, and he knew what defence counsel would do with footage of an interrogation that started to climb the walls. There would be endless applications and voir dires and nasty cross-examination, and he didn't need another lawyer in his face any more than he needed another ulcer. He backed off and changed subjects, asking Frank instead about that brief call to Scott Rourke.

"Oh, that," Frank said, sullen now, the heat seeping away from his cheeks. "I thought I'd call him up after practice shut down early, see if he wanted to go for a beer. Got his answering machine. Didn't bother leaving a message."

Leith looked at the phone records. "Thirty-two seconds. You waited through his recorded spiel, did you?"

"In case he was screening calls. Said 'pick up, asshole, it's me.' But he didn't."

"He screens his calls? Why?"

"I don't know. You'll have to ask him."

Leith closed the interview.

Chad Oman was brought in for a third round of questioning and said he didn't know anything about the breakup or another man in Kiera's life. He seemed genuinely surprised at the very idea.

Nobody the investigators spoke to over the course of the day, friends and family, Kiera's parents and her sister Grace, knew anything about it. In the late afternoon, after a long and tiresome day, Leith told his colleagues that frankly, in his opinion, the whole thing was a fiction in Stella Marshall's head, and she should be charged with mischief in the first degree.

In the late afternoon he chanced to run into Constable Dion in the detachment hallway that led to the rear exit and staff washrooms, and at the time it struck Leith as a good time to chat about that man's certain weak-kneed questioning of Stella Marshall last night, a witness who'd been apparently eager to talk and might well have had something important to divulge, even if it was an elaboration on a lie. "It's just one damn good example of when you should have pressed a witness for more information and didn't," he finished.

Dion listened through the advice, wide-eyed, and when Leith was done he gave a short *yessir* that sounded more like *fuck you*, and tried to trade places in the narrow hall and move on toward the men's.

But Leith wasn't done. He called after him, "If you hate this job so much, why don't you do yourself a favour and quit?"

"I love this job."

"You could fool me."

"I noticed."

"*What?*"

"Excuse me. Need to use the washroom."

Leith returned to Giroux's office with a scowl, just in time to hear her new theory, which was just a rehashing of an old theory, that maybe there *was* another man in the picture, and that his sin wasn't that he was married but that he was somebody too close for comfort. Namely, Frank's older brother. "Look at it," she said, standing by the large Google Earth printout they were using for a map, posted up on the wall and marked with points of interest. She moved her finger between points. "The Matax is halfway up the mountain, not far from Rob's worksite. What if Rob and Kiera agreed to meet halfway?"

"There's no calls between them in the phone records," Bosko said.

Giroux had an answer for that too. "Phone records are notoriously easy to check these days, so they thought they'd better set up their meetings the old-fashioned way."

"Smoke signals?" Leith said.

"Ha-ha," she said. "No. With good old-fashioned words. Set up in advance. They're both at the house often enough. Brush by each other in the kitchen, pretend to talk about the weather, but they're actually setting up a time and place. Saturday at 1:00 p.m. at the Matax trailhead, wink wink, slap on the ass. And next thing you know they're up there, sitting in his truck, whispering sweet nothings and managing to get their rocks off across the console."

Leith doubted it. He recalled getting his rocks offs with girls in vehicles — or one girl, one vehicle, one time — in his early twenties. It was an uncomfortable memory, in every sense of the word. But whatever was happening between Kiera and Rob, if anything, wasn't necessarily lewd. That was just Giroux, who had a way with words. Maybe the two were just talking, figuring out how to break it to Frank. Maybe they argued. Maybe one of them was putting some kind of pressure on the other. Maybe things went terribly wrong.

Aloud, he said, "Rob is alibied all Saturday, but that aside, you have to consider this. He's got access to a few acres of ripped ground and a backhoe. The ground's frozen, but if he banged at it long enough, found a soft spot, he could bury her so deep she'd never surface."

They all stood looking at the map and talking over Rob Law's alibi for Saturday in the hours of Kiera's disappearance. Six employees with a clear line of sight on him, or at least on his office trailer and his pickup, made for one solid alibi. If he'd gone anywhere that day, those six would have known it.

Leith said, "What about this one hour he had after his crew left at 6:00 p.m. and before he headed down the mountain at seven?"

"Doesn't work," Giroux said. "He'd have travelled down, stopped at her truck to call her name, and was home half an hour later. All that time would be taken in travel. Not enough time to deal with the body. And of course, soon after that the search began."

She was probably right; it didn't work. So it was earlier in the day or not at all.

Leith brought in the file box, and they looked through statements and evidence. There were loading slips that Rob had signed when rigs were loaded up and left the site, and there were times on those slips, and in all the scribbles the only window of opportunity emerged, a block of time when Rob Law had signed nothing and supposedly been in his trailer. Bosko wrote that window of opportunity on the whiteboard. One fifty-seven to two fifty-two, just under one hour, and all that time his truck had remained in place alongside all the others.

"So much for that," Leith said.

Giroux said, "Unless he walked."

Leith laughed aloud, but Giroux was once again running her finger along the map, not along the lengthy switchbacks of the Bell 3, but skimming over the pines as the crow flies. And suddenly it was not 12.7 kilometres between the cut block and the Matax trailhead, but perhaps three.

Leith was still smiling, arms crossed, but Bosko had his specs fixed on the new path she'd etched. "You think there's a way through, Renee?"

"Who knows," Giroux said. "Deer make paths. Winter brings those paths out nicely. Maybe it's a trail he's used before. The guy practically lives up there. Maybe he puts on his hiking boots and goes walking for exercise. Maybe he's gotten to know the lay of the land like the back of his hand."

"Lot of maybes," Leith said.

"Life is full of maybes," she said sharply. "Sometimes it's all we've got."

He couldn't deny that one. He looked at the Google Earth view again. He looked at Bosko, checked for skepticism, and saw none. He said, "Sending planes up for more aerials isn't going to help any, with this dense tree cover. We'll have to check it out on foot. But first firm up the theory before we go any further. I'll make some inquiries." To Giroux he said, "Can you organize a couple pairs of legs to walk the woods?"

"I'll put out a bid for volunteers," she said, and added with smug confidence, "My boys will be fighting over the chance to get outside and play in the snow. Just watch."

* * *

Sergeant Giroux stood at the threshold, asking who wanted to go for a nice hike in the woods on this beautiful winter day. She already had one volunteer, Jayne Spacey, but she needed one more. Everyone looked to the window, including Dion. The morning sun had been blown away by fast-moving rain clouds, and shrubs and treetops were thrashing about as if frightened by what was moving in. Giroux ignored the silence and went on outlining the assignment for them to find a route between the RL Logging site and the Matax trailhead — much like the intrepid Sir John Franklin, except without the ships, she said. Dion didn't know much about history, but he knew the Franklin expedition had not ended well.

Maybe everyone else was thinking of Franklin too. Giroux lost patience and snapped, "If nobody puts your hand up in two seconds, I'll have to raise it for you. I need somebody big and healthy and just bursting with vim." Still, nobody's hand went up, and just as Dion feared, she was looking at him. "Big and healthy, anyway. You've just volunteered. Thank you very much."

* * *

They gathered their gear and drove together up the mountain in the SUV, Spacey behind the wheel. She seemed to have gotten over her hatred enough to make small talk, but it was just speckles of cool commentary, and he didn't bother responding much. Up at the cut block, the rain had stopped but the temperature had plummeted. Rob Law was away, but his crew was at work. Spacey advised the foreman that she and Dion would be looking around the site for a bit, if that was okay. She didn't pose it as a question so much as a fact, and the foreman only rubbed his muddy nose and nodded.

The two constables walked up to the ridge behind the office trailer and explored its perimeter for twenty minutes before Spacey gave a victory shout. Dion worked his way through the brush toward her and they stood looking downslope together, facing southwest. There were mature conifers above and beyond as far as the eyes could see, giving the place a cathedral feel, and uninvitingly thick undergrowth, mostly bare-branched shrubs. Spacey had found what might be called a track leading through the undergrowth, just wide enough to allow a man through.

She said, "Deer trail. This is as good as it gets, and it's headed in the right direction. Stick close, and if you see anything at all of interest, notify me right away and I'll flag it. Got that?"

Dion zipped up his jacket and followed on her heels.

The jobsite fell behind, and with it the noise, and they soon were walking in wild isolation, through evergreen woods that rushed and creaked at the upper reaches, leaving a darkened dead zone below. They didn't talk, the only noise of their passage the soldierly thud of boots on soggy earth and the occasional muttered curse as they untangled themselves from low-hanging branches.

The trail lost definition and blurred into many small clearings. Sometimes it petered out and they had to wade through bushes until it picked up again. Sometimes it meandered in circles. Spacey marked their progress, tagging each fork with a strip of fluorescent ribbon, sometimes green, sometimes pink, occasionally blue. Sometimes she replaced the ribbons, one colour for another. She checked her compass and made notations in her log, and when Dion lagged for a third time, she told him if he wanted to go back, it was fine with her, she'd carry on alone.

Downhill rose to uphill, and the trees thinned and the path branched again, radiating every which way. Spacey stopped to catch a breath, damp and irritated. "It's a frickin' maze," she said. "Up or down?" It was herself she was asking, and herself who answered. "Up, I guess. Follow the compass needle, right?"

She started to climb, as if she'd never stop. Dion stopped to take off his jacket, tying it around his waist and elbowing sweat off his brow. He called out that she could take the upper trail and he'd take the lower, maybe they'd narrow it down faster.

"Oh, that makes a helluva lot of sense," she called back. "Let's get separated and when you get lost we'll just call in another search party. Giroux will be madly impressed."

"I wouldn't get lost," he shot back angrily. But he followed after her. A few minutes later, the trail became difficult, then impassable, and they had to double back, and to allow her to take the lead he needed to back himself into the bushes, scratching his face and hands as she edged by. He stood wiping blood off his cheek and swearing, and Spacey looked back at him with disgust. She said, "Tell you what. Go back to the truck and put a Band-Aid on that, then have a doughnut or two. I'll radio if I need you."

The doughnuts she spoke of were the half-dozen assorted that Giroux had given them to take along for the ride, what she must have thought of as a reward. He didn't need a Band-Aid and didn't want doughnuts, but he did want to stop trailing after a woman who treated him like pocket lint. He said, "We're supposed to stay together."

"It's a formality. Go on. I'll get in worse trouble if those cuts get infected and you die. Anyway, I'll get this done a lot faster on my own. Go."

He returned alone to the logging site and walked down to Spacey's SUV parked in the mud with several other vehicles. He stood looking for his keys. They weren't in his trousers, but they were in his jacket when he untied it from his waist and went through it. He also found something missing: his personal notebook.

"God," he said, standing in the parking lot, being stared at by passing workers. He tried beeping open the SUV to check if the book had fallen in there, but the doors remained locked. He looked at the keys in his hand and realized they were the wrong ones. These keys were to his cruiser. Spacey had the keys to the SUV.

He radioed Spacey and asked if she'd found a notebook on the trail. She said she hadn't. He told her about the keys, and she said he'd just have to come back and get them. He returned to the narrow little deer trail and headed down it, following the fluorescent ribbons and keeping an eye out for the little notebook in its black leather cover. Most likely, though, it had fallen when he'd taken off his jacket to tie around his waist. So why hadn't he seen it when he doubled back?

Because Spacey had seen it first.

The ribbons began to confuse him. He didn't understand Spacey's complicated system of colour-coding, and they soon led him into the middle of an unfamiliar glen, surrounded by trees, all identical and dizzying. He backtracked, looking for the flutter of neon plastic that had misled him, but now even that had disappeared in the maze.

Something seized in his chest, and the pain in his stomach began to cinch and twist. He radioed to Spacey again, and her voice, breaking up over the air, asked him where the hell he was. He said he didn't know. She called him a jerk-off. She asked if he had his whistle on him. He did. She said to blow it, hard, and to blow it every minute or so until she located him. He did as she said, and eventually heard her voice calling through the trees. He called back, and minutes later she stood before him, puffing out jets of vapour.

"Sorry," he said.

Spacey was sweaty and rosy-cheeked, stripped down to her shirtsleeves, jacket slung crookedly around her waist, but she looked pleased. "It's okay. I got through to the Matax. It's all ribboned out. We can head back."

"You didn't find my notebook?"

She walked backward to look at him. "How could you lose your notebook? My goodness, you're a dumb fuck, aren't you?"

Following her, also in his shirtsleeves, cap off and hooked to his gun belt, sweat soaking his back, he made it back to the SUV and climbed in. His faint hope that the notebook had fallen here died as he groped about under the seat. Spacey wasn't speaking to him at all now, not even in those cold soundbites, which suited him fine. In silence, they returned to the detachment, found it all but empty, and Spacey put the box of doughnuts, untouched, onto the table by the coffee machine.

Dion was searching his workstation, and it wasn't here either. Of course it wasn't, because he took it with him everywhere. He heard his name and turned around. He saw the notebook fluttering in the air, attached to Spacey's hand, being held up and flickered like a taunt. She was standing within punching distance, grinning at him.

"This is great stuff," she said. "My god, I didn't realize you were so good at listing things. All kinds of things that are so good to remember, like the names of the people you work with every day. There's maps to help you get around this very complicated village. Even a cute little diagram here, how to tie a tie. I thought you were dumb, but you're a very smart little boy, aren't you?"

He held out his hand, said, "Give it to me."

She flipped a page, searching. "I bet you've got instructions on how to make toast, too."

He grabbed for the book, and she stepped backward, but he was faster, and stronger, and had her wrist in his grip and was pressing her arm back, ready to break it if that's what it took. With a cry, Spacey let it fall. Dion shoved her hard, another bad call in a string of bad calls, and she crashed against a desk and from the desk to the floor. The clerk Pam popped her head around the corner and rushed over to help Spacey to her feet, but Spacey seemed winded, unable to move. *I broke her back*, Dion thought, dazed. Down the hall a door opened, and a man appeared saying, "What's going on here?"

Dion leaned to pick up his notebook where it lay near Spacey's shoulder, but was pulled upright by his arm, spun around, and propelled away, back against the nearest wall with a thud. Constable Leith had him pinned and was staring at him, close-up and angry, asking him what the hell was he was doing.

Spacey was back on her feet, supported by Pam, and he stared at her, knowing he hadn't broken her spine but finding no comfort in it. "He tried to break my arm. Look." Spacey exposed the pink friction burn on her wrist that was already starting to bruise. Dion twisted out of Leith's grip and looked with longing at his notebook on the floor. Not that it mattered now. She'd read it, she knew, and she'd tell everyone.

"You going to press charges?" he heard Pam asking her. It sounded not so much a question as a recommendation. He looked at Spacey and saw her face twisted like a gargoyle.

"Hell no, I'm not going to press charges. I'm going to have you crucified, that's what, fucking maniac." She scooped the notebook from the floor and thrust it at

Leith. "I found this. I opened it up to find out who it belonged to, and he went berserk. Pam saw it all."

Leith took the book and shook it at Dion. "Is that right?"

"No," Dion said. "She —"

"You want me to read you your fucking rights?" Leith's finger was pointed at Dion, in case he wasn't clear enough who was in trouble here. He said, "Better yet, get out. I'll book you tomorrow. You're fired. Get your shit and go. Guns, keys, badge, on the table, now."

Still damp and gritty from the mountain, Dion unloaded the key to his cruiser, his .22 Smith & Wesson, his RCMP ID card, on the desk in front of Leith, punched the front door open, and left the building. His face was wet with sweat and the tears of frustration, and the wind coming off the mountain seemed to turn him to ice as he crossed the highway to the Super 8.

* * *

Actually, Constable Leith had no authority to fire him, Dion knew. It was just a hotheaded temporary suspension. But it hardly mattered. The real shit would hit the fan over the next few weeks, and he wouldn't work another day. Criminal charges were unlikely, but the notebook would be examined, and the investigation into who he really was would be long and painful. He should have known, should have backed off, taken early retirement when it was offered. It wasn't just a matter of rebuilding muscle and reconnecting the synapses. It was his mind, not a missing limb. He'd lost depth, and now he finally understood that depth could not be restored at will.

He changed into his civvies and left the motel. His mind was oddly blank and carefree, or maybe he'd just blown a fuse. After some wait, he flagged the town's lone cab on the highway. There were only a couple of bars in the area, and he directed the cabbie to the one out in Old Town, which he'd stepped into briefly once before. The Old Town bar wasn't a cop hangout. The customers were mostly native, mostly young, all strangers. The music was too loud and too country, but he didn't care. The cavernous interior smelled of beer and deep-fried everything. He was eyed as he passed through, as if they sensed who he was or what he represented, but that didn't matter either. From experience he knew that if he ignored the world, the world returned the favour.

He chose a small round table near a side exit, where a low dividing wall and a fake palm tree buffered some of the noise, far from the pool tables where the brawls usually broke out. He had a simple contingency plan if a fight should break out: he would pick up and go.

With a double Scotch on order, he sat back to study the beer coaster. When he'd done with the coaster he watched the big-screen TV, which was tuned in to curling. The sound was muffled, so he couldn't hear the play-by-play or catch the rules, but the object of the game was simple enough: get the thing to land in the bull's eye.

He was on his second double, still fixed on the curlers, when Scottie Rourke slung into the chair beside him, a mug in his hand of that pale gold draft that everyone up here seemed to favour.

Rourke said, "Hey!"

"Evening," Dion said, not pleasantly. He hadn't expected company and didn't want it except in the most hands-off way. But company had found him, and he hadn't sunk low enough to get rude and tell Rourke where to go.

"Firstly," Rourke said, "I gotta tell you, I don't hold it against you personally, pulling in Frankie like you did. It's that SOB Leith out fishing. Gotta find his bad guy at any cost, right? Guilt or innocence? What's that? Nothing. It's the bottom line that matters." He waved his beer glass about, and he'd had a few already, by the looks of it. "You ran out of worthwhile leads, is that it? Just wanted to harass the locals, show you're earning your keep?"

"Maybe," Dion said. Flatly, to show he wasn't playing.

Rourke snorted. "And in the end you had to let him go, no charges laid, right? Well, am I right?"

"If you say so."

"Know what I think? I think you pulled him in just to stir things up. You were desperate. Maybe he'd crack under pressure, or maybe he'd confess just to get you off his back, hey? And who cares if he's innocent. It's happened before, and it will happen again. Well, am I right? Am I?"

"Don't ask me." Dion spoke with the huskiness of rising anger. "Could I just sit down and have a drink for once in my life?"

Rourke flipped his hands in startled surrender. "Okay, okay. Don't shoot, Officer."

"It's okay. Just don't grill me."

They sat quietly for a minute. Then Rourke wanted to know if Dion wanted to play some pool. Dion didn't, thinking sooner or later the man would get bored and leave. Instead, Rourke sipped his beer and looked settled. After a bit more silence he said, "How's the ticker?"

"Dead." Dion showed him his new multitasking miracle of technology. "Fifty bucks. Works like a charm. Should have done it in the first place, like you said."

Rourke frowned as he leaned forward, booze gusting out on his breath. "Gosh, no. I'm sorry. I really am. That thing means a lot to you."

"It's not your fault. Can't put the fucking thing on life support, can we? I threw it in the river."

Rourke was thrown back in his chair again, he was so shocked. "What? Why? You shouldn't have done that, man. That's kind of an antique. Maybe somebody else could have fixed it. And even if they couldn't, you could have got a few bucks for it, for its historical value or whatever." He sighed and dug in his pocket, bringing out his wallet, drawing out bills. "Here's your money back. No, I insist. I've been accused of a few things in my life, but I'm an honourable man."

"Keep your money," Dion said. "I don't care."

"No, hey —"

"I said forget it."

"Then I'll buy you a goddamn drink, how's that?"

"Fine."

Rourke bought a round and raised a toast. Then he sulked. Then he said, "Totally wrong place to throw something you love, the river."

"Seemed kind of poetic to me."

Rourke shook his head with conviction. "People say the river's beautiful, and it is, like a woman. But it's also a mean, dark bitch. Just try to step into it, even in midsummer. It'll freeze your nuts off then rip you to pieces. No, you want a good send-off, go upward. There's so much paradise around here to inter your loved ones, if you know where to look. You want somewhere open to the skies. The Gates of Heaven, that's where my ashes are going when my time comes."

On Dion's good days, he caught glimpses of paradise here in the north, but mostly he found it cold, badly lit, and monotonous. His own ashes, he had hoped, would sail out from the balcony of his North Vancouver high rise and join the city smog, and maybe a few molecules of him would drift farther out and be taken away by the ocean. But that wasn't going to happen. Even unemployed, he didn't have the heart to return to the Lower Mainland. He'd stay in the north, get some shitty job, end up in a no-name urn, buried in a grotty little graveyard in Smithers. "Gates of Heaven," he said. "What's that?"

"It's self-explanatory is what it is," Rourke said shortly, and Dion didn't care to pursue it. To take the small talk in a less tedious direction, he asked how come Evangeline hadn't come out barhopping with him.

Rourke swiped the air dismissively. "Evie's not the catch you seem to think, bro. She's a Calgarian whore, and I've told her to pack her bags, get the next bus back to Cowtown."

"That's a bad idea. Whatever kind of catch she is, she's probably your last."

Rourke was pleased, maybe because he too wanted off the topic of failure and death. Or maybe because fielding insults was more up his alley. "Fuck you too."

"So you picked her up in Calgary?"

"God, no. She was hitching through to Rupert to visit an aunt, so she says, and I gave her a lift, and she asked if I could spare a few bucks while I was at it, and I said 'Not for nothing, my dear.' So she came along to my trailer, and lo and behold, has been here ever since. But like I say, she's leaving. The thrill is gone. Brains of a chicka-dee, but she eats like a horse. And you'd think she'd pick up a broom once in a while and give the place a dust. No, I can't afford to sustain a duchess on my wages. Anyway, cheers. Here's to girls."

They clinked glasses.

"She's free then?" Dion said, half joking. "Single, available? Up for grabs?"

"All of the above. But if you hook up with her, take my advice and lock up your valuables."

It was getting late. Dion had come to the bar by taxi, and Rourke, who said he was temporarily without a proper vehicle for reasons he'd rather not get into, had come on his bicycle, a regular old one-speed of metallic blue. The two men stood outside the front doors around midnight, parting ways. The rain had let up by now, and for once the night was not so bitterly cold. Rourke said he could feel spring in the air. Dion said he couldn't. Rourke pushed off through the puddles on his two wheels, spraying mud and slush in his wake, and Dion started toward town on foot. He had enough cash for a cab ride back but felt he could use the walk.

Half an hour later he didn't feel like he could use the walk anymore, and had his phone out to call for the town's sole cabbie, but realized he didn't know the number. His was a regular cellphone, not a 3G with a brain that could pull information out of thin air, so he was stuck.

He continued walking until headlights coming from behind fanned a glare over the road ahead. A dog started to bark somewhere in the darkness, racing closer, a territorial warning but not aggressive enough to worry him. He turned to stick out his thumb at the approaching vehicle, the raised headlights of a large truck, the lights on high beam expanding at a speed that said it was going faster than anybody should be travelling on this kind of backroad, especially with a pedestrian here glowing like a jack-o-lantern.

The dog came pelting out of a driveway, and the truck veered away from the dog and straight at Dion, and his instincts already had him heading for the shoulders of the road. Drenched in light, he scrambled up the high snowbank, and the truck's bumper sheared off a great swath inches from his leg, straightened out sharply and kept going, fast.

Dion watched its tail lights disappearing. He heard a yelping and looked at the road and saw blood.

He stood over the injured dog, a shaggy black animal, middle-sized. The dog was no longer yelping, its eyes rolling at him sadly. The damage was bad. There were guts and crushed limbs, and he had his phone out to call 911. But you don't call 911 for animals, do you? You bundle them in your car and take them to the vet. Or as a last resort, you shoot them in the head.

He crouched down. An injured person shouldn't be moved, but did the same go for dogs? Out in the middle of the road like this, it posed a hazard. He scooped his arms carefully under the creature, embraced it, and with difficulty got to his feet, smelling feces and blood, feeling its rear end hanging heavy. "It's okay, it's okay," he said, rushing up the driveway from which the dog had appeared. The house at the end of the driveway was a tall A-frame with lots of fancy detailing, its front smothered in oversized, soggy looking bushes. The windows were lit with cold white light. He had no hands free, so he gave the door at the top of the steps a thump with his boot. A medium-strong thump, loud enough to be heard, not so loud as to frighten.

The door opened, and a woman looked out at him. She looked at his face, and then at the dog dying in his arms. "Oh my god, Coal," she said.

* * *

He knew who she was, Mercy Black-something, who managed the band. Coal lay on a blanket in the living room, beyond help. The woman was of average height, and slim and elegant, even in a thick bathrobe over long johns. Her long hair was light brown, clean and shiny and combed sleek. She knelt over the dog now, murmuring what sounded like a prayer.

The dog was no longer squirming and lay still. Dion looked around at the large, fairly bare living room. There was a two-seater and an armchair of white leather and chrome, which belonged more in a West Vancouver condo than a dilapidated Victorian in a tiny northern village. Three of the rough walls had been partially stripped down to show thin strips of wood nailed up at a diagonal, and the battered wood floor was strewn with old plaster. Sheet plastic lay here and there, and there was the strong smell of some kind of chemical in the air, varnish or paint stripper or glue thinner. A small wood stove crackled, but the room was cold. Or maybe it was just him, chilled by his close call with the truck, his horrific experiences with the dog. He looked from the woodstove to the one unmolested wall. A series of black-and-white photographs were up in frames, hanging over the blocky white-leather-and-chrome seating. The photographs were a series of some kind, some group shots, some showing individuals posed for the camera, and at a glance he knew they weren't family photos but stills from her professional life. The musicians she had managed in her past, probably.

The setup confused him. She'd been active and prosperous. She'd left the city with her furniture and photos, so she was here for a prolonged stay. It wasn't a happy stay, judging by her drawn face, yet she was undertaking renovations. By the looks of it, the renos were a DIY project and not gone at with any kind of expertise or organizational skill. Didn't she have the funds to hire a pro? From his quick scan, it felt to him like a mild form of madness.

"He's dead," the woman said. She stood.

Dion went to crouch down by the animal and double-check. He was no doctor, but he'd dealt with enough deaths over the years to know when a being wasn't coming back. He nodded at Mercy, and she said, "Could you please put him out on the back deck for me?" She crossed the room to an exterior door with a small square window and held it open for him. Dion lifted the dog again, wrapped in its blanket, and took it into what turned out to be a small, enclosed verandah.

"Put him there," the woman said, pointing to a place on the floor between a chest freezer and a basket chair. "I'll call somebody to take him away. Can't bury him here, his home, unfortunately. Ground's too hard. Poor Coal. I rescued him from the pound, you know. Just hours before he would have been put down."

Dion laid the dog down where she indicated and stood, rubbing his mucky hands on his mucky jeans. For the first time Mercy looked at him, and she gave a start, and reached out both hands, as if she wanted to either grab him or keep him at bay. "Oh no, you've got blood all over you."

He stepped back. He said, "It was a pickup, with a raised suspension, I think. Dark, quite new. Know anybody around here drives something like that?"

They were staring at each other, like two actors from two different plays on the same stage, confused but determined to get through it. She raked her hands through her hair, blinking. "Everybody," she said. "And everybody drives crazy fast on this road. You'll never catch him."

Dion wondered if the truck had veered to avoid the dog or was gunning at himself. He wondered if its bumper had smeared any identifying evidence into the snowbank. Jayne Spacey drove a little Rav, so it probably wasn't her. Her ex maybe, Shane. He could do some checking, but wouldn't. Not enough data and not enough interest to bother.

He followed Mercy to a bathroom, and she left him to wash off at the sink. The bathroom was large and its fixtures had once been grand but had become loose and rattly, the finish rubbed flat. The toiletries looked pricy and the towels were white and fluffy, too good for a filthy man to be washing off dog shit and blood, so he filled the sink with hot water and used his palms to scrub his face and neck. He used the hem of his T-shirt to dry off.

When he came out she was in the living room, and she had a tumbler of Scotch in each hand. She held out a glass and said, "You look like you need this. I know I sure do."

He took the drink and drained half the glass. He was studying her face, looking for signs of trauma. He'd never owned a dog, but Looch had, once. It was a terrier. The dog had died of old age, and it was the only time Dion had seen Looch break down and bawl. It had taken at least a week for the man to regain his spirits, but he'd never wanted another dog, that's how painful it had been.

Mercy seemed depressed, but he had the feeling she'd been depressed before he kicked the door. She said, "I put some more wood in. I'm already running low and rationing. This is my first real winter here, and I thought two cords would be plenty. It's impossible to keep this house warm. It's impossible to stay warm anywhere in this horrible place." She gave a shiver and then frowned with what he took to be anger at herself. "I'm sorry if I offended you. I didn't mean to insult your hometown. You're from around here?"

He wasn't offended. He wasn't actually listening, much, his mind still full of headlights and tail lights, and a dog in pain, a dog gone quiet, facing its own death but looking up, making contact in its last moments. He was still thinking of Looch's terrier, and close to tears, and hating himself for it. He hadn't cried in his life till waking from coma, and now look at him. Disgusting. Weak and weepy and afraid of everything, he couldn't get through a day without his eyes welling up, sometimes without warning. Sometimes out of the blue.

To hide the tears, he looked at the walls, fixing on the photographs, all those people and their instruments. Mercy featured in many of the photos. There she was in an outdoor shot, a casual but posed group photo. She stood between two men, an arm around each. The lighting was strange, not quite natural.

He was touched on the arm by icy fingers, gave a start, and looked aside, down, into her eyes. "Are you all right?" she asked. "Do you want to sit down?"

He finished his Scotch and handed her the glass. "No, thanks. I need to call a cab. I don't know the number."

"Oh, of course, you mentioned you were walking back to the highway." It was about all she knew of him, which way he was heading. She didn't know his name or that he was with the police, and since he actually was no longer with the police, it didn't really matter. She had a cellphone in hand, ready to call that cab for him, but paused and said, "I'm getting the feeling you're from elsewhere. What's your name?"

He didn't answer, distracted by her stare. It was unsettling. She was attractive, somewhere in her forties. She had clear skin and well-defined features, but most startling were her probing grey eyes. She was concerned about him, he could see, but the concern was scientific. She said, "Have we met? You look familiar."

"I doubt it. I live in Smithers."

"And what are you doing on this lonely road in the Hazeltons in the middle of the night?"

"Just finishing a job," he said.

"Oh. Who do you work for?"

"Odd jobs," he said, admiring his own ability to lie on the fly. Better yet, to lie without actually lying.

"That's kind of serendipitous," she said, with a lift of her brows. "Because as you can see, I'm in desperate need of an odd-jobber. I'm tackling this house on my own, and not too well. Maybe we can work something out." She didn't allow him to answer, moving on to a more immediate problem. "You're still quite dirty, you know. And you stink. You're welcome to have a shower. You're welcome to stay the night, if you're in no big hurry to leave."

True, he stank, and he took her words at face value. There was nothing scientific in her manner now, only concern. She said, "Sometimes a person can be more traumatized than he knows. I think you're traumatized. I probably am too, it just hasn't hit me yet."

He had a shower, but he didn't stay the night, though she offered again, almost insistently. Instead she drove him back to the hotel in a silver Beamer that might have been glamorous once but now had a cracked windshield and a great dent on one side. She kept her eyes on the road the entire way, as if enemies might pounce, and he wondered if her nerves had been shot by a recent MVA. Like his. She repeated her suggestion of hiring him to help with the renos.

"Also, I'll need Coal taken care of," she said. "Poor Coal. How about it? There's at least a month of work for you, with that drywall. You could stay at my place, of course. It's huge. You could have the whole top floor to yourself. I'll pay well, better than what you usually get."

"I don't think I'll be back this way," he said.

Her profile looked tense, angry. She said, "Still, take my number, in case you change your mind. And give me yours."

"I saw some ads on the bulletin board at the IGA, men looking for work."

"Hm," she said. "Okay."

At the parking lot of the Super 8, she idled the engine, wrote her number on the back of an old business card, and handed it over. He didn't offer his number in return. Then he climbed out and the Beamer scudded off, slithering on the entrance to the highway. One thing was for sure, he thought, watching the tail lights disappear: her send-off of Coal was about as moving as the flick of the fingers.

Ten

THE RUN

MORNING BROKE, WET and drizzly. A new document was up on the board when Leith arrived in the office, a large-scale aerial shot with a line arcing across in crooked formation. Giroux and Bosko stood in front of the board, talking about departures. Bosko was saying he was due back on the Lower Mainland in a day or so but would keep in touch; he just had to know how it all panned out.

"What pans out?" Leith said.

Giroux thumped the aerial shot with the side of her fist. "Spacey found a way through. We're zeroing in."

Leith looked at the photograph, at Spacey's trail drawn in black marker, at the mileage scale. Doing the quick and dirty math, he didn't think they were zeroing in at all, were just wasting taxpayers' money. The whole thing was crazy, as he went about telling his colleagues now. "That's at least five clicks. You can run five clicks in an hour, sure, on an even sidewalk. But we're talking woods here. We're talking incline, nasty weather, lot of weaving and climbing. And say he's fast enough to get there and back in the time frame — that doesn't leave him a lot of minutes to commit the crime, does it? Three, four minutes? What, he races up to the girl, hits her on the head, wheels about, and starts tearing back to the worksite? Face it, Renee, it's brilliant, but it's a write-off."

Giroux seemed unworried by his logic. "Right," she said. "So to put a mileage or timing on it, Spacey's going to run it again. Soon as she gets in, we'll set her up and get her on her way. I'll send Thackray out to spot her from a distance. He can't run, but he can handle a radio."

Leith gave up trying to convince her of anything, let alone who was in control here. He saw Bosko was studying the map up close, as if he could see a tiny runner making its way along the black line. Bosko said, "Jayne Spacey is quite the powerhouse, isn't she? Why hasn't she put in for promotion?"

"She has," Giroux said. "Twice. Always something gets in the way. Why, you're not thinking of stealing her away from me, are you?"

"She may just steal herself away."

Leith frowned at the back of Bosko, big and graceless, a circus bear in an off-the-rack suit. He'd never been great at reading between the lines, but it sounded to him like Spacey was going places, city-bound, to join that man in his shiny new Serious Crimes Unit. It didn't surprise him, but did tweak his professional jealousy, and he said grumpily, "Did Spacey tell you about the menace? Who I fired, by the way."

Bosko turned, eyes vanishing behind white sheen as his glasses caught the light. "You mean Dion," he said, as if he knew of the incident already.

Giroux was looking at Leith too, expressing overblown shock. "What d'you mean, you fired Dion? You can't do that. If any officer could fire any other officer, there would be no officers left to keep the peace."

"I know that," Leith said. "Let's just say he's suspended till you get him in front of the board, or whatever you have to do. I'm not saying this lightly, but he's got to go. He's worse than incompetent. He's dangerous. They were supposed to stay together on the mountain yesterday. He didn't. He abandoned the search, got lost in the woods, and Jayne had to go find him, wasting an hour in the bush. Then they get back to the office and he physically assaults her. He grabbed her arm and pushed her down, all witnessed by Pam. All over some dumbass misunderstanding."

Giroux was upset, her plans and diagrams on hold as she dealt with this troubling personnel issue. "Dion assaulted Spacey? Why? Was she hurt? How come she didn't mention it to me? Is she going to lodge a complaint?"

"Actually, I heard something about crucifixion," Leith muttered. He frowned at the awful ring of the word, reminded of the seriousness of being fired from the RCMP. It was tragedy to some officers, tantamount to execution to others. Dion struck him as an officer on the edge, the sort that might jump off a bridge. He glanced at Bosko, who was still looking at him, still shielded by the glare off his lenses.

"Spacey won't be pursuing the matter," Bosko said. "She and I discussed it last night. It was a rough day. Tempers flared. But she did mention something about a notebook?"

A demand was embedded in the question, Leith realized, and once again he felt there was some off-the-record connection between Bosko and Dion, and it worried him. "It's not his duty notebook, I think," he said, hesitantly. "It's personal."

"Right," Bosko said, still waiting.

Leith walked to his desk, unlocked it, and produced the little book, which he had flipped through last night, finding nothing remarkable, lists and diagrams, strange catalyst for a dust-up. Bosko took it from him and slipped it into an evidence bag.

"Well, excuse me," Giroux said. "If that's his personal property, you can't just seize it without cause and without warrant. Can you?"

"I have cause, and I can, actually," Bosko said. "Don't worry. He'll get it back."

She blinked at him. "So what am I supposed to do with him today? Send him packing?"

"Cancel the suspension, please," Bosko said. "Give him a warning to be good. He'll finish his week here then return to Smithers, where he'll get his orders. I don't have time to deal with it right now, but I'll be making arrangements."

"And why exactly is he your problem?" Leith asked.

"He's my problem because he's officially posted in North Vancouver," Bosko said pleasantly. "And that's my turf."

Giroux said, "Smithers isn't his first posting? Wow. We all thought he was fresh out of boot camp. Why didn't you tell us before?"

"I've only found out myself," Bosko said, and Leith thought it was a lie, and alarm bells were going off in his head now. No doubt about it, the troublesome Constable Dion was under investigation. He crossed his arms, wanting to ask more questions but afraid to step over the line, because a shadow crossed Bosko's face, the first Leith had ever seen, and it looked like impatience. He didn't know Bosko was capable of such thing. "Anyway," the man said. "Excuse me, I have to make some travel arrangements. Don't want to miss the bus." He gave an apologetic smile but was on his phone already, thumbing in a number as he left the room. The door banged shut behind him.

When he was safely out of earshot, Giroux said, "Who is that guy? I mean, really." She sat at her desk and pushed papers around for a bit, still upset. "Hang on," she said. "Dion. I know that name. Isn't he the detective in North Vancouver who crashed his car last year? His colleague was riding with him, and died? Remember that, Dave?"

If Leith had heard of the incident, it was long since forgotten. His memory banks were overstuffed with work-related crap these days, and didn't have room for much else. But Giroux was already answering herself. "Couldn't be him. The guy in the crash was older, and experienced. A vet. Our Dion's just a boy, and greener than spring." She checked a folder and said with triumph, "Yes, I'm right, he's the one. Crashed his car and was out of commission for a while. Lucky man, to walk out of that mess in once piece."

She assumed he'd been repaired. Leith wasn't so sure. Dion must have passed whatever tests they'd put him through, but somewhere along the way there'd been an error. With that attitude, that temper... He looked up as Jayne Spacey walked in, bright-eyed and sharp as a whip, a study in contrasts. She bounced to attention, telling Giroux she was ready to hit the trail again, this time with a stopwatch, and would have bounced right out the door to put her boots to the ground, but Giroux called her back. "Hang on there, Jayne. Come here. Look at me. What's wrong?"

Leith didn't see anything wrong with Jayne Spacey. No broken arm, no post-traumatic stress, no anger. She looked good as new, to him. A woman who was going places, places he would never see, damnit.

Spacey hung in the doorframe. "Nothing's wrong, boss."

"Don't give me that. You're sick."

"Bit of a cold. It's nothing."

And Leith saw it now too, that the young constable wasn't herself. Her voice was thick, nasally, and her eyes swam about, and it came to him in an epiphany that she had emptied her medicine cabinet to get her through this day. Nothing to do with the assault, probably, but yesterday's traipsing about in the cold. Traipsing about looking for Dion.

The women were arguing now, loudly, about Spacey's fitness to run the trail in this condition, and the argument was lively but brief, ending in Giroux physically marching the young woman to the door and telling her, "Go home. Now. Somebody else can do this."

With Spacey gone, Giroux was back at her roster, once again looking for volunteers. "So which of you wants to do it? I would, but I'm about half the size of Rob Law."

"Get Mike Bosko to do it," Leith grumbled.

Giroux gave him a sour look. "How about you? About time you shifted your weight."

Leith was fit enough, just barely, but desperately didn't want to run that trail. He said, "One of the constables, then. Thackray."

"I told you, Thackray can't run."

Leith's mood was starting a dangerous downhill slide. Maybe it was the fact that Spacey had been wooed away by Mike Bosko, while he hadn't even been courted. Maybe it was distrust of Bosko's weird agenda. More likely it was just the threat of having to run up a mountainside in the pouring rain. He raised his voice. "What d'you mean Thackray can't run? He's a cop. He's got to be able to run. It's a prerequisite."

"And Ecton's been working all night," Giroux went on, ignoring him. "Lynn Daniels couldn't compete with Rob Law any better than me. Well, a bit better. Augie's on another file that requires his undivided attention, and my other two are testifying in Prince George as we speak."

There were half a dozen others that she and Leith ran through before he gave up. They were out-of-towners, all good candidates, he thought. But Giroux seemed to think it unnecessary to pull them from their tasks when a perfectly good David Leith was going to be sitting around twiddling his thumbs all day.

He looked at the sleety grey window and saw himself slogging along at two thousand metres above sea level with a stopwatch. Exercise was not his thing these days, and so what he if was looking more solid than ten years ago? Alison said it looked good on him, and he agreed.

Giroux said, "Don't mope. You're not our last resort. Constable Dion can do it."

"Dion cannot do it," Leith snapped. "He'll fall and break his neck. And while he's at it, he'll cause an avalanche that'll wipe out your precious village."

But the Queen of the Hazeltons only nodded, a mule at heart. "He can do it. And he will. After he and I have a little talk."

Leith considered her stubborn face and considered the menace of Dion, and sighed. "No. I'll talk to him."

* * *

In civilian clothes, jeans and sweatshirt, boots and leather, Dion stepped into Giroux's office, finding not Giroux but Constable Leith standing by the window, his back to the outdoors. He looked more tired than usual, and pissed off in advance. "Weren't you told you're back on duty?" he asked, eying Dion's well-worn black jeans and leather car coat that said loud and clear *I'm not here to work.*

"It's probably not your choice to make," Dion said, sounding cool and firm, because he'd thought this out, every word planned in advance. "It's probably mine."

David Leith had only three expressions as Dion had counted them: fed up, indifferent, or angry. He looked the first right now. "I see," he said. "Quitting, are you?"

"I'm not quitting, but I'm leaving," Dion said, and then an unexpected surge of emotion swept him badly off script. "… and I don't know why. How did I mess up? Filed a few late reports? Got pushed and pushed back? Forgot to kowtow?"

"You screwed up every task you got, that's what," Leith said.

Dion bared his teeth and stepped forward. "Like what?"

The answer came at him in a near shout. "You really want me to count 'em off for you?" Leith tried to count it off on his fingers. "Shoddy paperwork, punctuality issues, snotty attitude. Insubordination. How about assaulting a fellow officer?"

All of it was true, and Dion felt his metabolism rising. "I'm not like this," he told Leith, hating the sound of his own voice, shaky and maybe insane. "I'm good. I'm better than you and everyone else here put together. I put in years of blood, sweat, and tears, and I got places. Look at my service record, then you go ahead and put my failures on a chart, put 'em against my accomplishments, you'll see what I am." He poked himself violently on the chest. "I'm the best. I'm down right now, but I was getting up, not with your help or anybody else's. If you couldn't see that, you're a worse fucking detective than I even thought."

He stopped, half blind with indignation, and got his bearings. He saw the vague outline of the man he was shouting at, who looked pale and bruised. "Right," Leith said. "I get it. You didn't get coddled like you wanted. So what are you waiting for? There's the door."

"I'm going," Dion said, and looked sideways at the open doorway. His eyes were clouded with inner heat, and the door seemed murky and distant, a challenge to reach.

A moment passed, and Leith said, "I may be a lousy detective, but even I can see you're not. Or did I get that wrong too?"

The room came into focus, but it shimmered and glitched. Past Leith were maps on the walls, the window looking out on New Hazelton, the flowering cactus on the sill, the desk with its clutter. Dion felt the breath socked right out of him. He moved toward the door and stalled again. From the corner of his eye he saw Leith had turned to face the window and was looking out, and he was speaking now matter-of-factly. The words were strange and incongruous in the moment, halting Dion in his tracks. "As you're in no big rush, I might have a job for you. Come here."

Dion joined him at the window. He followed Leith's gaze outside to the bleak scenery, the pelting rain.

"That trail you walked yesterday with Spacey," Leith said. "She can't time it now because she's sick. You have to go as fast as you can and log it for time and distance. Pretend you're a desperate man, not a moment to lose. Can you do that?"

"What?"

Leith laid out the details of the mission. "Sergeant Giroux says she's got a pedometer that'll do both measurements," he finished. "So you'll use that. Spacey's got the path all flagged out in pink ribbons, so it's just a matter of following 'em all the way to the Matax trailhead, making note of the time, and doing a fast return trip. Fast, but without breaking your neck. Ignore the blue and the green ribbons. They're dead ends. Stick with the pink. Think you can manage that?"

"Of course I can manage that," Dion said. "But why should I?"

"Because you couldn't walk out that door," Leith said, losing patience again. "Because you have something to prove, and here's your chance. And believe me, it's your very last."

Dion burst into scornful laughter, because he wasn't that much of a fool. "I get it. Give me the dirty job nobody else wants to do and dress it up like a big favour."

"Is that a no?"

Dion snorted. He looked again at the rain, and his first instinct of point-blank refusal was already complicated by a stronger desire to take on the challenge. A minute dragged by, and he knew that point-blank refusals had to be made point blank, not sometime later. He sniffed, and tried to match Leith's irritation with his own. "How much time did he have to get there and back?"

"Fifty-five minutes between loading slips. Anything else?"

There was something else, but it was touchy. "That thing you mentioned, is it easy to use?"

"Thing?" Leith said.

Dion narrowed his eyes at him. "For measuring distance."

"Oh, the pedometer? Easy as a wristwatch. Hang on."

Leith left the room and came back with the gadget. Dion paled as he took it, looking at its LCD display, numbers blinking at him as he thumbed one button then the other. He thought of his new Timex that beeped at him at odd moments throughout the day, and even with instructions he couldn't figure out why, or how to mute it, or how to make it beep when he needed it to. This was a hurdle he didn't need right now. But no sweat. He'd just go on the Internet when Leith wasn't looking. There was a how-to page for everything these days. Except somebody would catch him googling it. Spacey would notice. She'd point it out for all the world to see, him googling how to use an idiot-proof pedometer.

He had no choice but to back out now, tell Leith he couldn't do this run. His face burned, and the lump in his throat made it difficult to pull in air. Shallow breathing made his ribs ache and the room vibrate. He looked at Leith, and the face was a blur, starting to run, and still he couldn't put the words together.

Leith took the pedometer from him and dragged over a couple of chairs. "No problem," he said. "I'll show you."

* * *

Dion had no running gear, so he wore his casual civvies, the hiker-like boots from Mark's, his favourite black jeans, and on top the layers that somebody had suggested, tank, sweatshirt, patrol jacket, rain cape. He and Thackray drove up the mountain, that long, jouncing crawl with the heat blasting, to Rob Law's cut block. They parked and in the shelter of the SUV went over the plan. Thackray would wait in the vehicle, ears on alert, and be ready to respond in case there were any problems. If he didn't get any updates for fifteen minutes straight and couldn't get through to Dion, he'd call in backup and hit the path himself to see what was amiss. Thackray pressed his bony hands into a prayer and told Dion to please, please report in diligently, because he really, really didn't want to hit the path. Dion promised.

The crew was hard at work in the downpour, and Dion knew enough about the logging industry by now to understand that it was a seasonal scramble; they were racing against the spring melt, which would mire the north in mud, bringing operations to a standstill.

He shouted a question at one of the workers, and the answer was shouted back at him that Rob was out at the mill dealing with some sort of tally dispute, and would be back within the hour.

Dion climbed to the raw land behind the Atco trailer and stood in his flapping cape at the mouth of the trail, by Spacey's first ribbon, and set the pedometer as Leith had shown him. The forest ahead looked worse than yesterday. It hadn't rained on him yesterday, and the sky hadn't been smothered in blackish clouds that cast shades of nightfall over the land. Rain rattled on his cape and drizzled from the hood brim. He looked up at the sky and back some distance to the worksite, where it seemed half the crew stood watching him.

He pressed the start button and headed down the path at an easy stride, picked up speed only when out of sight of the spectators, and jogged along for some time, the cape catching on bushes. He stopped and struggled out of it and abandoned it by another of Spacey's markers, and now he was cold but unencumbered. Icy water coursed down his face and neck and back and rode up his pant legs as he ran, chilling him to the bone, but the exercise pumped his blood and warmed him. He hadn't moved, not really, since the crash. And this was no rehab treadmill but body in motion, complete with the hot rasp of his working lungs and the strain on his thighs.

He tired, recovered, and pressed on, faster, fast as he could push himself, straddling slippery logs, ducking under low branches, pounding through the mud puddles. He slowed when the path narrowed, and slowed further when it became treacherous, but mostly he jogged. He remembered in the nick of time to report in to Thackray, then ran downhill, slithered, righted himself. Splashed through another puddle, and now faced a long, steady slope of rocks, pathless but with pink ribbons marking the way across the scree, and up he went, soaked and grimed head to toe. At the top of the hill he looked down the valley, sweaty, sore, and breathless. Looking to his left, he could see off in the distance the three ribbons set in a triangle that he knew was the Matax trailhead. He clambered up through tall, dead grasses in time to hear, not ten metres beyond, the approaching roar of a truck and the drone of its brakes as it passed on its way down the mountainside on the Bell 3 Road.

One final climb and he stood on the road, almost directly across from the trailhead, the world quiet now except for the pattering of the rain that was softening to snowfall. He stopped the timer and checked. Nineteen minutes. He noted time and distance, contacted Thackray, and started back.

For the return trip he needed no markers. He was limping and nearing the end of his reserves when the upper reaches of the logging site came in view, and he walked like a cripple the last few metres to find the total time of the two runs, not counting the five-minute rest, was forty-four minutes, which as he understood it left the killer eleven minutes to commit his crime.

He stood making final notes in the small yellow book that Leith had given him, specially designed for wet-weather writing, and when he looked up again he found the killer himself stood facing him, a mere seven or eight feet away. He and the killer sized each other up, himself cold and wet and dirty, Rob Law dry and secure in gumboots and olive-green rain gear, eyes glinting from the shadows of his hood. Law was white-faced, fierce, and silent, and with the blackness of the forest at his back he looked like a samurai about to hoist his sword and lop off the enemy's head.

But Dion was armed and unworried. He squeegeed water off his face with a palm, and in the second it took to do it he'd lost his suspect. Law had turned and was walking back toward the worksite, not a word spoken. Dion called out, "Mr. Law? 'Scuse me. Could I borrow your office for a moment?"

But first he needed to let Thackray know. Down at the SUV, he fetched his gym bag and spoke to the constable, who sat reading a police manual in the warmth of its cab, studying for his next level exams, he'd said. Dion explained what the deal was, that he was going to change into dry things in the trailer, that Rob Law was there, to just keep an eye out. Ten minutes, max. Thackray wondered if it wouldn't be prudent if they went to the trailer together, considering Law was a suspect. Dion said he didn't think so, and Thackray went back to his reading.

The trailer inside was as dark as the outdoors, and not much warmer, but Law was working on getting the place running. A generator grumbled and then came a metallic whir, harsh light and dust-scented heat. "Place'll be too hot in about three minutes here," he said and went about making coffee in a slow, determined way, mixing sugar, no-name instant, and whitener in two mugs. Dion stripped off sweatshirt and tank and pulled on a clean, dry T-shirt. The jeans he would have to live in till he got back to his room, same with the wet boots. He bundled the soggy mess of used clothes into his bag and joined Law at the table, where a cup of coffee awaited him. As he took his chair, Law spoke so low it was hard to make out the words. "So, you have it all figured out?"

"I'm not the one who figures things out."

"Well, the path. You got that part figured."

Dion started to say he was just the runner, but found he couldn't. He was far from powerless, and to say otherwise would be a lie. He gave a noncommittal nod instead. The coffee he'd just gulped was hot and sweet and awful. Across from him, Law was thinking grim thoughts, if anything could be read in the teaspoon he was absently bending out of shape between two thumbs. But wet feet turning to ice and the fact of Thackray waiting in the truck both spurred Dion to get going, and after another gulp of the awful coffee, he stood. "Thanks for the warm-up. I'll be off now."

Law nodded, not moving from his chair, still in his rain gear, and he looked like he might sit like this all night. Dion saw depression, and it worried him. He walked back to the table and asked, "Is there a problem, Mr. Law?"

Law's throat worked. Eyes turned up, for a moment he looked younger than his years, almost juvenile. The moment passed, and he was himself again, a thirtysomething grown man, a mover of earth and trees without much of an education, now asking a strange question in a near snarl. "They still hang people?"

Dion was back in his chair, startled that anyone wouldn't know the basics of law and order in this country. But he supposed that if a man doesn't watch TV, doesn't listen to the radio, is maybe just not interested in how the world operates, he might go on believing there are still gallows set up in the backrooms of every penitentiary. "No, of course not."

Law pulled a cigarette from a box on the table then held out the open box. Dion, who hadn't stuck a cigarette in his mouth since the crash, shook his head. "I never been to jail," the killer said after lighting up, pulling in and streaming out the exhaust to one side, not to hit his guest in the face with it. "Scottie has, though, like I'm sure you know. Seven and a half years. Got off easy, considering what he did. Nearly killed the poor bastard. But it's 'cause it was done in the heat of the moment, he says. Beats me. How can a man be excused because he was pissed off? Don't understand the world. Never will."

Dion nodded in sympathy.

Law returned the nod, but he wasn't present, Dion could tell. He was elsewhere, talking, smoking, drinking coffee, all in a trance, going on in a low, fast mutter. "Jail just about killed him. He says it's kind of a chemistry, that you either cope or you don't, depends who you are. If you're too soft, you're better off dead. I'll cope, I think. I'm tough. Yeah, I'll cope." His eyes had widened in a blind stare at the tabletop in front of him, the mangled spoon that lay there. He seemed to lurch at a new thought, and this time the fear was sharp enough that he visibly paled. "Or electrocute?"

He wasn't being cute. Dion said, "There's no capital punishment in Canada."

Law watched him, registered the words, and that was about all. There were tears in his eyes, but they didn't fall yet. He couldn't seem to get the cigarette to his mouth now, and it smouldered between his fingers. Couldn't get another word out either, though it seemed he was trying.

Dion had been in much the same shape earlier today, but his problems were nothing compared to this man's right now. He said, "It's okay. I'll take you down in my vehicle. Gather what you need. I'll wait right here."

Law nodded. The tears were making creeks now, but he didn't crumple, didn't seem to even notice as he crushed out the cigarette and stood and looked around, wondering what he might need for the strangest trip of his life. Dion stood near the door and kept an eye on the patch of night sky through the window, but mostly he watched Rob Law, a man on a cliff right now, who might need catching.

Eleven

CONFESSION

"HE WHAT?" LEITH SAID.

"Confessed," Giroux said, again. "He killed Kiera Rilkoff."

The mountainside run had produced a helluva lot more than time and mileage, then. It had produced a prisoner, and quite possibly the end of the tunnel. Leith took it all in, one part relieved and three parts doubtful. Constable Dion had brought the prisoner in and was now at his desk in muddy jeans, dirt smudged across his face, writing down in ballpoint the conversation he'd had with Rob Law as verbatim as he could get it while it was fresh in his memory. From where he stood in Giroux's doorway, Leith could see the temp bent over his notebook, putting down the words so carefully he might have been tracing somebody else's scrawl.

Bosko hadn't left yet and was at Giroux's desk, on the phone, speaking with Crown counsel by the sounds of it. Giroux was at her board, considering the map, the path, the time and distance, and the possibilities. Leith joined her at the board.

"Okay, fine," she said. "If Rob's not just making this up to save his brother's neck, where's the body? Without a body, I say he's taking us for a ride. And what possible motive could he have for killing Kiera, hey?"

Leith thought about it, and when he answered it was more for Bosko's ears, Bosko who would be leaving soon, who hadn't once brought up the subject of Leith joining the bigger, smarter Serious Crimes Unit down in North Vancouver. "Taking us for a ride, for sure," he said. "He hasn't got the brains for this fancy alibi nonsense, loading slips and deer trails and all that. I just don't buy it. He's lying to cover for Frank, which points to his confidence in Frank's guilt, which is about the best thing we got from this whole damn exercise."

Giroux didn't argue. She stood deep in thought in front of her maps and charts. Bosko's ears had missed Leith's snappy logic altogether, and he was laughing about something with whoever he was on the phone with, a deep, comfortable laugh, a man who probably didn't know the meaning of self-doubt.

Giroux, who had got the ball rolling on this path theory in the first place, now in her contrary way began to tear it down. "So he signs these loading slips," she said, "Does a two-K run, kills his brother's girlfriend, does another two-K run, and then signs another loading slip. Before we talk to him, let's take another look at those papers, see what his signature tells us. A psychopath might be able to fake it, but that's not him. He was in tears and very scared, from what Dion says."

Leith wished he'd thought of it, checking the loading slips. Maybe that would have dazzled the man from the city. The only dazzling he'd done so far, he realized, was forcing John Potter into a premature death. He hauled the box out of the exhibit room and found the loading slips stored in a thick, grubby manila envelope. He pulled up a chair and emptied the flimsies out on Giroux's desk. Those from the Saturday Kiera disappeared were already separated out, and he put on his reading glasses, put the slips side by side on the desk, and inspected Rob Law's signatures, one against the other.

The writing he saw was sloping and immature, but practiced. It was just a signature that didn't say much of Rob Law's intellect, but it gave insight into his state of mind at the moment he put pen to paper. Leith knew from the records that Rob was a dropout, that writing wasn't his thing. Or reading, or high-tech anything, or current events. How strange, in this day and age, to be so insulated, nose to the ground, machines and money, payables and receivables, while the world accelerates into a breakneck spin around you. He shook his head. "Looks identical to me."

Giroux had done her own inexpert handwriting analysis, and agreed. "Right. He's either very cunning or he never left the worksite. Probably the latter. He's covering for Frank, and I'll bet he knows what really happened on Saturday. You want me to sit in with you, or do it alone?"

"Alone," Leith said. "This is going to be a piece of cake."

* * *

Rob Law told all. He sat in his work clothes, smelling of diesel fumes and the cold outdoors, avoiding Leith's eyes, not looking at him at all, and confessing to a variety of sins and crimes. "It's been going on for years," he said. "Me and Kiera. It just kind of happened. 'Course I felt bad. Every time it happened, I swore never again. But couldn't stay away from her. Last week she says she's going to tell Frank about it. I said no, we don't have to tell Frank nothing. We have to end it and pretend like it never happened. She was okay with ending it but still had it stuck in her head that she was going to tell him. So our last meeting there, we had a fight about it, and I ended up rattling her, and she hit her head on a rock and she just kind of stopped talking."

"How'd you arrange to meet?"

He shrugged. "We talked it over few days before. Time and place."

"What time and place was it."

To Leith's surprise, Rob answered promptly. "Two thirty, Saturday."

"Carry on, then."

"I tried to bring her back, but she was dead. I hid her as best I could and ran back to the site before they figured out I was away. After work, when all the guys had gone home, I drove my truck down to the Matax. I scooped her up and drove up the old Bell 6 a few miles, into the woods, buried her deep. I can try to find the place, but won't be easy. I was just in shock, eh. Doing things without much thinking. All I could think was I didn't want Frank to find out about me and her. Or that I'd killed her."

He bowed his head, about as genuinely miserable as a suspect could be. Leith said, "Took a shovel along, did you?"

The suspect nodded.

"Buried her and covered her back up?" Leith knew the ground was too hard to dig up — you'd break your shovel before you could make a dent — and already he was fixing a snare on the story, proving not that Rob was guilty, but that he wasn't, and the only charge he'd be slapped with was one of aggravated obstruction.

Rob nodded again, and he spoke now with an effort, pushing the words out in a hoarse whisper as he stared at the table. He looked revolted, horrified, maybe awed by what he'd done. "Ground's like iron. Can't dig. Found a pile of deadfall. Rolled her in. Heaped snow over top."

The snare had tripped, and all it had caught was what looked like genuine remorse. "Ah," Leith said. "You'll be able to find her for us, will you?"

Law nodded, wet-eyed. "Yeah, for sure."

Was it true, then, all of it? Had the logger actually done the killing, as he said, hidden the body, and was now coming clean? Maybe so, and if so, then Leith needed to switch modes. He was no longer bent on debunking Law's confession but hammering it into place, closing off any escape routes. "So tell me," he said. "Why the urgent need to meet her on Saturday at two in the afternoon?"

Law had a good answer for that one too. "Her and Frank and the others were planning an out-of-town trip in a couple days, playing at a dance down in Burns Lake, then another in Vanderhoof. It was about my last chance to talk to her alone. Convince her not to tell Frank."

"Vanderhoof is hardly the moon. They'd be back in a couple of days. Why not wait?"

"I couldn't wait. She was going to tell him, who knows when."

"Okay," Leith said. "One more thing I need to tie off before we head up the mountain. Tell me about your relationship with Charlene West."

There was a lengthy pause while the logger studied him. "Didn't work out," he said.

"Why's that?"

"I don't know. She got sick of me, or sick of this place, left a note and went back home. Why, did you talk to her?"

"We had a few words," Leith said, loading more meaning into the statement than it deserved. In fact, it was Jayne Spacey who'd done some investigation a few days back, and with help from the Dease Lake RCMP had tracked down Charlene West's cell number and given the girl a call to have a few words. And "few" was a stretch:

Q: *Ms. West, you lived with Robert Law down here in Kispiox, and his brothers Frank and Lenny last year?*

A: *Little bit, yeah.*

Q: *Why'd you leave?*

A: *Had a fight.*

Q: *Do you know Kiera Rilkoff?*

A: *Sure.*

Q: *She's missing; any idea what happened to her?*

A: *Nope.*

And that was about it, according to Spacey's transcription. But Rob didn't know any of that, so Leith used it for what it was worth, giving the suspect the quiet, confident stare that said *the gig's up, buddy, I had a good long talk with your ex and she spilled the beans on your dirty little secrets.*

But maybe Rob wasn't reading the stare, gawping back at him with dull and distant wonder, and finally blurting out, "Yeah? So?"

Leith rose to his feet and led Rob out to the main room, where they pulled on coats, hats, and gloves. Then they joined the others in the rear parking lot and climbed into trucks, bound for a search that would maybe turn up the remains of the Rockabilly Princess at last.

* * *

They had spent many long hours on the mountainside, traipsing about in a land without landmarks, hunting for a burial spot on the heels of the self-confessed killer, but no body had been found. Rob Law seemed as distressed about his failure as anybody. Just couldn't remember exactly which goddamn spur he had taken, he said.

He was back in his holding cell now, and Leith was at his own holding cell, Room 213 at the Super 8. Surprisingly, it was only seven o'clock, the evening sky cloudless for a change, sharp and clear, each star a bright sparkle against the heaviest blue. He was helping himself to a mickey of Scotch to soothe his nerves, sitting on his bed, on the phone with his wife. He told her of the new schedule, not a happy one, and he swore too much in the telling, until she told him to stop, because she didn't like that kind of language. Alison wasn't a prude, just sensible, and she saw no point in saying the F-word with every out-breath like most cops and criminals were prone to. It jarred the ears.

"Anyway," he told her, "he says he did it, and I think he did it, but he led us all over kingdom come and can't find her now in all those woods. So we're going to have to bus in a bunch of cadaver dogs from Rupert, George, Terrace, wherever we have kennels. So it'll be another few days at least. If that doesn't work, we're going to excavate the cut block, top to bottom. Yup, pull it all up, inch by fucking inch. Sorry. Because maybe he's just leading us on a wild goose chase miles uphill when really she's right there under our feet. Imagine that. He's got an eight-foot bucket at his disposal. Can you imagine the hole you can dig with that thing in about two minutes flat?"

"I can imagine," Alison said from across the miles, that warm and familiar voice that he missed so much. Time and distance made all the wrangling seem ridiculous now. The arguments about how he shut her out, about how she needed to lay off when he was tired, about having a second child (she wanted one, he didn't), about his opinions about certain of her family members, her opinions about certain of his, it all seemed trite now, and he only knew he loved her madly.

She let him ramble on a bit longer about the pursuit of a body and then interrupted, saying, "That's enough. You're really wound up, you know? You make my head spin. There is a world beyond crime, and you gotta get your mind off it. Go for a walk. Read a book. Listen to some music. Okay, hon? Then get some sleep."

"Okay, hon," he murmured. "Thinkin' of you, babe."

"Thinkin' of you too," she said.

He signed off, feeling better, wandered with his plastic tumbler of Scotch to the window, and gasped. Above the black rip-line of the mountains, a light-show played out in undulating waves of green and pink. The phone at his hip buzzed urgently, and it was Renee Giroux in his ear now, saying, "Finally. I tried your work phone, and it went to voicemail. So I tried this number, and it went to voicemail too, so I had to assume you're on a long call somewhere. You're worse than my thirteen-year-old niece. D'you see the goddamn sky?"

"I see the goddamn sky right now," Leith said, still lost in love. "It's the best goddamn sky I've seen in a long time."

"We're at the Black Bear," Giroux said. "Myself and Mike and Spacey. We're saving a spot for you. And make it fast because we need a distraction here in a big way. It's Mike's last night here, so he's pulling out all the stops, if you know what I mean. He's telling us in great detail the dynamics of aurora borealis, which I *so* do not want to know."

"Trashing the magic for you?"

"No, he couldn't do that. It's just really, really not interesting."

Leith smiled. "Sorry, but I'm not going anywhere. I've got my own bar right here in front of me. But I do have a question for you. Did anybody manage to contact the two little bears?"

Frank and Lenny Law, he meant. Since Rob Law's arrest, nothing had been heard of them, neither hide nor hair, and it was becoming worrisome.

"No," Giroux said. "I'll check with my people on the road, see what's happening, and call you back."

A few minutes later, she did call back, not with an update but breaking news. "Sorry, but we have to meet, like, now. Augie and Ecton just picked up Lenny. He was hitchhiking up the Old Town road. He's got something to say, they're telling me, but he's not saying it. Whatever it is, doesn't look good, Dave."

The detachment being just across the highway from the Super 8, Leith didn't have to drive, which would be breaking his own laws. He capped the mickey, pulled on jacket and boots, and made tracks.

* * *

The kid was a wreck. His mouth hung open. Bilious-looking, like he'd been into the liquor cabinet. Or the pharmaceuticals, maybe. And his eyes were swollen and bloodshot, sticky and heavy-lidded, like he'd been crying long and hard.

"What is it?" Leith asked him. "What happened?" He and Giroux sat with the youngest of the Law brothers in Giroux's office, trying not to loom over him, trying to make him comfortable. So far he hadn't said much of anything to anyone, and another minute passed, and finally he came out with it, but in a faraway voice, like someone — Leith imagined — sucked into the fourth dimension. "He's gone."

"Who's gone?"

"Frank."

"Where did he go?"

Lenny Law pointed more or less at Giroux. "Here. To see you."

Leith questioned Giroux with his eyes. She shook her head. "He's not here," he told Lenny. "He hasn't been here at all today."

"He dropped me at home and said he was coming here, and took off. An hour ago. He wouldn't let me go with him."

"Why was he coming here?"

"To tell you something."

"D'you know what he wanted to tell us?"

"What he's done," Lenny Law said in that airy voice that was beginning to give Leith the creeps.

He asked the boy to tell them everything he knew about what Frank had done, what exactly he had said, but the youngest brother wouldn't say. Leith asked him where they'd been all day, him and Frank, and did they drive there? If Frank was driving and had left half an hour earlier, he should have been here many minutes ago. Had he stopped somewhere along the way? Did he say where he might be stopping?

But Lenny was done divulging. It was Frank's thing now, and whatever Frank had to say he would have to say himself.

Giroux and Auxiliary Constable Daniels took Lenny back to his home to wait there, in case Frank changed his mind and returned. Leith stayed in the office, having instructed Constable Spacey to organize everyone on staff, on duty and off, including auxiliaries, to launch a dedicated search in the area for Frank and/or his green 1982 Jeep.

Spacey promised she'd scour the planet till she found him, no problem.

Spacey is a good cop, thought Leith, still with a mix of envy and admiration. *She'll go far*.

* * *

The sad warbling of a small bird buried deep under the snow woke Dion, and he looked at the ceiling. He didn't know which ceiling it was until the bird warbled again and he recognized the sound as his cellphone and the place as the Super 8, and he recalled he'd gotten off shift and lain down to rest and must have fallen into a deep sleep. He found the phone on the fourth ring, and Spacey's brittle voice was in his ear, telling him to get in to work right away.

He looked at his watch. "But —"

"Now," she said.

Across the highway he found the office fully lit, in spite of the late hour, and it looked like all were in attendance for whatever emergency this was. Spacey gave Dion and the others detailed instructions to grid-search certain areas of town for Frank Law and/or his vehicle. Dion took his copy of the bulletin and asked what was happening, and Spacey spoke in a low voice, for his ears only. "As I just finished explaining, but maybe you didn't click, word is he was on his way in to make a confession, but he disappeared en route. So if by chance you apprehend him, don't fuck up by having a nice little chat with him. Just shut up and bring him in and let somebody with a functioning brain get his statement. Okay?"

He worked on a mean, snappy reply, but not fast enough; she had moved on and was talking to somebody else. Dion drove out to find the area assigned to him, and it happened to be in the area to the west of the 7-Eleven mini-mall, and once within its quiet avenues and cul-de-sacs, he knew that this was the last place on earth Frank Law would be found. It was a small new subdivision with a middle-class feel to it, Hazelton's version of urban sprawl, and he knew Spacey had done it on purpose, given him the least likely zone to search. It was all about revenge with her.

He followed about half her instructions, visually checked driveways as he passed, but didn't stop at every closed garage or outbuilding and pester the residents about permission to search. It was cutting corners, but Frank wasn't here, not in plain sight and not hidden either.

Having cut so many corners, he was done sooner than the time allotted to him, and he turned his vehicle back onto the highway, tires scraping on ice, and saw that the skies to the east were strangely pink and writhing, as if the world on the far side of the mountains was ablaze. He was watching the sky as he drove along and almost didn't see the hitchhiker ahead, standing on the shoulder, a slouchy cap taming her long hair that fluttered sideways like a cape, and her thumb out. She pulled that thumb in fast when she saw the vehicle coming her way was a police cruiser, and at the same time he recognized her under the sickly orange glow of the street lamp. Evangeline Doyle, apparently on her way to a new life. He signalled, pulled over, and stepped from the car, and she gave a whoop of recognition and came forward in a weird lope, burdened by a large backpack. They stood on the shoulder, face to face, and he saw she was already road-weary, though not quite fatigued. Her pretty, round face broke into a grin. "Can you take me to Edmonton, Officer?"

"Bit late to be heading out of town. Why don't you wait till morning?"

"Nah. I'm a night bird."

"Still. Chances of getting a ride are slim, I think." At least with someone safe. He tried to tell her with a stern look what he thought of it, hitchhiking at all, but especially at night. And especially here, this notorious strip from Prince Rupert to Prince George that had earned the mournful name of Highway of Tears for good reason.

She sniffed and looked at the pink sky, now tinged with green. She nodded. "I suppose you're right. It's just Scottie's been in a really shitty mood lately, so we got in a bit of a yelling match, and I guess I burned my bridges. But one more night I guess I can put up with him. Would you look at that, though?"

They looked at the sky together, and then he looked at Evangeline, because the brim of her cap was sparkling pink under the lamplight, which reminded him of something, but he couldn't say what. She saw him staring at it, and said, "Problem?"

"Can I see it?" he said.

She took it off and handed it over. The cap was fake suede, with a stiff beak that was suede over card. He looked at the glitter, glued on in a deteriorating pattern along the brim. He touched the glitter and Evangeline said, "Careful, there's not much left, and it's an old favourite."

He looked at her and recalled the photo of her on the wall, the girl outside on a windy day, cap on and one gloved hand keeping it from flying away. He said, "Where are the gloves?"

Because it was a matching set, and the glove in the picture was grey, a soft knit fabric, with a little sparkling bow at the wrist, and though it was significant, he couldn't say why, or whether that significance attached to this file or something else altogether.

"Scottie lost them," Evangeline said, making a face of exasperation, a mother wearied by her child's pranks. "They're those tiny gloves that stretch and fit anybody, so the idiot borrowed them. Can you imagine a man wearing gloves with little pink bows? He probably stretched them all out of shape anyway. Do you mind if I ask why?"

He returned the cap, knowing the *why* might come to him, eventually. Probably too late to matter.

She put it back on and said with an attractive and challenging smirk, "Wouldn't be able to zip me over to his place, would you? It'll take you all of five minutes."

Zipping her over to Kispiox would be a lot more than five minutes. He phoned Spacey, told her he was finished the subdivision, and asked how about if he took a cruise through the outlying areas for a bit, then report back in. Spacey didn't care what he did. He loaded Evangeline's backpack into the trunk, and she got in the passenger seat, and he carved a U-turn on the highway and headed back toward Kispiox.

Which technically he shouldn't do. Technically, he should report in that he had a civilian in the car, and technically he could be disciplined for providing taxi service to the public. Technically, too, she should be in the rear seat, kept at bay by the bulletproof barrier. But technically he was at the nothing-to-lose stage of his career, and didn't really care what rules he broke. Anyway, he had a question or two for her, which made it less of a taxi ride and more business. "D'you know the Laws much?"

"Rob, Frank, and Lenny," she said. "Not too much. I've been to a couple parties over there. Scottie adores those guys. Funny, but he's more of a mother hen than you'd think."

"You don't have any idea where Frank could be right now?"

She didn't, and his duty was done. He said, "I can loan you bus fare if you want. Hitchhiking around here isn't a good idea. You know that, right?"

"I know that. I'm ready for it."

"I'll give you the bus fare."

She laughed. "I've got money, and I'll take the bus, if that makes you feel better."

They drove in silence for a bit and had left Two Mile behind, and Old Town, and were deep in the woods that flanked the Skeena when she said, "Hey, that's his bike."

"Whose bike?" Dion said, slowing the vehicle, looking at his passenger, following the line of her finger out to the woods.

"There. Scottie's bicycle."

Something blue shone from within the trees, and Dion pulled to the shoulder and reversed till he could see it better. "That's his bicycle?"

"That's his bicycle. Weird. It's the only way he gets around these days, 'cause his dirt bike's out of commission too, and he can't fix it. How dumb is that, Scottie the Fix-All can't fix his own bike. Great advertising."

Dion got out of the car and went to take a closer look. Sure enough, it was Scottie Rourke's crappy blue one-speed, leaned up against a tree off to the side of the highway. There was no lock and chain around it, and it seemed intact. Its tires were firm. With collar high against the cold, he looked up and down the dark, little-travelled byway that wound through forest toward the Law residence, and beyond that to Rourke's trailer, with a whole lot of nothingness in between.

The bike was pointing away from the village, so Scottie had been heading home, by the looks of it. He supposed it was no mystery; somebody had driven by and given him a lift. Not to Rourke's trailer, because why bother leaving the bike for subsequent pick-up if he was just about home anyway? No, he'd been given a lift back to the village, or somewhere else altogether. The police would be out crawling this road looking for Frank, so maybe Rourke had been picked up by one of the constables for questioning. But a pick-up would have been broadcast, and it hadn't been. Same if he'd gone to the pub or the Catalina. He'd have been scooped, and the scoop would have come across the police frequency. So the drive-by and the pick-up would have happened before the alert went out, and who would be driving by, by chance, on this remote road? One of the Laws. Not Lenny and not Rob. Frank in his old green Jeep. That's who.

He sat back behind the wheel and drove past the Law driveway, looking for police activity and seeing none, and a minute or two further to Rourke's trailer. The lights were off in the place except for one burning low in the area of the kitchen. He hauled Evangeline's pack from the trunk of the car and went up to the door with her. She had found a business card stuck in the jamb, and she showed it to him. Thackray had left his RCMP card with a note scribbled on the back to call this number ASAP.

Evangeline fished into an empty flowerpot and found the house key. She let herself into the trailer, and Dion followed and set down her pack. The place wasn't warm but not cold either. Evangeline was calling out for Scottie, and Scottie wasn't answering. She had turned up the heat, switched on lights, was pouring water into a kettle, and asking Dion if he wanted coffee or a beer or anything. How about some antioxidant tea with ginger?

He didn't. He stood in the middle of the tiny trailer kitchen, and it was coming to him like a home movie played without sound, everything that was happening. He remembered the photos on Rourke's wall, that snapshot of Rourke grinning at the camera, the grin cut in half by a terrible scar, an arm around each of the two older Law brothers' necks, throttling them with fatherly affection. That same suffocating love of Rourke's had destroyed a man and driven a woman to suicide. The crime was history, and maybe he'd mellowed, but it still ran in his veins, that terrible, overblown passion.

Dion experienced a fleeting moment of wonder at himself, that he was still here, knowing some things, not knowing a lot more, facing the end of life as he knew it, but still ticking away as if he must close the deal. He said, "Does Scottie have a gun?"

Evangeline didn't think so. "Why?"

And maybe he was totally off the wall, but in a further epiphany he could see *where* it was playing out, too, at least in vague composite form. Now he had to decide: call it in, alert the team what he thought and where they ought to go — or go there himself.

Time and space and a certainty that they'd drag their feet told him he didn't really have a choice. He would fire up his own engines and go there himself, now. Except he couldn't go there, because he still didn't know where *there* was. What he needed were coordinates. He said, "Evangeline."

She had her nose in the cabinets, looking for teabags. She turned and said, "Hm?"

"Do you know anything about the Gates of Heaven?"

She abandoned the cupboard and turned so she was facing him, no longer bustling but still and watchful. "The what, sorry?" He saw her glance to her right, at the knife rack, and to her left, at the door, and of course the question had scared her, put that way out of the blue, because psychos roamed the earth, even dressed as policemen. He explained there was a place Scottie had described to him the other day, and he needed to find it, fast, that was all. Did she have any idea?

Her shoulders relaxed, and she shook her head. "No. But tell me more. Maybe I can help."

Dion ploughed backward through that casual conversation at the Old Town Pub. "It's a place up on a mountain somewhere. It's got a great view. It's open to the skies. Scott wants his ashes scattered there when he dies. Ring any bells?"

"Oh, the place with the hubcaps?" she said.

"Hubcaps? Like a wrecking yard?"

"No, hubcaps like stuck on this big log arch thing. We buried the red-tail there."

This was hardly what he needed right now, more random puzzle bits. "The what?"

She said, "The red-tail, the hawk with the broken wing, last fall. We couldn't save it, and it died, and Scottie had a truck then, so we went up to the place with the hubcaps. He didn't call it the Gates of Heaven, far as I know, but it's something he'd do, Mister Schmaltz. He said he was going to build a cabin there, but raising the two posts and decorating them was about as far as he got. Anyway, he wanted to bury the bird. That was before the ground froze solid, right? So, great, except he wanted to bury it right on the edge there where its soul could soar free, blah-blah-blah, and he wanted me to stand with him as he did so and say prayers, but it was too scary, the edge, way too far down, eh? Made me dizzy. So he did it himself. He's not afraid of heights. He says he's got Mohawk blood in him that makes him not afraid of heights, but I don't believe him. It's wishful thinking. He's whiter than I am, and I am very white."

Dion was weeding words as she spoke, as best and as fast he could. He said, "This hubcap place, is it up the Matax trail, up that way somewhere?"

"No, no. It's a whole different mountain. It's over here." She poked the air to her left.

The Hazeltons were surrounded by mountains, so it wasn't a helpful poke. "D'you have a map? Could you show me where it is?"

She didn't have a map. He brought the one printed for tourists from his vehicle and flattened it on the kitchen counter, and Evangeline's pearly pink fingernail showed him it was pretty well just across the highway from the entrance to the Bell 3. An old logging road that didn't have a name, far as she knew.

"You take this road called McLeod, past this ranch, and then about five miles along there's a sign on your left warning people about logging trucks, and you take that. It's steep and gravelly, but not too bad, you don't need a four-by or anything…."

Her finger travelled up the mountainside, ended at more or less where she thought the plateau was located, and marked it with an X for him in ballpoint. "East Band," she said.

"What's that?"

"Scottie called it East Band. I don't know, East Band mountain, or road. He just said East Band."

When she was done, he told her to wait there. Out in his car he phoned directly to Jayne Spacey, his point person for the night, and told her where he was, at Scott Rourke's residence, and where he was going, up to a lookout on a logging road past McLeod, in an area possibly called East Band. He told her that he needed backup, because he believed Scott Rourke was up there with Frank Law, and it could be a dicey situation.

"What, where?" she said.

He looked at the map, so little of it marked with names. The lookout wasn't a tourist hotspot, and there was nothing to distinguish it from the rest of the green. There was no *East Band* that he could see. "I can't explain everything right now," he said. "But Evangeline Doyle's here. She'll give you directions, or maybe she can just take you out there. That would be better." He thought a moment, staring at his map, struggling through the logistics as the clock ticked. If the team had to come out to Rourke's trailer to get Evangeline, there would be a good half hour wasted, considering the road leading to the area she had pointed out started somewhere up Highway 37, not up Kispiox Road. The closest point between the detachment and the East Band, as he saw it, was Old Town.

He said, "I'll leave her at the Black Bear Lodge. You can meet her there. Get a team together. I'll go up ahead and see what I can find out, and wait there for backup. I'm not sure if Rourke is armed. You have to move fast on this. I don't know what exactly I'm headed into."

"Yes, fine," Spacey said.

He shut his phone and jogged back to the trailer to get Evangeline. She sat in the passenger seat and he fired the engine, aware that it was all wrong, somehow, him and Spacey, the games they were playing and the dynamite they had underfoot. But in this case she would have no choice but to act, and he could hardly sit here mulling it over anyway. Rourke had at least an hour's head start, and Dion was almost certain that if Frank wasn't dead already, all in the name of mercy, it was just a matter of time.

Twelve

THE GATES

THE SKIES WERE NO LONGER a weird, writhing pink but black velvet spangled with stars. He found McLeod Road, no problem, passed a ranch, and about five miles farther found a logging road jotting off his left, with a brown government sign warning about logging trucks. So far Evangeline had it all dead right.

The road started good and flat, and his high beams cut a white path before him as he sped along, exposing so many blurry kilometres of frozen gravel. Then it began to slant uphill, the grade increasing until the engine had to clear its throat and change gears.

The last of the ranch lands fell behind and the wilds closed in fast, and he became aware of his isolation, and almost worse than what he couldn't see before him was what he could, caught in the periphery of his lights, the flanks of nightmare forests. Something loomed in the headlights bigger than a deer and flashed away as he jumped on the brakes and slid into a spin across gravel and ice.

He sat breathing hard till his heart slowed, straightened out the vehicle, and carried on.

The road branched, and he braked at the unmarked crossroads and swore. Evangeline hadn't mentioned any branching. He left the car idling and went around to the back to dig out a reflective marker to leave for the team to know which branch he'd gambled on: the left.

From here the gravel steepened, deteriorated to ruts, and forced him to a crawl, and he knew he'd lost the race. It was time to find a good place to turn around, go back and wait at the crossroads for the backup that was bound to be just minutes behind him. Twenty minutes, he figured, if Spacey had jumped to it.

A fairly good place to turn around came up, but he passed it, thinking the next would be even better. Another chance didn't seem to come up, and he kept climbing the narrow road, higher and higher, alternately accelerating and braking, swerving to avoid the potholes, suspension jouncing crazily. When the gravel levelled out and gleamed away ahead of him, a pale blue ribbon touched with ice, he made a deal with himself that he would travel up this stretch as far as it went, and soon as it got rutty again he would turn back.

A kilometre into the stretch his headlights glanced against something man-made, off the road to his left. He pulled over again, this time shutting off engine and lights so the night's blackness invaded his lungs and made it hard to breathe.

Turning on the flashlight only made the blackness worse, so he flicked it off again. He backlit his wristwatch to show the time, calculated his backup ETA once more, tried his radio, got nothing but static, waited another full thirty seconds, then left the car, and with light on full blast headed toward the object downslope that had caught his headlights.

The object, as he'd thought, was a vehicle that had driven off the road across the dead grasses of a broad clearing, churning the snow and leaving twin tracks, and yes it was an old green Jeep. Frank's wheels. He touched the hood and found it cool but not icy. All doors were locked. There was nothing of interest visible inside. The footprints, two sets, headed off into the woods toward an opening in the trees. If he could read anything in the tracks, they seemed unhurried. Two friends ambling along.

He called out Frank's name, and Rourke's, and listened. This was where he would post himself, then, and wait for backup. Again he backlit his watch, and it dawned on him that there was something wrong with that ETA. He tried his cellphone again and found again no reception. That was what mountains did, threw walls up between towers, killed the signals.

And now he felt so tiny and alone, here in the vastness of the night. Grasses rustled, branches swished, wood creaked, but nothing in all those sounds warned him of company. The two friends were long gone. He could stand here and freeze, or he could return to the car and head back down the mountain, or he could follow those tracks. The risk, as he saw it, was moderate. Rourke didn't have a gun, at least not registered, and he, Dion, did.

The tracks didn't lead far. The trees formed a thick canopy that kept snow off the trail, and there were no signs of passage, leaving only the path itself as a guide.

The path was decent at times and at times became nothing, leaving him to cross boulders along the brink of what looked like a bottomless pit in his torch beam. When he'd gotten past the big rocks, the hillside dipped, and he could just make out the trail angling across its face. No footprints still, and he wondered again if he was going the wrong way. His feet propelled him downward in jerking strides through scrub and loose shale, until his passage caused a small avalanche and he lost his footing and went down in a slither, onto knees, then butt, then back, trying to dig in his heels as brakes but his weight carrying him down till some jagged obstruction brought him to an abrupt stop. Not just abrupt, but painful, and whatever had blocked his fall was sharp against his body. Worse, his flashlight had flown from his chilled grip. He lay still, eyes squeezed shut, listening to rocks clattering downhill.

The silence resettled, except for his own gasps. The pain drove up through his torso, flaring at his right side, and he eased upright and explored the area by touch. Something, a ragged branch stub probably, had ripped through his patrol jacket and gouged him. His hand came away wet.

For a minute he stayed where he was, in case the wound was fatal. According to plan, he tried to make his last moments not so lonely. Shivering, eyes closed, he imagined Kate leaning over, kissing him gently on the mouth. He waited a moment longer, still shivering. He opened his eyes and looked around. Down the slope a ways and stuck under a bush was a patch of light. He moved sideways and downward until he had the flashlight in hand again. He crawled back up to the path, got to his feet, used the light to check his wound. Not fatal, he decided. Hardly worth a bandage. Just an added aggravation in a difficult situation.

The path took him downward some distance farther and ended at a plateau of tall grasses poking up through the rain-tattered snow, and the sky opened before him into a dome, not quite black but a solemn midnight blue, and across the length of a football field, maybe, was the brink. He couldn't see it but could feel it, a hollowness, a near silent roar that told of empty space. This, he was sure, was the edge of the vista that had made Evangeline dizzy.

And there were voices, far away but distinct. They came from the brink, he believed, carried to him on the wind. He cast his light downward then flicked it off, and as he walked forward and as his eyes adjusted, a structure became visible, a hundred metres distant now, rough timbers raised to create a small silhouette against the sky. The hubcapped arch, the Gateway to Heaven. The voices came from there, and toward them he walked. He had found Frank Law, and since backup had screwed up, it was up to him to bring the guy back to town. Which he would do, no problem. He wasn't dead yet.

* * *

At half past ten Constable Spacey phoned with news for Leith. She was calling from the Black Bear Lodge, she said. She was talking to an Evangeline Doyle, the name ringing a bell faintly in Leith's mind. "I've notified Giroux and central dispatch," she said. "Dion called in an hour ago with some info, but he was in some kind of rush and didn't give me much to go on, so I wasted a hell of a lot of time trying to figure out what he was after. He mentioned Scott Rourke's girlfriend, Evangeline Doyle, so I tracked her down. She's here with me now at the Lodge, and she's saying Frank's gone up the Kispiox Range with Rourke, and that he might be in danger. Their destination is a bit convoluted, but I've got it pinpointed on a forestry map. I think it's called the East Band logging road. We've got to proceed with caution, sir. I think Dion's gone up ahead to see if he can find anything, but like I said, he wasn't too clear on the phone, and we only spoke briefly. I told him not to approach the subjects, to wait for backup. I suggest you get reinforcements together and we meet at the Black Bear parking lot. It's the closest landmark to the East Band I can think of to muster."

It was a lot to take in. Leith caught the gist, checked his watch and said, "All right, thanks. We'll be there soon as possible. Stay in touch."

* * *

There was no way he could walk in silence here, in the receding snow and the brittle grasses, but it didn't matter. The wind created a din across the bare patches of meadowland, and even if he wanted to call out and warn them of his presence, which was maybe the smarter move, he couldn't. Not yet. Only when he'd made it to a stone's throw from the two men he could make out the odd word fluttering back, and he could delineate against the blue-black their vague shapes bulked out by winter coats, both huddling, both wearing caps. He stopped to observe them, to get a handle on what was happening here. One man was seated on a bench between the hubcapped posts, his back to Dion, the other just barely recognizable as Scott Rourke. Rourke stood before the seated man and occasionally paced.

A small object passed between the men from time to time. A flask, Dion supposed. There was no snarl of anger in the voices, and maybe he'd been all wrong about Frank being in danger. As the breeze died down, he could make out broken conversation, Frank's voice, saying, "Too late for that. Lenny knows. They all know. Must have the bloodhounds out by now."

Rourke said something, broken by distance but patched together in Dion's mind to "We can work it out. I know the land. We got a whole network of friends. Have faith."

Frank had a strong voice, louder than Rourke's and twice as rude, and it carried well. "Yeah, like that dick pal of yours, Morris," he said. "What a warrior, long as there's beer in his belly and no cops in sight. Cops knock on the door, and suddenly his casa is no longer our casa. Anyway, we sure as shit can't stay here. I'm freezing my balls off, and I tell you, jail's starting to look kinda nice."

Rourke's voice spiked in anger. "Jail is never nice. It's hell. Haven't you heard a word I've said? It's hell on earth, and it'll kill you."

"Yeah, well, you do the crime —"

Rourke's interruption was harsh but too fragmented to hear. Then came silence. Then the rushing wind again, and the grasses fretted and flailed. Sheltered by the dark, Dion had a feeling that if he spoke now, the situation, peaceful as it seemed, would whip out of control, would possibly snap. He took a sideways stance, sighted down his pistol, and lowered it again. No chance. The two men had huddled closer together and become a solid blot. He moved forward a few paces with a vague plan: get close enough, beam his light, aim, and shout a warning. Get them both away from the cliff. It was the cliff that made him nervous. That and the heavy object Rourke was now holding loose in one hand, which wasn't a wine bottle, as he'd first believed. From the shape of it, and the relationship between hand and object, he believed it was a weapon. Gun, large hunting knife, or mallet. But probably gun.

Rourke made a turning motion and Dion dropped to his haunches. He heard Rourke say something about love. "You know what, Frank? It's all about love. All about love, little brother."

Frank said something that was whipped away by the wind, and Rourke spoke louder, making his point with passion. "I love all you guys. You're family to me. Always remember that."

It was the booze talking. Rourke had gotten himself tanked for courage, and it was strumming on his emotions, which was bad news, with drop-away cliffs and guns in the mix. And if it wasn't Dion's imagination, there was a note of farewell in those words.

Did Frank hear it too?

By now, Dion hoped that backup had gotten lost and would stay lost, because the situation had become fragile before his eyes. A swarm of officers now would just light the fuse. Rourke was on his feet again, pacing, and

Frank stood too, and instead of wandering into a safer zone, as Dion hoped, he moved closer to the madman, and there they stayed on the brink.

Rourke wouldn't push his friend over, Dion believed. That would be too cruel. He'd just take aim, when Frank wasn't looking, and splatter his brains to oblivion. And the moment was now, Frank taking in the view, Rourke's gun arm lifted, rigid at the elbow, pointed at the back of that man's skull, and it was like watching porcelain fall. Dion levelled both arms, torch and gun, and moved, three strides forward with a bellow that seemed to come from elsewhere, not himself: "*Scottie, stop!*" And the dynamics changed again, and it was a terrible lining up of bodies, both men frozen in his flashlight beam, Frank by the cliff, turned in surprise, partially cut off from view by Rourke at centre stage, gaping, white-faced, Dion lunging forward over rough terrain toward a handgun now aimed straight at his face.

He retreated a step and stopped. He raised both hands, and the light beam went up too, and all went dark, leaving Rourke a cardboard cut-out against the sky.

"Dion?" Rourke shouted. "What the fuck are you doing here?"

Dion shouted back, not at Rourke but Frank. "Move it, now. He's got a gun. Get away from the cliff."

As seemed to happen in Dion's world these days, things went from bad to worse. With bewildering speed, Rourke turned and seized the younger man by the scruff of the neck, it looked like, but it was probably his coat, and yanked him toward him into a chokehold. Just like in the snapshot, but without the sunshine or smiles.

"Oh, man," Rourke said now, more a whine than a roar. "You don't know what you've done here. He was going to go out painless. He wasn't going to know what hit him, you dumb shit. Look what you done."

Dion was doing just that, looking at what he'd done, and he felt that familiar slide of ice through his veins. He'd put Frank Law in a noose, gun muzzle against his temple, inches from a deadly fall. He watched Frank fight the grip, saw Rourke totter a bit, find his footing and hold fast, pure sinew, a wannabe Mohawk, a man not afraid of heights.

"I don't understand," Dion called out. He had knitted the plan together on the long drive up, custom designed for Scott Rourke, who was the home-grown religious type, rabid, reflexive, fiercely protective. Unless he had it all wrong, and having it wrong was a big possibility too, Rourke would rather see Frank dead than raped and ravaged in jail for the next twenty years. He called out, "He's not going to jail, Scott. You got it wrong. He didn't kill Kiera. We got a new lead on a guy, and it's not Frank, and it's not Rob either. It's one of Rob's employees. We have the guy locked up tight, man."

The air cracked at his left, and he dropped to a crouch and froze. The bullet had whistled past his ear, he could swear it was Rourke's way of saying "Don't bullshit me." He hitched his flashlight to his belt and stayed crouched. *Stretch this out*, he told himself. Things had shifted again, and yes, backup would be good now. They might not save the day, but they would resolve matters fast enough.

He could hear Rourke saying sorry to Frank, and he thought he heard a click, and he definitely heard Frank's yell of fear, almost a shriek, and it got him up out of his crouch to give it one last try, no longer a hostage negotiator talking but a pal to the rescue. "C'mon, Scott. We can sort this out. It's not the end of the world. You need help, and I can help you get it. And by the way, Frank wants to live as much as you and I. Right?"

"Frank doesn't know what he wants," Rourke shouted. "That's the problem, isn't it?"

Dion breathed hard. His options were running low, and a last-ditch plan had sprung to mind, and it was a shitty one. Worse, it was comical. But it was all he had, his last grenade. He raised his voice once more, trying for an emphasis he was not trained for. "Don't be an idiot, Scottie. You want to protect him? Well, guess what. I care too, and a lot more than you do."

If nothing else, Rourke would lose his train of thought, and that would buy some time. Rourke's response was angry but puzzled. "Hey? What d'you mean?"

"I mean I don't want him going to jail, and I have my reasons that are none of your business. And I'm going to keep him out of jail if it kills me, and you're going to help me by taking the rap. Right? I also have the means, and all you gotta do is hear me out."

He had Rourke's interest. The man's face lifted, tuned in, leery but wanting to hear more. "Don't know what the hell you're talking about here, Dion. Explain yourself, and make it fast."

Frank made a gagging noise, his boots scrabbling against the rocks and grit and grasses on the lip of a chasm. Dion could hear pebbles cascading, falling away into the abyss. He called out, "I'm not saying anything till you swear you'll take the rap for him. Would you do that? You love him enough to trade your soul for his?"

"'Course I would. Any day."

This was better than Dion expected. No bullets this time, but an actual dialogue. "Great, then I can make him get away with it. I can plant evidence. He'll get six months for being accessory after the fact, probably on probation. He can do that easy. But you'll go down for the murder itself. I'll see to it."

Rourke soaked up the information and then was bellowing again. "Why? Why would you do that? I don't get you. You're playing with my head here."

"I said I have my reasons," Dion bellowed back. "Take it or leave it."

Rourke seemed to lose patience and yanked Frank again, pulling him against him like a rag doll, cocking the gun against his skull, and again Frank cried out. Dion cried out too, the last resort, the punchline that would make him the laughingstock of the police community for years down the road. "I love him more than you ever will," he yelped. And cleared his throat and gave another hoarse shout. "You stupid bastard, that's why."

There. *Ha ha ha*, he had the asshole's undivided attention now. The muzzle lowered, and Rourke was staring his way. Dion spoke more calmly now, like a man who'd gotten a load off his chest, like there was nothing left but gentle persuasion. "I saw it in your eyes, Frank. You felt it too, didn't you? That night at the bar."

There was no night in the bar, no love at first sight. In fact, he hadn't seen the guitar man up close and in person until this very night. Frank made a noise, more a rodeo calf in distress than a man in love, but Rourke was diverted, still trying to get a handle on what he was hearing. "*You?* You have a thing for *Frankie*?"

"It's more than a thing," Dion said bitterly. "He's what gets me through my day. And I don't care if you don't feel the same for me, Frank. It doesn't change what I'm trying to do here. I'm going to get you off the hook, promise." He searched his mind for a handy catch-phrase, something gay-sounding, but drew a blank. He watched Frank struggle.

Rourke let loose a laugh. "Holy Jesus, and I thought you were into girls."

"You can't help what you're into. Let him go, and we'll talk it out, okay? We're all freezing to death, and we better get our story straight before we go back down that mountain."

"I can tell you one thing, Frankie's straight as an arrow," Rourke said. "Right, Frank?"

Frank snorted and kicked and tried to twist out of the older man's grip, but he was losing steam, starting to sag.

Dion was starting to sag too. Ridiculously, he still held gun in one hand, flashlight in the other, neither aimed anywhere meaningful. He looked at his own boots, inhaling the mountain air, trying to stay on track. It was the stress, the humiliation, the wound in his side. The grass and mucky snow beneath had a rotten earthy smell, and now that they'd all done shouting, there was quiet, and beyond that a muted conversation, millions of branches sawing together whenever the wind gathered force. And there was something else, too. Mountains were great auditoriums in the dead of night, and sound carried. He heard a distant grumble and knew what it was. Engines. Three or four gutsy V8s working upward at speed.

The timing was incredibly bad, too late and too soon. He raised his voice, which was worse than hoarse by now, breaking up like bad reception. "If you don't let him go, he's going to the pen, and he's going to end up with a scar like yours, but worse. Let him go. Let me save him. Only I can save him. I have an ironclad story for you to tell the cops, and long as you get it straight, this is going to work. But we have to get on it *now*."

The *now* was delivered in pure exhaustion and tired rage, designed to startle Rourke into action. Instead, Rourke become a dark, baffled silhouette, frozen in in-decision. Maybe he was having second thoughts about how much he loved Frank Law, if he was worth going to prison for. Maybe he just wasn't buying the lie, or maybe he was going back to the simpler Plan A, shoot the loved one to save him from grief.

Dion held out his arms. "Send him over here. You can do the time a lot better than he can. Nobody's going to mess with you, that's for sure."

"I think you're full of shit," Rourke said. "It's a trick, and a pretty sleazy one too."

One minute, two minutes, and they'd be coming down the ravine, and in a panic Rourke's trigger fin-ger would twitch, and blood would spray all over the hubcapped gates of heaven. Frank's blood. Frankly, Dion wasn't sure he cared any longer, or if so, why. Who was he trying to impress, now that he had nobody to impress? Not the RCMP, not Looch in his grave, not

Nadia from rehab, and not the old Indian Willy who thought they shared some kind of kinship but was dead wrong. He had nobody to impress, and what did it matter if Frank got a bullet in his head? In the spirit of resignation he told Rourke, "I'm coming forward so we can talk without yelling. Don't you fucking shoot me."

"I won't shoot you," Rourke said. "Just keep your hands up."

Gun holstered, flashlight slung in its loop, Dion linked chilled hands behind his head and stepped forward, coming close enough that Rourke's face became more than puddles of shadow. "I'm giving you my word, Scottie. All I want is for him to be free."

Rourke studied him with wonder, and with revulsion, and then something else creased his brow, some kind of understanding. "I feel for you, man," he said. "Being like that. Must be horrible."

"It is horrible." Dion reached out and touched Frank Law on the arm, claiming possession. Rourke released his chokehold, and Frank crashed to his knees. Dion helped him up and pulled him away from the madman, behind him to safety, and now that the danger was more or less passed, it crossed his mind almost irresistibly to whip out his own gun and put one through Rourke's face, if nothing else just to get back at him for all this crap he'd put him through tonight. Flying backward, Rourke would sail over the cliff. Soar free like the eagle he always wanted to be. And that would be that.

He said instead, "First off, you're going to have to break your alibi for the day Kiera died."

"I can do that," Rourke said.

"And I'm going to need your DNA."

"You're not getting my DNA how you're thinking, y'queer," Rourke said, but just joking.

"Spit into a baggie, that's all you have to do," Dion said. "Could you do me a favour and put that gun away? Makes me nervous."

"No chance," Rourke said. "You think I'm stupid?"

"I know you're stupid," Dion spat out, angrily, not wisely.

The engines were definitely there now, somewhere above, not loud but distinct. Rourke heard it too. "Cops," he said in a furious rasp, and his gun was up again, pointing at Dion. "You lying fucking cheating piece of shit."

"Wasn't me," Dion told him, too cold to care about the gun in his face, which he had come to realize wasn't going to discharge anyway. He just knew it. Probably wouldn't have discharged into Frank's skull either, and what he should have done, instead of charging like a fool to the rescue, was wait at the crossroads as he was supposed to, and these two fucking hillbillies would have finished their Scotch and returned down the mountainside, where they would have been arrested without incident. But he hadn't waited at the crossroads, and here he was in the middle of this big ugly mess he'd made, miles too late to go back, and so much explaining to do that it almost made his knees buckle. "They were going to track you down one way or another," he said. "Just be cool. They're going to arrest Frank, but they have nothing on him. I know the file. All they have is what Lenny's saying, but Lenny doesn't know anything, really, and he'll change his tune. So until Frank confesses, they have nothing, and long as he sticks to denial he's home free." He pulled something from his pocket, a granola bar wrapper he'd forgotten to dispose of, and held it out. "Spit into that."

Rourke did as he was told, and Dion pocketed the evidence that was supposed to dupe the entire North District Major Crimes Unit into a wrongful conviction. Rourke nodded at Frank, who was crouched down, massaging his neck, not returning the gaze. "Hear that, Frank? Don't stop denying, and you're home free, kiddo."

"Fucking maniac," Frank whispered, like his vocal cords were too sore to blare it out.

With no standing ovation for his grand performance, with nothing left to say, Dion puffed out a sigh and looked at the sky, and Rourke got the last word in, waving his gun. "One thing you better know, Constable Dion. You betray me, and I'll kill you. That I promise. I'll track you down and I'll kill you, and it'll be slow, and it will hurt."

Dion nodded. The engines had been purring into position up on the ridge, and now they were cut, and there came instead the telltale silence of a stealthy descent, peppered with discreet noises, the crunch of snow, the snap of ground cover and rustling of shrubs. He opened his eyes from a waking doze and said to Rourke, "Better throw your gun down, 'less you want to end it right here."

Rourke hesitated, maybe picturing that glorious showdown of his dreams, but his madness only took him so far into that imagined glory, and bottom line was he wanted to stay here, as most people did, eking it out until the last straw broke. Rourke leaned over and laid the gun in the grass. His hands were up as the team was still creeping forward. To speed things up, Dion might have shouted out to them, told them all was well, but he didn't. He was starting to flatline.

They materialized from the dark and took command of the situation, and he explained to David Leith in his SWAT-like gear that he'd put Scott Rourke under arrest for the murder of Kiera Rilkoff. Leith asked him about shots fired, but the question was not quite connecting. Dion knew only that he was cold, and told Leith so. Leith told him to hand over his firearm, and Dion did so. There was a party-like chaos now on the mountainside around him, lot of hubbub, Rourke being arrested, shouting something about Frank, Frank being arrested, shouting something about Rourke, and it was almost funny, until some kind of animal went screaming over Dion's head, a giant bat that was really just a piece of the sky flying off its axis. He raised an arm to fend it off, and when it was gone, so was the crowd, or most of it. A man's voice woke him from some distance, asking if he was coming or what?

He followed Leith up a difficult path, but not nearly so difficult as the one he'd taken earlier, and like everything else, he'd messed up his pathfinding and come the long way round. His feet took him into a clearing where the vehicles were parked. Engines were starting up, SUVs pushing off. He wasn't sure where Rourke had gone but knew somebody here must have the asshole under control. The ache in his side was now throbbing like a disco, and matching colours flashed behind his eyelids, red and blue and green. Leith asked him about keys, and he found them in his jacket pocket and handed them over. He was to ride with Leith back to the detachment, where he would give his statement. He wouldn't have to drive, and that was good news. He dropped into the passenger seat but found it wasn't the blessed relief he'd been hoping for. Folding himself into a seated position, the pain went from throbbing disco to mangling knife blades, and he felt the blood drain from his face.

He tried to keep his eyes open. The car woke, lurched, and was on its way. Leith spoke, but in a drone of foreign words. The car began its downhill journey, and with every jolt Dion felt warm liquid spurting from his midriff. He tried to pack the open wound by clamping his arm over it, but knew he'd been wrong, and it wasn't a minor scrape but a fatal split, and his guts were coming out. He was becoming a corpse even as he sat breathing the comforting warm automobile air and listening to Leith's intermittent drone.

This was what he wanted, to die in the line of duty, but he was desperately afraid. He was ice-cold and either very still or shaking hard, he couldn't say, even as he tried to look at his own hand. How would it all turn out without him? He should have written to Kate. Should have said sorry to Looch's widow. He should have been nicer, should have tried harder. Worst of all, maybe he'd been wrong about everything, and he'd been fighting his own shadow. Now that he was here at the end of the line, it was unbearably sad. He hoped he wasn't crying. The timing was wrong, that's all. Say something smart to Leith, he told himself. Something nice. He tried to speak, but nothing came out. He tried to raise an arm to wipe across his eyes, but lost the strength. The disco lights flared and went out.

* * *

Once they were on their way down the mountain, Leith launched into his lecture, not sure why he bothered. "She says she told you to wait for backup. You know what backup means? You want me to spell it out for you?"

Silence.

"Anyway, you're going to have to get it together. Rourke's gun's been fired, and I have to know who fired it and where the bullet went. How are you doing?"

Dion looked at him briefly, blankly, and didn't respond.

Feels stupid, Leith thought. *And so he should. Ballsy, going after Rourke on his own, and more than a little bewildering. But ultimately just stupid.*

Leaving the mountain behind him, upping the speed on straight flat rubble now, Leith glanced sideways and noted by the console lights that his passenger was leaning heavily back now, staring a bit too serenely at the windshield, that he was breathing shallow, that his arm was pressed across his torso in a peculiar manner. On a second glance he saw that the pale grey lining of Dion's patrol jacket, partially flipped back and visible, was black with a migrating wetness, and with a start he realized where that bullet had gone, and why he wasn't getting any answers.

"You've been shot," he said, hitting the strobes and siren toggles. "Hang on. I'll get you to emerg."

Ten minutes later, he pulled into the ambulance-only bay at the Wrinch Memorial, and a pre-notified team rushed out with a gurney, portable oxygen, and an arsenal of blood-staunching supplies. Dion was out cold now, unresponsive. He was wrangled from the car by two large medics, laid on a gurney and wheeled into the hospital with measured speed.

"Why didn't he say something?" Leith asked the nurse as he followed. "Why didn't he just bloody mention, oh, by the way, Dave, I've been shot?"

The nurse didn't know why, so he asked, more to the point, "Is he going to live?"

She couldn't answer that either. But things were crazy enough tonight, and Leith was needed elsewhere. He left a card at the nursing station with a request that they call the office as soon as they had news on the constable's condition, then rushed back to his car to head back to where the action was unfolding, anxious not to miss a beat.

* * *

There was to be no action for the rest of the night, as it turned out, because nobody wanted to talk, on either side of the thin blue line. So Scott Rourke and Frank Law were thawed out, fed, and given the usual one-size-fits-all coveralls and scratchy blankets for their night in the New Hazelton holding cells, which was full house by now. Leith went to his room at the Super 8 for a few hours' sleep, and the few hours went by too fast; his alarm went off at six thirty, and he was up and at it again.

There was a lot to sort out today, and as he ate breakfast in the motel's diner he tried to compartmentalize the problems in his mind. First problem, he now had three confessors to the killing of Kiera Rilkoff. Ironic, as he'd mentioned to Giroux last night, that three low-life bastards all wanted to claim responsibility for taking the life of one kind and talented young woman with a golden future. And they all claimed she was dear to them.

Giroux said it was plain that all three men knew what had happened to some extent or another, and each was trying to protect the others, and sooner or later the truth would emerge, whether they liked it or not. Just gotta keep hitting them till something breaks.

"Nothing like good ol' grassroots police tactics," Leith had told her, and added his own grassroots opinion that he hadn't seen such a schmozzle of false confessions in his life, and if he had his way they'd all do maximum time.

But in the end only one would face the most serious charge, and that man, at least, would get the royal treatment, twenty-five years eating over-boiled peas for dinner, staring at cement, and having a good long ponder on where he'd gone wrong.

His second current problem, taken as a thing in itself, was yesterday's incident on the East Band lookout, which had whipped itself up out of nowhere like a prairie twister, ending in two arrests and one officer down. How had Dion got himself up there alone? Wasn't he supposed to be grid-searching the new subdivision by the 7-Eleven? How was a wallflower like him always getting in the middle of the polka?

No, he revised. Not a wallflower. A thistle.

The third problem, taken as another thing in itself, was the timing of Jayne Spacey's call to him last night — ten thirty, as he'd logged it — mustering backup to charge up the East Band. He had nothing but a suspicion and a quick glance at the roster to go on, but something just didn't jive there, and would need looking into.

But first things first. It was seven thirty, bright and early, a great time to talk to three killers. He decided to start with his least favourite person in the world, Scottie Rourke. Rourke had twice declined the offer of counsel, but Leith wouldn't go forward with this until the prisoner had spoken to somebody, so it had happened. Rourke had been duly warned to shut the hell up and happily was apparently going to ignore that advice and spill all.

Leith popped a caffeine pill and went to the interrogation room, where he found Rourke wound up, twitchy, fierce-eyed. The two men sat face to face, and Rourke agreed he'd spoken to counsel and knew his rights. Leith gave him free rein to speak, which worked well with madmen, and Rourke told of encountering Kiera on the Saturday of her disappearance. She hadn't driven by but stopped to say hello. He'd made a grab for her, all in fun, and she'd slapped him, and he'd seen red, and next thing you know he had his hands around her neck.

"Where's her body?" Leith said.

"I buried her where you'll never find her," Rourke said.

Leith wondered if it was the same place Rob Law had buried her, where they'd never find her too. He wondered where Frank Law would claim to have buried her next. He wondered if the Rilkoff family would ever get their murdered daughter back. He said, "Without her body, I'm finding it hard to believe you actually killed her, Scott. And I've got a long day ahead of me, so —"

"You got piles of evidence against me," Rourke said. "You don't need her body. I want her to stay where I left her, out of respect for her, believe it or not. 'Cause I buried her right. She wasn't dumped like garbage. You can tell her folks that."

Oh, they will be immeasurably comforted, Leith almost said. Instead he asked, "And what evidence is that, that we have piled against you?" Already his pen was beating a fast tattoo on the desktop. He stopped it by crossing his arms and stopped his foot tapping by stretching out his legs and crossing the ankles.

"I choose to withhold that for now," Rourke said. "That's your job, to find it, I'd say."

"All right. So why are you telling me this?"

"Because it's fantastic. It's a comedy of errors. Rob and Frank each think the other did it, so they're trying to save each other's necks, which is insane because neither one should be going through this hell, when I'm the one who did it. Me." Rourke thumped himself on the chest. "That's why I'm telling you this. I have that much decency left in me to admit what I done, if it means saving those two bozos from themselves."

"Why did you and Frank go up to the lookout last night?"

"To talk."

"Your good friend Morris Fernholdt says you came by yesterday evening, you and Frank, and wanted to hide out there for a few days. He sent you packing. Why would Frank need to hide out if he hadn't done anything wrong?"

"Frank was just trying to help me out. He's a good man. Loyal."

"Sure. That's a nice .22 you got, by the way. Diamondback. Kind of rare specimen, isn't it?"

"They're still common as Ford F-150s, actually."

"Maybe. But far and few between up here in the sticks. How'd you come upon it?"

"Friend of a friend. An estate acquisition. Fifteen years ago, at least."

"Interesting. We'll have to do some tracking, find out when it went off the radar."

"I got hold of it before the radar was invented, sir, and before I got my firearms ban, by the way. It was an oversight. I guess I just stashed it away and forgot about it. Just doing some spring cleaning the other day and came upon it."

"And took it with you to talk with Frank on the lookout?"

"That was for cougars."

"You shot a cop, Mr. Rourke."

"Huh?"

"And since you're sitting here readily confessing to one homicide, is there anything else you should get off your chest? We got the gun, we'll get the riflings. We'll rummage the archives, and any place that gun shows up, every little gas station holdup, we'll have to assume you were there too. So save yourself the trouble of a bunch of long boring interrogations and give me the list now."

Rourke was looking appalled, and like all his emotions, it came across with exquisite exaggeration, Daffy Duck accused of murder. "What d'you mean, I shot a cop? I never shot a cop."

Leith's arms and ankles uncrossed themselves, and he sat forward. "Something wrong with your short-term memory? You shot him last night, right in the gut. He bled all over my car, and he's dying in the hospital as we speak. And you know what? Killing a cop is even worse than your regular civilian homicide."

Rourke jerked back in his chair. "You talking about Constable Dion here? I never shot him. Never."

Leith saw outrage, and it puzzled him. He didn't want to sound puzzled, so he said savagely, "Isn't that weird, because Frank's telling us the exact opposite." This was an on-the-spot invention, because he hadn't talked to Frank Law yet, but he'd never felt bad about lying to catch a shithead. He raised his voice as Rourke clambered to his feet in indignation and barked, "Sit the hell down."

"I shot over his head," Rourke said, back in his chair, still appalled and somehow hurt. "I never aimed anywhere near the jerk. I wouldn't do that."

There followed a dead spot in the interview. Rourke moped. Leith sat tapping his pen again, studying the man's face and wondering.

He left the room to talk to Giroux and found instead a big bear at her desk, Mike Bosko, who was supposed to have caught the sheriff shuttle to Prince George this morning but apparently hadn't. Like a bad rash, he'd take his time fading away.

Bosko looked up, smiled, said, "How's it going with Rourke?"

"He says he didn't shoot Dion," Leith told him. "And he's full of hot air on every point except this. Are we sure it's actually a bullet that got him?"

Giroux stepped in, sparing Bosko the trouble of saying *I don't know* in his long-winded way. "Not a bullet, guys," she said. "Just heard from the hospital. He woke up long enough to confirm what the doctor suspected. It was a jab, not a bullet. And self-inflicted."

Naturally, Leith thought.

The same blast of contempt had maybe crossed Giroux's mind, the way she tossed her hands. She said, "Seems he impaled himself on a branch during a fall. Lost some blood, but no vital organs. Exhaustion is the diagnosis, few stitches and rest is the cure. So he'll be okay, but we can't talk to him till they say so."

"Well, they better say so fast," Leith said.

On the other hand, he wasn't too concerned about what Dion had to say. Frank's confession had been in the works last night, and the East Band was just an aggravating little diversion masterminded by that idiot Rourke. Now they were back on track, and Frank was being brought in for his turn at the podium, and Leith felt cautiously optimistic that this would be the grand finale. The interview that would close the file forever.

* * *

Things seemed to go well, at first. Frank Law, in a choppy, solemn way, told Leith that after a day of reflecting, sitting up at Sunday Lake with Lenny, chilled to the bone, he'd known what he had to do: come clean with what had happened to Kiera, and for the first time in a long time Leith's hopefulness marched forward. He nodded encouragement to this intelligent young man who could see the writing on the wall, who was going to do the right thing now and save everybody a lot of time and trouble and admit he'd done it.

Frank took a deep breath and said, "Scott Rourke killed her."

Leith went through the motions in his mind of slamming the table and howling rude words at the heavens. But only in his mind. He gave Frank his steadiest gaze, rimed with ice, and waited for more.

The not-so-intelligent young man nodded, something earnest in his demeanour, almost sweet, and Leith thought about juries and their fallibility. "Ask him," Frank said. "He'll tell you."

So the long way around they would have to go. Some cases were quick wraps, others were like playing musical chairs in a fevered dream. Leith put Kiera aside for the moment, made a note to himself, and got onto the more recent past, asking about the shootout on the East Band lookout.

"Not much to tell," Frank replied. "I'd just dropped Lenny back at home, was on my way here, to tell you guys everything. But met Scottie, he was heading home on his bicycle, and I made the mistake of stopping to say hi, and he said he wanted to talk about something, so he hopped in my Jeep and we went up to the lookout."

"Long ways to go for a chat in the middle of the night."

"Around here, man, logging roads are entertainment."

"You went straight up the mountain, then?"

Frank shrugged uncomfortably. "First we went over to Morris's place. Scottie was saying he'd be needing a place to lie low for a while. He has this idea that he's got friends all over the planet who'll hide him till the heat blows over. I think he's kind of delusional."

"You think? Well, what happened at Morris's?"

"Cops knocked on the door, but we'd seen 'em coming, and Scottie yanked me into the back bedroom. Morris got rid of 'em, then he came and told us the cops were looking for me and he wanted us to get lost in a big way. So we did. Went on up to the lookout, and Scottie had some hooch, and I wanted to get bombed, so we went to the arch and were just talking about shit when the constable jumped out at us from nowhere and was yelling at Scottie to let me go. And suddenly Scottie's got me in a chokehold with his gun shoved up my nostril, so I don't know, but I think that cop had things a bit backward. Anyway, I can tell you, I was pretty damn confused."

Which makes two of us, Leith thought. "So it was some kind of standoff?"

"Don't ask me what it was. Scottie would never shoot me. He's not that kind of guy. Anyway, him and the cop yelled back and forth for a while, and Scottie fired at the cop but didn't hit him, and finally he let me go." The young man pulled a face, brows up, mouth turned down, a mime portraying bewilderment.

"What happened between the gunshot and him letting you go? What changed his mind?"

Frank's stare went distant, and Leith thought he was blushing, but it was maybe just the central heat parching the air. A big chunk of the story had just been skipped over, it seemed, and Leith waited, but Frank didn't carry on and fill in the blanks. He said, "I don't know why he changed his mind. Probably because there was a cop telling him to let me go, so he did. I still can't believe Scottie killed Kiera."

"Neither can I," Leith said. "And I don't. It's time to cut the bullshit, Frank. We all know Rourke didn't kill Kiera. The truth will come out one way or another, and it'll be a hell of a lot better for your own interests if it comes from you, here, now. Her family is waiting for closure. You're not a bad person. You know what's right."

Frank hung his head, pressing fingertips against his eyelids. After a minute of the hung head, he said he was going to heed his lawyer's advice and say no more.

Leith took him back to cells and then joined Mike Bosko in the monitor room. Bosko was eating a sandwich and didn't look nearly as steamed as Leith felt. He said, "Well, you can hardly blame him for not looking the gift horse in the mouth."

What did that even mean? Leith said, "So that's it, then. We can't hold him. Rourke's going to claim responsibility, and unless we get something solid, we're going to have to go with it, right down the line till trial. Do I have all that right?"

Bosko shrugged. He put the sandwich aside and said, "There's something I want to ask you about. Let's go to the case room for a minute." He lumbered out of his chair and led the way. In the case room he sorted through folders, found one, flipped through statements, and folded the clipped pages back on one where he'd put a sticky note. The statement was of Chad Oman, and the handwriting was not Leith's, but Leith's scribe of the day, Constable Dion. Bosko put his finger on a notation appended to the end that was in Leith's handwriting and read it aloud. "'*Constable Dion suggests he's lying but can't say why.*' What's that about?"

Leith skimmed through the statement to refresh his memory. "I interviewed Oman," he said. "Dion's notes were useless, and he'd forgotten to press 'record,' so all he got was dead air. We ended up writing out the interview from memory. My memory, because he didn't have any. At the end he apologized for messing up, then added that he thought Oman was lying. I tried to get out of him what he meant, lying about what, and he couldn't elaborate. In the end I figured he was just trying to impress me, the old *newbie with keen intuition senses a witness is lying and breaks case wide open* scenario. I was going to ignore it altogether, but next day, when my hand wasn't so sore, I decided I'd better add that note. And that's about all I can tell you."

"Good thing you did," Bosko said. "Since as we now know, he's not a newbie at all. Right?"

Leith had to acknowledge something that had been niggling at him; maybe saving Dion's life made Leith his *guardian ad litem*, in a sense, or maybe it was just his own dislike of loose ends, but he needed to know. "What's going to happen to him?"

Bosko looked at him with interest. "The man's had a serious head injury. It wasn't something headquarters wanted to advertise, but it is something they need to monitor, and that's what they're doing, if it makes you feel better."

"Is that why you're here, to monitor one of your constables?"

Bosko grinned. "For one thing, he's not my constable. He left North Vancouver before I moved in, so we haven't crossed paths till now. For another, I wouldn't be flying halfway across the province and taking lodgings to watch one brain-damaged constable. Wouldn't be very cost-effective, would it? The locals in charge were supposed to send in regular reports, however, for the first six months, which they've been doing, but Renee didn't notice the letter that accompanied her temp, and Willoughby didn't stress the importance of the letter, so between them, he's kind of dropped off the radar. Kind of frightening, isn't it?"

Very, Leith thought. He crossed his arms, then uncrossed them and stuck his hands in his trouser pockets. When Bosko was reticent, it bothered him. When he was forthcoming, it bothered him even more. Bottom line, he still didn't trust the man or his agenda.

"I wouldn't worry about it," Bosko said. "We've got our eye on him. All right?"

It wasn't all right. Head injuries changed people, diminished them. Leith had never heard of a head injury improving on a man's powers or personality, and Dion was clearly no exception to the rule. Maybe he'd been a prodigy, as he claimed, but he was now just bad news. If he didn't get somebody else killed, he'd kill himself. Neither struck Leith as *all right.*

Bosko was looking at the document in question again. He said, "His abilities aside, do you have any idea what he thought Oman was lying about?"

Leith shook his head. "No clue."

"Then talk to Oman again, go over the same ground, and watch for tells. Get tough if you have to. And ask Dion what he recalls, soon as he's back in the now."

"How about I get Giroux to grill him?" Leith asked. "Whenever I talk to the man, I get these homicidal thoughts."

Bosko was amused, but only for a moment. "Seriously, I think you should deal with him yourself. I think you have a way with him. And try to be patient, Dave."

A way with him? Leith ground his teeth. He wasn't sure Constable Dion would ever be *in the now,* or could recall what he ate for breakfast, let alone the nuances of Chad Oman's veracity over a week ago. And now, thanks to that brain damaged cop's whimsical *I think he was lying* remark, he, Leith, was going to have to play bad cop with the drummer, a man who was quite possibly blameless, and that was a role he didn't relish. Yes, it rankled. His phone buzzed before he could put his resentment to words, and speak of the devil, it was the hospital calling to say Dion was ready to talk.

Thirteen

WHITE LIES

WAKING HAD BEEN BAD, but not hellish. Not like rising from the coma last year, when he'd dragged his own broken body through a dark, wet corridor for endless miles in pain, confusion, and bouts of genuine terror. This was easy, dry, bright, and the painkillers worked wonders. Dion sat on a straight-backed chair in his hospital room waiting for his ride from the hospital. His side hurt, but it was nothing next to the thudding in his chest. He rested his face in his palms, trying not to imagine the hilarity, and imaging it all the same. Frank had told all, by now, every last excruciating tidbit, and the story would have gone viral. They'd be laughing hard. Spacey would laugh hardest.

The thought of the story doing the rounds in this detachment and spreading to others, probably eventually reaching the world at large, sickened him, literally, and he limped into the bathroom and leaned over the throne, hands splayed on the tank, ready to barf up his hospital breakfast, whatever that had been. The nurse came up behind him as he stood contemplating the plumbing and asked if he was all right. He straightened, wiped his mouth, and accepted the glass of water she offered. Somehow the dizziness had passed, and so had the nausea, and even the rip in his side didn't seem so bad. Only the worry remained. "I'm okay," he told her.

"I don't think you are," she said.

She went to get him a couple of T3s, and he thought about fleeing the scene, walking, jumping on a bus, hitchhiking, anything, just getting out of there, fast. Cross the border, sink into anonymity, become a bearded street person.

But there was a hitch in that he had no jacket. They had taken it away, along with the uniform he'd been wearing during the farcical confrontation with Scott Rourke last night. He now wore the clothes somebody had brought in from his room at the Super 8, the winter-weight joggers and sweater he usually wore on his days off, the black leather Nike runners, and a scarf around his throat. The scarf he'd wrapped around twice, depressed.

"Hi there," Thackray said, poking his head around the door. "Ready to go?"

Ten minutes later they walked into the detachment, and Dion found it quiet inside, nobody laughing. Spacey was nowhere to be seen. Leith stood from his desk and said, "Hey, glad you're okay," then summoned him down the hall to the "soft" interview room.

They sat across from each other, like accuser and accused, and Leith said, "I really thought you'd caught a bullet. Took you down Code 3, man, made quite a scene."

"Yeah, sorry about that."

Leith seemed glad to be done with the small talk and got down to business, opening a file that turned out to be an interview with Chad Oman. He told Dion the date and time of the interview and asked Dion if he remembered it.

Of course Dion remembered it. He answered coldly. "Right, it was last week."

Leith read out what they had written out together at the end of that miserable interview, after the disaster with the recording device. He finished reading and said, "You told me you thought he was lying about something but couldn't remember what it was. But you were flustered then. Maybe now something's twigged, huh?"

Dion pulled the statement across the table and read it again, trying to put himself back in the moment, imagining the witness in the room. He couldn't remember what had prompted him to say Oman was lying. Oman had been loud, a fast talker, hard to track, and his own regrettable comment about lying had come out of him spontaneous as a sneeze.

He shook his head. "I don't know. There was that bit where Oman paused here, said something was funny, then wouldn't say what he thought was funny. Maybe it was there."

"That's kind of what I was thinking. But that's not really a lie, is it? At worst, that's holding something back."

"I don't know, then."

Leith looked far from shocked and closed the folder. Now it was time for another painful rehashing: what happened on the East Band last night. He let Dion run through the narrative first, no questions asked. Dion did his best and told what he could remember, which was just about everything, from picking up Evangeline, to spotting the abandoned bicycle, to the directions he'd gotten to the Gates of Heaven, to calling Spacey for backup. He told of his drive up the mountain, expecting reinforcements that didn't seem to be coming, his hesitation, and his ultimate decision to plough on. He told of his conversation with Scott Rourke, and his final ploy of giving Rourke a false motive for not wanting Frank Law to go to jail. Here he fell silent, unable to finish.

Leith said, "Yes? And what was that false motive?"

"I told him Frank and I were friends," Dion said. Which was the truth. Not the whole truth, but enough. He watched Leith's face, expecting he'd already got the punchline out of Frank and was just holding back the guffaw. But there wasn't even a smirk. Just an intense and skeptical gaze.

"And he believed it?" Leith asked.

Dion basked in relief for a moment. So Frank was just as embarrassed about the whole thing as he was and hadn't said anything about love at first sight or any of the rest. Maybe it would never come to light. He sat straighter and gave a shrug. "I guess Rourke believed me. He let Frank go. Then you and the others finally got there, and you know the rest. What took you so long, by the way?"

Leith skirted the question, saying, "Any idea why Scott Rourke wanted to blow Frank's head off in the first place?"

"Like I said, he thought Frank was going to jail. He wanted to preserve him from a fate worse than death."

"Honestly? Sounds like a stretch to me. How about he, Rourke, killed Kiera, and Frank knew it. Rourke thought Frank was going to report him, so he had to silence him."

Dion shook his head. "Everything we said up there pointed to a mercy kill. Or that's the way it looked to me at the time. I figured the only thing that might stop him was my promise that I'd keep Frank out of jail. For personal reasons. So I ad libbed."

"You think he would have actually shot him?"

"No, I don't," Dion said glumly. "I should have just sat at the crossroads and waited, and they'd have probably wrapped up their drinking party and come down and met us. But I did what I did, and what happened happened. I don't expect any medals. I'm just glad nobody got killed, because then I'd really be up to my neck in it, wouldn't I?"

Leith agreed. He said, "There's a lot more we have to talk about yet. You and Scott Rourke, and his girlfriend, Doyle. I don't know you've broken any rules, fraternizing with witnesses, but you've sure bent common sense out of shape. Pretty soon you're going to have to tell me all about it."

"Sure," Dion said. He felt unburdened, empty but free. It was all coming together, reaching a conclusion. Things were wrapping up, and he could walk away with few regrets. He thought about his watch, running slow, the source of all this mess. The watch lay on an icy riverbed now and would rust there till eternity. Looch was dead, which had its advantages, and Cloverdale was worlds away. Everything seemed good. He could breathe.

"But for now," Leith said, having ended the interview, turned off the tape recorder, and signed off on his notes, "We're going to have another chat with Chad Oman. I want you to sit in and pay attention, and maybe you'll catch it again, whatever you thought he was lying about the first time, for what it's worth. And just one more thing. You called Spacey last night, and we know the time of your call from the records. I just can't figure out how it took her an hour to get things moving. She says your message was garbled or unclear, and she had a helluva time trying to locate Evangeline and find out what was really going on. Any comment?"

"It wasn't complicated. I was clear as I could be. She doesn't like me, and she lets it get in the way. When can I get off this case and go back to Smithers? You must have it figured out by now, I'm not much help here."

Leith nodded. "I'll see if I can get you back on the road tomorrow. You might have to return to give further statements, but maybe we can get 'em over the phone. Now, go grab a bite, and I'll get Thackray to bring Oman in. Report back here at eleven twenty. Okay?"

He gathered his things and left the room. Dion remained for a few minutes, trying to program his watch to beep at eleven, giving himself a good margin of error, but couldn't get the sequence right. Too many buttons, too little brains. So he wrote it in ballpoint on his palm, "Oman 11:20." If that failed, he thought, he'd throw himself in the river too.

* * *

The band's drummer seemed to have lost weight since his first interview, and a good deal of vim, too. *But hey*, Leith thought, *reality's finally set in. Kiera's gone, and she's not coming back.* Before her disappearance, these kids were just embarking on an endless party, fun, fame, and good times. Now it was the brink of humdrum for Oman. A slow climb to department manager at the local Home Hardware. Two-inch nails and miscellaneous fasteners. Even without Kiera they could have carried on, led by Frank. Mercy Blackwood seemed to think it was possible, maybe even better, to carry on without Kiera. But now Frank was possibly going away too, and that left, what? Not much. Oman was just a drummer, and no matter how good he was, he would never be the next Ginger Baker.

Quite a shock to the system to lose all that in the space of two weeks.

Yet the guy seemed somehow okay with his lot when they first sat down, exchanging the small talk. Maybe he was a flat-bottomed boat, a survivor. Doggedly upbeat, with that off-centre smile on his round, healthy, brown face.

Dion sat in, as agreed. He looked physically unfit, still suffering from the stitches and the drugs, but he was doing his best to listen. Oman stuck faithfully to his story the first time around, and Leith could find no cracks to get a fingerhold in, to flip him upside down and get to his vulnerable side, so he did what he had to do, as rotten as it felt, and got mean. He eased into meanness with, "I hate to say it, Chad, but I'm finding it hard to believe what you're telling me here."

Oman looked stunned, and being a bit of a ham, he overdid it, eyes agog, mouth dropped open. "About what?"

"About Kiera leaving the house without her coat on, for one. It was a bitch of a cold day, as I remember it. Snow was bombing down. Temperatures well below zero, right?"

Oman's eyes roved the room and settled back on Leith with some indignation. "She was wearing a pretty good sweater. I figured she was going to jump in her

Rodeo, go to town, get something, come back. We're all of us born and raised in the snow, hey? So that's what I figured, she was just hopping out for something."

"So you clearly remember her leaving without a coat?"

"Yeah, I do. She turned around, put her hands in her front pockets, her jeans, like this, said see you later, or back soon, or something like that, and she stepped out backward, kind of, and shut the door. I can see it like it's happening right now."

"But when she arrived that day she came in wearing a coat, right?"

"I don't know. I got a pretty good photogenic memory, but to a point, eh."

Leith didn't break the flow to correct the kid's vocabulary and went on ramping up the tension. "It was a rough day. Everyone was upset, including Frank. Kiera didn't leave on her own, did she? Frank went with her."

"Yes, sir, she left on her own."

"You sure of that?"

"Yes, sir."

And there's the tell, Leith thought. The *yes sir, yes sir, three bags full, sir.* His own bad cop routine was a well-worn thing, simple and not very imaginative, but effective, especially with the young and the inexperienced. It was the arctic blast stare-down. He stared Oman down with icicles and said, "You know where this is going to lead, Chad? You don't tell me the truth, it's not going to be good."

"Yeah, how so?" Oman snapped back, maybe more aware of his rights than Leith gave him credit for, maybe knowing where threats and inducements would lead, eventually. Nowhere.

Leith crossed his arms but toned down the bullying. "How so in that you'll be charged with obstruction, is how. It's not the kind of thing you can wiggle out of, you sitting here telling me she left alone, then later it comes out she didn't. You're going to turn on your heels then? How?"

"It's what I saw," Oman stated.

"You actually watched her walk out the door alone?" Leith asked, and held up a warning hand. "Here's where you better be damned sure you're telling the truth, because here's where there's no going back. Understand?"

Oman hesitated. He said, "Yeah, she walked out the door alone, cross my heart and hope to die."

"Where was Frank when she walked out the door alone? You might want to cross your heart again, now."

Oman was silent. Leith watched him, still as a rock, like he would sit here still as a rock all day and all night, if that's what it took.

Oman said, "I think he …"

"He what, Chad?"

"I think he might have stepped out too, a minute or two before her. For a smoke, maybe. But I'm not a hundred percent on that."

"Right," Leith said. He was buzzing within now but speaking calmly, as if he was merely hammering down the details of facts he already had. "And Stella Marshall, where was she when Kiera walked out the door?"

"She was around. In the room there with us."

"So she saw Frank leave?"

"I guess so."

"And Lenny?"

"I'm not sure on that. He wasn't around, but probably in his room. I think he left afterward."

"So you're in the house, and Frank's gone out, maybe for a smoke, and a minute or two later Kiera goes out as well, and now they're both outside. Did you watch them from the window at all, see where they went at all, what they did out there?"

"No."

"Hear any vehicles starting up?"

Oman paused and admitted he hadn't heard any vehicles starting up, and it looked to Leith like a dishonest pause but an honest admission. Which was interesting.

"When you left the Law house that day, her Rodeo was still there, wasn't it?"

Oman shook his head vaguely.

"Yes or no?" Leith said, wanting something for the record.

"No, I don't think it was," Oman said.

"For how long were they out there, Frank and Kiera?"

Oman's bluff facade was breaking down, nearly gone. He said in a low and husky voice, "I never saw Kiera again."

"Sure. What about Frank, when did you see him again?"

"He came back."

Leith raised his voice, just enough to give the kid a jolt. "I know he came back, and I know damn well *when* he came back. I want to know when *you* say he came back so I don't have to waste any more time writing up criminal charges here. This is a homicide we're dealing with, right? If you think I'm grim to deal with, think again. Next to the prosecutor, I'm a pretty nice guy."

"Yeah, sorry, I was just trying to think, is all. I'd say … ten."

"Ten what?"

"He was out for ten minutes, maybe," Oman said, and looked away, rosy-cheeked and wet-eyed. "Fuck."

Fuck said it all, in Leith's mind. The drummer boy's last hope for a rosy future had just gone up in smoke.

* * *

With Dion dismissed for the night, back to his room at the Super 8 to sleep off the pain pills, Leith was on his own now, interviewing Stella Marshall. It didn't go well. However much he bullied her, she stuck to her original story, that Kiera had left on her own, that she'd left in her truck, and that Frank had stepped out earlier for a smoke, but had come back, and he had nothing to do with her disappearance. Breezily, she went about shooting down the case built up against Frank by Chad Oman's latest admissions. Chad, she said, had been smoking some pretty high-grade zombie all morning and wasn't firing on all cylinders to begin with. "Let's just say he's pliable," she said, lounging in her interrogation chair, inspecting Leith with those pale marble eyes as she twined her hair about a finger. "Especially in the face of a policeman with lots to lose, right? I'm sure you didn't exactly handle him with kid gloves, as they say. Did you?"

This lady really should get into politics, Leith thought. He said, "First I've heard of zombie."

"It's the kind of thing you don't blather about to cops if you don't need to."

"Everybody was smoking hard?"

"No. I only smoke on weekdays, and only what I can bum off friends. Frank only had a toke after Lenny left, so he doesn't set a bad example. Very old-lady, Frank is, when it comes to Lenny. If he only knew. Kiera tokes once in a blue moon, and I don't recall her smoking that day. So it was just Chad indulging."

"What d'you mean, if Frank only knew. Only knew what?"

"The kid's a total pothead, when big brother's not looking."

"Where do y'all get your weed?"

"I really don't know," Stella said.

Like hell she didn't.

When he'd let her go too, Lenny Law took the seat next and told Leith that Kiera's Rodeo was gone when Tex had picked him up that day for their trip to George. And you could hypnotize him or put him through a lie detector, and you'd get the same answer, he said, swear to god.

Even without the swearing to god, Leith believed the kid. He considered pressing him about the weed angle, but it was barely a tangent at this point, and he didn't want the trouble. So that was the end of his eyewitness list, barring Frank, who on the advice of counsel continued his right to say nothing. Not a word.

* * *

They didn't arrest Frank. Crown counsel didn't think they had enough and didn't want to blow it by jumping the gun. You can't base an arrest on a boatload of *probablys* and one witness's foggy say-so. So the team heads sat about with take-out dinner and a steady supply of caffeine and brainstormed, looking for a solid bit of proof. There was the matter of Kiera's coat, and it bothered Leith enough that he went over it again. And again. A striking purple coat, with embroidered cuffs and flamboyant fake fur trim, as described by her family and friends, that hadn't been found, either at her own home, or at the Law house in the woods, anywhere on the property, or in her vehicle or anybody else's. It was nowhere. So it was presumed to have been on her back when she'd been taken and was maybe buried with her now. Except Chad Oman had sworn she'd left the house without that or any other coat on, just the sweater, and in that respect Leith believed him.

All of which led him to the conclusion that somewhere between her walking out of the house that day and vanishing into the unknown, she had somehow been reunited with her famous purple coat, and that coat had gone with her to the grave. Probably it had been in her Rodeo, and she'd gone out and put it on, before or after her interaction with Frank.

In the prevailing theory, Frank had killed her, there in the woods near the home, even though a pair of dogs with keen nostrils had snuffled about the whole five acres and located no trace of cadavers or shed blood. So the killing had been clean, a strangulation, maybe, or suffocation.

And then? Then he had left her there, and later, when the band had gone, with Lenny safely packed off with Tex to Prince George — or so he thought — he had placed her into her Rodeo, which despite what Lenny

said remained in the driveway, and driven her somewhere and disposed of her, either alone or with the
help of his lying, cheating friends. But there the theory
became impossibly dilute.

The windows were solid black when Jayne Spacey
said, "What's this?"

She tossed over a photograph that Leith recognized
as one of the printouts from Frank Law's iPhone. The
image was tilted, blurred, and would have been deleted
off the phone immediately if Frank had been the efficient type, a shot of Chad Oman doing what many kids
did these days to show how smart they are, giving the
camera the two-handed middle-finger salute.

"Why do they do that?" Leith said. "In my day we
smiled and said cheese."

"Fuddy-duddy," Spacey said. She leaned, pointed.
"It's this blue thing here."

Giroux pulled more photos now, crime scene shots,
spreading them around and hovering over them like a
plump little human scanner. "Holy smokes. I don't see it
anywhere. It's gone."

Leith looked at the blue thing in the blurry shot of
Chad flipping the bird. It was there in the background,
barely a smudge. Could be a garment, he thought. Her
coat? *Gotta see if we can find a picture of her in her coat*,
he thought. "Her family called it purple, not blue. This
is definitely blue."

"Frank's still got the old iPhone," Spacey said. "Not
great at handling some colours."

Leith inspected the photo as close as his not-so-great
eyes would allow without reading glasses. "There's this

paler stuff around the top. That could be the fake fur trim her sister mentioned."

Spacey and Giroux agreed, it could be furry trim. Spacey said, "We'll show it to her family. They'll be able to identify it better for us."

If the blue smudge in the photo was indeed Kiera's coat, the find was significant. Leith stood and paced, playing the devil's advocate. "Like Stella said, Chad was stoned. So he forgot he'd seen her walk out with her coat under her arm."

"Chad's description of her leaving the house was convincingly detailed," Spacey countered. "He saw her with both hands in her pockets. There's nowhere for a coat to hide in that memory."

"Hooked under her arm, like this?"

"It's a bulky winter coat. It would have been part of his mental image."

"Maybe this blue thing is a different coat altogether. Maybe it belongs to Lenny, and it went with him when he left for Prince George. Or Chad's or Stella's."

"All will have to be checked," Giroux said. "But I agree with Spacey here. I'm pretty sure that's her coat."

So, Leith thought, assuming for the moment it was Kiera's coat. *The door's closed, and Kiera's out there in the cold with only a sweater and jeans.* Ten minutes later Frank had returned. The Rodeo was gone, according to Stella and Lenny; maybe so, according to Chad. Whatever the case, the coat was in the house when she left, and wasn't there when the police photographer showed up with the ident team the next day, and nobody had an explanation. If nothing else, that showed somebody in the house was covering his or her tracks.

Spacey took the photograph and went to visit Kiera's parents. She phoned back with the results half an hour later. "Yes, it's her coat," she said. "Ninety-nine percent positive."

Leith spent an hour on the phone with Crown counsel, in spite of the hour, and that same night Frank Law was arrested and charged with the murder of Kiera Rilkoff.

Fourteen

FOUND IN TRANSLATION

MORNING CAME, ALONG WITH a steady fall of big snowflakes, fat and wet. The case wasn't over, not even close. After six hours of interrogation, Frank stood firm that he was innocent, and there was nothing Leith could do but keep scrounging for evidence.

On this day Mike Bosko was truly and finally abandoning ship, hitching a ride with the sheriffs on the prisoner shuttle and flying out from George, as he'd planned to do so many days ago. "It just kept getting more interesting," he said in his cheerful way to Leith and Giroux. Leith was glad to see the last of him. Bosko was a grating reminder of what Leith had no chance of becoming. Too smart, too high-ranking for his age, and to top it off, he didn't even seem to realize it. Too big, too worldly, too modest, and quite possibly a vegetarian, were some of his flaws. And he was slow. Right now he wasn't snapping up his briefcase and flying out the door, as he should be, but finishing a cup of coffee and chatting with Giroux about something anthropological, a native legend about frogs, or foxes, or the reinvention of self.

Mike Bosko probably knew more about First Nations culture than Giroux, by the looks of her face as she listened, awe mixed with offence. Leith only tuned in when the conversation somehow tied back in to the case, Bosko and Giroux back to an earlier debate about Scottie Rourke's intentions up on the East Band lookout, holding a gun to Frank Law's head when Frank wasn't looking, a supposed act of euthanasia against the ills to come. "Oh, you bet Rourke would have shot the kid," Bosko told Giroux. "Then he might well have shot himself to wrap it up, but I doubt it. Anyway, that's my take on it."

Leith stashed that takeaway to think about later, but for now Bosko had turned to him, reaching out a hand. "You know," he said, as they shook, "I know it wouldn't be easy, leaving the north, but think about it. I'm looking for the best for my new team, out with the old SCU and in with the new, and I could sure use a guy of your talents and energy."

Leith stood blinking. Talent? Energy? "Yes, sir, thanks, sir," he said, and it came out in a blurt after his first stunned silence. "I'll sure think about it. Thanks."

"Excellent. Be hearing from you soon, then, I hope?"

"Yes, sir. Thanks. Was great working with you. Safe travels. I'll be in touch."

Now it was Giroux's turn. Unlike Leith, she didn't blather like a drunken lotto winner, but promised to keep Bosko posted about the Rilkoff case. "Things aren't over till they're over, right?"

Leith watched Bosko out the window, somewhat infatuated. The big man stood and chatted with the sheriffs from Prince Rupert, who had been waiting patiently at their transport van. The snow fell, and the sheriffs seemed content to stand chatting for a while longer with a man they didn't know. They were pointing toward Hagwilget Peak, talking geography now, probably. Talking stats. Sharing hiking stories. *God*, Leith thought. *He wants me.*

Finally, they all piled into the van and it trundled off, full of cops and robbers making the world go round. "Sad," Giroux said. "Just when you get used to somebody in your life, poof, they're gone."

"Yes, and I'm next," Leith said, two thumbs up, thinking about Ali and Izzy, cranky wife and truculent daughter, home and haven. His big smile and two thumbs up seemed to bother Giroux, and he understood why. This was her universe, this little spattering of villages, and she couldn't imagine anyone wanting to leave.

Not that it was over, quite yet. There would be many interviews to conduct over the next day or so. He recalled another unpleasant item on his mental agenda, and with a sigh told Giroux about Spacey and her disturbing lack of expediency when it came to mustering backup to the East Band lookout, night before last. He told her of Dion's version of the delay. Giroux listened, her fierce black eyes shooting sparks, and Leith noticed for the first time that she was going grey at the temples. Just like Alison, who'd told him last month during one of their tiffs, "I'm going grey, take it or leave it."

He would take it, of course he would. But with Renee

Giroux he felt a pang of pity. Maybe because she was a firecracker that would sail high but burn fast, and she would never reach the stars.

"No way," she exclaimed in answer to his ratting out of young Spacey. "No way would she put anybody's life at risk, dragging her feet like that. If she complained that Dion had been unclear on the phone, then he had been unclear on the phone. Unclear is his middle name, for Pete's sake."

So it'll go into the personnel cold case files, Leith thought. An unsolved case of *he said, she said.* Like Giroux, he believed the *she.*

Back at his desk in the main room, he was struggling through the paperwork of Frank's arrest when he was distracted by a commotion. Constable Thackray had arrived, helping a little old native lady up the front steps and into the detachment, bringing gusts of brisk air and a swirl of snow crystals. Leith delayed a phone call to observe the little old lady, who looked older than the village itself, and wondered what it must be like to have existed before the escalation of convenience, before mass transportation, mass media, mass instantaneous gratification had set in. Must have been slow days, then. Must have been kind of nice, listening to the crickets at night. For entertainment you sat on the front stoop, watching the sunset, having a real conversation about real things with real people.

His iPhone buzzed, a text from home: *When?* He texted back: *ASAP.* With a happy face.

It was amusing, anyway, watching Thackray, the lanky young constable, trying to communicate with the little old lady, but she wasn't speaking the language, except in fragments. Thackray tried Police Pidgin, then a kind of ad lib sign language, then sighed and caught Leith's eye and said, "She wants to report something, but I can't understand what the problem is."

Dion had arrived, not in uniform but civvies, looking preoccupied. He brushed past Thackray, went to his cleared-off desk, and started searching for something in the drawers and behind the computer monitor.

Leith asked Thackray, "Don't you guys have an on-call translator?"

"Yeah, we do, but she's out of town."

Dion said, "My keys."

Leith said, "I gave 'em to Thackray."

Thackray pointed at the bulletin board on the wall, where he'd tacked Dion's keys. Dion stuck them in his pocket and headed for the exit, but didn't get far. The little old lady stepped in front of him and spoke to him in tongues. Even after he told her he didn't speak her language, she kept at it. Leith wasn't sure why she picked on Dion. Maybe because he had dark hair and dark eyes and looked like he could be at least part native. In the right light.

Like Thackray before him, Dion did his best, making a yacking gesture with his hand at his mouth, shaking his head at the woman, saying, "Sorry." Leith and Thackray grinned at each other, and the old lady went quiet. Dion turned to Leith with arm outstretched, pointing at the wall, and said, "Willy's at the Super 8 diner every morning about seven. You must have seen him there, old Indian guy, white hair. He could translate for you. Ken could probably tell you how to reach him."

"Willy ..." Vaguely, Leith recalled a white-haired gentleman in the Super 8's little gingham-tabled restaurant, sitting at the window booth, outlined by predawn darkness, drinking coffee. "Ken," he said. "Who's that?"

Dion stared at him. "He serves you breakfast every morning. Right? Ken Cheng?"

And with that he was reaching for the door handle again, and Leith wondered if this was it, he would now just climb into his cruiser and shoot away back to his home posting of Smithers, a one hour's drive south, without so much as a goodbye or a swell to know you. Recalling the paperwork Giroux had been flapping about earlier, Leith shouted after him, "You have to clear it with the boss before you go, right?"

"I did," Dion shouted back, and was gone, out into the falling snow.

The old native lady looked exasperated, and Thackray said to the door, "Goodbye, Mr. Sunshine."

* * *

Getting a translator for the little old lady was Thackray's problem, really, but Leith decided a change of pace to the day would be good for him, and he offered to do it himself. Sometimes to run a simple errand is rejuvenating. Solve an easy puzzle and feel good about yourself for a change.

He crossed the highway on foot to the Super 8 and talked to the short-spoken little Asian fellow who served him and the other out-of-towners breakfast every morning — sure enough, the name was Ken Cheng — and asked him about a customer named Willy. Mr. Cheng told him, yeah, Willy hung out here most mornings — in fact, he left about an hour ago. He didn't have a lot of money, taught languages at the Continuing Ed place sometimes, for free. But not many people were interested in language learning, so Willy mostly just walked about town or went fishing in the season. Mr. Cheng didn't know Willy's address.

Leith re-crossed the highway on foot, jumped into his SUV, and drove to the Continuing Education building, where he spoke to a woman there who knew Willy and had his address on file. No phone number, sorry. She told Leith that Willy wasn't a translator, really, not too good with English, more a teacher of the old language, but he'd probably be able to help out in a pinch.

Not feeling much rejuvenated, Leith punched the address into his GPS and drove to the address the woman gave him, a rundown apartment low-rise in the poorest nook of the village. He climbed the stairs and knocked on the door. He heard loud music and loud shouting and a loud dog barking incessantly, all from behind thin walls, and his nerves danced. Nobody answered his knocking, but the shouting in the next apartment went quiet, and a native teenager who should have been in school looked out and asked him what he wanted. Leith told him he was looking for Willy. The kid said, "What's Willy done?"

Being in plainclothes, Leith mentally bellowed, *Now why d'you assume I'm a cop? I could be the old guy's perennial fishing pal.* But on reflection he realized he couldn't be anybody's fishing pal; in this scenario, he could be nothing else but a cop. He said, "Willy's not in trouble. I need him to translate for me. D'you know anybody else who could translate?"

"Translate what?"

Leith realized he didn't have any idea. "Gitxsan, I'm pretty sure."

The kid shook his head.

"Thanks," Leith said.

"No problem," the kid said and shut the door, and the shouting started all over again, and Leith realized it was aggressive but not angry shouting, and there was laughter thrown in, so it wasn't murder after all, just some kind of party. The shouting was in English, but it wasn't good English. It was slurred and mangled. Leith was glad he was white and middle-class and didn't have to live next to these noisy bastards. Better yet, he didn't have to *be* these noisy bastards. Poor Willy. No wonder he wandered the town.

Outside, the snow was ankle-deep but heavy and wet. His mission was a failure, and he felt far from good about himself, and it was high time to hand it back to Thackray, say go find your own damn translator. But then he saw him, a shambling figure walking along the side of the highway, head bowed, heavily dressed, and Leith said aloud, "I'll bet my right arm that's our man."

He stopped the SUV and approached with his ID out, and the shambling figure stopped to watch him come in stony silence.

"Hi, excuse me, I'm looking for William Lloyd?"

"Why?" came the answer. "What's ol' Willy done?"

This wasn't the first time Leith had lost his right arm, and he knew it wouldn't be the last. He pocketed his ID. "Any idea where he is right now?"

The man who wasn't Willy pointed to the big yellow sign on the main drag not too far ahead.

Leith drove the two blocks to the Catalina, stepped inside, and found a table where four native men sat. There were three middle-aged men speaking English — something about construction of a new road — and one old guy with wild white hair and mismatched eyes, one milky blue, who seemed to be mostly just listening. All four men looked at Leith as he walked over. This time there could be no doubt which was Willy.

There were greetings all around, and he was invited to sit down, in spite of being a fair-skinned, hazel-eyed detective from Prince Rupert. The three men listened while Leith spoke with Willy, asking him if he could do some translating for him. He didn't mention the complainant's name, Paula Chester, in case one of the three men listening was somehow involved in the crime. Who knew?

Willy said sure, he could do that, and his English didn't seem so bad, actually. "Now?"

Leith called the detachment, and Thackray said Mrs. Chester had left, but he would pick her up again and bring her back. Fifteen minutes? Leith would have left with Willy then, except one of the three men had bought him a coffee. This guy too was from Prince Rupert but hadn't been back in a while and wanted to know how things were going in the City of Rainbows.

After the unwanted coffee and chat, Leith drove Willy back to the detachment and found Thackray hadn't yet returned with Mrs. Chester, so he left the old man in the more comfortable interview room, which would be the best place, he thought, for the translation process. Then he went back to his desk to get stuff done. The cute little errand hadn't been so cute in the end, not the mood-boost he'd been aiming for.

As he was to find out later, it was some minutes after he'd left Willy in that room that the old man must have gotten bored with sitting looking at travel magazines and got up and wandered about the detachment a bit, finding himself in the primary case room, which should have been locked but wasn't, and which took the Hazelton case on a whole new trajectory.

* * *

The apartment, which Dion had rented partially furnished when he'd moved to Smithers five months ago, still had the echo of an unloved place, and now on his return it had also the chill of vacancy. He dropped his gym bag to the floor and turned up the thermostat. The baseboards ticked alive, and in time the iciness began to thaw from walls and furniture.

One of the first things he'd bought after landing in Smithers had been a Sony ghetto blaster from the local stereo store, and he stooped now to bang in a synthpop CD to scare away the silence. On the kitchen counter stood another welcome-back bonus, five beer left over from a twelve-pack he'd started on before heading out on the out-of-town assignment so many days ago.

With a beer in hand and the music blaring, he sat on the sofa and worked on forgetting the dirty backwaters of the Hazeltons and all its troubles. He was glad to be out of there and back into this pocket-sized city, with its fast food and yuppie pub and its strip mall. But there was a sense of something left unresolved, and it wasn't just the full and sworn statements he had yet to give. It was mixed somewhere in the faces and the conversations that had flowed at and around him in the strange little settlement under that big mountain. There were conversations yet to be had and faces yet to be met, it seemed, and it was a weird and unsettling notion that nagged him even as he shook it off, finished a second beer, and bobbed his head to the music.

Whatever.

He had picked up a pile of mail from his box in the lobby, and he sat on the sofa and sorted through it. Most of it was junk and flew into the waste bin. Some bills to set aside and deal with later. There was also one slim envelope from Kate, which he looked at in wonder. She still wrote. After all his cold shouldering.

When he was in rehab, he'd refused to see her because his face was skewed and bruised, and he drooled when he spoke. He'd sent her a note saying the accident made them strangers, so she'd better delete his number from her list, find someone else. Even after his face straightened out and he learned to control his tongue, he knew he was far from fixed, and wouldn't see her. He returned home, and since he'd been battling the RCMP to keep his job, he'd been in no mood to see her then either. So "just go" were the exact words he used at his apartment door as she stood there with a bottle of wine in her hand. He'd been blunt. "Don't call, don't write. When I'm good again, I'll be in touch."

The letter he held now was proof she just didn't get it.

He went to add it to her other three envelopes he'd received since arriving in Smithers, stored away in a shoebox on the shelf, but it occurred to him that things had shifted again, and the faint hope of Kate was no longer even faint. He tapped all four envelopes on the counter until they were nicely square with each other, hesitated once more, and tore them in half. It hurt, but in a good way, he told himself, as he dropped the tatters in the wastebasket with the other junk mail. It was just another lightening of the load.

* * *

The old man named Willy was looking at the photographs still up on the bulletin board in the case room when Leith came looking for him. The photograph he seemed most interested in was that of Frank Law, blown up from a snapshot to show his handsome, smiling face. Frank's front tooth was chipped, but otherwise his teeth were straight and white. And ask any local girl, she'd say the damage only added to his charms.

Leith said, "Sir, sorry, but this room —"

And Willy said, "Where has his girl gone?"

Leith stood next to him and looked at the picture of Frank. Posted within inches was the photo of Kiera, but Willy didn't seem interested in her, which didn't mesh with the question he'd just asked.

"She hasn't been found," Leith told him. "We're still looking. We'll never stop looking."

Willy nodded, still studying Frank.

Leith frowned. Maybe the old guy was blindish. He

put his finger under Kiera's picture and said, "D'you know her, sir? Ever met her in person?"

Willy looked at him and at the photo he was indicating. He looked harder at the picture and said, "Nope."

"She's the singer who went missing. Kiera Rilkoff?"

"Yes, yes." Willy nodded in recognition at the name. "It's a sad story."

There was still something off-key with this whole exchange. "She's Frank's girl. You know that, right?"

Willy grinned. "He got a lot of girls."

"Hey?"

Willy stopped grinning and said something in his native tongue, but only to himself.

Leith tried for the unequivocal approach. "You asked about his girl. You mean her?" His finger was on Kiera's picture again.

"No," Willy said. "The Laxgibuu. Wolf House. Bilaam is her name. The singer."

Leith puffed out a breath. What he needed was a translator for this translator. Willy appeared to be searching his mind too, and finally he said, "Charles West. Bilaam. His girl. Never came back to finish up. I ask around, nobody know."

"Charlie?" Leith said.

Willy nodded and smiled. "Charlie."

Leith nodded now, relieved that they were finally getting somewhere. "Charlie West went back to Dease Lake. That's where she's from."

"From Gitlakdamix," Willy said, correcting him. "New Aiyansh. Whole family went up to Dease. They follow the jobs, eh. Mom and dad died. Car accident, you know? Horrible. Sad."

"Right, okay. So you know her well, Charlie? What makes you say she's Frank's girl?"

"She come by with this boy, to the school. Frank, he wants to see too."

"See what?"

Willy, so brief till now, suddenly spouted off at length. "Come to see her sing her own words. I teach her the words. She grow up away from all what made her, you know? Lost it all, but they're coming back. I am bringing them back to her."

To Leith this was becoming one big, irrelevant headache. Rob Law's ex-fiancée was taking language lessons, or singing lessons, or find-your-roots lessons, or some combination, from this old guy, and she had taken Frank with her to one of their sessions because he was interested, and the old guy assumed they were a couple. So what? "When was this that she came by with Frank for lessons?"

Willy said it was late last summer. September. He nodded at his memories. "Good singer. Smart. I hope she comes back and finishes up. Her music is fine and good things. You give me her phone number, hey? And I will call her. Maybe she does not understand that I will be gone soon. And then so will her songs be gone."

Leith went to the files and found the phone number for Charlie West in Dease Lake to give to the old teacher of the old language.

And that would have been the end of it, but the next morning he encountered by chance Willy in the Super

8's diner and asked him if he'd talked to Charlie, and Willy told him no, he'd talked to Charlie's sister, and the sister said Charlie had never made it home.

Which was puzzling and worrisome. Leith didn't want to get into another painstaking back-and-forth with the old man, so he went across to the office and dug up the file once more. He looked at Spacey's transcription of her call to Dease some seven days ago.

Q: *Ms. West, you lived with Robert Law down here in Kispiox and his brothers Frank and Leonard last year?*

A: *Little bit, yeah.*

Q: *Why'd you leave?*

A: *Had a fight.*

Q: *Do you know Kiera Rilkoff?*

A: *Sure.*

Q: *She's missing … any idea what happened to her?*

A: *Nope.*

Charlie was a nickname. Her real name, as on Spacey's notes, was Charlene. Wasn't it? Well, wasn't it? If there was a sister, could the nickname be some kind of … hell, no, that was impossible. He grimaced. Knowing the impossible was often called *shit happens*, he made some calls himself and learned with dismay that, yes indeed, there had been some gross miscommunication, that Charlene West was Charlie's sister, one year younger, that Charlie's legal name was Charlotte, that as far as Dease Lake knew, twenty-year-old Charlotte had gone to live with Rob Law in Kispiox. She hadn't been home since.

Why hadn't Rob corrected the mistake when Leith had brought the issue forward in interrogation?

Charlene. He recalled now that Rob had paused, had seemed baffled, but then gone on and let it pass. Maybe the logger had motive to uphold the lie; more likely he saw no point in correcting the dumb bull asking him questions.

Following some hours of telephone tag, Leith was able to connect with Charlene herself, and he put her statement to her over the line. "You told Constable Spacey last week that you lived with Rob Law."

"Well, stayed with," Charlene said. "Yeah. That week."

Lived or stayed with, Leith thought. Amazing how a slip of semantics could throw a case so badly off the rails. "What week?" he asked grimly.

Charlene was a girl of short patience, and already she was speaking loudly to show she didn't appreciate the interrogation. "Sometime April last year. Thought I might move down too, but then we had a big blow-up and I came home. Why?"

"What was the fight about?"

"My drinking, that's what," she said, and added belligerently, "But I quit, you know."

"Good for you." He said it gravely, wanting her to know he meant it, that he admired anybody who got off that road to ruin, that he hoped she stuck with the program. He said, "Do you know she left Kispiox?"

"Yes, I know."

"I'm looking to contact her. It's important. Do you have a number or address for her?"

There was silence on the line, and she said, "Why are you asking about Charlie? What's going on?"

"Just a few questions about the case. She's not in trouble."

She remained tense. "I haven't heard from her since September. She called from a pay phone, but the line was bad, and all I got out of her was she's got some big decisions to make, something about her music. Said she may go away a while, has a lot to deal with, not to worry. I didn't know 'a while' to her is six fucking months. I'm this close to reporting her missing." She paused, and she seemed to listen to his silence, and there was sudden stoniness to her next words. "She *is* missing, isn't she?"

"To tell the truth, we thought she was up in Dease Lake with you till now, so we haven't been looking too hard. Which means she's probably okay, Charlene. I hear she's an independent girl. What else did she tell you in that phone call?"

Instead of an answer she said, "We weren't tight. You understand? You'd think we would be, after all we've been through. But it just got in between us, which is how he wanted it, right? Divide and conquer. He's dead now, which is sweet, and like I said, I kicked the booze, and I think we'll be okay now, me and her. Just wish she'd call."

Leith asked her who "he" was and what he'd done.

"Uncle Norm. Norman Wesley. And what he did is none of your business. He's dead now. It doesn't matter."

Leith knew the name, Norman Wesley, a Dease Lake resident who'd got himself murdered last September. He could guess what Wesley had *done*. So Wesley was Charlie's uncle, and he'd been murdered in September, which was when she'd left home, which was interesting.

Charlene said, "Charlie's got a way with words. You wouldn't know it if you talked to her, but she does. And she wrote these songs, she says, and she's got 'em on CD, and she's going to go sell 'em to a recording company and get rich and famous. She was kidding, you know, about the rich and famous, but she wasn't kidding about trying. Sounded to me like she was heading south, to the city. Scary place for a girl like her. I told her come home to Dease, but for the first time in her life she stuck to her guns, and I guess that's a good thing. But I know what's going to happen. She's just going to get trampled all over again."

"What d'you mean?"

Charlene's answer was vague and peppered with language Leith didn't quite get, but the sense he got was her wayward older sister knew what she wanted, but just didn't have the strength to get there without being dragged back.

"Dragged back by what?" Leith asked her.

"By a man," she said. "She's with some fucking guy, probably. And she's native, right? So she's got nowhere to take cover when he gets mean, which they all do in the end. No cover in Dease, no cover in Vancouver. Really, when you come down to it, she's got nowhere."

"Sure," Leith said, knowing what she meant.

Charlene paused, maybe to take a breath, maybe to puff at a cigarette. She said with forced cheer, "Anyway, this isn't really about Charlie, is it? It's all about that missing chick, Rilkoff, right?"

"Yeah, it is," he said. Though really this was becoming more about Charlie West than Kiera Rilkoff. Well, actually it was about both. Two girls gone missing, two singers, mysteriously silent, as he was going to have to tell Charlene now, break the news. He'd also have to get all she'd just told him taken down in a proper statement via the Dease Lake detachment.

The case was far from over, then. In a way it had just begun.

* * *

Leith had talked to Giroux, and they agreed to talk to Willy again, find out more about this song writing, because music, it seemed, was at the heart of this tragedy. They needed to learn how intimate Frank had been with this other singer, Charlie West.

Leith talked with Frank, but Frank had spoken to his lawyer again and was still saying nothing. Mercy Blackwood told him Charlie West had submitted a song, but Kiera didn't like it, and it had been scrapped. As far as Mercy knew, Charlie had left town soon after that, and they'd lost contact. Rob Law had nothing to add, aside from a few words explaining how he met Charlie up north on an equipment-buying expedition. In the end, nobody had anything constructive to say about Charlie West, who seemed not much more than a ghost meandering through this whole affair, saying little but humming a tune.

Leith got Willy back in and brought in a translator for the translator, a serious Nisga'a girl who was studying the language. She did a good job of it, Leith thought. Translating in bits and pieces, she relayed a whole raft of rhetoric on Willy's behalf. Like, "If you don't teach the children the language, how will they speak to their ancestors, and if they can't speak to their ancestors, how will they be taught right from wrong?"

Leith had been brought up Catholic and still swore on the Bible in court, but deep down, he knew the job had more or less bullied the religion right out of him. These days he had little patience for spiritual types of any make or model, to the dismay of his parents and brother, all churchgoers who still prayed over every meal.

"There was a time," the Nisga'a girl translated, "people knew right from wrong."

Leith highly doubted that too. He asked for more about Frank and Charlie, how they acted together that day they visited the school. The girl translated that Frank and Charlie seemed to be good friends. But no, they didn't hold hands, didn't kiss, nothing like that.

Leith asked for more details on the music itself and learned Charlie West was shy about her singing. She told Willy she had made a CD of the songs she wanted to translate, and she'd bring it next time. She sang one song, and it was a good and beautiful thing, Willy said. He had told her that translation would not be easy, that really she would have to learn the language, be fluent at it, before she could sing those words in a meaningful way, but that he would help as best he could.

Leith asked if Willy remembered any of the words to that song.

The translator spoke to Willy and then spoke to Leith. "It was a love song."

Every other song, in Leith's experience, was a love song. But then every other thought in a young person's mind was about love. And this was about love, as it should be. "Did Frank say anything through all this?"

The translator spoke to Willy some more — it was a lot of back and forthing this time — and finally gave Leith the gist. "Frank said nothing, except forgiveness. He kept telling Charlie about forgiveness."

Forgiveness? Leith thought, startled. About what? Kiera? This was last September, long before Kiera went missing. Was it no crime of passion, then, but a long-planned act, a conspiracy between Frank and Charlie? "What do you mean, forgiveness?" he asked, tamping down a growing impatience. "Forgiveness for what? What did he say exactly?"

But Willy didn't know. Mostly Frank had just stood around waiting, except for those few words overheard.

Leith jotted it down, underlined it twice, and finally asked the man, "So did she bring you her CD, as promised?"

No, she didn't. Willy never saw her or Frank again. He had one last thing to say, through the translator, as Leith stood to signal the interview was over. "I hope you find her, Bilaam. I'm very worried. She is water."

"Water?" Leith asked.

After some more back and forthing, the translator corrected herself. "Dew. She is a dewdrop."

* * *

Leith needed a break. He had made some calls to arrange for time off, five days in which he would return home to Prince Rupert to recharge, and today was the day. This was also the day Scott Rourke was released from lockup in Smithers.

Rourke reported in to the Hazelton detachment, where he met with a probation officer and went over the terms of his recognizance. It was a strict one, loaded with conditions, one being to stay clear of the Law residence. He signed his name, gave the PO a piece of his mind — which Leith and everybody else heard — then was let loose, back onto the streets. Giroux stood at her office window, looking out, and laughed. "There he goes," she said. "Bow-legged old greaseball. I don't often say this, but that is one scrawny waste of skin."

Leith joined her, peering outward. "Who are those guys?"

"Look vaguely familiar. He's chatting 'em up pretty good. Must be friends."

Two men stood on the sidewalk, one white, one native, both in their late forties, dumpy and on the rough side, truckers or loggers by the looks of it. And she was right, they were chatting with Rourke. The conversation looked friendly. Rourke flapped a hand at the police station, then all three sauntered off toward a beat-up pickup parked at the curb.

"Should we be worried?" Leith said.

"About what?" Giroux said.

"He's said it himself, he's got friends far and wide. A network of anarchists. He'll go into hiding."

"Good riddance. Waste of taxpayers' money, putting him through trial. For what, being a goof?"

"He tried to kill two people, one of them a police officer. That's goofy to you, is it?"

"Public disturbance and careless use of a firearm. I don't care what Mike says, Rourke wouldn't have shot anybody up there. He was being, what d'you call it, Shakespearean."

"You're forgetting he nearly bludgeoned a guy to death, Renee?"

"That was different. It was libido-driven. This was dramatic flair, and our fellow Dion just made it worse. Probably what happened was he startled Rourke's trigger finger."

Leith shrugged irritably. Giroux was the worst to argue with, inflexible, swift and resilient. Still, he tried to implant in his memory the faces of the men who'd wafted Rourke away, in case it came up again later. He did the same with their vehicles as they spat exhaust and tore off onto the adjacent highway, but didn't catch a single licence plate number in the process. Which meant he didn't only need reading glasses; pretty soon he'd need distance glasses too. Or like his dad, those god-awful bifocals. As much as he loved his dad, the idea of becoming him was pretty damn scary.

He left instructions for the hunt to continue in his absence and went out to his truck for the long drive home. Normally he'd be whistling a merry tune, heading home after such a grind. But there was nothing to whistle about today. Midday and he was pushing into a dark highway, high beams on against the falling snow, mission far from accomplished.

* * *

Leith's week off was antsy and far from restful. He spent much of his time on the phone with his team, drank too much, slept too little, made love with his wife only once, and barely noticed his daughter toddling about destroying whatever she could get her tiny hands on. He also caught a bad cold. He returned to New Hazelton, drugged and more tired than ever, to pick up the pursuit, the search for Charlie West, still haunted by the notion that Charlie was somehow involved in Kiera's disappearance, that maybe if he tracked her down, he'd have tracked down the motive, if nothing else.

Mike Bosko was back in the North Van SCU, re-immersed in big city crime, no doubt, the Hazeltons just a fading memory in his busy mind. Dion was no longer around, which was just plain nice. And Spacey was gone too. Promoted to some more glamorous place, Leith thought, but Giroux told him no, there was no glamour to Spacey's whereabouts. She was in big trouble, facing some serious allegations. Allegations that Giroux herself had made.

The news startled Leith, like he'd just learned of a death in the family. "What happened?"

"We had words. She was having problems in her life. Messy divorce. Her ex filed for a restraining order, and so did his girlfriend, who's the bartender at the Black Bear you met, Megan. I love Spacey like a daughter, but I see now she's not looking for a mother. She's looking for a punching bag. Your life's out of balance, I told her. She told me to get stuffed, except not so politely."

Beating around the bush like this wasn't Giroux's way, normally, and neither was looking wounded. "Anyhow," she said, "I pulled up the East Band issue again, her calling for backup. The timing was so off that I had to get to the bottom of it. She maintained it's Dion's fault. I told her I didn't believe her. And I still don't, because you know what? When that young man wants to talk, he talks better than you and me. And so I wrote it up. I had to. She said she'd fight it to the end, but she won't. She'll see the writing on the wall. She'll resign."

They stood a moment in silence, and it really was like a death in the family. Not some distant aunt, but a beloved cousin. Leith couldn't help but blame Dion for the loss. And Giroux. He said, "Was it really worth losing a good officer over that? She made a bad judgment call. Didn't jump to it quite fast enough. You or I might have done the same in the circumstances."

Giroux shook her head. "At great expense and difficulty, I pulled in Evangeline Doyle, all the way from Edmonton. What she says fits with Dion's version, not Spacey's. It's not a trivial matter. Spacey lied. She tried to take credit away from Dion and tried to make him look the fool, and in the process she put his life in jeopardy. You can't turn a blind eye to that kind of behaviour, now, can you?"

"No, ma'am," Leith agreed.

But it still hurt. There was a sense of deconstruction here, now that the group had shrunk to so few familiar faces, and in an odd way, Leith missed all those who were gone. As for the Law boys, Giroux wondered if Frank would be deemed by the circuit judge to be neither a flight risk nor a danger to the public and would be let go on a condition-laden recognizance. It would be good, she said. For a little while at least the three bears would be together in their home in the woods.

Leith doubted it. Frank might not be a flight risk, but Kiera was still missing, and if her bones lay too close to the surface, somewhere out there in the ever-shrinking snow mass, there was a danger the killer would steal out one night and make sure she was never found.

Dismantle her, scatter her to the winds. And then how would the poor girl ever rest in peace?

Fifteen

SMITHERS

NOT ALLOWED BACK TO WORK till he got his doctor's okay, Dion was learning the fine art of being idle.
After a solidly overcast week, he opened the drapes one
morning and saw the sky had shed its murk and become
a broad, dazzling blue vista over Smithers, shot through
with sunlight so sharp it made him wince. The stitches
in his side were out, but it still hurt when he inhaled too
deeply. When he eventually returned to work, they said
he'd be put on light duties for at least a month.

It seemed to him that if his duties got any lighter he
would turn into a puff of smoke and disappear. Two days
ago he'd been sat down for assessment with the Internal
Investigations people, but they hadn't seemed too worried
about the Spacey incident or anything else he'd done wrong.
They'd asked a few questions, returned his confiscated
notebook, nothing said, and basically told him to carry on.

He'd have preferred it if they'd bellowed warnings in
his face and slammed down a list of conditions to meet

before they'd let him back in the door. Instead there was that eerie silence, and he knew what it amounted to. They were going to gently downsize him till he vanished.

He didn't want to go out like that. He looked out the window, up to the snowy peaks. He imagined if a hiker went missing up there, they'd search for a week then call it off. He'd climb so high the winds would batter him to death. So high they wouldn't find him till he was bits of bone, white and pure. He decided to go for a walk.

A taxi took him to the base of a popular trail that wound up the ski hill just west of Smithers. Up there past the trodden path he would find pure wilderness, he knew, endless peaks and valleys. But even before he left the car he hit a snag, as the heavy-bellied middle-aged native cabbie he'd never met before balked instead of taking his cash. "What, you're going to walk up the mountain?" the cabbie asked. "Dressed like that? S'a long haul, you know. It's not Sunday afternoon in Stanley Park, hey."

"I know. I'm okay."

"You got no canteen, no provisions. You start walking, you'll get thirsty, and you'll look around and realize you're miles from anything. No Starbucks up there, my friend. It's dangerous. It's a full day to the top, and that's with all the proper gear. Soon as you're out of the sun it'll drop below zero. I've never seen anyone go up here without a pack."

"So I'll go halfway and come down again."

"You got gloves? No, look at you, man, you don't even got gloves!"

Dion sat with the passenger door wide open, exasperated. What was the problem? This guy wasn't his mother, and even if he were, it wouldn't be her business. "I'll be okay," he said again, and stood.

"And how you going to get back to town once you get back to this point, thirsty and hungry and cold? Even right here there's no good cell service, you know. Let alone up there, you got nothing."

Dion hadn't thought it out this far, that the cabbie would report him to the police as a self-destructive lunatic, and they'd come and fetch him, and so much for going out with dignity.

"Tell you what," the cabbie said. "There's a road I know, gets you pretty high up the base of the glacier there out past the Johnsons' farm on the 16. You can do the hike, it's about three quarters of an hour, to this really spectacular kind of waterfall thing, then you come back down and I'll pick you up at —" he looked at his watch "— one o'clock. How 'bout it?"

Following the cabbie's orders, he was driven to a different trailhead, and he walked up a gravelly path fit for geri-atrics, passing a few other hikers on the way, who all smiled hello at him. At the top he looked at the glacier and the waterfall and stood on a sightseer's platform and listened to the wind. The wind slapped him hard but didn't try to kill him. By the time he arrived back to the parking lot at five minutes to one, he was thirsty, hungry, and numbed. He was grateful when the cab pulled in a few minutes later.

"I brought you some coffee," the cabbie said. "Knew you'd need it."

Later, back in his apartment, Dion considered how easily he'd been dissuaded from suicide, and had to ac-cept that he just wasn't ready for it. He also wondered if the cabbie was just being nice, or really just wanted that big tip he'd ended up getting. His own judgment in all things was bad, following the crash, and one big fear of his was being taken for a sucker. Maybe that was why he thought through everything about four times longer than the average man, and sometimes forgot to say thank you.

While he was eating a late lunch in the silence of his apartment, he decided that the cabbie was for sure happy to get that big tip, but it wasn't what drove him. Niceness was the purest of motives, in the cabbie's case. Or caring, or common decency. Just as Scottie Rourke was nice, however off-the-rails he was. And Frank Law seemed like a good man, at least through hearsay. No doubt Kiera was good too. Stella Marshall might have been nice, in the right circumstances. Willy, who'd taught him how to say *foolish* and *rabbit* in the Nisga'a tongue, was very nice, and he missed Willy's early morning company. Bunch of nice people, really.

He thought of Mercy Blackwood. For all her hospitality, she wasn't nice. It wasn't just the way she blew off the death of her dog. It went deeper than that. She was worse than not nice. She was just like him, bloodless, heartless, and cold to the touch.

Sixteen

THAW

LATE MARCH, AND THE GROUND was still frozen, but the snow was on the wane. Spring break-up was washing over the central interior, and 90 percent of logging operations had shut down to ride it out. When Leith arrived at the Law home the sky was pelting rain and the midday light was muted to a premature dusk. Frank Law had been released pending his remand hearing but hadn't been home more than a week before he'd screwed up badly, caught drinking and driving, and was sent back to the slammer. In Terrace. So much for reprieve. The youngest bear, Lenny, opened the door to Leith's knock and directed him out back to the fleet of oversized Tonka toys in the yard, in particular to what he called the grapple-skidder. Leith had no solid idea what a grapple-skidder was, so he walked between the half-dozen machines until he found one emitting a clanging noise. He climbed the rungs and looked in to find Rob lying sideways on the operator's seat, wrestling at something within the manifold with a wrench in each hand. His bare arms were striped with grease and his face contorted. He glanced around irritably when Leith rapped his knuckles against the mud-spattered, projectile-proof glass.

"Need to talk," Leith shouted.

He waited between the machines until Rob came to earth with a thud and asked what he wanted.

"Charlie West," Leith said. "Where exactly did she go when she left?"

"Charlie? Went north, I thought. But now I'm hearing she went south, so I'm guessing Vancouver. I told you, the lawyers said not to talk to you guys."

"Thing is, she didn't get to Dease Lake. Her sister hasn't heard from her since last September, around the time she left you. No news of her showing up elsewhere either. With that in mind, d'you have any suggestion where she may be now?"

Rob shook his head, eyes squinched with fatigue or impatience, or both. He gestured at the house. "Gotta go clean up, get out of the rain."

Leith followed him across the yard. "Has Frank been in contact with her since she left?"

Rob's voice was dispirited. "Why should he be in contact with Charlie?"

"Why d'you think?"

They were inside the house, in the kitchen now, Rob running hot water, dousing a rag in soap. He didn't pursue the *why*, and that said it all. He shrugged and spoke to the soap. "Seems to be a rumour Frank was screwing around with her. No clue why. He wasn't interested in her whatsoever. Doesn't matter. He'll get his trial next month, and then he'll probably go away for a long time. We got other things on our minds. She's gone, hell knows where, and the last thing we need —"

"We're concerned about her," Leith said. "I understand you don't want to hear this, but she's missing, and I plan to find her, and you're my best lead. Okay? So help me out."

Rob made a noise, part disgust and part defeat. He said, "I'm having a beer. Want one?"

Leith said no to the beer but followed him into the living room, where Rob in his dirty coveralls sat heavily in an armchair, leaned back, and closed his eyes. The can of Labatt's dangled in one hand, popped open but untouched.

The silence stretched until Leith broke it, putting to words what had bothered him since the last round of phone calls with the girl's hometown. "She's dead, isn't she?"

"Dead," Rob said, still slumped in his armchair. "Why should she be dead?"

"Well, I don't know. You tell me. You might as well, because I'm going to dig up the Hazeltons till I find her. How did it happen, Rob?"

Rob gave him a hard look. "She left in September. We never should have got together, me and her. Nothing in common. But no, I didn't kill her, and Frank didn't kill her. You'll have to look elsewhere."

Leith set his mouth, depressed at the odds against finding her. The land here was too broad, too hostile, too easy to vanish within, dead or alive. "Tell me again how you met Charlie."

"Wesley Logging had equipment to sell," Law said wearily. "I went up to take a look. Met Wesley's niece,

Charlie, we partied, thought we'd party for the rest of our life together, and came back to Kispiox. Didn't turn out quite that way. Didn't even last a year."

Leith knew the name well. "Wesley Logging, run by Norm Wesley?"

"That's the dude. Ended up spread eagle in the mud flats last September, as I hear it, full of buckshot." Law didn't look hugely affected by the loss, just a little disappointed. "Never got any equipment off him in the end. It was standing shit and rust, that's what."

* * *

The killer of Norman Wesley had never been found, Leith knew. It occurred to him that maybe they had a suspect at last. Wesley had a bad reputation in the community as a child molester and wife beater, and maybe Charlie was a victim. It was an interesting enough idea that he made the two-hour drive to the Terrace remand centre to visit Frank Law. Frank was brought to the interview room, where he reiterated without spirit that he wasn't going to say anything. Not because he'd done anything wrong except try to protect Scottie, but just he wasn't supposed to talk.

"Sure, I understand," Leith said. "But this isn't about Kiera or Scott Rourke. This isn't even a formal statement. I'm talking to you right now as a regular witness. It's about Charlie West, your brother's ex-fiancée."

Nothing glinted in Frank's eyes except irritation. "What about her?"

"I asked you about her before, and you wouldn't talk. But I'm here asking you, if you care about her at all, to help me out. Nobody's heard from her since September. Her own sister Charlene hasn't heard from her. Charlene's worried."

More than worried, Charlene was frantic, on her way down to the Hazeltons to spearhead a search that would probably end up being quite the solitary march.

Frank said, "If I could help you, I would. I can't. Sorry."

"What do you know about Norman Wesley?"

The name was familiar to Frank. Somebody Rob had dealt with up in Dease. Leith said, "It's her uncle. She didn't mention him before she left?"

"Nope," Frank said.

Leith worked at filling the other gaps that riddled his case. "You were close to Charlie, weren't you? You took her to William Lloyd, a Nisga'a translator, to help her get language lessons. Why?"

"I wasn't close to her, but we needed her, to write our songs. She was a great songwriter."

"How did that come about?"

"She lived with us, was going to marry Rob. I guess Lenny had a crush on her. Never realized that, but it makes sense. They're closer in age and both quirky, and Lenny spent a lot more time with her than Rob did, so I can see how they got friendly. More than that, though, and you're probably thinking sex, but it wasn't. I come home one day and hear a girl singing. Snuck down to the studio and couldn't believe my eyes. Charlie was singing, using one of my acoustic guitars, and Lenny was at the mixing boards. She wasn't too great on the guitar, but the song was, wow. Totally self-taught, I could just tell, and totally original. They didn't see me there till I clapped and whistled."

He half smiled at the memory. "For sure they were hiding something from me, the way they stopped and Lenny jumped up. Probably he was using the equipment to record her, which is no big deal. Don't know why they were so secretive about it, but maybe that's just Charlie being shy."

"Any idea where that CD is now?"

"No. Lenny said he didn't burn one, and he's a bad liar, but I wasn't going to push it. But I did tell Mercy in the next day or so how Charlie's this fabulous diamond in the rough she's looking for, and she came right over and tried to get Charlie to show us what she could do, but Charlie just clammed up. She did show us the lyrics, though, and Mercy loved 'em. Mercy had this idea that Charlie would write for us. Me and the others had mixed feelings. I was cool either way. Kiera didn't like it at all. She tried singing one of Charlie's songs, with Charlie's help, but couldn't make it work. I'm not much of a singer, but I gave it a try, and it fit me like a glove. The song, I mean. Everybody said I'd got it just right, including Charlie. But didn't matter in the end, because Charlie herself, well, I found out she had other ideas altogether. Like I said, she's shy, not a big talker, and I had to figure it out myself, reading between the lines, how she wanted to go after her roots, write for her own people in her own language. So there she was teetering. Mercy wrote a big fat cheque to show Charlie how profitable it would be staying with us. Charlie almost took it, almost signed Mercy's contract. But something got fucked up."

Frank's lip had curled at the word *contract*. "What got fucked up?" Leith asked.

The curl was gone, and Frank's face lit up with something close to humour, maybe even happiness. "Probably Lenny. He never liked Mercy, or the direction she was taking us, and I think he told Charlie to dump us all and follow her dreams. Whatever. Charlie came to me, said she was sorry, but she had to do what she needed to do. I said don't worry about it. I even gave her a ride to see the old Indian guy. And once I was there, seeing her talking to him, I knew Lenny was right. She should go her own way. We'd just mess with her mind. I bet she'll end up with big pots of money anyway, once she shows the world what she can do. I told her so, too. I said forget the translation for now, you can do that later. Go to Vancouver and wow the studios. She just laughed. But maybe that's what she did in the end, went south. And power to her."

A word in Leith's notebook reminded him of the mystery word of the day. He said, "When you took Charlie to see William Lloyd, he overheard you talking to her about forgiveness. What was that all about?"

Before Frank could say hell if he knew, it came to Leith in an epiphany. The word had simply been lost in translation. He said, "Could it be *mercy,* not forgiveness? You were telling Charlie about Mercy Blackwood?"

"Oh, ah-ha," Frank said, dully. "That's it. I told her Mercy wanted her to stay, write songs, and be our magic money-making machine. I said, 'You better go break it to her yourself, because I sure don't want to.' I also warned her to stand firm, because Mercy can be damned persuasive." His mood shifted now into a sulk.

"I should know. She's got me on the hook so good. We'd have to sell at least one album, and it better be successful, because if we don't, we'll have to pay her back, all the money she sunk into us. And there's lots. A helluva lot more than I expected. It's all there in the fine print."

Leith raised his brows.

Frank nodded. "I know, why did we go signing shit without thinking? It's because she had us believing we would make it big if we hired her. No money up front. Great deal. Now look at me, stuck in a vice. If I get out of jail, I have to work for the bitch for the rest of my life and make her rich. If I don't, she'll go after me for all I've got. I can sell the equipment and the instruments, but it won't be anything near what I owe her. Professional photographers, posters, web design, all the studio gear and instruments, she covered it all. I used to wrap my shitty second-hand guitar in a sleeping bag when we went on the road. Now I have a top-of-the-line Gibson with its own coffin. Velvet-lined. I wish I could go back to my sleeping bag, man. I really do. Me and Kiera, hitting the road, happy as fleas."

Leith's brows were still up. He said, "That's no contract. You should have taken it straight to a lawyer. Any first-year law student would have it in the shredder in no time."

Now Frank's brows were up too. "Really?"

"Really. But we didn't find any contract in your papers."

Frank looked embarrassed. "I ripped it up after our CD fell through, flushed it down the crapper. Pretty dumb, I guess."

And childish. It wasn't the end of the world, but it would add complication to Frank's efforts of extricating himself from a bad deal. Leith sighed and went back to the point of this meeting, Charlie West, a spirit that was both meek and willful. "Did Charlie tell Mercy she was leaving?"

"Nope. She told me she'd think it over, go walk-about, but she never showed, never called. Mercy was super ticked-off about it." He frowned. "I was playing in Smithers last summer, thought I saw her, Charlie returned from her walkabout, passing by the stage. I thought she'd come to tell me what she decided. But must have been somebody else. Sorry I can't help you. I hope she's okay."

"Didn't any of you try to contact her?"

"Only girl in the world without a cellphone."

"How about calling her sister in Dease Lake?"

"No. Why would I go chasing her down?"

"You weren't worried about her?"

"To tell the truth, I haven't thought about her till now, you asking about her. She's not somebody you worry about. She's one of those super-independent types. Goes for long walks all by herself, used to stay out all night sometimes in summer. She's the kind of girl you can imagine building a cabin from scratch and living off the land. Anyway, she'd burned her bridges with us, leaving in September like that. Once she left Rob, he didn't want to hear her name, so 'Charlie' became a taboo word in the house. Mercy got over it. She says I'll just have to write my own hit tunes, like it's easy as picking apples. Well, it isn't. Especially when your life's gone down the shithole. Know what I mean?"

Leith said he knew, and then sat in silence. He'd learn-ed a lot, and none of it was useful. Frank sat motionless too, lashes down, a promising young man whose fabu-lous future was falling away fast. Leith considered the long drive back and the coming night. He was shifting out of his chair, ready to call it a day, when Frank said calmly, "I killed her."

Leith stared, but not for long. He eased back into his chair and blanked his face, not to spoil this fragile moment. But it hardly mattered, since Frank was still looking down at his hands or the tabletop, mute now. Leith said gently, "You killed Kiera, Frank?"

"Yes."

Leith brought from his wallet the little card, which had printed on it every detainee's constitutional rights, to be followed by a repeat of the Brydges warning, advising of access to free legal counsel. Somewhere down the road a lawyer would be grilling Leith about this moment, over and over, ad nauseam, whether Frank understood what he'd just done, whether the confession should stand.

Leith believed it bloody well would. Frank Law hadn't been bullied into this disclosure. He'd come to it on his own. Just plain ran out of steam.

* * *

Over the next hour and a half, Frank talked, of how Kiera had arrived at the house on Saturday morning cold and angry. He had asked her what was wrong, but she wouldn't say, because Chad and Stella were going to show up at any minute. "We'll talk later," she told him. The others arrived, and they played through a song six times, more like random noises, before they all knew it was a write-off. Frank put some food out, but nobody ate, and when he could stand her cold shoulder no longer, he told Kiera to step outside and tell him what was bothering her.

They did, boots on but too wrapped up in themselves to think about coats. Oblivious to the cold, they walked away from the house, down the path to a low bluff over the river, and here they argued. Her rant was so chaotic that he couldn't pin down what she was accusing him of. He was conspiring against her, fucking other women, wanted to dump her, and she never wanted to see him again, it was over, and damned if she'd bang a tambourine in the background for him and that bitch. He tried to get her to calm down and speak clearly, but she was thumping her fist on his chest, threatening to hit him across the face. "I saw the proof," she told him, and called him a cheating bastard, and she'd gone for his face again like she wanted to rip it off, and he'd grabbed her wrists. She tried to knee him in the groin, and he'd pushed her. Backward. Forgetting they were on a bit of a rise there overlooking the riverbanks, and there were rocks below.

He'd scrambled down to where she lay, hoping she was just dazed, but she was so still, eyes closed. He'd carried her up, laid her in the snow, knelt down and tried to rattle her back to life, but she didn't move, didn't breathe. There was no blood, that he could see, but no pulse either, no heartbeat. He stood in the falling snow, stunned, and gradually it had come to him like a vision, all that would now happen, the arrest, the trial, prison. He imagined Rob being left alone. Rob was a tough guy without much of a life, and all he had for a friend was Frank. Lenny was just a kid, and needed him even more.

Frank was brother, mom, and dad to Lenny. Leaving these guys just wasn't going to happen.

He took Kiera's keys, jumped in her Rodeo, and drove it around back to the equipment yard. Then he went back inside and told Stella and Chad that Kiera had taken off. He called Tex and told him to pick up Lenny, take him to Prince George for a few days, have some fun. Then he ushered Stella and Chad out the door, saying he was tired. Tex picked up Lenny, and now, alone, he called Scott Rourke, who was always on hand to help out in a crisis. Rourke was over within minutes. He worked on reviving Kiera, applying his CPR skills and everything else he could think of, but it was futile. Rourke told Frank to go back in the house and forget this happened. He should stick to his story that Kiera left in her Rodeo. He, Rourke, would deal with the body.

Frank returned to the house. Scott came in and grabbed Kiera's purple coat, and any other belongings she'd had with her that day, and went back out. Frank went to the bathroom and took a bunch of pills, whatever he could find in the medicine cabinet, Aspirin, and some old prescription Tylenol and a fistful of Rob's Sleep-Eze, laid down on his bed, and tried to die. Obviously, it hadn't worked.

Pretty soon the phone rang, Rourke on the line with some elaborate instructions — it frankly didn't sound much like Rourke's mindset — telling Frank to get that mixer nerd over, Parker, soon as possible to set an alibi, and Kiera would send a text. If Parker was present, Frank was to respond with *WTF*. Code for "Parker's here."

Frank, doped on painkillers and feeling ill, called Parker, and Parker, who had no life, came over right away, and they worked on the day's recording. Parker was amazed at how bad it was. *What's wrong with you guys?* he'd asked. A text had come through, Kiera's fictitious "*screw you*" line. He'd responded with "*WTF,*" and "*where are you*"? Done.

Parker left shortly afterward, and that was it. From there, Frank was genuinely in the dark about what had happened to Kiera. "But Scott knows," he said. "Ask him."

Leith was almost too tired to think by now. He squeezed his eyes shut and recounted all the phone calls back and forth. He would have to check the records, once he was back at the Hazelton office, and start firming up the story. He would have to go over the statement with Frank in greater detail, too. But at this point he believed all he'd heard. Kiera's death was classic and pathetic, the end result of a lover's tiff, but at least it had been quick. He was halfway to finding her, bringing her home, but to finish the job there was one more son-of-a-bitch to clamp down on: that meddling dishrag Scott Rourke.

* * *

Back in New Hazelton the following day, Leith was distressed to find that Rourke hadn't been located. He calmed himself, scheduled some follow-up interviews, filed his report with Crown counsel, then got to work on the phone records, lining them up with Frank's story, and he waited for the constables to bring in Scott Rourke for the big wrap. It didn't happen. Day darkened into evening, and still no word. The man had vanished off the face of the earth. Leith leaned in the doorway of Giroux's office and asked her how in hell people around here could just up and disappear without a trace.

"Are you blaming me?" she said.

"Yes, I am."

"Well, blame me for Stella Marshall too, then."

"What?"

"Gone. Sit down a minute."

Leith took a chair in front of her desk and buried his face in his hands. Giroux said, "Don't worry. I'm sure she's gone on her own volition. Neighbours say she packed up her little red Sunbird and took off. South. Like I said before, she's more involved in this thing than we know. She's smart and she's observant and she's sneaky. Put yourself there. She's at this miserable rehearsal. Frank and Kiera are in some kind of cold war. She'll have observed their mood, even if they were trying to keep it to themselves. The lovers leave the house to duke it out in the privacy of the woods. Frank comes back in ten or fifteen minutes, alone. Stella's antenna is up. Not Chad's, he's a guy, and guys don't notice stuff that's happening around them —"

"Thanks."

"You're welcome. But Stella does. Frank tells them Kiera just took off. Stella has her doubts. I'll bet you anything she went back after dropping Chad off to check out the situation. She sees Rourke's dirt bike there. She doesn't go in the house but follows the footprints down to the riverside, and maybe meets Rourke carrying Kiera to the Rodeo. I bet she masterminded the whole cover-up. Rourke doesn't have the brains."

Leith's regrets doubled. He had let Rourke walk out, the man with critical information, and he should have followed his instincts and kept custody of him. Trumped up charges, if that was what it took. But he hadn't. Now he had Stella to eat at his conscience. He said, "I'll find her."

"Bet you won't."

Giroux was probably right. He made arrangements to get Stella's picture out, as he'd done for Scott Rourke, the borders and all cars put on high alert. Fugitives like this rarely got far, but in the case of Stella Marshall, he had a funny feeling the dragnet would fail, and she'd just sail on through, broomstick and all. Rourke was another story. Dig up enough rat-holes and he'd come squealing to the surface, no problem.

* * *

Giroux had a pleasant little house at the edge of town, just where the woods began. After Leith's busy day, she tried to soothe his nerves by inviting him over for dinner. He brought wine, though Giroux wasn't much of a drinker. "I could be," she warned when he offered to fill her glass. "But I'm smarter than that." She sipped her half glass and Leith downed the rest of the bottle over the course of the meal, loosened up, and went from griping about his own incompetence to griping about his rocky marriage.

Giroux's response was an insinuation that he should know better than to let his marriage hit the rocks. "You're an adult," she said. "Get it together or you'll end up like me. Old and alone."

If much of the conversation wasn't great, the stew had been excellent. Leith helped clear the dishes and said, "Can we talk about this truck now? You said you had thoughts."

The mysterious white truck with the black window seen barrelling down the mountain on the day of Kiera's disappearance. "Yes, I had thoughts," Giroux said. "And I'm an idiot not to get this earlier. And so are you. I probably wouldn't have gone down this road, except Frank, as you say, said Mercy is crazy."

"Right," Leith said. "And we placed her under the microscope again, and she couldn't be involved."

"Sure, but listen to me. It's not easy to get a hold of temporary wheels in a small town where everybody knows everybody and what they drive, right? But what if you're a mechanic? You got temporary wheels parked in your garage all the time, right? And you got the keys in your pocket."

"Jim Duncan, Duncan's Auto Repair," Leith said. He stood by Giroux's picture window, looking out at the night, weighing the possibility. He summoned an image of the skinny mechanic with his long brown hippy hair and moustache, John Lennon glasses, serious, never smiling. A possible accomplice, sure. "Huh."

"Not Jim," Giroux snapped. "He rescues anything that limps, for crying out loud. His sister, Mercy, I'm talking about."

"Mercy Blackwood is Jim Duncan's sister? I didn't even know they're related."

"Well, I told you, Dave, in plain English. I said they're twins. That makes them related, right?"

He turned to face her. To face her he had to look down quite steeply, her being nearly a foot shorter than him. He recalled the conversation vaguely, driving with Giroux down the main strip through New Hazelton, passing the IGA parking lot, spotting the mechanic Jim Duncan chatting with Fling's manager Mercy Blackwood, both in their heavy winter outfits. One of them had been loading groceries into a little black pickup, the other just talking and gusting cigarette smoke; he couldn't remember which had been doing what. Or maybe it wasn't cigarette smoke but just classic northern breath clouds. Whatever the case, Giroux behind the wheel had nodded in their direction and said simply, "Twins."

None of it mattered to Leith just now, aside from the revelation that Mercy might have had access to a stranger's vehicle. Handy, if you're going to commit a crime, like having access to an unregistered handgun. He looked out the window again and murmured, "I thought you meant something else."

"What else could I possibly mean?"

"I don't know. That they look alike?"

"Well, they don't, much, do they, given his big moustache."

"From behind, maybe, sort of?"

She was a word miser, that was part of the problem. Instead of saying "Twins," that day, she could have said, *Hey, Dave, did you know those two are twins?* Which he couldn't possibly have misinterpreted as metaphor. But she hadn't, and he couldn't really blame her, because he was the same way. At New Year's, when Alison's family was up visiting, Alison had called him surly, right in front of everybody. Maybe it was a cop thing to dole out words like they each cost five ninety-nine, punctuation sold separately. He said, "You couldn't have thought of this sooner?"

"Mercy Blackwood never hit my radar as suspicious, okay? If she had, I would have."

"Yes, well, we all pretty well discounted her. And I still do. Her alibis are scattered for the whole day, but if you thread them together, they're solid." He thought of the different surnames, Duncan, Blackwood. So the woman was married, and why was he surprised? There was just something untouchable about her, and maybe she hadn't been exactly off his radar after all. He said, "We'll have to grab Mr. Duncan's records, see what's been through his shop lately."

"Thackray's already on it."

Leith reflected that if the mechanic felt no obligation to cover for his sister's crimes and opened his books without a fuss, that would be great. If he dug in his heels and made Thackray go for a warrant, that would be pretty darn interesting. The other scenario, of course, was Mercy had already taken care of those records, with or without her brother's help, and nothing would be found at all. The fourth and most likely scenario, as he told Giroux now, was that her little brainstorm was just one big make-work fuss over nothing.

"Yes," she agreed, with a sigh. "Probably. Dessert?"

* * *

An early morning mist lay low over the Hazeltons. Leith noticed on the grounds surrounding the RCMP office that the grass was starting to show through, surprisingly green and perky, as the snow receded. On his drive out to Mercy Blackwood's house in Old Town, he saw in some of the gardens that the vegetable beds had already been turned, getting ready for the snow peas and other hardy whatnots to go in. The growing season in the north was good, in some ways, in that it was longer than down south. Colder, but longer. More daylight hours. So a garden could produce some damn big northern zucchinis. Leith knew it because he'd eaten a damn lot of damn big northern zucchini over the years.

It was too early now for even the most avid gardeners to be out. Nobody was out but one determined detective on his way to show up unannounced on a perp's doorstep, catch her off guard. It was smarter to show up in twos, a wall of solidarity, but he'd decided to come alone in the case of this particular perp, an aider and abettor, possibly, but not a killer. So unannounced and alone, early on this crisp cold misty Wednesday morning, just when most decent human beings were smacking their alarm clocks to snooze, he knocked on Mercy Blackwood's door.

It was a handsome old house, lovingly decorated once upon a time with scrollwork and spindles and fish scale accents, but the paint had long faded, the spindles cracked, many scales knocked loose. The porch floorboards felt wobbly under foot, worn dangerously thin. A faded silver BMW coupe sat in the driveway, and firewood was stacked high along the side of the house. The chimney was smoking badly, which meant whoever stoked the fire didn't know what they were doing, or didn't care.

Mercy Blackwood opened the door and blinked at him. Taken off guard, she wore no makeup and her sleek brown hair was mussed. But she looked prettier than ever. She held a cup of something in her hand, the cup emitting steam. She wore a plush black dressing gown, tied at the waist, black tights, and moccasins on her feet. She looked, as always, cold and miserable.

"Morning," Leith said. He reintroduced himself, apologizing for the crazy hour to be knocking on her door. "May I come in for a word or two?"

She was clearly not delighted. "I'm kind of in the middle of things. I'll come down to the station in an hour or so, if you want."

"It'll only be five minutes."

They smiled tensely at each other, and she said, "Yes. Of course."

He stepped inside, angling toward the living room he could see to his left, but she said, "Not there, sorry. I'm renovating, and it's a bit of a mess. My office is over here. This way. I'll make you some tea, as I don't have coffee, if that's all right."

"Thanks," he said. He didn't want tea, but a moment alone to snoop about her office wouldn't be bad.

He followed her through a passage, past a kitchen with crumbly green walls, but well equipped with modern appliances, and farther along to what was probably once a bedroom, converted now to a sparse office, with a tiny window, a desk, a computer. Mercy had brought along a kitchen chair, and she placed it down before the desk and said, "You can sit, if you like." That said, she went to get him the promised tea.

He didn't sit or remove his parka, the air chilly enough in here to condense a man's breath. He listened to her moving about her kitchen, discreet noises of running water and clinking dishes, and he looked at her desk, the papers on it, unrevealing, bills and receipts — some marked overdue — nothing on her computer monitor when he sidled around to take a look, but a screensaver shot of horses racing across a misty field. There were framed CDs and certificates on the wall, proof of professional conquests.

A kettle shrieked, and a moment later she was back in the room with two cups of simple but chic design, bone-white and delicate. Her hair was combed smooth now and tied back, but she had put on no makeup, not worried about impressing him. He sat, and she placed a cup of tea before him, seated herself behind her computer, looked at him in that direct, somewhat disconsolate manner he had become familiar with, and waited.

He said in a jovial way, "So I hear you're a twin."

His friendliness didn't move her. She only nodded and pursed her mouth. He drank some tea, but it tasted funny, and he set the cup down. He asked how she got along with Jim. She said she got along with him fine. He asked if she would ever go over to the garage for any reason. She said she'd been there a couple of times. He asked if she'd been there at all in February. She said she'd gone there last week, actually, to talk over some estate matters with Jim.

Of course she had, he didn't doubt it. And Jim Duncan would confirm it, and even if Giroux's theory was right, it was quite possibly unprovable. He chipped away at it a bit longer, hoping she would give herself away, but she didn't. The woman was either innocent or shock-proof. He gave up on the garage angle and said, "You've heard Frank will be indicted?"

She nodded. "I've heard. I'm not surprised. Did he actually confess?"

"Sorry, I can't discuss it. I do want to ask you something, though. He signed a contract with you. I'm wondering how his incarceration will affect the deal."

She pulled a *who knows* face. "It null and voids it, I guess."

"Can I see it?"

She opened a drawer, riffled through papers, and placed one before him. It was a computer printout, wordy and professional-looking, under Mercy Blackwood's letterhead. He looked it over, looked at her, and said, "You wrote this?"

"It's boilerplate, with a few adjustments."

It was dated March of last year, soon after she had discovered the band at that Valentine's dance. It was signed by Frank and Kiera. "You think it's binding?"

She shivered and tugged the collar of her robe tighter around her throat. "Probably not, if it came down to a legal battle. I didn't write it expecting trouble, but just trying to cover my own ass. Fling's not just some noble artistic endeavour to me. It's income. An investment. I sunk a lot of money into those kids, which in retrospect was, well, hare-brained stupid."

She paused and seemed to listen to the echo of her own words. She caught his eye, gave one of her tense little smiles, and he could almost see her flipping the facade back into place.

He said, "Things didn't work out, did they?"

"Spectacularly, no. I'll probably never recoup."

"You must be angry."

"I feel used, yes," she said. She gazed at him, reflecting, and said, "It's all over now, and I guess I can tell you how they played me along from the start. They promised to work hard and strive for success, and I put my faith in them. Frank complained of the quality of their studio equipment and instruments. I thought it over, took the gamble, cashed in my investments, and paid for what they needed to propel them forward. Turns out I lost the gamble. They didn't work hard. They took all my advice and expertise and ignored it. They partied hearty and missed deadlines. Not malicious, just callous. As I said, I'm not surprised their lives ended in violence." She shrugged. "It doesn't matter. It's over now. I'm fixing up this house, as you can see. Then I'll sell, soon as possible. I'll get a good price for it. I'll be all right."

Leith looked around at the walls she gestured at. Like the kitchen, they crumbled. The cost of repairs would be astronomical, and the market in areas like this was worse than soft, and he should tell her to cut her losses and sell as is. "Probably should get some advice before you put too much money into it," he said.

She nodded curtly, and he guessed that her life was a string of hits and misses, richly embellished with poor choices. Like Fling. He thought of her characterization of Frank and Kiera as lazy, cruel, and conniving. He recalled too Frank calling Mercy a bitch, and Lenny calling her a black worm, corrupting good people with false ambitions. Probably there were shards of truth in all that maligning, but not much more. Angry little shards left over from a bad breakup.

He switched to his other big concern, doubting she could add anything useful. "Charlie West is still missing. I asked you about her a few days ago, and you didn't have much to say. Is there anything you can add now?"

"I'm sorry, there isn't. Charlie is another example of their self-destructive behaviour. She was a special kind of talent. She wrote amazing music. She was what Kiera and Frank needed to break out, but they were afraid of change. Especially Kiera. She'd let Charlie write their music over her cold, dead … well."

A faux pas. Leith watched her for blushing and shame, but Mercy only became whiter and smaller. He said, "I heard Charlie made a demo CD. We haven't found any evidence of one, either physically or on the studio equipment, and Frank says he knows nothing about it. Were you part of that?"

The CD looked like news to Mercy, and a dark annoyance seemed to spark from her eyes. "No, I apparently was not. Who did you hear that from?"

"I also hear she wanted to follow a different path, and Frank only helped her out because he felt it was the right thing to do."

Her sour expression said otherwise. "She could have been something. They all could have. See what happens when everyone works against each other, each wanting to get their own way, instead of pulling together? Charlie's nowhere, and Fling is history. It's a lose-lose situation. I guess I'm the lucky one in all this mess. Now, I'm sorry, Officer, but I'm not going to cry over spilled milk any longer. Your five minutes are up. If you need anything else, please call and I'll willingly come to the station."

They walked down the hall, past the kitchen, to the small foyer, and he glanced into the living room again, and he smelled the rubble, saw the haze of dust, saw a wall stripped down to its antiquated bones. "Lathe and plaster," he remarked, recalling renovations from his own pre-RCMP days, when he'd worked for a salvage company back in Saskatoon. "You're not seriously thinking of replacing all this with Gyproc, are you?"

"That's the plan."

"You'll have to hire professionals," he said, sticking his nose officiously where it didn't belong. "Believe me, every problem you fix will uncover four more."

"I'll be hiring muscle," she said with a wry smile. "Promise." She went to open the door for him, but he was zipping up his jacket and still looking through the arched entrance leading to the living room, at the mess, the furniture draped in painters' cloth, at a series of photographs visible along one undamaged wall.

"Is that Joe Forte and his gang?" he asked, looking at the closest shot. "And that's you there with them. May I?"

Take a closer look, he meant, and even as she tightly smiled her permission, he saw that unmistakable *No, get the fuck out of my house* glint in her eyes, a look he'd seen often enough over the course of his career. He walked over and studied the photograph of a much younger Mercy standing in a group of two guys and two girls. The wildly bearded Joe Forte had his arm across her shoulder, and both looked happy. He said,

"You'd still be working with them now, if he hadn't died, I guess."

"Oh yes, things would have turned out a whole lot differently."

He looked at the other photographs, four altogether, and recognized one he'd seen quite recently, in passing. On TV, or a magazine, or online maybe. It showed a popular bunch of musicians called the Midlanders, the one Mercy said she'd had to give up for medical reasons. A recent nomination and the upcoming Junos had put them in the news. In this framed photograph Mercy stood smiling at the camera next to Jerry and his all-male band, out in somebody's backyard, by the looks of it, a casual but formal shot with all faces forward.

From Leith's recall of this particular group shot, he didn't recall any woman being in there. He looked closer. Behind him, Mercy said with a dry laugh, "Okay, I confess. It's Photoshopped. It's a case of a dozen pictures taken, I look great in one, they look great in another, let's put 'em together. Cut, paste, blend, and presto. You've just reinvented history. It was done for nobody's benefit but my own. I just wanted a nice picture of us all together."

"Ah," Leith said. Nose to the photo again, he said, "Right. The lighting looks a little funny. Otherwise you'd never guess."

"It's done more often than you'd think, in show biz," she said.

The word "fraudulent" crossed Leith's mind, and then in another brilliant flash he believed he had solved one more mystery in this thickening file. He glanced at Mercy as he was transported back some days to the New

Hazelton detachment, to the earnest, middle-aged wait-ress from the Catalina seated across from him, telling him Kiera had called Mercy a frog.

It might have been funny, but it wasn't. It was all part of an ongoing tragedy. He said, "Did Kiera see this photograph? Did she catch you out? Is that what she was accusing you of, at the Catalina? Fraud?"

Mercy was not shaken. "Maybe that's what it was," she said. "I don't recall much of that conversation." She stood looking lost in this ravaged room, lit but unwarmed by the slow-blooming light of morning. Something banged on metal somewhere on the property, a rhythmic tinny thudding, water melting off the eaves.

Leith thought about Kiera's ranting on that Saturday morning as she battered Frank with her fists. Where had that sprung from? It was no evolution of discontent, but a spark. Something had set her off. He put it to Mercy in his kind but firm *no-point-in-denying-it* voice. "Kiera came by here, early on Saturday, before she went to Kispiox."

Mercy denied it. "Of course not. I'd have told you if she had, wouldn't I?"

He said, "She told Frank she had proof of something he'd done behind her back, and I can only think of a few things that would upset her that badly. Did you tell her something to set her off? Did you show her proof? A contract that excluded her? You wanted her gone. That would do it, wouldn't it?"

He was giving her the eye that worked best with people like her, borderline criminals, educated and for the most part decent, those who just needed a nudge to walk out from the lies and into the light. He told her with that gaze that there would be proof somewhere, and sooner or later it would be found, and she might as well cut the crap and tell him now. She stared at him, and to his surprise, a tear ran down her stony face, first from one eye, then the other. Like Constable Dion, she was too numbed by misery to realize she was crying.

She said, "I was just making a point. I wasn't trying to fool her. How could I? Frank would tell her there was no contract, that it was all a lie. But she took it for face value, like it was written in stone. I didn't know it would end like this. I just wanted them to see what was best."

"You wanted them to split."

"If that's what it took."

"Show me the document."

"I burned it."

"You faked Frank's signature?"

She nodded. "It was a whim. I had it done up in advance, expecting they would finally get it, that this was the only workable arrangement, put Frank up front, Kiera on backup vocals, or leave. She's really not born to sing lead, you know. Her voice, it's nothing special. In the perfect world I would get that prodigy Charlie up on stage, but she's too damn shy. And dumpy. She'd need to get herself in shape, work on appearance, projection, style. But we could handle it, we could make it perfect, if they'd all just …"

Leith watched her fade, her eyes down on her hands now, all her great ideas turning to dust. She said, "I didn't know they'd fight, that Kiera would die." Her eyes shifted toward him, widening. "Do you even know for sure she's dead? Maybe she's still out there. Maybe she's lying in wait."

"Lying in wait for what?"

"For me," Mercy whispered.

She was no longer crying, the tears smudged away with the back of her hand. Now she was back to square one, cold and miserable, and by the sounds of it a little cracked. The sunrays angled in to light her face, showing her age, not the mid-thirties as Leith had thought at their first meeting, but closer to fifty.

He said, "I think it would be a good idea if you sit down, have some tea, and let me take a look around."

She shook her head briskly. She'd found a Kleenex and was pressing it against her nostrils, tidying up the mess, pulling herself together. "I can't allow that. I'm sorry."

After all her admissions, he had expected meek acquiescence. What more did she have to hide, then? More bullshit, probably. False certificates on her wall, a hard drive full of malfeasance. He said, "I can get a warrant within the hour, ma'am."

"I've done nothing criminal."

He wasn't so sure about that, at this point. Especially with this shift of demeanour, a wall of defensiveness that seemed to spring from nowhere. He pulled out his cellphone, and she said sharply, "Go ahead, then. Take my computer. Just take it."

There was haste in those words, heightened anxiety. He looked into her steady grey eyes, and a chill went through him. He looked toward the office, and she stepped that way too as though to usher him along. *Yes, get the computer*, she was saying with body language, which was foolish of her. She stopped when he didn't move and followed his eyes back to the living room, ripped apart in such haphazard fashion. He looked at the wooden floors. They had been highly polished once upon a time but were sanded down by decades of neglect. On the floor in front of the woodstove he saw dark stains, and he walked over, crouched down, had a closer look. He was aware of Mercy walking around behind him, from his right to his left. He watched her where she stood now, backlit. Behind her were windows and a door leading out to an enclosed porch.

"My dog was struck by a vehicle," she said, tense and angry. "He was bleeding. A man brought him in for me, laid him down, and the blood seeped through the blanket. I tried cleaning it off, but it stained the wood. These floors are going to be redone, so I just left it. I want you to leave, right now, or I'm going to call 911."

Leith rose to his full height, only interested in one thing now. Why was she guarding the door at her back? What did she so badly not want him to find? He pulled out his BlackBerry and made the call for backup. He put his phone away and moved toward her, to push past her, to get to that door, and to hell with warrants. The blood gave him reasonable cause, didn't it?

She grabbed his arm as it reached for the knob, so he snapped it free and grasped her by the upper arm, pressing her backward, telling her the only smart thing for her to do right now was stand back and be quiet, because for all he knew, Kiera was out there, held captive on the porch or an outbuilding, and he didn't have time for niceties.

Still gripping her arm, he opened the door and pulled her out with him onto the porch. "Where is she?" he asked, roughly. "It's over. Tell me."

The porch was bright and frigid cold. Hardly airtight, with bits of card flapping where panes had fallen out, fabric shifting and something thudding rhythmically when the wind gusted. At the end of the verandah he saw a large chest freezer, and the disappointment he felt was like a jab to the heart.

"You need a warrant for this," Mercy said, grasping at him so they were both hanging on to each other. She pulled one way, he pulled another. She said, "Go and get your fucking warrant."

He no longer cared to keep custody of her, however unsafe it might be. He undid her grip with force and started toward the freezer, and as he brushed past her she hissed at him, "This is ricin spray. You're dead."

Her arm was outstretched, and she blasted something at his face.

He released her in a panic to bring his arms to his face, eyes squeezed shut, mouth closed, but he was enveloped in the mist and could taste it on his tongue, smell it, feel it burning up his nostrils. He stumbled back, crashed into the freezer, managed to stay upright.

He coughed, hacked, spat out the poison. His throat was cinching. He doubled forward and coughed violently, like a barking dog, wheezing on the inhalations. He opened his eyes to slits and they were watering so badly he could barely see. Mercy was gone. He peered down at his hands and thought of Alison, of Izzy. He said, "Fuck." One eye too painful to keep open, the other nearly blind, he turned to the freezer, hooked a finger at one end of the latch, not to disturb whatever prints would eventually be dusted off the thing, and pulled the top open, and squinted in. He saw bags of frozen peas, lots of them.

Too many frozen peas for any sane person to keep on hand. His lungs were shutting down. The pain was unbearable, spearing at his tender organs, spreading fast into his bowels and up his spinal cord, into his brain, numbing him. The numbness coursed down his arms, turned his fingers into useless sausages. He began to shiver.

He flexed his stiffening hand till it cooperated, enough that he could pull aside frozen peas, pawing through the bags to find crinkly orange tarpaulin fabric. He found the edge, a rusty grommet, peeled the tarp back, and found the contours of flesh, skin, a nose in profile, a face twisted at an unlikely angle in her fetal curl. Her face was turned in three-quarter profile, and her visible eye was open and rolled up toward him, a pinpoint of light within a muddy iris, returning his one-eyed stare. Brown hair was matted in a stiff river against her cheek. Her skin was a pale, silvery grey.

In the tumult of Leith's emotions, he didn't see her as dead. He saw her as sick but alive. He reached down to touch her cheek with affection, because at least he'd done this. He'd saved the Rockabilly Princess.

The sounds of the outdoors came through the verandah as easily as the wind, and he heard a vehicle scud away, off toward the Kispiox Mountain, Mercy making her getaway. A second later he heard distant sirens coming from the other direction. He pulled out his phone to text a message to Alison, *I love you,* but realized it was a bad idea. She would freak out, getting a mysterious dead-end text like that. Anyway, his hands were shot. He sank to the floorboards, back against the freezer, and waited for the end.

* * *

He went bravely, with Constables Thackray and Ecton, to the hospital. Still able to walk on his own, still half blind, still gasping and hacking, he attended emergency and stripped down, as instructed, and gave the nurse his particulars, and tried to get out his phone to call Alison, but the nurse wouldn't let him. "That'll wait," she said, though he told her quite loudly, between coughs, that actually it wouldn't. She gave him an eyewash, took his vitals, listened to his horror story, and called the doctor. The doctor came, and Leith repeated his story, that he'd been sprayed with ricin, had breathed in god knew how much, couldn't breathe, had no feeling in his extremities.

"Yeah?" the doctor said, a young guy with a pink, bristly face. "How long ago?"

Leith peered at his watch, weakly. "Forty-five minutes, I guess."

"Hm," the doctor said. "You're sure it was ricin? How do you know it was ricin?"

Leith knew it was ricin because a madwoman, a witch with a dead woman in her freezer, had told him so. "I was told so," he croaked. "She sprayed it right in my face. I also drank some pretty weird-tasting tea. Shouldn't you be running tests? Flushing me out? Do something. Please."

"You seem to be breathing okay," the doctor said, stethoscope wandering around Leith's chest, then his back. "Blood pressure's fine. Your temperature's a little high. Feel this?"

"No," Leith said as the soles of his feet were poked here and there with something sharpish. "Yes," he revised.

The doctor sat back. "You sure it wasn't pepper spray?"

It had never occurred to Leith that it was pepper spray. His thoughts went scrambling back to his own experiences with the stuff, back in training depot. Was it the same taste, smell, sensation? Hope began to pound at his temples, more like a headache than relief. He realized he actually did have feeling in his extremities, that he could breathe quite well, that the pains in his torso could be from violent and prolonged coughing.

"You look like you got pepper-sprayed," the doctor said. "Looks like you avoided a full-on attack, though. Doubt you'd be upright and functioning if you got the works. How far away was she?"

"She was right next to me. Must have had the stuff in her robe. What kind of person runs around with ricin spray in their pocket?"

The doctor looked a touch exasperated. "I really doubt it's ricin spray. Probably an expired can of mace or pepper spray, and you only got a bit on you. You'll be fine pretty quick."

"Well, that would be great, wouldn't it? But what if it *is* ricin?"

"I think by now you'd be feeling far more alarming effects. Sit tight. We'll monitor you for a while."

Leith had a few sarcastic things to say about sitting tight and waiting to die, but the doctor was gone. Just like that, gone. He began to feel better. He sat on the bed and thumbed a message to Alison on his phone, going through the various stages of embarrassment. Denial, anger, and finally happiness. He didn't tell Alison in his text that he'd just gone to hell and back in a virtual body bag. He only said he loved her.

She texted back "*Me too.*" And moments later, because she was a worrier, "*U ok?*"

To which he replied, "*Fantastic, Y?*"

Which he was, absolutely. He pulled in a deep, cleansing breath, felt no numbness in the extremities or pain in the plumbing, wriggled fingers and toes, and smirked at himself for believing for a second that he'd actually been in danger. *Pepper spray, the lying bitch.*

He made other calls, harassing the office, asking if they'd caught Blackwood yet. He feared the worst, another viper slipping away into the shadows. Finally he got word they had her. Her BMW had gone off the road, and she'd been on foot, racing down the road in her bathrobe and gumboots, due north.

* * *

A lot happened over the next five hours as Leith remained under observation in hospital, though by hour three he insisted he was okay to leave. A prisoner now of his own paranoia, he made all his calls from the patient's lounge, getting updates about the search of Mercy Blackwood's house, recovery of the long-lost body of Kiera Rilkoff, the media frenzy, journalists converging from every corner of the province to get the scoop. What time he didn't spend on the phone being updated he spent on the phone arguing with his higher-ups for the right to be the one to interrogate the prisoner as soon as he got out.

His higher-ups, Staff Sergeant Prentice and certain brass from North District, didn't think he could be considered impartial, considering Ms. Blackwood had just tried to kill him. They stuck to their guns even when the tests came back, blood and urine analysis, A-okay. Ident had also scoured her kitchen for the poison she might have put in his tea and found nothing more insidious than a soggy little bag of No-Name chai.

"She didn't try to kill me," he told Prentice for the fifth time, free from the hospital, back at the New Hazelton detachment, Renee Giroux listening in and rolling her eyes. "She tried to distract me from that freezer, sir. She thought I'd peel out of there to save my own life, giving her a chance to hide the evidence, is what she thought."

"That's insane," Prentice told him.

"Half this village is insane," Leith answered. "And Mercy Blackwood leads the pack."

The brass talked some more, and finally caved and told him to carry on, just to watch his P's and Q's. As soon as he felt he was too emotionally involved, he should hand the case over to someone else.

Before sitting down with Mercy, Leith sat down with Renee Giroux in person and the rest of the team via teleconference, from wherever they had scattered to: Terrace, Prince George, Prince Rupert. The meeting lasted two hours as they picked over every aspect of the case with its shifted dynamics, now that there was a body. Kiera had been transported by plane to Vancouver for autopsy, accompanied by Corporal Fairchild and the constable in charge of exhibits. The team talked at length over what Mercy's tack might be, what approach to take, any pitfalls to avoid. But there was no right approach, Leith knew. Whenever he thought he had her scoped out, she morphed into something entirely different. That left him with the least desirable "wing it" tactic. "I'll begin with respect," he said.

Late in the evening, she was brought to the interview room from the cells in her prison coveralls. He had her unshackled, and they sat across from each other, saying nothing. She appeared to him much the same as the first time they'd met, chilly, polite, and subdued. He himself was calm. Nobody looking on would have guessed at their recent melodrama. He asked if she'd spoken to counsel, if she was satisfied with the advice she'd received. She said she had and she was. He asked her to tell him everything. She said she would, if she could get a sweater or blanket.

He had her fixed up with a blanket and a mug of hot tea. After her first sip, she put down the cup and said, "I'm very sorry about the ricin thing. I do these things, sometimes. It's like I'm possessed. I always carry that pepper spray around with me, since I moved up here. Lot of vicious dogs running around. I don't feel safe."

The apology sounded dry but genuine. He ignored it and said, "Start from the beginning. How did we end up here?"

"All of them have been to my house, Frank and Kiera, Stella and Chad, back when things were good between us. They knew their way around. They must have broken in that day and hid her in the freezer. When I say *they*, I can only guess who was involved."

"Who?"

"Stella. It was only days later I discovered the body in my freezer, wrapped in a tarp. I didn't look closer, but of course it was Kiera. I didn't touch the body. I phoned Stella. She said it was a terrible accident, and they didn't know what else to do with her. She told me to say nothing. If I reported it, they would implicate me. Of course, I still considered phoning it in, and I should have. But I hesitated. And the minute I hesitated, I became a criminal. And I knew it. I said nothing. I have been living in a cold sweat ever since."

She was done, the shortest police statement in history. Cold sweat summed her up perfectly, Leith realized. She'd been in a cold sweat every time he saw her. He said, "What about the truck you borrowed from Jim's garage?"

"I didn't."

"Sure you did. You had keys. Jim says so. The shop closes at noon on Saturdays, but somebody let themselves in after closing that day, took a truck out, and returned it much later that same night. We found the truck that was used. The proof's on the odometer. And there's surveillance video too."

The footage was not from Duncan's garage but the Home Hardware up the block, and all it showed was a vehicle leaving the lot, with a time stamp. But he wasn't about to say so. He didn't mention either the black fabric and tape found in the garage's dumpster, or the tape residue on the truck's rear window. He said, "You let yourself in, found the keys, drove that truck out. Brought it back. Hung the keys up. Let yourself out again."

She was appalled but not surprised. "God," she said, "she must have taken the key."

"Stella knew you had a key to his garage, did she? And knew where to find it?"

"Obviously."

But Leith had more. He said, "D'you know who dumped all those frozen vegetables over Kiera's body in the freezer?"

Her crinkled brow said she was losing patience. "They did, apparently. Stella and whoever she was working with."

Leith said, "If you want, I'll show you the IGA surveillance tape. Sunday, the day after, you're buying a lot of frozen peas. Enough to feed an army. Do you want to explain that?"

She considered his face, her brow smooth now. She pulled the itchy grey blanket snugger around her shoulders and said blandly, "Well, I suppose it wasn't several days later I discovered the body. I must be mistaken about that. That's right, it was the next day. Yes, I did buy the frozen vegetables to cover her up. I'm sorry. I know it was wrong. I know her family will never forgive me, and I know I will be criminally charged. Is there anything else?"

* * *

Leith stayed at his desk at the detachment and worked late into the night, writing his report and looking at the facts, knowing her story had to be a whitewash. Or in her case, a greywash. How did Kiera's body get from riverbank to shallow grave on the Matax trailhead to

Mercy Blackwood's freezer? What was the story there? He suspected that until Scott Rourke and/or Stella Marshall showed up and spilled the beans, he may never know the whole truth. Blackwood's house was undergoing a thorough search, autopsy results were pending, but it wouldn't tell him what he needed to know, who did what, when. He told himself that at least Kiera's family would have a body to bury, whatever peace that brought.

He called in an off-duty Constable Thackray, the exhibit custodian for the Blackwood search. Thackray arrived in civvies, looking unkempt and dazed. Leith told him he needed to see Blackwood's phone. Thackray brought it from the lockers and sat by while Leith went through the phone's databanks. He found one number of interest, called several times over the last ten days. He ran the number down on his computer. It was a cellular that belonged to a Van Edwards. "Who's Van Edwards?" he asked Thackray. "Name mean anything to you?"

"Local guy," Thackray said. "Unemployed. Does odd jobs around."

Leith punched out Renee Giroux's number on his BlackBerry. She sounded as if she might have been asleep, and she asked if he knew what time it was. He looked at the wall clock and realized it was a quarter past two in the morning.

"Sorry," he said. "But I was thinking. I'm mining Blackwood's phone here. She's been in touch lately with a local odd-jobber named Van Edwards. Maybe she was planning to hire him to remove the body. She couldn't do it herself, could she? Why now, though? Why not soon as possible?"

"Too many cops around," Giroux suggested.

He agreed that was possible. But it was something else, deeper and darker, that nagged. "She suggested Kiera wasn't dead, was lying in wait, would come after her. That's when we were talking, before I found the body."

Giroux said, "A ruse to throw you off the scent."

It continued to bother him. He thought of the photographs of Mercy on the wall, from not so long ago, before she left the city. She'd been wholesome-looking, round-cheeked and smiling. In the span of a year or so she had shrunk to her present state. Forever cold. He relayed the thought, more or less, to Giroux.

Giroux said, "Of course she's shrunk. So would you if you were hiding a corpse in your freezer. A corpse you were at least in part responsible for by spreading false rumours and counterfeit documents, which sparked the fight that killed her. It's called guilty conscience."

He sighed, knowing she was right. "I don't know," he said, spinning a pen on the desktop and frowning. "Something bothers me about this whole thing."

"Huh, well," Giroux said. "Here's a suggestion. Sleep on it." She disconnected.

* * *

After sleeping on it, he was no wiser. First thing in the morning he spoke to a sombre, hulking twenty-two-year-old who Giroux knew as troublesome but harmless, Van Edwards, a good-looking native boy of impressive height and width. Edwards told Leith how Mercy

Blackwood had found his number on the bulletin board at the IGA last week and called him up, wondering if he could help renovate her house. He was up for it. He'd shifted some junk, he said, got a hundred bucks off her, and not much else so far. He was losing faith that he'd ever see any real money from the job. "She tried to seduce me," he added.

Leith was somewhat expecting it. Mercy needed not just muscle but devotion when it came to moving a human body. She was probably hoping the young guy would fall head over heels for her, do anything she asked, and cover for her crimes. He said, "And did it work?"

"Course," Van said, grinning. "Worked three times. Weren't bad at all, too."

They talked for another hour, Leith trying his best not to lead, trying to find out if Mercy had told the man anything that might shed light on his own murky suspicions. Not leading got him nowhere, so finally he made a suggestion. "Did she ever mention an upcoming job that might not be totally legal, say?"

"Nope."

Leith pondered. "There's a blood stain on her floor in front of her woodstove," he said, thinking of Mercy's story of an injured dog, which he hadn't believed for a moment. The floorboards had been cut out and were away for analysis, but he wouldn't have an answer for a while whether the blood was indeed human. Kiera hadn't bled out, from what he'd seen and what he'd been told, but he was certain that bloodstain was somehow integral to whatever happened in Mercy's house that day. "Know where that came from?"

"Dog," Van said. "Got hit by a car."

So she'd given him the same lie. Leith crossed his arms.

"She was weird about that dog," Van went on. "It got killed a week or two before she first hired me, but she was always talking about it. Fact she still had it in her freezer. I go, what? You put it in your freezer? That's where your food goes. She says the freezer's old and shitty and she wants it taken to the dump, dog and all. I says, I'll need help with that, you'll have to hire another guy, somebody with a flat-deck. Then she changed her mind, says she wants the dog buried." He reflected a moment and then nodded. "Yeah, weird how she's always going on about that damned dog. She said she watched it die, how horrible it was, how it scared her at night, knowing it was there on the verandah, and she was always hearing things. Jumpy. Zombie dogs, eh. Ha. That's why she wanted me staying overnight all the time, I guess, so she wasn't alone, that's how freaked out she was. I said, well, fuck, just get rid of it. I'll take it out to the woods for you. Can't, she says. Not yet. Soon. She wanted to give it a proper burial when the time was right. Said she'd pay me good money for it. Up in the hills, she says. Way far away from town." Van rolled his eyes in mock fear. "Weird lady. Kind of gave me the creeps sometimes, when we're lying in bed, and she's hanging on to me like her life depends on it, staring at the doorway like she can see something coming. I don't scare easy, but I tell you, I was pretty well ready to quit that bitch."

"Did you ever look at the dog in the freezer?"

"No. I tried, but she wouldn't let me."

"When would the time be right, for this burial, did she say?"

"Soon as the ground thaws," Van said with a shrug, and now his eyes gleamed with interest. "So what's she done wrong?"

Leith thought of the gardeners out in their yards with their forks and shovels, and the dripping eaves, and the softening ground. He would talk to her again, and this time he'd get mean. A call came in just then from Corporal Fairchild. Members following Leith's directions had been re-reviewing security footages from the vicinity of the Blackwell residence from the day of Kiera's disappearance, and had discovered something he ought to see.

* * *

Leith and Mercy were talking again, because Leith now had what he hoped was proof of collusion. Down the block from Mercy's house stood the Royal Bank where Stella worked. The Royal Bank had a surveillance cam, and the footage on that cam provided proof that he was now advising her of. On Saturday, the day Kiera disappeared, Mercy had met Scott Rourke on the street, and they had spoken. This was at 2:15 p.m., soon after Rourke had learned of Kiera's death, according to Leith's timeline. He wanted to know now what they had talked about.

Mercy was silent, so he let her know, with rising anger, that she'd better come clean and tell the truth this time. All of it.

She flinched, and he could see that a night in cells had worn down her bravado. Finally, she nodded.

"Saturday afternoon. I was on my way to the bank. I ran into Scott Rourke on the street. I almost walked on by, but he looked jittery, more than usual. He's a high-strung man, but that day he looked like he'd seen a ghost. I asked what was wrong, and he told me about Kiera. That Frank had killed her. It was an accident."

"Just like that?" Leith asked.

"Yes. He's a babbler, the last person you'd want to trust your secrets with. But Frank had apparently done just that, called up Scott and told him all about it. And now Scott was telling me. He said Stella was involved too. While Frank stayed at home and buried his head in the sand, Stella and Scott wrapped Kiera's body in a tarp, put her in the back of her Rodeo, and drove up the mountain to bury her in the snow off the Matax."

"How'd they get back down?"

"They drove in tandem. Stella took Frank's Jeep. She thought the police would blame it on the Pickup Killer. She got Scott to call Frank and tell him what the plan was. Frank should set up an alibi with Parker, our sound guy. Something about a text message sent from Kiera's phone before they ditched it. Also, Scott would tell the cops he'd seen Kiera driving by, and it had to be during the time Parker was at the house. Stella's sharp, but not as sharp as she thinks she is. When I heard all this, I told Scott it was a terrible cover-up. The body would be found and traced back to Frank in no time at all. What they should have done is go straight to the police. If it was an accident like Frank said, then he was in trouble, but he wouldn't get much. Maybe a year, maybe just probation. But now he was in it up to his neck. And so were they. And so was I, for even talking to Scott like I was."

She glowered back at those crossroads she'd stood upon, and the really bad fork she'd chosen. She said, "I told Scott he'd better go back up the mountain and get the body, hide it for a day or two, then take her away, somewhere remote. He just sat there moaning. He said driving Frank's Jeep up the first time was horribly risky, and a second time could be disastrous. It would be recognized. He had a point. So I gave him the key to Jim's garage. Jim always had a truck or two in the bay, waiting for service. Scott took the key, promised he'd bring it back, and left. I was already full of regret, of course, and scared out of my wits, but it was too late. I carried on as planned, spent the day in town, doing errands, making sure I was seen by lots of people. Establishing my own alibi."

Again she paused, and Leith could see her gathering her thoughts. He didn't like suspects gathering their thoughts much, but he waited in silence.

She said, "I came home that evening and saw someone had been on my back verandah. The floor was wet. I had a bad feeling. I looked in the freezer and saw something was in there, under the food. Large, wrapped not so well in an old orange tarp. I realized that those two angels had found a really great hiding spot for the body."

She hung her head now, done. Leith wasn't, quite. "Tell me about your dog," he said.

Her face lifted, and she stared at him.

He said, "You said your dog was hit by a vehicle, and a man brought it inside. I need to verify it. What's his name, the man?"

"He was a stranger, walking by. I asked for his name, but he never told me. He said he's from Smithers, does odd jobs around. I asked if he was interested in doing renovation work for me, but that never went anywhere. We were both in a daze."

"Describe him, then," Leith said. It was all an invention to explain that mysterious blood stain, he knew, and now she would go on to describe a tall, dark stranger.

"Young," she said. "Tall. Good looking. Dark hair, dark eyes. May have been native, but I don't think so. I drove him to the Super 8."

What a load of crap, Leith thought. He leaned forward and said, "How about this instead. There was no dog. It was Kiera you watched die. You opened the freezer and found her there, but she wasn't dead. She was looking up at you, asking for help. That's what's left you in a cold sweat. That's what's giving you nightmares." He stood, leaned both hands on the tabletop and raised his voice at her. "She's going to tell us from that autopsy table, every last detail. So out with it. Tell me. Tell me the damned truth."

Mercy shrank away from him. "No, that's not true at all."

"It *is* true," he shouted and slammed the table with both palms, hard, and for the first time in his career his anger was more than interrogatory theatrics. He had a connection with Kiera, stronger than he ought to have allowed develop. She had become his own personal missing loved one, and he couldn't bear to think of her suffering, yet everything in his mind pointed to that terrible death, without foundation or confirmation, without one tangible clue. He said it again, feeling the ulcer at work in the pit of his stomach, the veins popping at his throat, the wet heat in his eyes. "You damn well could have saved her, and you shut the lid, didn't you? Slammed it down and left her in the dark to die. Didn't you?"

"Yes," she said. She was crying freely now, sobbing and huddling as if to burrow away from the memories. "But it was too late. There was no going back."

"Why?" he asked. "Why in hell would you not help her, even if it was too late? To save Stella? Scott? Frank?"

It was a while before she answered. She straightened, popped her eyes wide, and spoke like an automaton now, gazing at the wall. "Just Frank," she said. "My beautiful, brilliant Frank. When this all blew over I would take him places. He was always the star of the show, just didn't know it. With his curb appeal and Charlie's music, we would have broken through for sure."

Leith buzzed for the guard to take her away, and his own heart was beating madly as the door swung shut behind them. He looked at the lens of the video camera set up to record this interview and realized it was still rolling, and he was still swearing. He straightened his shirt collar and stood to switch it off.

* * *

Over the next few days Leith tackled the loose ends of the file. More came to light about Mercy Blackwell the fraud. Her departure from Vancouver had nothing to do with a medical crisis and everything to do with being fired by the Midlanders, a lawsuit related to another bad contract, and the looming shadow of bankruptcy. Her dying grandmother had been more a stroke of luck to Mercy than an act of kindness, a place to go, temporary accommodations. The luck had gone south when she discovered Fling. Promoting the little band of musicians was her effort to get back on her feet, but instead it had landed her in jail, maybe for life. A purple coat came to light as well, stuffed into the attic in a garbage bag, another nail in her coffin.

She was now in the care of a fairly high-profile lawyer from the Lower Mainland. There was still no word of Charlie West, and her shy, plain face joined the league of missing girl postings. Stella Marshall was still gone, untrackable. Scott Rourke seemed to have followed her into the void; he had never showed up at his ratty little trailer, which was watched round the clock, and none of his associates had seen him for several days.

Just as Leith was preparing to leave the Hazeltons and head back to Rupert, leaving those loose ends for someone else to tie, he received some grisly news. A hiker had been exploring a defunct highway running from the main road to Two Mile, a stretch of crumbly blacktop left to the mosses and weeds. The man had been walking along, taking pictures. Took a shot of this, of that, pointed his lens upward at a massive cottonwood arching over the road, and jumped out of his skin.

Ident were now on scene, trying to deal with the hiker's find. From the side of their vehicle, Leith and Giroux shielded their eyes and looked up. Limned against the fuzzy grey sky a thin scrap of adult male hung, tattered and weathered. On his feet were saggy socks. Cowboy boots lay below, tossed wide. The boots had already been marked with little yellow numbers. Judging from the way the head was angled, Leith saw it wasn't a professional hitch that had broken Rourke's neck, but an amateur's knot that would have slowly throttled him.

Leith winced. He didn't like Scott Rourke, but nobody deserved an end like that.

He watched as the body was cut down, lowered to earth, and the processing began. He said, "I'll have to pass this one on to someone else, or I'll never get back home."

"Kind of like a bad dream, isn't it?" Giroux said. She too seemed sobered by this death, whatever she had called Rourke just days earlier. "It's the people that make a community," she said. "Good, bad, or weird as hell. When you think of it, those were a bunch of friends to die for. Stella, Scottie, Chad. Risking everything to save Frank. Have you ever had a friend who'd do that for you?"

Leith hadn't. He thought of Mercy's remark about these kids working against each other. Well, they'd been very much working together, in fact. And still would be, if she hadn't come along. He said, "What they did was not only criminal, but mind-blowingly stupid, all of it. They put the family through hell and burned through a year's worth of man hours that could have been spent elsewhere."

Giroux nodded. "Still. And they'd have done the same if it was the other way around, if it was Frank they thought dead. Except Kiera would have refused to go along with it. She's a woman. She's got brains."

"You know you're a real female chauvinist pig? Stella's a woman too, and she was the mastermind behind it all. What d'you say to that?"

"Stella's not a woman; she's an anomaly."

You couldn't win with Renee Giroux. Leith huddled and swore under his breath.

"Hmph," Giroux said, not to their argument but to the body lying before them. "I hate this. For whatever his sins, he was one of us."

"Any idea who did it? Those two guys we saw him with outside the detachment, by any chance?"

An ident officer brought something over in a plastic exhibit bag. "Was in his pocket, sir."

Leith and Giroux read the suicide note. Leith saw authenticity in the calligraphy and the prose, but no outright reason given. He winced, imagining the weight of guilt floating about this town. This was no mob lynching, then. Just self-annihilation. He said, "Rourke's the do-gooder from hell. He tried to save Frank's neck, but failed. But I don't think that's it. I think he found out Kiera wasn't dead when he dumped her in the freezer. That's what he couldn't live with."

Giroux was irritated. "That's a hell of an assumption. How could he possibly know that?"

"I don't know," he grumbled. "Maybe he didn't know, but suspected. Maybe she twitched as he laid her inside, but like Mercy, he knew it was too late to save her."

"Maybe this *is* all a bad dream," Giroux said. "Did you hear about the dog?"

He stared down at her. "What dog?"

"The dead dog behind Mercy's house. In the bushes. Looks like it had been hit by a car. And the blood on her floorboards is animal, not human."

Leith said nothing. Watching Rourke's body zipped into its body bag, he told Giroux of his big decision, his new posting, fast-tracked by the amazing Mike Bosko. "Yeah, looks like I'll be gone April 20th, heading for the bright lights of North Vancouver," he said, jetting his hand southbound across the continent to more exciting places, a part of him hoping to make Giroux just a little bit jealous.

"Yeah?" she said flatly. "My condolences." And she meant it.

Seventeen

UNFOND FAREWELLS

KIERA'S BODY WAS COMING HOME, and on this same weekend an outdoor festival was held in Smithers, all along Main Street, with a stage set up at the rondo at one end. As Dion understood it, the festival was in celebration of Kiera's life, combined with a fundraiser for women at risk. The turnout was good. These early April days were still too cold for outdoor events, really, but people bundled up in parkas and long johns under their jeans, wearing mitts and toques and big smiles. They brought folding chairs or wandered and listened to the live bands playing and the speeches and comedians and fundraising auctions and whatever else climbed the stage and took the mic. There were midway games, food booths, plenty of native arts and crafts on sale, *I Love Kiera* T-shirts, and Fling's first and only CD selling like hotcakes.

Dion had arrived with Penny at noon. Now at half past three they found a bench near the stage to sit down and eat corn dogs. A new band was setting up, country rockers from Prince George. This wasn't the fall fair, but it felt much the same to Dion as the guitars were tuned and the mics tested. A woman on stage introduced the members of her band. She talked about Kiera, and of violence against women, and of the changes that would now be made. There were cheers and applause to her proclamation, and Dion kept his doubts to himself. Her first song was titled "Captivity."

"Not as good as Kiera," Penny murmured as the song played. "Nobody can ever be as good as Kiera."

Penny mourned Kiera but had no regrets for Frank, facing charges of second-degree murder. The posters had come down off her wall, and he'd been flicked into the scum bin in her mind, but she still knew nothing of men. "That guy's pretty hot," she said, looking toward the stage and meaning either the guy on guitar or the guy on drums. The song ended. There was another round of applause, and Dion clapped too, knowing he was going to be here in this town forever, attending concerts with Penny and feeling nothing.

"Oh," she said, waving. She had spotted some friends and wanted to go join them. Dion told her to go ahead, he'd catch up with her later. In the middle of a song, which struck him as rude, she got up and headed toward her pals on the far side of the street. He called out, "Hey, Penny," and held out the small plush penguin he'd won for her on the mini midway.

She mouthed "Later," and kept going.

He sat ignoring the music, considering his position, the new secret to add to his stockpile. He'd maintain the lie, because nothing would be gained by confession.

He'd been in Mercy Blackwell's house. He'd laid the dog at the foot of the freezer, inside which lay the body of the missing singer. Maybe he'd left fingerprints; maybe they'd be found; maybe he'd be interrogated for hours, even suspected of being involved. But he doubted it.

Anyway, in the big picture it hardly mattered. His crimes were a lot bigger than that. He'd killed a man. His justification would be laughed out of court, and they'd put him away for good. *That* was something to worry about.

There had been a witness, doing whatever she was doing in that gravel pit that night. She had jumped on her bicycle and pedalled off, and she'd got a good head start, but he'd jumped into his Dodge, Looch in the passenger seat, and went after her with intent, pedal to the metal, and crashed instead, and now that witness was out there, somewhere, a fat girl with pink hair who visited him in his dreams. That was something to worry about too.

He blew out a breath and told himself again that everything would be cool. He'd finally been cleared to return to light duties at the Smithers detachment, starting tomorrow. He was doing okay. He'd come a long way over the course of the winter. He'd found his gloves, knew how to steer out of a skid on sheer ice. Penny's family still liked him, and he was determined to work harder at getting along with the guys he worked with. He still talked to Looch sometimes, when nobody was listening, but even that was a habit he had just about kicked. There was plenty to celebrate.

He pulled a pack of Rothman's from his shirt pocket, knocked out a cigarette, and searched himself for a lighter. It was part of his celebration, taking up smoking again. Penny had been shocked and disgusted when he'd lit up in front of her, but he didn't care. He liked the hit of nicotine in his lungs. It steadied his nerves and took him back to the man he'd once been. He waited till the set was over and then left the bench, little plush penguin in hand, and started down Main toward the highway, with plans of stepping into the Alpenhorn Pub. He had a new mission in mind: get to the bar and grab some matches. There was a smoking section out back where he could sit and have a pint in peace and quiet.

As it happened, he didn't make it as far as the Alpenhorn, sidetracked by a chance encounter. The man stood in a concession stand lineup, someone he'd known briefly, and not so well, what felt like half a lifetime ago. Riding on the man's broad shoulders was a small child with curly blond hair, the curls tossing like a halo in the afternoon sunlight. The man wore dark shades. He happened to look sidelong through the drift of passersby, straight at Dion, lowered the dark shades and peered, then lifted an obligatory hand in greeting, and the expression on his face said *damn*.

* * *

It was Constable Dion, of course, in the act of passing by, almost a stranger in jeans, hoody, dark blue baseball cap. He'd filled out a bit, which suited him well, and but for the plush toy in hand he looked like any other twentysomething jock on his way to the pub. Leith expected the jock to return the salute with his usual diffidence and keep going, but instead he sauntered over, gave a surprisingly friendly nod to Leith, then looked up at Izzy and said hello to her too.

Izzy was silent, of course, and Leith couldn't see her face, but he knew she would be staring imperiously down at the stranger, sizing him up. He said, "Say hello to Constable Dion, Izzy," because he was in the process of teaching her good manners. Izzy said hello, and now it was Leith's turn. "Hi, how's it going?"

"Pretty good." Dion turned and pointed toward the stage. "Been listening to the bands and speeches. Good stuff."

Leith nodded. "Caught a few songs myself, but the kid here doesn't have the patience."

The lineup shuffled ahead, a few steps closer to that hot dog he really shouldn't be getting. He had one worried eye out for Alison, lost in the crowd. She'd give him hell if she found him feeding Izzy junk food. Dion didn't say *okay, well,* and leave, as expected, but moved along with the lineup and said, "I heard how you found Kiera. Congratulations."

"Thanks."

"So what brings you to Smithers?"

Leith looked at him sidelong. Maybe Dion's brick-wall personality in the Hazeltons had just been a stage in his recovery. Maybe he'd improved, had found his own humanity, had become a regular nice guy. Which was always a good thing. "Still mopping up after John Potter," he told Dion. "Seems he had work down here around September last year on a roofing crew. Big contract, upgrading the tar and gravel roof at the courthouse. So we're going over any missing persons cases, see if he did his best at touching this community as well while he was hereabouts."

Dion nodded. "I know. I heard about it. I also saw in the news this morning that Charlie West's listed as missing. I thought she was located in Dease. I thought Spacey talked to her."

"That turns out to be a miscommunication," Leith said.

Dion nodded again, up and down, a bit too much. Trying too hard, but trying for what? He had a cigarette between his fingers, and he stuck it in his mouth.

It was news to Leith that Dion was a smoker, and it irked him. It was no fault of Dion's; it was just that being an ex-smoker himself, Leith didn't appreciate others enjoying that heady blend of toxins in his presence. He said, "I'm just here for a couple days, actually, passing the Potter file over to Paul Foley, 'cause it looks like I'm transferring out, be gone by the end of the month." The looming move was one reason he'd brought Alison and Izzy along on this police-business trip, trying to spend as much time with them as possible before he left. He would leave them in Rupert while he firmed things up down in North Van, bring them down only when he was sure it was going to work out. "You'll probably be meeting Paul in the next few days. I don't think smoking is allowed here, eh. Public place."

Dion was still nodding, cigarette in mouth, unlit. "Sure, I know. Where are you transferring to?"

"North Van. Joining Mike Bosko's unit. Serious Crimes."

Dion had stopped nodding like a bobble-head, maybe getting a sore neck. He said, "North Vancouver. Wow. That's great."

"Your old turf, right?"

Which apparently Dion didn't hear. He stared off down Main Street, jerry-rigged into festival grounds, and above the crowds into the cold blue sky, and said, "Any chance I can look at that file?"

"What file?"

"The Potter file. You've brought it with you, right?"

Leith's bonhomie seeped away. "Why?"

Dion looked down and seemed to notice the object in his own hand for the first time, a stuffed toy with a yellow beak and yellow feet, some kind of duck. A midway prize, made in China, a dollar a dozen, Leith thought. "Sharpshooter, are you?"

"Okay if I give this to your little girl?"

"Sure. Thanks. You'll make her day."

Dion handed the duck up to Izzy, who snatched it out of Leith's sight. Leith told her to say thank-you, and she did, kicking her heels against his chest in a happy way as she inspected her new toy.

Leith repeated his question to the off-duty constable. "Why?"

Dion was no longer smiling or nodding or looking concertedly casual. With one eye squinted against the afternoon glare and the other challenging Leith point blank, he said, "I might have seen him. Potter."

* * *

They looked over the file in the Smithers case room, Leith and his colleague Foley and Constable Dion, who always got into the middle of the polka. Dion zipped through the documentation, zoning in on certain information, skimming most. He read a bulletin, found photographs, laid them out. A photograph of a building, the Smithers courthouse, with several workers up top, then an outdated portrait photograph of the missing Charlie West. He went back to the courthouse photo and studied the workers on its roof with an intensity that Leith hadn't seen in him before, had frankly not thought possible.

Dion directed his words at Foley, maybe because Leith was transferring out and in his mind was already gone. "The man I saw wore a red cap, like this. Was tall and skinny, like this. I think this is him. And I think this is her."

In the end, though, it didn't matter, Leith realized. If it was true, and not some kind of ghoulish coincidence, that last September this cop had seen that killer following that victim, it pinned matters down, gave them a timeline to work with, but it really didn't get them anywhere. It all was moot, since the killer was dead now.

But everyone wanted Charlie West to be found, especially her sister Charlene, and if she was found dead, then they needed her to be given the dignity of a proper burial. Dion's information maybe at least gave them the basis to bring in the cadaver dogs and set them to work.

Foley left the case room to make enquiries, and Leith stopped Dion from following for a final word in private, a last rebuke. "You could have said something, back in September. At least filed a report."

"I had scant information. I saw nothing that could have been put down in black and white. And if I had, it would have come to nothing."

"I realize that, but that's not the point. The point is, you didn't even try. You're part of a team, and I'm still not sure you get it. Bottom line is, you gotta ask yourself, are you really cut out for this?"

Dion appeared to consider his answer carefully. "No, I'm not cut out for this," he said finally, with vehemence, indicating the detachment walls around them and missing the point altogether. "I'm cut out for that office you're headed for in North Vancouver. That's *my* desk you'll be sitting across from. But that's okay, because you know what? Someday I'll be in that chair again. Maybe someday you'll be calling *me* sir."

It was maybe his idea of a joke, but even so he had stepped over the line, and in a big way. Leith felt himself pinkening in anger. Just like that, it had become one of their famous confrontations, with lots of eye contact and no understanding. Dion was pink, too, as if he knew he'd said too much, and if he had any sense, he'd apologize. He didn't. Leith tried to sound not just crisp, but authoritative. "With your attitude, un-fucking-likely. Especially if I have any say in the matter. More likely, if you don't shape up, you'll be looking at the job boards. It's still your choice, Constable, but pretty soon it won't be. Get it?"

Dion's eyes glimmered with what looked like antipathy, but he seemed to have run out of smart comebacks. He sealed his mouth into a line, flicked the brim of his baseball cap, said "See you," and walked out.

Unbelievable. Standing alone and shaking his head, Leith packed the folders back in the box. He shut the lid and hauled it out for lockup. Barring disaster, it was the last he'd ever see of bloody Constable Dion. "At least I got the last word in," he said with grim triumph.

Not until the following day, driving home to Rupert with Alison and Izzy and recounting the conversation in his mind, did he realize he actually hadn't.

Eighteen

LAST SNOW

A WEEK AFTER DION had said his farewell to Constable Leith, he was hard at work on a pile of General Investigations dockets in the Smithers office when his desk phone rang. He picked up and said, "Dion."

"Hello, Calvin," a woman's voice buzzed in his ear, not one he recognized immediately. "It's Theresa Stein. How are you doing?"

It was a ghost, Inspector Stein from North Vancouver, an ex-supervisor from before the crash, before his transfer. The voice set his teeth on edge and cooled the blood in his veins. He wheeled his chair into a better alignment, sat up straighter, ready to get up and run. "Yeah, hi," he said. "Good. Not bad. You?"

"I'm doing just fine. I've been hearing good things about you, Cal."

Stein was good at plunging the knife in deep, giving it a little twist. Over the time he'd known her, she'd made sarcasm an art. He braved it out, waiting for the punchline.

She said, "Do you remember Mike Bosko?"

Big guy in a white dress shirt, black suit, cheesy necktie, glasses, who'd never spoken to or looked at Dion except in a glancing way. His cooled blood froze, and the knot was back in his stomach, tighter than ever. "Sure. He was involved in the Hazelton case in February that I was on."

"You got along well?"

He listened to the silence that followed her words, trying to read her. "I don't think he registered my presence much, so yes, I guess we did."

"Really?" Stein was puzzled. "Isn't that funny. Because he asked me about you at some length the other day."

The knot gave a painful cinch, and he dragged a hand down his face. He'd found peace of sorts here in Smithers. He'd stopped trying to go back, or forward, had accepted the now. He had started to believe this call would never come, and he'd be safe. But he should have known better.

Stein said, "Maybe you've heard, we're reorganizing down here. There's a new gang-control unit, and Serious Crimes is being shuffled around and moving away from drugs, so to speak, and it's for all intents Bosko's department now. He's done wonders, really."

He still couldn't read her, but knew where she was going. It was a subpoena, casually thrown at him, with threats attached. It was a noose. He said, "Yes, and?" Bluffing now, playing his ignorance card. "If this is about what happened in Hazelton, and what he has to say about it, I don't get why I should care. He can tell his story and I'll tell mine. Send me an appointment or a questionnaire or whatever the hell, and I'll answer. One thing for sure,

I'm about as far north as you can send me, so if you're thinking of some iceberg off the Bering Strait —"

Stein cut in, suddenly irate, her voice jumping an octave. "What are you going on about, icebergs? I'm asking if you're ready to return to North Vancouver. Bosko's recommended your placement in SCU. The ultimate decision is mine, of course, and the way you're blathering I'm not sure you're ready for this. I really am not. Do you want to discuss this reinstatement, or not?"

The words took a moment to sink in. Dion wheeled his chair closer to his desk so he could lean against it, catch his breath. Penny McKenzie grinned up at him from a picture frame, freckle-faced and sweet. He squeezed his eyes shut.

"Well?" Stein said.

He opened them again. "You're saying I'm being transferred? Back to North Van?"

"I'm saying there's a suggestion you might be, if you feel you're up for it."

Up for it. For a moment he dared to believe, but the cold shadow soon followed, and he fully understood. Bosko didn't have anything on him, not yet, but he was working on it. The distance was a hindrance, so he wanted to drag his suspect up close where he could keep an eye on him, read his mail, put a bug on him. Well, fuck Bosko. That wasn't going to happen. He answered Stein shortly. "I'm okay where I am. Thanks for calling. Appreciate it. Bye."

He hung up firmly and got back to his filing, but he was shaking inside. It was too late, and she'd blown his peace to shrapnel. Because what if he was wrong about

Bosko? What if in his paranoia he was passing up a chance to go home? He looked beyond the personal peril and saw the greater danger, a wild bar graph of a skyline, noise, and traffic, sirens weaving through the grid work sprawl. The briny stink of a polluted ocean, the road rage, the rampant crime. He could see himself back among friends, back with Kate, back on top of the world. Sick with a longing that hadn't let up since he'd got off the Greyhound nearly a year ago, he called Stein back and asked if it would still be an option tomorrow, the offer, once he'd had time to think about it.

"Of course it'll still be an option," she said. "This isn't eBay."

He set down the receiver with care and stared at it, wondering what it was, really, a telephone receiver or a baited hook.

"North Van," he said, chewing his lip. He smiled.

* * *

The next day it snowed across the north. Winter's last stand, as Dion had heard people say. On this day as well, Charlie West was found. He'd been following the progress, profilers circling some regions, studying the aerials. Volunteer bushwhackers and native trackers on foot had discovered an abandoned camp, and finally today a cadaver dog had zoned in on a piece of disturbed ground, not too far from the cold remains of a fire pit. The dog had sat its rump down to say the search was over.

A brother officer had come by Dion's apartment in the evening to tell him about it, describing how the body had been almost for sure identified by a distinctive tattoo, that she was found too late in the day to be fully exhumed and would stay *in situ* until morning. Dion had the officer point out where, on a map, and then borrowed the man's four-by-four and headed out. First he drove twelve kilometres south from Smithers, nearing the much smaller community of Telkwa, then struck up a level grit road heading east off Highway 16. In the headlights he watched the road shooting ahead through rolling hills covered in scrub, then the woodlands closing in. Pebbles banged the chassis for another twenty minutes until he saw a figure in his headlights, and took his foot off the gas.

She walked the road ahead of him, a girl, her back to him, trudging along, bent against the cold of the night. Way out here in the middle of nowhere. He slowed further as he approached and stared at her hard. She started to glance around, and he saw her long black hair, whipping in a ponytail, and the curve of her cheek lit by his headlights as he slowed even further, slowed to a crawl. Her hand went up to hold back her fluttering hair, and he stopped the truck and waited, and watched her turn all the way around, and he wouldn't look away, not this time. He saw her face, just as he imagined it would be, and he gasped, almost a sob.

He was looking at the girl from the fall fair. She walked toward him. He scrolled down the window. The cold blew in, and she was looking up at him in the high cab of the truck. She said, "Oh my god, I been walkin' all fuckin' night. Think I'm going to freeze to death. Gimme a ride?"

"'Course," he said.

She climbed into the passenger seat and said, "Try anything, you're dead."

He didn't doubt it. "Where are you going?" he asked, but he already knew.

"Be with my sister. She's buried somewhere around here. There's supposed to be a cop car sitting there guarding it, and I know they won't let me see her, but I just want to be near her."

Tears glinted in her dark eyes, black as onyx. She'd taken off her packsack and held it tight against her chest like a child. Dion drove farther, another twenty minutes, till pylons glowed ahead, marking the spot. He parked behind a lone RCMP Suburban and told the girl to wait there. He left the truck and found a constable he worked with sitting behind the wheel of the RCMP vehicle, keeping guard. They talked about the burial site, and the constable agreed to escort him there.

"I picked up her sister on the way," Dion said. "She can come with us, far as the barricade?"

"I guess that'll be okay."

Dion beckoned, and the girl joined them. She trailed the men at some distance as they walked into the trees. "You knew the victim?" the constable asked Dion.

"Kind of. Was anything else found?"

"Just bits of things in the fire pit. A CD, burned to shit, and some documents."

They continued up a narrow footpath flagged for ingress and egress, mostly uphill, for fifteen minutes. They arrived at an abandoned camp with scant evidence of a squatter in the scrub, and the constable pointed Dion to the gravesite itself, a little farther into the trees, where crime scene tape billowed. He said, "I'll watch from here, if you don't mind."

Dion said he'd be five minutes, max. He walked with the sister up a knoll to the marked grave, and saw it was covered by a blue tarp.

"Charlie," said the girl. She stared at the tarp for a long moment, then began to talk to her sister, telling her those things she'd failed to say in life. There was lament in her words, mixed with harangue, and a little bit of teasing thrown in.

Dion turned off his flashlight to let the night press down. Snow drifted over the tarp and the surrounding grasses and shrubs, paling the world. He gazed at where she lay and thought of Leith's admonition: you should have said something, at least tried. But what could he have said, or what would anybody have done if he'd said it? *I have a bad feeling.*

There'd been nothing he could have done then. There was nothing he could do now except keep her in mind and move on. "You can't stay here," he told Charlie's sister, and she nodded. They rejoined the constable where he stood waiting, and together they headed down the path toward the road. Dion lagged behind and stopped once to look back. A new kind of sorrow passed through him like a draught, unlike anything he'd experienced before. Unthinkable, that he was walking away, bound for the warmth of his apartment, and would leave her there in the cold dirt, alone.

Hard to believe he could do such a thing. He turned and followed his flashlight beam to the truck, said goodnight to the constable on guard duty, and with his passenger beside him drove back westward toward Highway 16.

Next to him the girl pulled a book from her pack, a hefty black hardcover. She turned it over like a mysterious package, looking at it from all sides.

"What's that?" Dion asked.

"Frank's kid brother Lenny gave it to me. When I stopped by their house looking for info." She frowned at the title. "It's about hitchhiking. What the fuck, eh?"

Dion was thinking more or less the same.

"*Guide to the Galaxy*," she read out. "Weird. He says it's for Charlie. He says, give her this when you see her."

She flipped through the pages, stopped, and said, "Oh, hey."

Dion glanced over and saw her pull a slim CD case from the innards of the book. So it wasn't a book, really, but a receptacle. A square hollow hiding place had been cut into its pages. He thought of the little sliver of paper he'd found by Frank's woodstove, the leftovers from an X-Acto blade cut, and the words on that sliver he'd copied into his notebook. All he recalled now was *suddenly*.

"It says 'copy,'" Charlene said, reading the scribbles on the disk, holding it up to the glow of the dashboard. "Ten songs here. Says 'demo.' Oh my God. This is amazing. Isn't it amazing?"

He agreed it was amazing. So Charlie had found at least one good friend in the world: Lenny Law. And she'd left her mark, ten songs. Too bad everything else just got in the way.

He drove Charlene back to Highway 16, where she wanted to be let out. He asked her where she was staying, and she said it was a B&B right down the road here in Telkwa, and she could get there from here on foot. He said he'd take her to its doorstep, no problem, it was only a few minutes out of his way. She refused. "I really want to walk," she said. "I'll be okay. You think anybody's going to mess with *me?*"

"The kinds of men —" he said.

She shut him up with a lifted palm. "I know. Men are bastards. But not all of them. Okay? You're proof."

He put the truck in park at the crossroads, and she climbed out, clutching her bag. She'd stashed the CD into its depths but left the book on the seat. The door slammed shut. He watched her go, because she was dead wrong about men. And especially about him. She turned and waved, not just goodbye, but go, get lost.

He flicked the signal and joined the highway traffic, back toward Smithers, and pulled a U-turn only when far enough away that she wouldn't notice. Back in the settlement, he cruised till he spotted her under the street lamps. He pulled over and from the shoulder watched the girl walk down a side street. He eased the truck forward and killed the engine as she climbed the stairs of a respectable-looking home. She pressed the bell. The door opened, light shone out, and she went inside.

The chill was seeping into the truck's cab. He remained at the wheel, looking ahead, not thinking about the girl in the house or the girl in the ground, but the map in his mind, that slow line crawling down the province through Prince George, Williams Lake, 100 Mile House, Hope. He cranked the key, turned the truck around, and headed back to the lights of Smithers, so dazzling in winter's last snow.

ACKNOWLEDGEMENTS

In 2013 I was lucky enough to meet two excellent, award-winning writers, Holley Rubinsky and Deryn Collier, two very different authors who had teamed up to lead a mystery writers' workshop in Kaslo. I signed up for what turned out to be an eye-opening week of learning in the most beautiful little town. I owe a ton of debt to Holley and Deryn. Their knowledge, generosity, and support spurred me on to enter *Cold Girl* into the 2014 Arthur Ellis Awards — the Unhanged category for unpublished first novels. I effusively thank the Crime Writers of Canada and Dundurn Press for hosting this program of awards and celebrations; it's such a great help to artists in a difficult field.

I thank my literary agent, Carolyn Swayze, who took the reins with style and grace. I'd be floundering without her. I am so pleased to be working with Dundurn Press, Carrie Gleason and her friendly and efficient team. Thank you again for this amazing opportunity. And I thank editor Allister Thompson, for the intensive and productive days he put into this novel.

In the bigger picture, I thank my parents, gone now, but remembered always. And the important guys in my life, my husband and brothers and son, who keep me stable in the wildest weather.

Most of all I thank you, reader. If this story clicks with you, that's what matters most!

* * *

The overall geography in this book is real, but some locales, roads, and businesses named are fictitious, and the people are strictly imaginary.

DUNDURN

VISIT US AT

Dundurn.com
@dundurnpress
Facebook.com/dundurnpress
Pinterest.com/dundurnpress